HOW TO FLIRT WITH A WITCH

BY TIANA WARNER

ROGUE CANNON PUBLISHING

Content Warnings and Information

This book contains sex (exclusively f/f), magical violence, animal attacks, and mentions of blood, injuries, and death of a loved one. There is no animal death, and all sex is consensual.

CHAPTER 1

Call the Vet and Maybe an Exorcist

THE BEDROOM DOOR RATTLES against my sweaty palms as Lucy claws furiously at the other side.

"*Mrawwwrrrr...*"

"I think I should crawl out the window," I say, my heart pounding.

From the laptop on my unmade bed, Hazel's voice is stern. "You listen to me, Katie. You're going to take a big breath, open the door, and trap that kitten under your laundry hamper like your life depends on it."

There's a terrible pause as we both seem to wonder the same thing. *Does* my life depend on it? What, exactly, does this cat want to do to me?

"You saw my arms!" Adrenaline pumping, I turn around and lean back against the only barrier between myself and mortal peril.

"So put a jacket on before you touch her!"

"More like a hazmat suit." I look heavenward. My skin stings so fiercely that tears well in my eyes. Aside from the bloody scratches, boils have erupted on my hands, arms, and neck, resembling gigantic, pus-filled versions of the zits I used to get in high school.

But Hazel's right. I have to take Lucy to the vet. And possibly take myself to the hospital, depending on what the vet says.

"You're sure you haven't developed an allergy to cats?" Hazel asks. "It's been a long time since you had one." On my laptop screen, she paces in and out of the frame, flapping her hands in her signature *oh-my-god oh-my-god* gesture. She's ready for class in jeans and flannel, with her dark hair braided and her makeup done. She's three hours ahead in Toronto, so it'll be ten there. Guilt twists my stomach for delaying her like this. But the rising panic pushes it aside.

"It's not allergies. I'm not sneezing. It's..." I scrunch my face. How do I explain without sounding like I've lost my mind? "The way Lucy's acting, there's something wrong with her. I know the shelter checked her health, but..."

But I don't think there's a test for whatever this is, I finish in my head. In the corner, her food bowl sits melted to the floor, a lump of pink ceramic with ash in it that was once kibble. The charred scent still hangs in the air. Beside it, the kibble bag slumps where I left it when I jumped back screaming, letting the flood of spiders scuttle out and disappear to God-knows-where.

These are not your typical symptoms.

Which is why they're probably unrelated incidents, right?

There's no sound of a tiny paw trying to turn a doorknob, so I dart to my closet, grab the laundry hamper, and empty it onto the carpet. Then I rummage through the hangers for a few layers of protection. "Can you research boils for me?"

A chair scrapes as Hazel sits in front of her laptop. "Yeah, for sure. Skin boils from cat scratches... aggressive behavior... anything more?"

Yes. A lot more.

I shake my head, unable to say it. I'm afraid of what's happened, afraid of sounding unhinged, and afraid of what it all might mean. "That's it. Look for a condition that could transfer from cats to humans."

"On it."

The frantic *tap-tap-tap* of Hazel's keyboard rings out from my laptop, the noise reassuring me that I'm not alone.

My heart fills with gratitude as I pull my ski jacket off its hanger. Where would I be without her? Even from across the country, she's here for me—the same way it's been since we met in Grade 10. Back then, we were two multiracial girls adrift in a small-town high school—me, Filipino and German, her, Japanese and Italian—and the cliquey nature of our class meant neither of us was sure which social group we belonged in. Too white to be one of the Asian kids, too Asian to be one of the white kids, not athletic enough for sports, too studious for the rebels, not into gaming... So we formed our own group, just the two of us. It's always the two of us.

My ski jacket swallows my small frame as I zip it up over the moon-phases t-shirt I use as pajamas. It's like I'm donning armor for a battle I never signed up for. I put on winter gloves and a balaclava for extra coverage, then jeans to try to bring some normalcy to the look.

Hazel groans, sending a jolt of dread through me. That is *not* something you want to hear when you've asked someone to research what sort of disease you might have contracted.

"What is it?" My panicked voice is muffled through the balaclava. I race over to the laptop and lean down.

Her brown eyes flick to me through the screen. She doesn't laugh at my appearance, which is a testament to both our friendship and the grimness of the situation. The visible part of my face is clammy, my normally rosy-beige complexion drained and ashen. My dark eyes are wide, and light brown tresses poke out from the balaclava, which I tuck away so I don't look like a mad scientist.

"Come on. Hit me." I clap my gloved hands and make a 'bring it' gesture. "This day can't get any worse. Might as well know what I'm dealing with."

"Well, I'm not sure," Hazel says calmly. "But it might be some kind of... worm or parasite? None of the pictures look exactly like what you've got going on, but it's the closest I can find."

A wave of nausea crashes over me. The idea of these boils being *worms* under my skin makes me light-headed. I lean on the bed for support. "Th-there's a cure for that sort of thing, right?"

"Of course." Hazel types something else. "A twenty-four-hour vet is a few minutes away from you. *Helping Paws Vancouver Animal Hospital and Emergency.*"

"Helping Paws." Easy to remember. *Help,* like what I desperately need right now. "Got it. Thanks."

Lucy yowls from beyond the door.

Hazel stands to resume her pacing and *oh-my-god* hands.

I draw a steadying breath. As usual, my roommate and upstairs landlords aren't home, leaving me alone and in silence except for the gutter runoff splattering on the stone walkway outside my window. It's a jarring change after growing up with three sisters and a very vocal husky.

I take out the little blue kennel I used for Lucy when I adopted her four days ago. A pang of sadness pierces the adrenaline. My sweet girl. Our life together, possibly over before it began. She was supposed to solve my loneliness in this new city, and now look at us. Why does nothing ever go the way I imagined it?

A burning sensation prickles at the corners of my eyes, and I grit my teeth. I refuse to give up on her. First, she's already been abandoned once in her short life, and I could never bring myself to return her to the shelter. Second, I'm an Alexander, and Alexanders don't give up.

With the kennel open, the laundry hamper dangling from my fist, and a red fleece blanket sitting by in case I have to throw it on her, I go to the door.

My pulse pounds as I grip the knob with a gloved hand.

Lucy stops yowling, and a heavy silence falls.

She knows.

I scan the room for things that could go wrong.

Window shut. Closet closed. The storage platform bed leaves no room for hiding underneath. My nightstand, desk, and shelves hold lamps, plants, textbooks, romance novels, the diffuser I use to mask the dank basement smell, three years' worth of pictures of Hazel and me, and a lifetime's worth with my sisters. It can all handle being knocked over. The plush cat bed, scratching post, and toys I bought her sit in the corner, mocking me.

"I'm doing it." My voice trembles. "If things go south, call an ambulance."

"Okay..." A note of worry tinges Hazel's tone. Maybe she's wondering how helpful she'll be from across the country.

I raise the hamper like a shield, draw a breath, and muster all my resolve. Then, I whip open the door.

"Heyyy, girl."

Lucy is sitting in the hall, a white fluff ball on the beige vinyl, her stubby tail sticking out like a cotton swab. She's ten weeks old, her beige-tipped ears suggesting she could be part ragdoll. There's a tiny brown smudge on her left rear paw like she dipped her toe in chocolate.

I fell in love with her the moment I saw her. But now...

A glint in her eyes makes dread creep up my spine. Maybe I'm imagining it, but I swear her retinas have turned purple. They're gleaming, unnatural, like a little alien.

The lights flicker, sending a chill through me.

"C'mere!" I swipe the hamper down, but before I can trap her, she darts between my legs and into the bedroom.

"Crap." I spin around, gritting my teeth.

"Katie, look out!" Hazel cries.

Searing pain shoots through my thigh. The kitten is latched onto me, clawing and biting.

I scream, kicking my leg. "She's trying to infect me!"

"Grab her!" Hazel shouts.

I seize Lucy's tiny body, and she spins to attack my glove. Her claws break through the material, and I yelp, shaking her off onto the bed.

"Get—off—" My big toe slams into something, making my eyes water. "Ow!"

It's my biology textbook, lying in the middle of the floor.

Wait, where did that come from? Weren't all my books on my desk a second ago?

I stare at it, mentally fumbling all the strange stuff that's been happening, trying to connect them into a reasonable explanation.

Before I can reach any conclusion that isn't "my brain is broken," a gust of wind and a flapping sound pulls my attention.

I gasp.

A crow has flown through the window and is circling my room in a panic. It hits the walls in the tiny space, cawing. Wind whistles in and sends a draft through the room, lifting papers from my desk. Loose pages and feathers float like confetti, raining down in a chaotic mess.

What—is—happening?

"Why did you leave the window open?" Hazel shouts.

"I didn't!" In pain everywhere, I lunge for the fleece blanket. "Hazel, I *swear* it was closed. There's something weird going on. I think I'm losing my mind."

This infection—it's got to be making me hallucinate. Objects moving on their own, a crow in my room, my kitten trying to commit murder... this can't all be real.

But the stabbing pain all over is real enough. Same with Hazel's screaming.

While the crow continues in frantic circles, Lucy scampers over the bed and up the wall like a squirrel, her claws gripping the drywall.

"She's going to crawl across the ceiling!" I cry.

"Oh, God, it's like *The Exorcist*!" Hazel shouts.

I bat away the crow. "I don't think there's any ceiling crawling in *The Exorcist*!"

"Well, I don't know, I haven't seen it!"

My potted aloe plant hits the carpet, dirt spilling.

"Yes, you have! Remember in—"

"Shut up and trap her before she escapes!" Hazel yells.

Point taken. I crawl onto the bed, hurl myself at the wall, and trap Lucy beneath the fleece blanket before she gets to the ceiling.

She yowls louder than ever, thrashing. I bring my hands together to keep her inside the blanket, falling sideways.

Hazel screams as I roll across the duvet, holding Lucy to my chest, and hit the floor. Panicked sobs escape my lips as I crawl for the kennel.

"Hold her tight!" Hazel cries.

I drag the kennel closer and stuff the bundle inside. Sucking in rattling breaths, I swing the door shut. Victory surges in my chest. "She's in—"

There's a crash, and I flinch. The floating shelf with all my pictures has fallen off the wall. I stay focused, pinching the latch to lock it.

Lucy frees herself from the blanket and lunges at the metal grate. Her fuzzy little arms stick through, claws out, trying to destroy my fingers. The purple glint in her eyes is brighter than ever, a flame roaring to life.

I yank my hands away and slump back, gulping down air and coughing. The crow is still circling, cawing loudly—but I can deal with that in a second. The more important problem is contained.

"I did it!" My room might be in shambles, but relief floods through me, leaving me light and shaky.

"Yes!" On my laptop, Hazel jumps up and down, pumping her fist.

Lucy is the only one not celebrating. "*Mrawwwrrrr...*"

The kennel shakes as she throws herself at the sides, hissing and spitting.

My heart does the same thing against my ribs, fear smothering my victory as Lucy's eyes blaze. Stinging everywhere, I grab the handle, praying the vet will know what's happening to us.

CHAPTER 2

Doctor Zacharias's Diagnosis

As I burst into the waiting room in my balaclava, the vet technician behind the front desk freezes, her eyes widening. I guess I do look like I'm about to rob the place.

I set the hissing kennel at my feet. "Help. My cat has something contagious, and now I have it, and I'm sorry for coming here with an infectious disease but I didn't know what else to do."

"Okay," she says flatly—and oh, the things this young woman must have seen to react so calmly. She reaches for a clipboard, glancing past me to where half a dozen people with dogs and cats fill the sterile white room. "We have a bit of a wait, but—"

"I can't wait." I'm breathless as panic tightens my chest and the boils prickle my skin. "I need to cure her as soon as possible. You don't understand."

I'm not sure *I* understand, but what I know is that the bus broke down on the way here, and while walking a half-hour in the rain, my shoulder got clipped by a car mirror, I stepped in something brown and sticky, and I rolled my ankle on the curb hidden beneath all the dead leaves. And I swear to God, this is Lucy's fault. In the four days since I adopted her, each day has been worse than the last. It feels like my luck is about to run out at any moment—like the kennel at my feet is housing a ticking bomb.

"I can relay your concerns to the vet," the vet tech says, her calmness infuriating, "but we have a priority sequence—"

I splay my gloved hands on the desk, standing on my toes to lean closer. "This is your new top priority!"

She pushes the clipboard toward me, her expression blank, totally impervious to my panic. "Please fill out this intake form, and we'll get you into the queue."

Frustration and disbelief bubble inside me. Sweat prickles under all my layers. Can't she see my desperation through the slit in my balaclava?

The clipboard slips off the counter and lands on the toe of my sneaker, corner first. Pain jolts through my foot and up my leg. "Motherf..."

I grit my teeth against it. The stroke of bad luck isn't even surprising.

"I don't—have time—for paperwork." My voice is quiet and desperate. With how things are going, I'll bleed out from a paper cut if I try to fill it out.

Another vet tech, a twentysomething woman with a purple bob, sidles behind her and rummages through a file folder, casting me nervous glances.

"I understand how stressful it is when our pets are unwell," the first one says, her expression pitying.

The door to an examination room opens, and an elderly man walks out carrying a chihuahua. Flanking him is a middle-aged man in a white coat.

The vet!

"My kitten is making me break out in boils!" I shout, stepping closer. I peel off a glove to show him my disgusting, lumpy hand. "It might be a parasite or something, but—"

The vet puts his palms up. "Miss, I need you to wait your turn—"

"This is urgent!" I'm aware of the eyes on me and the hush that falls over the room. But public humiliation is the least of my worries right now.

"You're at the emergency clinic," the first vet tech says, standing. Her calm demeanor is starting to crack. "Everything here is ur—"

"My window opened without my control when I was trying to crate her," I say. "Her food bowl melted to the floor this morning. I found a dead scorpion in my slipper last night with her little teeth marks. A *scorpion*. In *Canada*. Doctor, please."

The entire waiting room goes still. The vet drops his hands, staring at me.

My insides twist. I shouldn't have said all those things. How must I sound?

The doctor turns to the vet techs, his expression solemn. "Get her into quarantine. Call Doctor Zacharias."

Both girls freeze. Their shoulders tense, their eyes going huge. They exchange a glance I can't interpret. Fear? Excitement? Both?

Whatever their reactions mean, it doesn't matter. He's put a name to the solution: *Doctor Zacharias.* My savior.

Without a word, the girl with purple hair leads me into a windowless room at the back of the office. Pictures of puppies hang on the pastel blue walls, an attempt to cheer up the clinical space. The door slams with a little too much force.

Hollow silence and the buzz of fluorescent lights replace the comforting hum of people. Alone with Lucy again, I shiver, my jeans damp from the rain, cold sweat prickling beneath my ski jacket.

I place Lucy's kennel on the metal examination table, the thump filling the room. I sit in a creaky wooden chair, vigilant, scanning for anything that could hurt me. Medical supplies are safely inside jars, cupboards, and drawers.

My gaze snags on the ceiling tile overhead. Is it a little loose?

I shift the chair so I'm not underneath it.

The kennel is eerily silent. I peek in to see Lucy sitting on the fleece blanket, staring at me with that purple glint in her eyes. Her little tail swishes, promising violence if she gets free.

Bouncing my knee, I pull out my phone. It's 8:44—and the battery is at ten percent.

"No…" I moan. My lifeline to Hazel is slipping away.

Dread turns into irritation. I *know* I plugged in my phone last night. But with the luck I'm having, what did I expect?

I message Hazel, feeling less alone knowing she's expecting an update.

Katie

> Waiting in a quarantine room for an on-call specialist to arrive

Hazel

> Praying for you

Katie

> At this rate, I'm going to miss my morning lectures… and I have midterms next week… ugh

Hazel

> You'll be ok. Can you ask a classmate to send you their notes?

Katie

> I don't know anyone in my classes

My face burns, shame creeping up as Hazel takes a minute to reply. She's likely shocked and confused that I haven't made friends in the six whole weeks since term started. Meanwhile, she goes to parties every weekend and makes friends in every class.

A twinge of envy bubbles up. Not all of us can be social butterflies.

Hazel

I promise it's easy to make friends in university. Everyone is in the same boat. Say hi to the person next to you in class, and say yes to department events. Trust me.

Katie

Ok ok. I will

Even the prospect makes me shift uncomfortably.

Growing up in Toronto together, I got used to having Hazel as a crutch in social situations. She's popular; I'm a wallflower. She talks; I tag along. That's how we work. I meet new people through her. That's why university would be easier if she were here—but she got a scholarship to the University of Toronto, and I got a scholarship to the University of British Columbia. As much as we wanted to attend the same institution, we both knew it would be ridiculous to prioritize our codependence over our future careers. So here I am, a five-hour flight away from my family, bestie, and everything I've ever known.

Footsteps approach on the other side of the door. "Yes, Doctor. Quarantined."

I jolt to attention in the chair, putting my phone away. My savior is here—even as the word *quarantine* hangs like a death sentence.

The door swings open, and a tall woman in an open white lab coat, black V-neck tee, and tight jeans strides in, clipboard in hand. Her muscular arms fill out the lab coat, and her long legs are—um—very nicely toned. Is it hot in here?

"Miss Alexander?"

I meet her eyes, and my heart does a backflip. "H-hi. Yes. Hi."

"I'm Doctor Zacharias." Her voice is a low purr, rumbling through me and down to my toes.

This woman... is going to make everything better.

This woman is also making my brain stall.

She oozes confidence, turning my knees to jelly as I look up at her. It's hard to breathe as I take in her features—her light, freckled skin, arched eyebrows, straight nose, and God help me, her heart-shaped lips. Behind copper eyeshadow, her dark brown eyes seem to glow, pinning me in place, warning me to answer every question she asks. Her thick brown hair is swept deeply to one side, all the volume and length cascading over her left shoulder. A few small braids peek through the locks, woven with strands of green and yellow. I never thought side-swept hair would be my downfall, but that was before I met this woman side-sweeps were made for.

She turns to close the door, giving me half a second to compose myself.

Despite the maturity in her eyes, she must be only a couple of years older than me, maybe in her early twenties. How does a person become a vet so young? Shouldn't she still be in school? Personally, I'm expecting to be in university for seven years before I can start my career as a psychologist.

I perch forward in the chair, suddenly invested in her life story. But as she looks at the kennel, I shake myself back to reality, remembering why I'm here.

"Thank you for waiting," she murmurs.

"No problem." My voice is muffled through the balaclava.

Oh God, I'm still wearing the balaclava and ski jacket in front of this gorgeous woman.

She leans down to peer into the crate. Lucy yowls and hisses, and the whole thing shakes as she lunges at the door. Her paw swipes through the grate, claws extended.

Doctor Zacharias doesn't flinch. She just studies the kitten with a neutral expression. Either she's seen this before or she's really good at pretending this isn't alarming. "Tell me what you've been experiencing since getting the cat."

Interesting wording. Not "tell me the cat's symptoms," but rather, "tell me what you've been experiencing." I think I've found the right person.

"It started when I adopted her four days ago..."

She lays the clipboard on the examination table, and with deft fingers, grabs the penlight from her breast pocket and shines it into the kennel. Lucy hisses.

Considering they called this room *quarantine*, she's dressed casually. No mask, no gloves. It's comforting—like maybe I panicked too much.

Then Lucy makes a low, threatening growl, and that cold fear returns.

"Go on," the vet says, her dark gaze flicking to me. The look both reassures me it's safe to continue while giving me no choice.

"She's been acting rabid, but it's more than that." It's hard to look at someone so effortlessly gorgeous while I'm at my lowest, so I relay everything that's happened to the tile floor, scorpion in my slipper and all.

I expect her to recoil or gasp, but her demeanor doesn't change. "I see."

Should I be reassured or annoyed by how calm she is? "Have... have you seen this before?"

"Maybe." She clicks off the light and straightens up, facing me with crossed arms. "Where did you get her?"

I furrow my brow at her non-answer. "The shelter. Someone found her abandoned in a box outside an apartment building and brought her in."

"Alone or with a litter?"

"Alone."

"And out of all the cats at the shelter, why did you adopt this one?"

Another interesting question. "I... thought she was cute?"

"But what attracted you to her? Why did you get this cat in particular?"

The way she purrs the word 'attracted' makes my heart miss a beat.

I try to find words to explain the pull I felt toward Lucy. She's adorable, but a lot of adorable kittens were up for adoption. Something drew me to her like a paperclip to a magnet. "I don't know. I just liked her."

Doctor Zacharias's eyes remain as enigmatic as ever, so I can't tell if this answer is sufficient. Or why it matters. This whole line of questions is weird.

She scans my outfit, a cute crease appearing between her eyebrows. "Take off your coat and show me the boils."

Embarrassment and dread churn inside me. Why does the second half of that sentence have to be a thing?

With a sigh of resignation, I shed my winter garb, letting the cool air hit my irritated skin. I'm clammy because it's nowhere near cold enough to wear all these layers.

I can feel Doctor Zacharias's gaze like a flame as it roves over my body—all five-foot-two of me, small and defeated. Our eyes meet, and something flickers in hers. Disgust? Pity? I look away, not wanting to know.

She clears her throat and bends closer to study my arms. She doesn't touch me, just looks with the same focus as when she examined Lucy.

The closeness sends a pleasant ripple through me. I'm not prepared to be hit with her scent—warm, calming, like a mug of herbal tea in the winter. I want to lean in and inhale deeper. But I don't because that would be weird.

She straightens up, taking a step back. "Those will go away by to-morrow. They aren't contagious—just a reaction. Avoid showering or putting any lotions on for the next twenty-four hours so you don't agitate them."

Relief washes over me so intensely that I slump back in the chair. I didn't realize how much I was bracing for the worst until now, as the tension drains from me and leaves me tingly. I can handle not showering or moisturizing for a day. It's not like I'm going anywhere like this.

She scans the clipboard. "Are you okay other than that? No other health problems came up?"

Other than the absolute chaos of the last four days? Other than all the stuff that made me question reality? "All good."

"Your breathing feels normal?" Her concerned tone makes me melt a little.

I nod. "Is that a symptom?"

"Sometimes." She scribbles something down. "Well, Miss Alexander, I was called in because my specialty is rare infectious diseases. I'm sorry to say your cat has carried a disease into your home."

"Oh." A strange feeling settles in my gut—not fear about being told it's a disease, but some kind of... disappointment. The straightforward diagnosis isn't enough to explain everything that's happened.

She wraps her slender fingers around the kennel's handle. "I'll take the cat to the lab for testing—"

"Take her?" I straighten up as if zapped, my voice rising as panic grips my throat. "Is she going to be okay?"

She raises one of those perfect, arched eyebrows. "You want her back? After the way she's been... behaving?"

I stand, ready to seize the kennel. "Yes! She's my kitten!"

The vet's brow pinches in bewilderment. "But she's..."

Something in my expression makes her trail off.

Indignation rushes through me, sharpening my next words. "People would never abandon a loved one because they're sick, so why would I do that to my pet? This lack of empathy is everything that's wrong with the world!"

Her mouth opens a little as if she's surprised by my outburst. But as heat rises in my cheeks, she softens and drops her gaze. "You're right. I—I'm sure I'll be able to cure her, Miss Alexander. I'll have the front desk call you when she's ready for pickup. I promise she'll be in good hands."

I nod, a little embarrassed by the tone I took with her but grateful for her response.

An ache forms in my chest as she steps back with the kennel. As chaotic as Lucy was, she was still my furry companion, and now I'm returning to an empty house.

"What's the disease called?" I ask, my mouth dry. I'll feel better if I can look it up when I get home.

"I'm afraid I can't disclose that."

My heart sinks. What kind of doctor withholds critical information from a patient? I narrow my eyes and take another approach. "What diseases do you specialize in?"

"Ones most people have never heard of."

"Try me," I shoot back.

The corner of her mouth quirks, but she just lifts the kennel to peer into it again. Lucy growls.

Annoyance twists in my gut. I don't like her lack of answers or eye contact. Is her work so classified that an infected person can't know what they've contracted?

"You're young to be a vet." It's not an accusation, exactly, but this is all really weird.

"I did an accelerated program." She's still inspecting Lucy. "I knew what I wanted to be from a young age."

I cock an eyebrow. "So you're a genius too?"

"What do you mean, *too*?"

Heat rushes into my cheeks. She must know she's a knockout, right? Like, people must always tell her she's the full package of looks and brains?

I cross my arms, wincing as the boils press against each other, and redirect the topic. "I guess that makes sense. I also knew what I wanted to be as a kid. I'm taking psychology, and I used to make my sisters lay on the couch and tell me their problems like I was psychoanalyzing them."

There's a pause, and the heat in my face intensifies. I was hoping to make her laugh. She doesn't.

Well, we found out why I hate talking to strangers. Dammit, Hazel.

Abruptly, she grabs my upper arm, pulling me toward her. My heart jumps, both at her strong hand and the suddenness.

As our chests bump, a burst of debris smashes over the ground and hits our ankles. The loose ceiling tile I was afraid of lies in a dozen pieces, a cloud of dust rising.

I cough and wave my hand, turning my face to avoid inhaling it. Doctor Zacharias's expression hasn't changed—like she's as unsurprised by the event as I am. Did she even flinch? The way she grabbed my arm and pulled me out of the way was so calm, like she might as well have said, "*Ah, yes, this again.*"

We're close enough that I can feel the heat of her body. As we lock eyes, she drops her hand, leaving my arm tingling.

She nods firmly. "We'll call you when your cat is cured and ready for pickup."

She leaves the room with the kennel, plunging me back into silence.

I huff, my frustration replaced by a hollow sense of loss. I didn't expect to be returning to my place alone today.

I step around the debris and shrug into my jacket, today's events swirling through my head. Doctor Zacharias's vague diagnosis isn't enough to explain it all. Rather than answer my questions, she planted a seed of suspicion. What's she keeping from me?

I pull out my phone and open the browser. Something is going on—something bigger than a disease. She's hiding the truth, and I'm going to figure out what it is.

CHAPTER 3

Friends on this Side of the Country

As the boils subside over the following days, I keep my phone beside me, which becomes both a source of hope and a torture device. Every time it buzzes, I fumble for it, the jolt of anticipation followed by a sinking disappointment. By day five, a dreary, rainy Monday, I've lost count of how many times I've called Helping Paws to ask for an update.

"I just want to know if Lucy's okay," I tell the annoyed vet tech, pacing my room. "Can I please speak to Doctor Zacharias?"

"I'm sorry, but we can't give out her number. We'll call you."

I hang up without a goodbye and throw my phone on my bed. A hot surge of anger rises in me. Would it kill her to relay a message? I fight the urge to pick up something else and throw it too. This state of not knowing is eating me alive.

My fingers tremble as I weave my hair into its familiar braid over my right shoulder. As I pull on a knit sweater and jeans, with nothing but swishing clothes and pattering rain filling my ears, a lump forms in my throat. Lucy's absence leaves a void, not to mention a constant reminder of this freaky mystery. To ward off the homesickness, Hazel and I have been video chatting every night—sometimes, we'll leave our call running in the background while we study in parallel. It helps a smidge.

When I get to the biology lecture hall, amid a hum of conversations and the shuffle of papers and backpacks, I grab a seat along the far left wall. The cavernous room is cold, smelling like damp coats and old books. The tablet-desk seating is designed for right-handed people to write in tiny notebooks, so I carefully balance my phone in the space beside my laptop.

My browser is still open to a page on rare infectious diseases. I close it quickly before anyone can look over my shoulder and see the words *full-body skin boils*. All this gory research and I still haven't been able to figure out what Lucy had. Should I be worried about more cats like her popping up? Are there any lasting effects of whatever I contracted?

The prof gets organized at the front, firing up a slide deck. We're reviewing the unit today before Wednesday's midterm. I have yet to get the class notes I missed last week—my entire focus has been on trying to determine what Lucy had and who Doctor Zacharias is.

I hesitate with my fingers on the keyboard, then turn down my screen's brightness and open the browser again. In the search bar, I type,

dr zacharias vancouver veterinarian

The results list many Doctor Zacharias's, and I pick up where I left off yesterday, clicking through them one by one. A frustrating wave of hope and disappointment rolls through me with each click, each failed attempt to find her annoyingly gorgeous face.

I try another search.

dr zacharias infectious diseases

The results give me more doctors who aren't her.

After searching all week, I might have to conclude that she doesn't exist online. But *why*? Wouldn't a doctor be listed *somewhere*?

Dark possibilities swirl through my mind. Can she be trusted? Is Lucy really safe with her?

A part of me knows I'm spiraling. I should focus on studying and trust the professionals. But what if I'm missing something crucial? What if I regret not figuring this out and my inaction leads to something terrible—for Lucy, for myself, for anyone else in the world who's been exposed to whatever this is?

A coat rustles and a plastic chair creaks as someone sits next to me. I close the browser window.

I look over, and our gazes catch. He's a lanky white guy with a crew cut and soft blue eyes, wearing a zip-up hoodie open over a green polo shirt.

"Hey," he says.

"Hey."

Silence.

Last night, Hazel asked if I struck up a conversation with anybody yet. I told her defensively that I said hi to my roommate, who showed up for the first time in a week to swap her wardrobe before heading back to her boyfriend's place.

Ugh, Hazel's right. I need to make friends who live on the same side of the country as me. I thought a kitten would fix the loneliness of moving to a new city, and look how that played out.

My phone lights up, and I lean over to check, but it's an email from my calculus professor reminding us of this week's midterm.

The guy beside me points to my background, an angelic picture of Lucy. "Aww."

Okay, that's my cue. It's time.

"Her name's Lucy." My face heats up as the threat of a conversation becomes a reality. "I just got her."

"I take it you don't live in a dorm?" He casts me a lopsided smile. "Unless you have a secret about how you smuggled in a pet."

"I'm renting off-campus." A decision that was probably not great for making new friends. "You?"

"I'm in Totem." He leans back, slinging an arm over the back of the empty seat on his other side before bringing it down again. He's projecting confidence, but it doesn't quite fit. Maybe he spent his high school years shy and nerdy, and now that he's in university, he's trying to start fresh with a Cool Guy persona. "Ever come on campus to party?"

"Sometimes," I lie. Not once have I partied since being here.

"Well, if you ever want to come out, we're always doing something. My roommate and I throw good parties." He says this with the pride of a kid showing you what he drew.

I return his smile. "Thanks."

Wow, that *was* easy. I can't wait to tell Hazel I got invited to a party.

The prof starts talking, and the guy opens his laptop to take notes.

"I'm so behind," he murmurs. "I was too hungover this weekend to study. Beer pong tourney."

I humor him with a breath of laughter. His casual brag about being too much of a party guy to study checks out. The folders on his desktop—PHYS, CALC, BIOL, CHEM—tell me he was definitely a brainy kid in high school. He's probably on a several-week bender now that he's free from parents and teachers.

"Hey, did you happen to get notes last Wednesday?" I whisper. "I missed class that day."

He brightens. "Yeah, I can send them to you. What's your email?"

A party invite *and* the notes I missed! Look at me go!

As I reach over to type my email address into his laptop, he doesn't lean back, which means my arm brushes his chest. This feels akin to giving him my number, and I hope he's not getting the wrong idea.

"Katie." He tips the screen back toward him. "I'm Clayton."

I return his smile.

My phone rings, and I reach for it so fast that I nearly send my laptop crashing to the floor.

The name on the display infuses me with hope. It's Helping Paws. I'm finally going to get answers about Lucy.

After class, when Doctor Zacharias meets me at the front desk of Helping Paws with Lucy's kennel, my heart skips for two reasons.

First, obviously, Lucy.

Second... Doctor Zacharias is even more striking than I remember. Even in the harsh lighting of the vet's office, her jawline and cheekbones are so sculpted that she could be at the top of a Google image search for the perfect facial structure. She stands with a cool confidence, and seriously, she should publish her leg-day gym routine for the benefit of humanity. Her commanding presence seems to take up all the space in the waiting room—and all the air.

"I'm glad to see the boils went away," she says in that low purr of hers.

Though she's looking at me clinically, *not* checking me out, the way her gaze travels up and down my body weakens my knees.

"Same," I stammer, tugging my knit sweater straight. "How is she?"

A little meow comes from inside the kennel, nothing like the angry yowling from a week ago.

Doctor Zacharias tilts her head, a lock of hair fluttering across her eyes. "Restored to health."

"Thank you." My shoulders sag in relief. She's coming home with me! Before I lose my nerve, I add sternly, "You took a long time to get back to me."

"It took a long time to cure her," she says, unfazed by my tone.

I feel a lot of gazes on us. Doctor Zacharias seems to have caught the attention of everyone else in the waiting room, including the vet tech, whose gaze keeps flicking away from the computer.

I do my best to ignore them. "I would have appreciated a call. I tried to find your contact info, but you're not online anywhere."

She arches an eyebrow, which makes my indignance turn into a flutter. This woman is infuriating. "I keep my business information private. Sensitive nature of the work."

"Am I allowed to know which disease she had now?" I ask, dreading the answer.

She shakes her head once. "Classified."

Irritation swells inside me. "I have a right to know what happened to my cat."

"And certain organizations have a right to withhold information from the public."

I roll my eyes. "I didn't realize I was talking to a Secret Service agent."

Doctor Zacharias's lips twitch as if she's about to smile. "Infectious diseases like this need to remain classified until they're better understood. We don't want to cause panic."

I scowl. Fine, that sort of makes sense.

But I still think she's full of shit. What kind of infectious disease involves the ability to summon a crow through a window? I know what I saw, and if she expects me to move on without asking questions, she's mistaken. After all, I'm getting a degree in psychology, and my job one day will be to ask people a lot of questions—to uncover the truth beneath all the lies people tell themselves and others.

If she won't give me answers, I'll find them myself.

Lucy meows, a tiny, pitiful sound.

"Don't worry, you're going home," Doctor Zacharias says. She lifts the kennel to let me see inside. The fleece blanket I used to trap Lucy is folded nicely, as cozy as a bird's nest. She's sitting at the back, gazing at me with big blue eyes.

Blue, not purple. *This* is the angelic kitten I adopted—and to top it off, there's a pink ribbon around her neck.

"Oh, she looks so cute." My anger melts away, replaced with a wave of relief and gratitude over having her back. "Hi, sweetie."

She meows again, flashing her little teeth.

"I wanted to make her presentable for her return," Doctor Zacharias says.

I meet her gaze. "You put the ribbon on?"

She presses her lips together, almost bashful.

Dammit, now I feel bad for getting snippy. "I—well—thank you. I'm glad she's safe and healthy."

Something I can't decipher glints in her brown eyes. "And I'm glad she's going to a home where she'll be loved deeply."

Her voice reverberates in my chest like a subwoofer.

As she passes the kennel to me by the handle, our fingers entwine. A ridiculous giggle escapes me as I try to ignore the heat zapping up my arm. "Oop—got it."

Oop? What's wrong with me?

My skin tingles where her warm, soft fingers slid between mine.

Lucy gives a tiny meow, as if asking if we can go now.

"I know, baby, we'll cuddle as soon as we get back," I tell her.

Doctor Zacharias turns to fidget with the pens on the front desk. "Is she your first cat?"

The question feels more personal than clinical, catching me off-guard. I nod. "I'm just here for school and wanted a study buddy."

"Just for school? You think you won't like Vancouver enough to stay?" Her tone is teasing, a peek at a different side of her.

I lift a shoulder. "It's nice here, but... it's not home."

She studies me as I try to act like mentioning home didn't just punch a hole in my heart. Why did I think applying to a university across the country was a good idea?

The door swings open with a soft *whoosh*, letting in a gust of cool autumn air. A girl my age runs in, holding a squirming golden retriever puppy. "My dog swallowed a bunch of LEGO," she cries, her eyes watery.

The vet tech grabs a clipboard. "Please fill this out," she says in the same flat tone she used with me.

I step toward the door with Lucy's kennel, the handle firm and comforting in my grip. "Thanks again." I swallow hard. "Can I at least have your first name?"

She pauses for a fraction of a second. "Natalie."

"Natalie. I'm Katie."

She must have known that already, but she nods anyway, her dark eyes gleaming.

I wave and turn away. Will this be the last time I see her? On the one hand, that would be a good thing, given her job in infectious diseases. On the other hand... it's been at least a year since anyone made me feel like fireflies were waking up inside me.

Natalie. Nat. Doctor Natalie Zacharias.

Any way I spin it, it's hot.

I dip my chin to hide my smile. She might be unwilling to tell me anything, but I'm as determined as ever to unravel who she is and why she's keeping secrets. And now I have one more piece of information I can use. *Natalie.*

CHAPTER 4

Midterms and Impostors

LUCY POUNCES, A BALL of fur and energy as I move my hand beneath the duvet. I'm cross-legged on the bed, my laptop casting a pale glow through the dark room, Hazel on a video chat. A swarm of tabs is open, each one a fruitless search.

"I've hit a wall," I tell her after catching her up on what happened. "I might never know what I was exposed to. Should I be worried?"

"You're not in quarantine, so I'd say no." Hazel pauses as she washes her face. She's bringing me with her as she gets ready for bed. "The vet would be monitoring you or would have scheduled a checkup if there was something to be concerned about, right?"

The uncertainty in her tone does little to soothe my nerves. "I guess."

I swish my hand under the blanket, and Lucy's tiny body makes a *thwap* as she pounces on it.

Something I can't decipher tingles in the back of my mind. Unease. A warning.

Maybe it's the trauma of what happened to Lucy—and nothing to reassure me she's cured except the word of a woman who's definitely hiding something.

I move my hand again. *Swish.* She pounces. *Thwap.*

"Do you have any other info to go on?" Hazel's background shifts as she takes me out of the bathroom. She's home with her family tonight. Framed photos of her and her sister decorate the hallway, and her dad's massive *Great Wave off Kanagawa* print makes a brief appearance behind her before she plunks down in front of the familiar red brick of their fireplace. A pang goes through my chest. I'd give anything to be able to randomly drive home for a night or two.

"Just her first name." *Swish.* "Natalie."

Thwap.

I let her name linger on my tongue. I like saying it, even though it's attached to a woman wrapped in an infuriating mystery.

"Natalie," she repeats, sounding like a detective on a case. "I'll look her up. I want a picture."

"Don't bother. She's nowhere." Defeat weighs heavily over me. I was so sure I could find something. *Anything.* All I found was a Reddit post from three years ago where someone asked about an excellent piano tuner in Vancouver named Natalie Zacharias, who seemed to have disappeared overnight. A local news article from two years ago also named her as an employee in a thrift shop that got robbed.

But what does this tell me? Maybe she had part-time jobs while completing her degree. Or these were different people with the same name.

"Ugh, that's so weird." Hazel puckers her lips, a deep crease between her eyebrows.

I know that look. It's the one she makes when she's trying to solve a tough problem. And Doctor Natalie Zacharias is a tough problem.

Lucy crouches and wiggles her butt, then does the most ferocious pounce yet. Hazel and I both laugh, and the sense of dread thaws a little.

Is it safe to trust that she's been cured? She's acting like a normal kitten and is definitely more playful now.

"I think I need to give up and accept that I'll never know what happened to us." Resigned, I drag the laptop closer and open my class notes. "Anyway, I've got midterms to cram for. I can't believe I have four next week. This sucks."

"I know." Hazel's voice is muffled behind her hands. "It feels like term just started."

Exhaustion pulls me down, and I lean back against my pillows with my laptop on my thighs. My motivation is at an all-time low after the chaos of the last few days. How am I supposed to buckle down? As much as I want to follow my own advice and give up, I can't force my mind away from Natalie—or the image of Lucy's blazing purple eyes.

She flops around on the duvet, having the time of her life while I move my foot. Still, the nagging worry is there, a sense that I'm missing something important.

"I've started a study group with a bunch of other CompSci students," Hazel says. "One of them is literally the smartest person I've ever met in my life. He's been helping me with assignments." The determined edge in her voice is all too familiar. We're both overachievers who deal with pressure from our parents, but she tends to take it to the next level. She wants to start her own tech company that helps the environment in some way.

"Good to hear you're making friends so you can use them for their brains," I tease.

"It's a fair trade." She fidgets with something off-screen, a flush in her cheeks. "I give him free cinnamon buns from work."

I raise an eyebrow. There's more here. "And how often is he coming by for cinnamon buns?"

Hazel does a little awkward giggle that totally confirms my suspicion.

I gasp, excitement surging. "Oh my God!"

"We haven't gone out yet! But I think we're both getting up the nerve to ask." She covers her face, a gleam in her eyes.

"Who is he?" I shout, leaning closer to my laptop. Hazel's adorably giddy when she has a crush.

The video gets blurry as she rushes to her bedroom, presumably so her parents don't listen in. When she sits, her lips twist into a suppressed smile. "His name's Sean. We met in the Computer Science Student Society and... I guess we've both been showing up in the study lounge a little more than necessary."

I clap. "Ahh, this is so cute! I'm so happy for you." And painfully aware that this is a perfect example of how meeting people starts with being social. She's always been good at this. She met her last boyfriend on a dodgeball team. I'd die before joining a team that requires athletic and social competence.

Lucy flops on her side with her claws locked onto the blanket over my foot. I watch her little paws bat it, feeling them patter against my toes. My gaze keeps traveling to her eyes, searching, like I'm expecting them to turn purple again.

"Our flirting is so awkward and shameless," Hazel says into her hands. "You'd cringe if you saw it."

I laugh. "At least you know how to show someone you're interested."

"Uh-huh. Speaking of *crushes*." Hazel grins, seeing right through me. "Maybe you should get to know Natalie a bit better."

I splutter something that isn't even words, not ready for the abrupt turn in the conversation. I finally choke out a sarcastic, "Yeah, okay."

"Why not?"

"Even if she wasn't weirdly cryptic, and even if I *did* trust her..." Longing fills me at the mere prospect of going out with someone that hot, that smart, and that confident. "A person of her... caliber... would never be interested in me."

"How do you know?" Hazel asks optimistically. Bless her.

"I read the room."

"What room? A vet's office?"

I say nothing, my attention suddenly veering to Lucy, who's lying on her side and purring. *Wait a second.*

"Not exactly a flirty place," Hazel says, oblivious to my shift in focus. "Come on, you said after Mansplainy Matt that you were ready to date girls again. I can see your infatuation from here."

I'm frozen, staring at the kitten on my bed. A chill creeps over me. Where is the brown smudge on her back paw?

A cold knot forms in my stomach as I lean forward, picking her up despite her meow of protest. I sift through the fur on her paw, searching. Could she have shed the brown hairs?

No, it's been less than a week since I last saw her.

"Katie?" Hazel's voice filters through my frantic thoughts. "You good?"

My phone is in my hand before I register moving, my fingers flipping through every picture of Lucy since the day I got her. I hold the kitten up next to my phone, comparing.

No—effing—way.

Disbelief and betrayal slice through me, leaving me breathless.

"Katie?" Hazel's tone has an edge as she picks up on my panic.

"I—" My hands are shaking. I gaze into the kitten's big blue eyes, which are wider set than in the photo. "Hazel, this isn't Lucy."

"Helping Paws Vancouver Anim—"

"Hi, this is Katie Alexander," I interrupt, gripping my phone so hard that my hand cramps. "I picked up my cat from Doctor Zacharias today. Can you have her call me? It's urgent."

My room is dead silent except for the rain lashing against the window, leaving streaks between me and the pitch black night. My candles sway in a draft, casting shadows over the walls.

"If it's urgent, we recommend you bring your cat in for an exam," the vet tech says.

"Please just have her call me." I pinch the bridge of my nose. "I have follow-up questions."

A pause. "Okay. What's the best number to reach you?"

I give her my number, and before I can ask how long it will be, the line goes dead.

I flop sideways on the bed and draw my knees to my chest. Hazel is still on my laptop, walking in and out of the frame as she paces her room and flaps her hands.

Not-Lucy comes to curl up beside my face. I pet her.

"Whose cat are you, then?" I whisper, and she purrs, oblivious to my turmoil.

"There has to be an explanation," Hazel says calmly. "A vet could get in serious trouble for something like this. They could be sued, or shut down, or... get a really bad review on Google."

I moan incoherently into the duvet.

The minutes tick by with excruciating slowness. I turn on my desk lamp and try to study, re-reading the same notes over and over, praying they sink in so I don't fail my first university midterms.

It's hopeless.

After an hour, Hazel and I have to end our call so she can go to sleep.

Finally, as I lie in bed and prepare to stare at the ceiling all night, an unknown number lights up my phone.

I sit up and answer with a trembling hand. "Where's the real Lucy?"

Silence. An exhale. "What are you talking about?"

Natalie's voice disorients me. It purrs through the speaker, making me tingle everywhere.

I scowl. "Don't give me that! You swapped my cat."

The silence goes on for longer this time. "What makes you say that?"

I fling the blankets off me and get up, pacing the dark room. The ambient light from the street lamps outside casts a faint glow over the bed. "First of all, her whole personality is different, but I chalked that up to her being cured from... whatever she had going on. But it's her back paw. The real Lucy has a smudge there, and this kitten doesn't."

"Do you not like this kitten?"

The question makes my heart jump. "So you admit it. This isn't Lucy."

"And you don't like her?"

I look down at the little fluff ball on my pillow with her big eyes and beige-tipped ears. "That's not the point."

"Miss Alexander, trust me when I say you're better off this way."

I freeze mid-step, a scoff escaping. "I don't trust you! You've given me no reason to!"

She says nothing. I want to reach through the phone and shake a real answer out of her.

"Is this why you put the ribbon on her?" I ask. "To distract me?"

"No. Maybe."

I growl in frustration, acid rising inside me. "You're despicable. Is Lucy still alive?"

"I have to go, Miss Alexander. Please understand that you've got the cat you were meant to have."

"What is that supposed to—"

Beep beep beep. The call disconnects.

I gape at the phone, fury bubbling up. The jerk hung up on me!

I can't even call her back because her number is private.

My hands are shaking. I can't believe her. She lied about Lucy being restored to health, she lied about her contracting a curable disease, and now...

My eyes prickle, a lump forming in my throat.

No. Don't go there.

She has to be okay. Only a monster would harm a kitten.

I tap the number for the vet's office.

"Helping Paws, please hold," the vet tech says in a rush.

"Wait—"

Hold music blares in my ears. I pull the phone away a few inches, continuing to pace because there's no way I could sit still right now.

A long minute passes before she comes back. "How can I help you?"

"Hi, it's Katie Alexander again. I have another important question for Doctor Zacharias. Can you please have her call me?" I barely refrain from referring to her as 'that asshole.'

"I just spoke with her," the vet tech says, sounding a little snippy, "and she told me to tell you that Lucy's illness is resolved and there is no further reason for you to contact us."

My face burns. She's made it sound like I'm stalking her.

Too humiliated to argue, I swallow. "Oh. Sorry for..." I mumble something incoherent and hang up.

My room is quiet. Not-Lucy is asleep. Even the rain has ceased, leaving me in a heavy, suffocating silence.

These dead ends won't stop me. I refuse to let the real Lucy down by giving up on her.

But 'Doctor' Natalie Zacharias seems to be a pro at this. Like maybe she does this sort of thing all the time. What if Lucy isn't the only victim? Have there been other cases like hers—at other vet offices, even?

I grab my laptop, determination settling over me like armor. I'm ready to do whatever it takes to break this secret open... even if that means making a reckless plan.

CHAPTER 5

The Haunted Flea Market

T HE FOLLOWING FRIDAY, I drop my head into my hands as I finish writing my last midterm. Sighs and rustling pages fill the lecture hall, and the prof comes around to gather our exam papers.

Well, that sucked. Cold regret pulses through me as reality hits. I wasn't as prepared as I should have been for any of the exams. But aside from trying to study for four tests at once, it's impossible to concentrate on topics like neural structures when there are mysteries to solve. Namely, who is Natalie Zacharias and why is she so infuriating?

Between studying, I phoned a bunch of veterinarians and asked if they knew of her. Turns out, she's on call for specific symptoms at every vet's office from here to Abbotsford, which is far enough from Vancouver to have its own international airport. When I asked which symptoms she's on call for, they all said they couldn't share that information. They also wouldn't provide me with her contact info.

Frustration burns a hole in my abdomen. No matter how deep I dig, I'm no closer to the truth—and no closer to finding the real Lucy.

A loose plan is slowly taking form. If Natalie does this sort of thing, whatever *this* is, then I should track down another kitten with the same condition and bring it to a vet so they call her in.

The problem: how am I supposed to find another Lucy? Do I volunteer at the shelter and watch if any kittens start triggering strange occurrences?

I shuffle out of the lecture hall and into the chilly outdoors, swallowed by a sea of students. The quiet, somber mood tells me everybody was just as defeated by that test. Few things are as humbling as being told you're gifted in high school only to become painfully average in university.

Footsteps thump on the concrete, and Clayton catches up, his breath misting in the autumn air. "How'd you do?"

"Terribly. You?"

"Same. At least if we all did, the prof will have to move the bell curve, right?"

"There's always that."

We have two classes together and have been sitting beside each other in both. I don't mind. It's comforting to know someone. I'm just going to have to get creative with ways to turn down dorm parties.

He zips up his hoodie, hunching against the wind. "A few of us are going to Granville Island later to celebrate finishing midterms. Want to come?"

My default answer is on my tongue, but wouldn't it be nice to meet more people? Also, I have yet to see Vancouver's famous sights.

"There's a haunted flea market happening," he adds, his blue eyes hopeful. "Halloween-themed. Sounds like it's worth checking out, yeah?"

Hazel's voice whispers in the back of my mind. *"Say yes. Make friends."*

After these terrible couple of weeks, it would be good for me to do something social and take my focus off Natalie and Lucy. I'm getting obsessive about it.

I smile, pushing past my reluctance. "Cool. Sounds fun."

Clayton's expression is like the sun breaking through the clouds. And I can't help smiling back.

As a demonic clown and a convincingly grotesque zombie lumber by, I'm no longer sure if a haunted flea market is my idea of fun. The crowd is shoulder-to-shoulder, invading my space, and there must be a theater troupe here because the creepy costumes are *way* too detailed. Screams punctuate the buzz of conversations.

We weave through the disorienting maze of tables, which fills a huge building and continues outside under white tents. Clayton's friends, Johnny, Mo, and Andrea, live on campus in Totem Park as well. Andrea is wearing devil horns and all red, and Clayton has one of those headbands that looks like he's been stabbed in the brain with a dagger. Johnny and Mo are in jeans and coats, same as me. The only thing on my head is a giant clip. I'm not opposed to dressing up—Hazel and I were ketchup and mustard last year—but I didn't have time to buy anything today.

"...oh, and the beer gardens," Clayton says, still talking about parties. "We should check out both..."

"Look at this nineties stuff! I *love* the nineties," Andrea cries, pulling me to a cluttered table. She's been clinging to me since we got here, towing behind me by the strap of my backpack. "Oh my gosh, I *love* Furbies. Look how cute."

She picks up the fuzzy white toy. Its beak is open and it stares at me with glassy, dead eyes. Maybe the setting is getting to me, but I wouldn't use the word 'cute' to describe it.

She's still clamped onto my backpack with the weight of an anchor, making the straps dig into my shoulders. The way she's clinging to me to stop me from leaving her behind, doing everything to make sure I don't forget she's there, I get the sense she's struggled with holding onto friendships.

Fighting the sense of being smothered, I repeat my mantra—*I want to be here, I want to make friends.* But lying in bed with a book and a kitten curled up beside me sounds more fun. Am I doomed to not fit in at university?

"Yo, we should buy this for our floor," Mo says from the next table, inspecting some kind of plastic fountain.

"What is it?" Clayton asks.

"Fondue maker! For parties, you know?"

A girl with scary-good demon makeup brushes past, and I turn away. Maybe this isn't the best place to come after getting attacked by a possessed cat.

While the guys bicker over whether a fondue maker is a good idea, I walk on to check out more booths, and Andrea drags along behind me.

What would happen if I grabbed her backpack strap in return? Would we keep walking in a circle like a snake eating its own tail, stuck in an infinite loop until someone comes and pries one of our hands away?

The next table is full of vintage dolls—Cabbage Patch Kids, Trolls, Barbies, Care Bears, and a bunch more that I recognize but don't know the names of. They all stare at me with vacant eyes.

"Cuuute!" Andrea cries.

The elderly woman behind the table smiles at us. "Let me know if you have questions."

"Thanks." I'm about to keep walking when a weird, icy sensation travels down my back and into my legs, freezing me in place.

My gaze pulls to a porcelain doll. I step closer. It's like she's cast a fishing line and sunk a hook into me. She's a foot high with cream skin, rosy cheeks, periwinkle eyes, golden ringlets, and a frilly purple dress.

I furrow my brow. This doll means nothing to me, so why is my face going numb? Why do I feel like something is urging me to lean in, pick it up, and ask questions?

I point to it. "What's the story with this one?"

The woman stands up from her chair to peer over the mound of dolls. "Oh, that's Rebecca. I collected her in Boston about... ah, I'd say thirty years ago."

"It's creepy," Andrea says in a pouty tone.

I can't disagree. But that inner tug hasn't gone away. My legs are rooted, my heart slamming into my ribs like I'm sprinting. "From an antique shop or...?"

"Toy store. Walked past with my husband and had to have her for the collection!"

I nod. Natalie's words simmer in the back of my mind, asking me what attracted me to Lucy. I liked her because she was cute and playful, but wasn't it more than that? Wasn't there something I couldn't explain? It was a feeling in my core, a tug like the way you have to keep watching a thriller to find out what happens. My pulse quickened, my skin tingled, and I couldn't turn away.

That feeling is back as I look at the porcelain doll. My chest skips like I've set eyes on something historians have been searching for. This dead-eyed, creeptastic toy named Rebecca is important.

I need it. For the same inexplicable reason I had to adopt Lucy, I have to buy this doll.

This is how I get a hold of Natalie Zacharias.

"Nice, you getting something?" Clayton asks, stepping up beside me. He sees the doll and flinches. "Jesus Christ."

"It reminds me of… one my grandma had," I lie.

Andrea says nothing, watching in horror as I exchange payment with the woman and accept my purchase.

The feel of her is as creepy as her appearance. The frilly dress loses volume as my fingers close around her formless body. She's a couple of pounds. Whatever I expected her to feel like, this isn't it.

I can't look at her. Maybe it's the way her head is tilted or the way age has put little chips and smudges all over her face.

"I'll get you a bag to protect her from the rain," the woman says.

"Yes. Thank you," I say with a sigh of relief.

She puts Rebecca in a paper bag with handles, and it immediately rips. "Oops. That's weird," she says and gets me a new one.

I chew my lip. *Coincidence?*

Her second attempt at bagging the doll is successful. I let out a breath and roll my shoulders, shaking off my anxiety.

We continue through the flea market, me with the porcelain doll swinging from my arm in a paper bag, Andrea with her hand glued to my backpack, and the guys getting excited about random items like old video games. Mo buys a lava lamp and a neon beer sign for his dorm room.

We head to the outdoor portion of the market, and I zip up my jacket. It's dark, but there are enough lights to see the water and the Granville Bridge passing over it. The wind has picked up, making the tents groan and the string lights sway. Vendors scramble to secure loose papers and tablecloths.

"What do you think of Granville Island?" Clayton asks, falling into step beside me.

"I like it," I say truthfully. "Not sure about the creepy costumes, but the place itself is nice. I'd like to come here by day."

A grim reaper lumbers past, the person in the costume on stilts.

Clayton grins at me. "We should go to the improv theater one night. It's a lot of fun."

His words dangle in the air. I can't tell if he means 'we' as in the two of us.

"I'm starving," Andrea says. "Can we get dinner?"

"Same," I say quickly, grateful for her interruption.

"Let's head to the Mexican restaurant over there," Mo says, pointing.

Suddenly, a buzz ripples overhead, snapping the market's vibrant colors into darkness. People cry out, their voices rising over each other. I stop walking, blinking to try and adjust my eyes.

"Power's out," someone beside us murmurs, the echo of those words carrying on the wind as everyone comes to the same conclusion. Shouts, screams, and ghostly "*wooo*" noises erupt as some people decide this is a good opportunity to scare their friends.

My heart beats faster. *Another coincidence?*

I don't like this one bit. I need to get back to my basement suite so I can call Helping Paws, and fast.

Andrea's hand on my bag gets heavier, like she's tightened her grip. "The restaurants will have to close," she says. "Let's head back to fourth."

People take out their phones, and we join a throng of silhouettes shuffling toward the road. Even the traffic lights are out, the power outage far-reaching.

By the time we get to 4th Avenue, we're all quiet. I'm hungry, socially drained, and the doll weighs more on my arm with each passing minute.

"I'm going to head back to my place," I say. The others will catch a bus heading back to UBC, so I point across to my stop. "I'll see you—"

"Whoa!" Andrea yells and pulls me back by the strap she's holding. My backpack jolts against my shoulders, tipping me off-balance.

Clayton swears and jumps back.

I regain my footing and follow their wide gazes down to the road. A black snake slithers past, right where I was about to step. It's got to be as long as a car.

"What the hell?" Johnny exclaims.

"It must have escaped from somewhere." Mo looks around as if to find the owner running after it with an empty cage.

I stare after it, a chill settling deep inside me. *Oh no, no, no... Get home. Get home now.* My mouth is dry, my voice shaky. "I—I have to go. Thanks for inviting me—"

"Look out!" someone shouts, and before I can turn my head, they slam into my shoulder, knocking the wind out of my lungs.

In my periphery, a cyclist wobbles, skids, and regains his balance—and I land hard on my butt, the unforgiving concrete sending a stab of pain up my back.

"You okay?" someone asks.

I blink, disoriented, and catch my breath. Did I just *fall over*?

My hands sting where I caught myself on the sidewalk. Gravel is embedded in my palms, and I'm definitely bleeding.

Heat rushes into my face as Clayton and Johnny haul me back to my feet.

"Thanks," I mumble, too mortified to meet anyone's eye.

"Asshole didn't even look back," Clayton says, glaring after the cyclist.

"Some luck we're having tonight, huh?" Andrea says bitterly, crossing her arms.

"No kidding," Mo says.

My embarrassment gives way to cold terror as I dust myself off, my palms stinging and my breaths coming faster.

I clutch the bag with the doll inside. *Rebecca.*

What have I done?

The hairs on the back of my neck prickle. My pulse quickens. These aren't coincidences—they're connected. I don't understand why, but I know this is a chain of consequences. And I'm about to find out just how far the chain goes.

Certainty slams into my gut like a second bicycle: I might have just made a huge mistake.

CHAPTER 6

Rebecca's Revenge

ALL THE TRAFFIC LIGHTS are out, so the bus moves at a snail's pace. I would walk if I weren't afraid of getting run over by another cyclist, or worse.

My stomach churns as shadows flicker past the windows and the stale air fills my nostrils. The engine rumbles, making the paper bag at my feet vibrate as if the doll is about to explode.

Okay, I just have to stay calm until I get back to my suite and can call Helping Paws.

Needing a distraction, I put in my earbuds and tap my soothing study playlist.

"Total Eclipse of the Heart" by Bonnie Tyler comes on.

I pick a different playlist—bossa nova music.

"Total Eclipse of the Heart" by Bonnie Tyler.

What the fuck?

I try several more playlists, growing more frantic with each attempt. Pop, classical, death metal—it doesn't matter. My phone keeps jumping to the same song.

Oookay then.

Slumping lower in my seat, I abandon my music app and call Helping Paws. I don't think I can wait until I get back. "Hi, it's Katie Alexander again."

The vet tech sighs. "Miss, Doctor Zacharias clearly said Lucy is—"

"This is different." I grip the phone tighter, my palms sweating. "I adopted another pet that has the same symptoms. I don't want to come in person because it's contagious."

"Right..." She sounds unconvinced. "I'll pass on the message, but I'll warn you now that this isn't how our appointments work, and she might not call back unless you come in with the sick animal."

"Noted. Just please tell her it's urgent, and I'm sure it's the same disease as before." I hesitate. What if she doesn't believe me? What if I get stuck with this potentially dangerous doll? "Tell her it's really rabid. Worse than last time."

As we end the call, I rub my face, praying this works. The staff at Helping Paws might think I'm a stalker or a weirdo or both, but I'm in deep now, and there's no going back.

I bounce my knee as I wait to get close enough to my place that it's safe to get off. I try the podcast app instead and tap the first one that comes up.

"Total Eclipse of the Heart" resumes.

Resigned, I let the song play, taking slow breaths.

But a shiver crawls up my spine, lifting the hairs on the back of my neck. Is the song trying to send me a message?

I check over my shoulder.

The guy seated behind me meets my gaze and offers a pursed-lip smile.

I return it and face forward again. I'm being paranoid.

By the time I rush into my basement suite, my movements are jerky and frantic. My hunger from skipping dinner doesn't help. I slap the light switch, but the power is also out here.

"Dammit."

"*Meew!*" Not-Lucy trots over to greet me.

I pick her up and clutch her to my chest, her presence and baby-soft fur comforting. I haven't given up on the real Lucy, but I have grown attached to this one. She's playful and cuddly and everything I wanted. If—*when*—I get the original Lucy back, I'll have two cats.

I take her to my room and place her on top of her scratching post, safely away from the doll.

"Stay there," I say, a nervous tremor in my voice.

I light all three candles I own, which helps cut the darkness, then take Rebecca The Creeptastic Doll out of the bag and put her on my bed. Her glassy stare bores into me, the candlelight glinting off her face and making each flaw look like an open wound.

From her scratching post, Not-Lucy stands up, arches her back, and hisses.

Her reaction makes my heart jump.

"You feel it too, huh?" I murmur.

As I look at Not-Lucy, something happens in the corner of my eye—the doll shifts.

I gasp and leap back, throwing my hands up in defense.

But when I look at the doll, nothing's changed.

I blink, waiting, keeping my fists up. Nothing happens. The candlelight flickers over her chipped face and dress.

I tear my gaze from her, my heart thudding. There it is again—the shift.

My breath catches, but I force myself to keep my eyes on Not-Lucy. The effect is only in my periphery. It's like when you're in a dark bathroom and you catch a glimpse of your reflection in the mirror, and there's a half a second when you think it's a ghost or a murderer.

In the edge of my vision, the doll's eyes gleam red. Her mouth is open in a silent scream of rage. Her dress is black and tattered, and her little white shoes have morphed into crow feet.

I flick my gaze to her again. Blue eyes and a frilly purple dress.

And then away. A demon in my periphery.

My face tingles as unease settles over me.

Okay, I'm *really* going to need Natalie to call me back.

My phone makes a noise, and I lunge for it before the sound registers. It's not ringing—it's "Total Eclipse of the Heart."

"God dammit!" With a trembling finger, I smash the pause button.

Should I grab a weapon in case this doll decides to pull a Lucy and go rabid on me?

I sidle over to my desk and yank open the drawer. Even a pair of scissors is better than nothing.

But where my scissors should be, a long, hairy leg pokes out from the depths of the drawer.

I freeze.

Another leg extends, and sick horror wells inside me as an engorged body appears.

I leap back, a blood-curdling shriek tearing from my throat as a spider as big as Not-Lucy scuttles out.

"Ew, ew, ew!" I jump onto the bed, curling my legs under me. I don't know if it's a tarantula or a wolf spider or something else, but it's the most disgusting thing I've ever seen in my life.

It reaches the corner behind my door and stops, two legs on the wall, the rest on the carpet.

Panicked breaths escaping, I lean over and grab Not-Lucy from her scratching post, hugging her close. Do spiders eat kittens?

My phone rings for real, and I scramble to answer. "Hello?"

"You adopted another one?" Natalie shouts.

Though she's yelling, the relief at hearing her voice is so great that I sink onto the bed, my shoulders slumping.

"It's a doll." I try not to panic as I keep both Rebecca and the spider in view. How am I going to get that thing outside? I don't have a cup big enough to trap it, nor do I want to step anywhere near it.

"Explain," Natalie says.

"I was at a flea market, and I had the same feeling as when I saw Lucy in the shelter. I knew it had the same... problem." I don't know what to call it, because it's definitely not an infectious disease.

Natalie's breath hitches. "So you bought it?"

"Tell me where Lucy is," I retort. I can't lose sight of why I brought this doll home in the first place.

Hollow footsteps thump in the background, like she's pacing or maybe walking somewhere. What's she thinking during all these long silences?

Finally, she huffs. "What's your address?"

Nothing like a hot girl coming over to abruptly shift your priorities. In the twenty minutes before Natalie arrives, I frantically shove dirty dishes into drawers and laundry into the closet, make the bed, wipe dust off every surface, and wave candles around to mask the musty basement smell. I give the spider a wide berth, still unsure how to get rid of it.

Out of breath, I glance out the dark window, seeing only my reflected silhouette. My hair is a mess, falling loose from its clip. I tame it with shaking hands.

The solar floodlight illuminates the path. A pair of brown Blundstones strides past.

Oh God. She's here.

I grab Not-Lucy and take her with me, speed-walking down the hallway and through the kitchen.

Doctor Natalie Zacharias is *at my place.*

She knocks twice, the sound piercing the quiet.

I stop, take a half a second to try and look composed, and open the door.

My greeting comes out like a breathy, "Hi-i…"

Her hair is pulled back into a low ponytail, loose strands framing her face. She's wearing an oversized black blazer over a tiny white bralet and straight-leg jeans, showing off her toned abs. Behind her familiar shade of copper eyeshadow, her gaze is hard and serious. "Where's the doll?"

I point down the hall, where candlelight flickers from my room. "On my bed."

She kicks off her boots in a rush and strides past me. Her warm, herbal scent hits my nostrils, rooting me in place for a second before I slam the door and trot after her. Those little braids with hints of green and yellow peek through her ponytail, which comes halfway down her back.

Heat floods my cheeks. Doctor Natalie Zacharias is *in my bedroom.*

She puts an arm out to stop me from passing, staring at the doll on the bed. "You touched her?"

A jolt runs through me as her arm brushes my chest. I step back. "I mean, to buy her—"

She spins, scanning me up and down. I suddenly feel underdressed in my flannel, ripped jeans, and moccasins.

"Are you okay?" Her tone is soft, but her eyes are blazing and her jaw is tight.

I shift. Am I itchy? Nauseous? I can't tell what's real and what's in my head. "I think I'm fine."

She rummages in an inner pocket of her blazer, the swaying material wafting her scent at me. "I'll take the doll with me. Are there any, uh, side effects I need to take care of while I'm here?"

Catching her meaning, I point. "There's a spider in the corner."

Not-Lucy hisses and leaps from my grasp, her needle-sharp claws digging into my forearms.

"Ow! Hey, no!" I cry, trying to catch her.

She hits the floor with a thump and zooms from the room in a white blur. My eyes water in pain, my skin burning where her claws sliced me open.

"Leave her!" Natalie extends a hand. "I need your help."

A crackling noise fills the air, and it dawns on me what the kitten was hissing at. The doll contorts, bending backward, her angelic face melting like hot wax.

Terror seizes me, weakening my legs. I scream.

"Okay, new plan." Natalie takes a glass vial from her inner coat pocket. It's thumb-sized, tubular, with a cork stopper to keep the shimmering amber substance inside. "We're doing this here. I have to get this onto the doll, but she's going to resist."

"What's in the vial?" The second part of that sentence registers, and a chill ripples through me. "What do you mean *resist*?"

Her dark, molten eyes meet mine. "I'm not going to let you get hurt. But I need you to do exactly as I say."

She uncorks the vial. The *pop* is drowned by something louder—the *whoosh* of my window opening.

A cold draft blows in, lifting the strands of hair framing her face and raising goosebumps on my arms. The candlelight shudders, casting moving shadows over everything.

Uncertainty crosses Natalie's expression. "You really shouldn't have brought that doll home."

She lunges for Rebecca, and I hurtle toward the window to shut it.

I'm too slow. A massive bird swoops in, knocking me back a step. It heads straight for Natalie.

"No!" I lurch after it, trying to shoo it away as its talons close over Natalie's wrist. For an absurd moment, the word *pterodactyl* comes to mind. Then logic kicks in. It's a hawk.

Good God, there's a hawk in my bedroom.

At least my landlords aren't home.

Natalie roars in pain, blood oozing between the claws on her wrist.

"Get off her!" Icy fear shoots through me. She came here because of me, and I can't let this happen.

In an explosion of sound, music blares from my desk.

Natalie looks around, a hand on the bird's neck as she tries to pry it off. "What—is—that?"

Heat invades my face. "My phone."

"Total Eclipse of the Heart" has resumed, blaring at full volume, filling the room until my head throbs.

"Why?!" Natalie shouts.

"I don't know! Ask the doll!"

Fine, it was the last song I listened to. I have a playlist of power ballads that Hazel and I love to bellow at the top of our lungs, and I may or may not have been reminiscing earlier.

I would dive for my phone and turn it off, but the hawk is still on Natalie's arm, and whatever is in that vial is in danger of spilling.

I charge and seize the bird around the middle. Its bony wings flap against me, its soft feathers smushing between my fingers. Its shrieks shred my eardrums.

Something catches my eye on the bed.

From the melted porcelain and crumpled purple lace that used to be Rebecca, a black shape emerges. It breaks apart, trickling over the duvet. In the darkness, it takes me a moment to process what's going on.

"Spiders!" I shriek.

A nest hatches from the lump that was a doll, scattering across the room.

Shit, shit… What have I unleashed? Are these poisonous? Will they spread through the city and—

Wait. The huge one in the corner… It's gone. And there's something on my pant leg.

I look down to see the monster spider from earlier scuttling up my jeans. A scream tears from my lips, fear clouding my head so all I can do is kick and thrash.

Somehow, amid my tap dancing, I slap it back to the floor. In the millisecond that its spindly legs and soft body touch my palm, the heebie-jeebies rocket through me.

"Katie!" Natalie grits out.

Right, the hawk!

With a roar, I grab it again, pull it away from her, and throw it at the window before it can sink its sharp beak into me. It lands on the windowsill with the agility of a cat landing on its feet.

Natalie stumbles, her wrist bleeding freely. "Hold it off!" she shouts over the blaring music.

The hawk takes flight in the bedroom, and I wave my arms to keep it away from her, crushing spiders beneath my moccasins with every step.

This is so out of hand. I've unleashed an arachnid infestation on the city *and* we're both going to die from a rabid bird attack.

I look back at Natalie—and freeze, my brain derailing as I try to process what I'm seeing. Her palm hovers over the vial, and the amber contents have risen out of it, morphing in the air like an amoeba. It's not a liquid, more like the slime my sisters and I used to make as kids. And it's *floating*.

A thud pulls my attention. A candle on my desk has fallen to the floor, the carpet smoldering.

"Shit!" I grab the nearest container of water—my diffuser—and dump it on the smoke before anything catches fire.

I've unleashed an arachnid infestation *and* we're going to die *and* the house is going to burn down.

The was-a-doll throbs, pulsing like a black heart at the center of the chaos. Pictures fall off shelves. My lamp hits the floor. Gasping for air, I seize a textbook from my desk for self-defense and send the whole pile crashing down.

"Hurry!" I cry, praying that whatever amber substance Natalie unleashed from that vial is enough to stop all this.

The goo hits the was-a-doll with a wet *slap*, warping and stretching until it engulfs it.

The song crescendos, and I bellow over Bonnie Tyler's voice, swinging at the hawk before it can bite my face.

The goo-covered was-a-doll sizzles and spits, steam rising. A scent like burnt sugar curls in my nostrils.

Ohmygod ohmygod...

The hawk circles. Spiders scuttle. We gulp down air, Natalie on all fours on my bed, me frozen in place with the textbook raised.

I drop the textbook and step closer, but she puts a hand out. "Stay there."

"Is it...?" I trail off, not sure how to finish the sentence. Dead? Deactivated?

From the kitchen, the microwave beeps, the fridge hums, and ambient light brightens the room by a fraction. The power is back on. My bedroom light remains off, the candles dancing as if in a high wind.

A spark comes from the shimmering amber goo-covered was-a-doll, snagging my attention. *Zap. Zap.*

"Cover your ears!" Natalie shouts, launching off the bed.

She throws herself at me, smothering me with her body and pinning me against the wall as an explosion rattles the bedroom.

CHAPTER 7

A Bit of a Mess

NATALIE WRAPS ME IN a protective cocoon against the wall as the explosion rips through the room. Her body, warm and solid, presses into mine. Her absurdly soft skin brushes my temple, and her forearms bracket my head as she covers her ears.

The blast rattles my bones, sending wisps of torn bed linens into the air.

As it dissipates, I take my hands away from my ears to cover my mouth, trying to keep the dust out. It's on my lips, bitter and dry. I'm cold, trembling, my breaths fast and shallow—but as Natalie's scent mixes with the acrid smoke, a sense of safety wraps around me like a blanket.

I can't believe she protected me like that. Her back was totally exposed.

Where the doll was, there's a black, jagged crater in the bed, as if a mine detonated.

I'm going to need a new mattress.

The rest of my room is in shambles, looking like a home demolition in progress.

I try to ask Natalie if she's okay but can't find my voice, terror constricting my airway. Loose strands of her hair tickle my face, and she's so close that her breath brushes over my lips, cool and minty. The candles have extinguished, their light replaced by the soft glow from the street lamps outside. It bathes her face in shadows, accentuating her jawline, her narrowed gaze, her pinched brow. She's furious.

"What were you *thinking*?" she growls.

"I—I didn't know it would do that." My voice quakes, and I swallow hard, clinging to the comfort of having her between me and the wreckage.

But she steps away, leaving a chill where her body used to be. Fear rushes back, and I fold my arms over my stomach.

She turns on the bedroom light, and in the sudden brightness, I blink, my eyes stinging.

Three vibrant purple butterflies rise from the crater, spiraling in a hypnotic dance before flying out the open window. Another butterfly circles where the hawk was, and there's another that I can only assume was the massive spider—or has taken the place of the spider? Animals don't morph into butterflies. That's impossible.

Their wings flap in chaotic blurs, and then they dart through the window too, disappearing into the blackness and leaving me wondering if they were just a hallucination.

"Total Eclipse of the Heart" ends, then starts over. I grab my phone and hit pause, and a ringing silence descends in place of the power ballad.

I gulp down air, willing my hands to stop shaking. It's over. Rebecca is gone.

Natalie walks back to me, her expression smoldering. "You saw how the cat was. Why would you want another...?" she grinds her teeth, leaving me to wonder how that sentence is supposed to end.

"Another *what*?" My voice is still weak. "I don't understand what Lucy and an old doll have in common."

"So you bought the doll to try and figure it out?"

I feel small as I look up at her. "I got it because I knew that was how I could see you again."

The crease between her eyebrows softens. She searches my face. "And you wanted to see me again because..."

"The kitten," I say quickly, heat flooding my face. "Because of Lucy. Not like—not like in a stalker way, like I'm trying to force you to see me—" My tongue is suddenly too big, tripping me into silence.

Oh, God, put me out of my misery.

The corner of Natalie's mouth twitches for the briefest moment, revealing a dimple, and then her scowl returns. She steps back. "If you're hoping I'll give you back your old cat, you're fighting a losing battle."

"Why? What did you do with her?" My focus pulls to the crater in my bed, nausea overcoming me. "Did you dump a vial on her and make her melt—"

"No, I didn't melt a kitten! Jesus Christ." She lets out an exasperated growl, turning away. "That cat wasn't a *her*. It wasn't even a *cat*. That—" She points to Not-Lucy, who's returned to watch us curiously from the doorway. "*That* is a cat. That's the one you were meant to have. Not that other thing."

"What do you mean, she wasn't a cat?" My words come out roughly, hurting my throat. My grip on reality is slipping away, leaving me grasping at nothing.

She runs both hands over her head, raising her arms in a way that shows off the curve of her waist beneath the open blazer. "Katie..."

My brain stalls, pausing my bewilderment over everything that just happened. It's the first time she's called me that instead of *Miss Alexander*, and I like the sound of it coming from her lips.

When she drops her arms, her expression softens. "I can't explain the way you want me to."

I clench my teeth, frustration rising. None of this makes sense, but what choice do I have but to accept it?

She must see my helpless confusion because her shoulders sag. She glances between me and the kitten, exhaling slowly. "What's her name?"

The kitten meows—in protest, probably, because what kind of a name is Not-Lucy?

"Ethel," I decide. My older sister went through a phase of binging old TV shows like *I Love Lucy*. I guess it fits. Lucy was the chaotic one.

Natalie's mouth quirks, teasing me with a grin that doesn't quite come. I have yet to see her smile, and it makes me yearn for what I'm missing out on.

"I hoped you wouldn't notice Ethel wasn't the same cat," she says. "I wanted you to be able to move on."

I furrow my brow, the pieces coming together. "Is that why you took so long to get back to me? You were searching for a replacement kitten who looked like her?"

She hesitates, then turns toward the bed, answering with her back to me. "Yes."

"Oh." As furious as I want to be with her, she went to a lot of trouble for me. "You could have told me she died."

Natalie shakes her head once. "I could tell how much that would've upset you."

I watch her, numb, as she pries a lump out of the mattress. The whole doll seems to have shrunken into a purple gemstone. She pockets it.

Something strange is happening inside me, weakening my legs until I have to sit down in my desk chair. It was sweet of her to find me a new kitten—but a conclusion settles over me, heavy and somber.

Lucy is gone. Worse, she never really was.

But if she wasn't a cat, what was she?

I rub my face. This is all so confusing and impossible.

I've stopped shaking, my pulse returning to normal—but as the adrenaline leaves my body, a sharp sting comes to my attention on the backs of my hands and forearms. I'm bleeding where Ethel used me as a ramp to dive for safety. The cuts have slowed to an ooze, but the red has smudged across my skin, making it look worse.

Natalie notices and sucks in a breath. "Are you okay?"

I nod. "It was Ethel. She got scared of Rebecca."

She raises an eyebrow. "Rebecca?"

"The doll's name."

The dimple makes another appearance.

Her reddened hand snags my attention, and my stomach lurches. She didn't get through unscathed, either. Her sleeve covers her wrist where the hawk tried to eat her, but blood trickles down to her fingers.

My fault. The reality of what I've done hits me like a kick in the ribs. "How about you?" I ask. "Do you need stitches or… a rabies vaccine?"

She tugs her sleeve further down. "I'll take care of it at home."

We stare at each other, a stalemate.

Natalie swears under her breath and walks a small circle, rubbing a hand over her throat. "I can't believe you saw—this wasn't supposed to—"

Guilt rises in me to see her distressed, but I can't give in. I want an explanation.

"Listen, you *cannot* tell anyone about this." Her tone is firm, but her eyebrows arch downward—something desperate hiding beneath her expression.

Her moment of weakness bolsters me. I cross my arms, my need for answers surging back full-force. "Uh-huh. In exchange for keeping your secret, are you going to tell me what's going on and why my room is in shambles?"

A muscle in her jaw flexes, a storm passing behind her eyes. "You shouldn't have brought that doll home. That's on you."

A familiar defiance sparks inside me. "How was I supposed to know it was dangerous? You haven't told me anything! I just felt the same feeling I did with Lucy, and…"

"About that." She picks up the psychology textbook I used as a weapon, looks at the cover, and places it back on my desk. "What, exactly, did you feel?"

I try to recall the sensations in my body when I saw the doll—the ones that strangely lined up with seeing Lucy at the shelter. "It's like my heart jumps, and there's a pull toward it, like I have to have it. I don't know." I try to find more words, but nothing comes. "It's hard to explain."

"Hm." She picks up another textbook, and I clue in that she's tidying up.

"It's okay," I say quickly. "I'll clean up. Don't worry about it."

She gives me a look like, "Yeah, right," and picks my lamp off the floor.

I hurry to help, going to the photos that fell off the shelf before she can get to them. She doesn't need a tour of all the absurd selfies I've taken with Hazel and my sisters over the years.

We work in silence for a moment, the tension as thick as the dust settling over every surface. The idea of her picking up my personal belongings, touching the intimate pieces of my life, twists my stomach.

"Are you studying psychology because you're good at reading people?" Natalie asks.

"Maybe. Friends have told me I'm good at listening. Good at empathizing."

She sets the fallen candles on my desk. "Would you say you're an empath?"

I lift a shoulder. I've used the word, but when a high school classmate once rolled her eyes at it, I stopped. "Maybe."

She picks up one of the books that were in a neat stack beside the photos—a spicy romance novel with two women making out on the cover.

"I'll—I'll get those," I splutter, snatching it out of her hand and stooping to collect the rest. My face is so hot I could cook an egg on it.

I feel her gaze on me for an unbearably long moment before she turns to fix my pillows.

And now she's touching my bed.

Breathe, Katie.

"You say that word a lot," Natalie says.

I fight to get my brain back on track. "What word?"

"*Maybe.* Like you're afraid to commit to an answer."

Oh, thank God, she's moving on with the conversation without mentioning my smut pile.

"Well, I grew up with three opinionated sisters," I say. "Life's easier if I roll with things."

She comes back to look at the photos I placed on the shelf, and there goes my plan to avoid that awkwardness. She moves close, the heat of her body tingling on my left side. There's her scent again, comforting, almost woodsy, like cozying up in a cabin while it snows outside.

"Are you the eldest?" she asks, her voice rippling through me.

My mouth is dry. "Second-eldest."

She studies a picture of my sisters and me with our arms over each other's shoulders. It's the least absurd photo, to my intense relief.

"That was at Alyssa's bachelorette party last year. She's the oldest." I point to Alyssa in her white dress with the veil hairpiece. The rest of us are in little black dresses. As Natalie stares, I'm uncomfortably aware of how low-cut mine is. "Alyssa's married now and trying to have a baby. Which is... soon, if you ask me. She's twenty-three. But she's been talking about babies for years, so..." I shrug. "And that's Pearl—she's finishing high school this year—and Nicky's in Grade 10."

Natalie's eyes are soft and curious. "Who are you closest with?"

"Pearl and I were always a pair. Middle kids, I guess. But we all get along."

My throat tightens as I talk about them. Pearl is the first person I tell about major life events. She was the first person I came out to in Grade

10. With her support and encouraging smile, I knew I'd be able to handle telling the rest of the family I was dating a girl.

As Natalie peers into my world, I'm hyper-aware of her—every fleck of dust clinging to her skin, the sheen of sweat on her neck, her slow, even breaths.

"Was it hard to leave them to come to Vancouver?" she murmurs.

"Meh, a little." The real answer makes my eyes sting. I turn away, ready to change the subject back to the matter at hand. "Thanks for helping me clean up. It looks—" I gasp. The bed is repaired. Completely. There's not even a dent. "You—you fixed it!"

"Fixed what?" she asks, still facing the photos.

"The crater!" I wave my hands at the bed.

She cocks an eyebrow. "What crater?"

I glare at her. "Don't you dare."

"What?" she asks, infuriatingly innocent.

"I'm not that dense, and what you're doing is called gaslighting, jerk."

Her mouth opens in surprise, and before I can feel guilty about calling her a jerk, she grimaces. "Okay. I'm sorry."

She rubs the back of her neck, looking genuinely ashamed.

The apology catches me off-guard. "It's fine. Just don't insult my intelligence again."

She nods.

"And tell me how you fixed the bed," I say.

The corners of her lips tug upward. "Not a chance."

I huff. It was worth a shot.

"Look..." She steps closer, making my breath hitch. Her gaze locks mine, forcing me to tilt my head back. "It's not my intention to lie to you, Katie. But I have to. You don't understand what you're prying into, and you're going to regret it."

"You say that like you know me."

Natalie backs up, glancing out the window. She tugs her blazer straight.

"Are you really a doctor?" I scan the coat for clues about what other mysterious vials she might be keeping in secret pockets.

"I'm not faking my title."

"Okay..." It feels like she dodged the question. "So you have a Ph.D?"

"In a way." She meets my eye for a fraction of a second. "I'm not a veterinarian, and I didn't study at a traditional university."

"But you went to... a non-traditional one?"

"The equivalent of one. I studied for a long time and earned something like a doctorate."

I wait for her to go on, but she doesn't.

"What if this happens again?" I ask. Not that I would go out of my way to find another Rebecca, but I could by accident.

She looks at me sharply. "Don't tell me you anticipate this happening again."

I shrug. "It's hard to know what to anticipate when I don't even know what's going on."

She sighs pointedly.

"And you're still not going to tell me," I say, more of a statement than a question.

"Nope."

I sigh back. "You know that makes me even more determined to figure it out."

She frowns, her expression getting further from the smile I keep hoping for. "For your sake, Katie, I hope you don't."

Her words settle over me the same way the sight of the giant spider did. She's dead serious.

But so am I. I might believe her about Lucy—that the kitten wasn't what I thought, and I'm not going to get her back—but as for Natalie? She's a mystery that needs to be solved. I've crossed over a threshold, peeled back the covers on a dark secret, and there's no coming back from it.

I need to be able to contact her again. I don't want this to be goodbye.

As she turns to the door, my heartbeat quickens. My mouth goes dry as the question I want to ask burns in my throat.

Say it. Just say it.

"Can I have your number?" My lips tingle as the words come out. I dip my chin and look up at her, trying to seem small and harmless. "Just in case?"

Natalie hesitates. I give her my best innocent face—one that says, *in case I need you to come rescue me again?*

Not the truth, which is, *so I can crack you open like a puzzle box and find out what you're hiding.*

I tuck a lock of hair behind my ear, casually letting the bloody scratches on my arm linger in her line of sight. Poor me, so helpless.

I'm taking a chance here. I know this would work on a man—putting them in the position to become a hero in the face of a damsel in distress. The question is: does Natalie Zacharias care about a damsel?

Her gaze roves over me. She catches her bottom lip on her teeth, thinking.

Slowly, her expression softens. There's a subtle lift in her posture as she breaks.

As she crosses to my desk and writes her phone number on a sticky note, I press my lips together to keep from smiling.

CHAPTER 8

An Alexander Christmas

S o Natalie is not an ordinary veterinarian. She's not even an ordinary *person*. She has something to do with possessed cats and dolls, and the need to figure it out consumes me day and night until my dreams are full of exploding dolls and purple butterflies.

Is 'possessed' the right word? Are we dealing with demons? Hazel's petrified shouts are burned into my memory as Lucy climbed my bedroom wall. I thought that night was the scariest of my life, but little did I know what hell awaited me at a flea market.

As the days pass, I sometimes catch my reflection in the bathroom mirror to find haunted eyes staring back—the face of someone who's realized the world isn't the safe, predictable place she'd always believed it to be. Other times, the phantom sensation of Natalie's body shielding mine rushes back, tingling through me, betraying me with a burning attraction to this woman I can't trust. The woman who's lied to me over and over again.

Huddled in a campus cafe one December afternoon, desperately trying to focus on studying for finals, I tip my laptop screen away from my study buddies and do a quick internet search on exorcism.

I'm with Clayton, Johnny, Mo, Andrea, and three others, a coffee on my left and an open statistics textbook on my right. We've been meeting on Tuesdays and Thursdays to study between classes, a big change from my old routine of sitting in the library with headphones on.

Look at me, making friends.

Wikipedia tells me exorcism tends to involve some kind of ritual, religious amulet, or recitation—none of which match what Natalie did. But I could argue that the shimmering substance in the vial was holy water. Or... holy goo.

I grab my phone to text Natalie.

Katie

> I figured it out. You're an exorcist, and Rebecca and Lucy were possessed by demons.

I've texted her a few other theories since she gave me her number, and while I was hesitant to bother her and make her pull back, my messages don't seem unwelcome.

"What possessed me to take calculus?" Andrea moans into her hands.

The word *possessed* makes me look up.

"Katie's taking calculus," Clayton says, perking up. "I bet she can help."

"Um—sure." I blink, pulling my focus away from my phone. It's been more challenging to study lately with my mind constantly circling Natalie. I'll be mid-sentence on a paper, and suddenly, I'm reading an article on jinxes.

"Do you have any idea what I did wrong?" Andrea pushes her notebook across the table to me, and I mold my brain around the equation.

"Katie's a genius." Clayton leans in and gives me a not-so-subtle flirty nudge. He always manages to sit beside me and never misses an opportunity for a poke or elbow.

I keep my gaze on Andrea's page. "Just a perfectionist who doesn't give up on solving a problem."

"That's why you're going to ace everything," he says.

Clayton failed two midterms, which was obviously an awakening because he's been less concerned about being the Party Guy since then. Now, his approach is to ask me to get together and study instead of inviting me to parties.

"You almost had it," I tell Andrea. I scribble down the solution and slide the paper back to her.

She looks it over. "Oh my gosh, I *love* you."

My phone buzzes, and my heart skips a beat.

Natalie

> If I were exorcizing demons, how would that change your world view? Would you adopt a certain religion?

I press my lips together, hearing the text in my head in her low voice. Typical Natalie, skirting the answer.

Katie

> It's a little infuriating how you don't confirm or deny any of my theories. At least give me a hint.

Natalie

> Have you considered a zombie outbreak? Rebecca was looking a little undead before she exploded…

Katie

> You're such a brat

I sip my coffee to hide my smile. I don't need Clayton asking me what I'm smirking at.

The playfulness in Natalie's texts is... surprising. Encouraging. If she didn't want me messaging her, she would tell me, right? She was certainly direct about it before.

But something's changed since the doll incident. She's more open.

I scroll back through our message history. Of all my scattered and ridiculous theories, I keep coming back to one word: *cursed*. I think Lucy and Rebecca were carrying curses. What else could bring powerful strokes of bad luck? What else could cause electrical outages, hatch spiders on my bed, and open the window to let aggressive birds fly into my room?

Two weeks ago, I texted the word to Natalie. Her response, also a single word, was as noncommittal as ever: *Interesting*.

"You going home over the break?" Clayton's voice breaks through my thoughts. He leans forward, folding his arms across his textbook and forcing himself into my line of sight.

"My family's actually coming here," I reply, setting my phone down. "They've never been to Vancouver. You?"

An excited jitter goes through me at the promise of seeing my family. Homesickness has been my constant companion since September, curled up against my belly right beside Ethel.

As he tells me about catching up with his high school buddies out in the suburbs, a pang of sadness hits me. I'd kill to see Hazel over the holidays. Ever since the guy in her program, Sean, asked her out in November, they've been blissfully attached. Glued together, really. It's great to see her so happy, but it means I haven't had a chance to tell her about the exploding doll or the fact that Natalie and I have been texting.

And although she was adamant that I don't tell anyone... I can't hold in something that weird. It's eating away at me, and I have to bounce ideas off my bestie—starting with the theory that I accidentally adopted a cursed kitten.

Standing in the domestic terminal at Vancouver International Airport, my mouth falls open as I process the sight of a familiar face walking toward me. She's in ripped jeans and a black varsity jacket, her hair in a loose braid, and a full backpack over her shoulders, looking effortlessly cool until we spot each other.

"Hazel!" I scream, dropping my cardboard sign.

She screams back, and we meet in a jumping hug.

"Surprise!"

"Oh my God! How long are you staying?" My voice is muffled against her shoulder.

"Just three days. I need to go home for my family's Christmas thing—"

"Of course."

"—but I had to come visit you while I could."

My heart is ready to burst as we step apart. "We have to jam-pack these three days. Ugh, we have a lot to catch up on."

Hazel raises her eyebrows, and my stomach twists in anticipation. Finally, I'll be able to get her opinion, and she can help me come up with a plan.

Over her shoulder, my family pushes through the crowd rolling their carry-on luggage, all smiles and waves.

I scramble to pick up my handmade cardboard sign, holding it high.

Welcome home from prison, Alyssa, Pearl, and Nicky!

They dissolve into giggles, enveloping me in a group hug—my sisters, Hazel, Mom, and Dad. Everyone looks the same as ever, a reminder that it hasn't been as long as it feels. Alyssa is in full makeup and a knee-length trench coat, with fresh highlights lightening her brown tresses. Pearl is sporting her usual ponytail, her coat open over loose jeans and a white tee. Nicky's dark hair is long and wavy, her willowy legs peeking out from beneath a down jacket and a short skirt—definitely something that would've sparked an argument with Mom about bare legs in the winter. Dad towers over us in aviators and a jean jacket that make him look helplessly like Alan Grant from Jurassic Park. Mom, the shortest of us all, is swathed in a calf-length down jacket, leaving only her round, smiling face, signature pearl earrings, and black bob exposed to the cold.

To my horror, my eyes prickle and my vision blurs. When was the last time I hugged someone who wasn't a cat? It feels like thawing out by the fireplace after a long day in the snow.

Luckily, nobody notices my watery eyes because everyone is shouting over each other.

"Nicky was sitting next to a guy who snored the whole flight—" Pearl shouts.

"I had to pee so bad—" Nicky says.

"I tried to flirt my way into getting bumped up to first class—" Alyssa says.

They keep it up during the entire van ride to the vacation rental, which is a few blocks from my place. I'm going to bring Ethel over and stay with them for the week.

"We have to visit Grouse Mountain—"

"—and Stanley Park—"

"Will you show us the UBC campus?" Hazel adds, contributing to the din and earning her title as an honorary Alexander sister.

"—a day trip to Whistler—"

"Can we eat sushi every day?"

I laugh, my shoulders dropping as my homesickness melts away. "Yes to all of it."

I promised the sushi in Vancouver is better than anything they've ever had at home, and I can't wait to prove it.

A skip of excitement shoots through me at the prospect of showing them around. It hasn't felt like my city to show until this moment.

Maybe there's hope that it'll one day feel like home.

With a few hours left in the day, we hit the Christmas market downtown. Snowflakes drift gently, dusting the ground and making the North Shore mountains look even more picturesque. I'm wrapped in my ski jacket, which now hopelessly reminds me of the chaotic day I met Natalie.

"Hey, brought you something," Pearl says, nudging me with her arm. "I had to fight Nicky for the last one."

She pushes a sandwich bag into my hands. In it is a slightly crumbled butter tart—Auntie Jan's famous recipe.

I gasp. "You're the best."

"You owe me," she sings, skipping off to join the others.

A huge, unstoppable smile tugs my cheeks. It's the simple things that make me miss home so much—family recipes, Pearl's energy, the non-stop chatter.

I share the butter tart with Hazel as we wander through displays and vendors, overindulging in sugar and taking ridiculous photos that will end up on my shelf. The air is filled with the scent of soft pretzels and gingerbread, bursts of warmth hitting me as we pass heat lamps.

Eventually, my parents and sisters go in separate directions to explore different stalls, leaving Hazel and me with our hot chocolates.

"Have you met someone?" she blurts, seizing the moment to ask about my love life.

I laugh. "No." My traitorous thoughts jump to Natalie. I sip my hot chocolate. "How's Sean?"

Hazel grins, oblivious to my deflection. "Great! I met his parents a few days ago."

"Ooh, big step! How'd it go?"

She recounts the slightly awkward dinner while we browse the vendors. Tables are full of candles, soap, ornaments, flavored popcorn, candy... It's all disappointingly normal.

"Are you looking for something in particular?" Hazel asks, maybe noticing the way I'm studying everything we pass.

"I'll know it if I see it." I've done this a couple of times since the doll—once in a used bookstore and once at a consignment store I walked by. Nothing has triggered the same reaction as the doll and Lucy. "I've still been trying to figure out what happened to Lucy. I don't believe it was a disease."

Hazel nods, looking thoughtful. "Same. I told Sean about that whole thing, and he—"

"You did?" I exclaim.

She chews her lip. "Was I not supposed to?"

I hesitate. I guess I never told her not to tell anyone. It's just such a bizarre situation, and after Natalie warned me to keep quiet about it, I feel like we should be careful. "It's okay. Go on."

"Well, he plays Dungeons and Dragons, and he said it sounds like Lucy was carrying like... a jinx, or a hex, or a curse."

I grab her arm as a wave of relief hits me. "I had the same idea."

Her validation is like a hug, a reassurance that I'm not losing my mind.

Hazel leans in, flashing a smile. "Have you told Natalie what you think?"

"I've texted her my theories, and—"

"You've been *texting*?" She balls her fists in front of her mouth, her eyes gleaming.

"Theories! And she won't confirm or deny anything I say." Frustration creeps back, and I crush my empty cup and toss it away. The hot chocolate's warmth is dissipating, leaving me hunched against the cold.

"Hm..." A table of candles lures Hazel in. She picks up a pine-scented one and smells it. "You should try to find another pet with the same problem so you have an excuse to give her another call."

Here we go—the part where I tell her I already found another curse, and her name was Rebecca.

I bury my chin deeper into my scarf. "The thing is, I kind of stumbled on something..."

Hazel gasps. "What?"

"A doll at a flea market," I say like it was no big deal, even as my brain replays my screams of terror as a thousand spiders scuttled across my bedroom. "Weird, right? A toy showing the same symptoms as Lucy?"

Hazel's mouth opens and closes as she processes the news. "Do you think she's even a vet?"

"I think being a vet is a small part of her job, and she deals with anything carrying a curse." We continue to the next table, which has knitted scarves, mittens, and toques. I poke at a mound of wool, relishing its softness. "What would you do if you were me?"

Hazel tries on a pair of red mittens with reindeer on the backs, wiggling her fingers as if to test them out. "I see two options. One, you can drop it and move on with life."

I deflate, gazing blankly at a white scarf as I consider abandoning this mystery and never talking to Natalie again.

Hazel searches my face. "Do you really have to figure this out? What if it's better for your sanity if you let it go?"

Letting it go would be easier, sure. But how can I? "I need to know the truth about her," I say easily.

She keeps watching me, her brow furrowed, as if reading the meaning beneath my words. My fierce desire to understand people has always been my guiding force in life—the whole reason I'm here studying psychology on a scholarship. I just think if everyone took the time to understand each other a little better, the world would be a kinder place. Like, I would've had an easier time making friends—and I wouldn't have been called weird in Grade 7 for being quiet when I was really just shy. And then there's Pearl, who wouldn't struggle so much with being neurodivergent if people took the time to understand what that means. And more people in Nicky's life would empathize with her anxiety instead of getting frustrated. This is about more than just solving a mystery. Learning about people, fully understanding them, is who I am.

Hazel smiles, knowing this without my needing to say it. "I would expect nothing less from you, Katie."

I smile back.

"Plus, you like Natalie, right?" she adds.

Heat rises in my face, her bluntness catching me off-guard. I could deny it, but what's the point? "A little."

She thinks for a long moment, returning the mittens to their rack. "What if..."

"What?" I press.

"No, it's a bad idea."

"Tell me!"

She faces me, uncertainty crossing her expression. "You know how Sean kept coming to my cafe to buy cinnamon buns? It gave us a chance to talk and get to know each other, and it kind of... showed me he was interested."

I narrow my eyes, trying to follow. "Okay..."

"What if you did a version of that? She obviously works with curses, so what if you bring her another one?"

"What, like a penguin bringing a pebble to its mate?"

A smirk plays on her lips. "It's a way to see her again, *and* it'll make her realize you're not going to give up on figuring out what's going on."

My pulse quickens at the thought of finding another cursed object. Is it a coincidence that a second one fell into my lap, or is it easy now that I've opened a door into this world? Maybe curses are everywhere, and it just takes awareness in order to see them.

But do I *want* to touch another one? The risk of unleashing hell sends a shiver down my spine—and at the same time, a thrill races through me at the prospect of seeing Natalie again.

"It's a ridiculous idea," Hazel says, walking on. "It's one thing to show up at your crush's work to buy a cinnamon bun. It's a whole other thing to search for a potentially dangerous object because your crush happens to be... whatever she is."

"That is the question," I murmur. What's the name for someone who explodes cursed objects?

We stop at a table of wooden nutcrackers. They range from the size of my hand to several feet tall—the one standing beside the table is my height. They gaze at me with sad, dead eyes, tufts of clown-like white hair poking out from under their hats, their toothy grins ajar as they wait to be given something to crunch.

They're super creepy. Like, Rebecca creepy.

As I focus on a particularly sad-looking one with his mouth open unnaturally wide, something twists inside me.

Was this the same sensation as when I set eyes on Rebecca? Or am I just feeling it because I'm thinking about the way the doll contorted on my bed?

Ugh, this situation has me questioning everything lately, including my own senses.

Footsteps and festive jingling rush up behind us, and all three sisters appear wearing antlers with bells. They're holding two more.

"We bought these for pictures!" Pearl wrestles one onto my head. The jingling beside me tells me Alyssa is doing the same to Hazel.

Although I laugh, frustration cinches around my stomach. I can't decipher what I'm feeling when I look at this nutcracker. Is this another item worth telling Natalie about, or am I imagining it?

As my sisters tug us over to the five-foot tall one and tell us to smile for a selfie, Hazel glances from me to the creepy one I was staring at, her eyebrows raised.

"I'm gonna do it," I whisper to her. "I'll be a penguin bringing pebbles."

Very dangerous pebbles.

CHAPTER 9

Becoming a Penguin

I PUT THE CREEPY nutcracker on my bed, my heart thudding as I wait for something bad to happen. Ethel purrs loudly in Hazel's arms, nuzzling under her chin.

"You're so cute I could eat you," Hazel says through her teeth, looking at Ethel like she's really thinking about it.

I told my family I'd meet them at the vacation rental in an hour—I just have to get Ethel and shove a week's worth of clothes into a bag. Hazel came to help.

Away from them, this gives us a chance to check out the nutcracker.

"What do you think?" I ask Ethel, studying her for a reaction. "Cursed?"

She ignores it, batting Hazel's braid. At nearly five months old, she has the energy of a kitten but the confidence of a fully grown cat, making her a sassy menace.

Disappointment trickles through me—followed by shame for feeling disappointed. I *should* be relieved I haven't found another curse. But I can only think about what this means for our become-a-penguin idea.

"Would a curse have made weird stuff happen by now?" Hazel asks.

"Maybe." I scowl, arms crossed, then point to it like a cop in an interrogation. "Let's see if you're really who you say you are, *Mr. Nutcracker*."

I go search the pantry for nuts—but I don't buy whole nuts and my roommate doesn't keep food here, so I don't know why I bother. The most nut-shaped things I find are peanut-butter stuffed pretzels. I grab one and return to the bedroom.

I put it in the nutcracker's mouth and press the cold wooden lever on its back. Nothing happens. I push harder, the flimsy wood straining under the pressure, until the pretzel pops out and rolls across the floor. Ethel leaps off the bed to chase it.

"What kind of nutcracker can't even crush a pretzel?" Hazel asks.

"Exactly," I say suspiciously, tossing it back onto the bed.

We study it with crossed arms while Ethel bats the pretzel like it's a toy.

I sigh. "Let's pack my stuff. Give it a minute to see if we get attacked by spiders."

"Um—" Hazel starts.

I wave a hand. "Don't worry about it."

I'm piling clothes into my suitcase when there's a *pop* behind me, and Hazel screams.

I spin, dropping the sweater I was holding. "What happened?"

"All good." She shakes her head. "I unplugged your laptop and it sparked."

I snap my gaze to the charging cord stretched across the bed. The wire is exposed. "Weird," I say pointedly. "Maybe a stroke of *bad luck*?"

Hazel's eyes widen.

The nutcracker is where I left it, staring at the ceiling with dead eyes.

Ethel comes to sit in my doorway, her tail swishing. The pretzel she was batting around is probably under the couch.

What if I've stumbled on another Rebecca?

"Just call her," Hazel says, plunking down on the bed. "It's better to be safe."

The excited gleam in her eyes tells me she might have an ulterior motive.

Honestly, I might too. "Okay."

Hazel lets out a squee, confirming my suspicion.

My hands tremble as I pick up my phone, my insides doing a jig. I hover over Natalie's name until my screen dims, then suck in a breath and tap it. I put it on speaker.

It rings twice.

"Katie?"

My stomach swoops. The smooth way she says my name will be the death of me.

"I bought a nutcracker from the Christmas market, and I can't tell if it's cursed." I sit on the bed next to Hazel, and she leans in.

"Jesus... One sec." There's a scuffle. People talk in the background—maybe Natalie is somewhere for the holidays. Her voice comes back closer than before, firm and brusque. "What's it doing?"

"It doesn't work, for starters."

A pause. "Maybe it's supposed to be decorative."

I meet Hazel's eye. She grimaces, and my cheeks warm. Dammit, that might be true.

"Okay, but my laptop cord just sparked," I say.

"Has Ethel been entertaining herself with it while you're not looking?"

I spin toward Ethel, who stares back. The heat in my face intensifies. Natalie might be right about this too.

I glare at the useless decorative nutcracker.

"Anything else?" Her voice is tight, like she's trying not to laugh.

My insides squirm, and I stand, pacing the room. "Yes. I tried to make banana waffles last week with a new waffle maker, and they turned out disgusting. Could the waffle maker be cursed?"

"Where'd you find the recipe?"

"TikTok."

She sighs.

Fine, I'm smarter than this, and I'm overlooking the obvious. Time to get to the point.

I stop pacing, gripping the phone tighter. "I can't help noticing that you didn't correct me when I used the word *cursed*."

She says nothing.

My heart does a victory leap. *Ah-ha!*

Hazel clenches her fists under her jaw like she's going to burst.

"Anything else leading you to believe the nutcracker is cursed?" Natalie asks. "Any more boils? Can you breathe okay?"

There's the breathing question again.

I inhale deeply. No problems. "I'm fine. So you admit Lucy and Rebecca were cursed, then."

Hazel's mouth drops open. My face tingles. Did I just get an actual piece of information?

Natalie's breath hits the phone. "Katie, you're trying so hard to solve a mystery... but what if this is tough to figure out because you're not *meant* to figure it out?"

"Everything is meant to be figured out."

"Spoken like a true scientist."

The mysterious vial lingers in my mind's eye. "Is that what you are? A scientist?"

"Depends how you define science."

"What was in the vial?"

She pauses.

I chew my lip, waiting for her answer.

Hazel tugs me back to sit next to her. She leans close to the phone again and puts a hand over her mouth to stay silent.

In the background of wherever Natalie is, people talk and shout to each other. She moves away from the noise, her voice returning in a low purr. "Are you ever going to let this drop?"

"What do you think?"

"It would really be in your best interest to drop it."

"Good to know."

There's a shout, a hiss, a bang, and Hazel and I both lean away from the phone as it crackles.

We exchange a bewildered look.

Hazel mouths, *Where is she?*

I shrug.

Someone shouts Natalie's name.

"Coming!" she calls back, then returns with a note of urgency. "Okay. I've been thinking, and there are a few things I can explain. But I need you to do me a favor in return. Are you free to meet up tomorrow?"

Hazel grabs my arm as the words jolt through me like a lightning strike.

Meet up? *In person?*

"I—I can't until after Christmas," I say. "My family's visiting. How about the 28th in the afternoon?"

It's the day my family leaves. I can go straight to Natalie after saying bye at the airport.

"I'll pick you up at your place at three."

Hazel's grip is so tight on my arm that I can tell she's going to detonate like a bomb the second we hang up.

"Okay," I say, breathless.

Natalie ends the call before I can ask what the favor is.

I turn to Hazel. My inner victory dance is reflected on her face. *I did it.* The plan worked, and Natalie is finally going to answer some questions!

I just have to wonder what changed... and what favor she could possibly need from me.

Natalie steps out of a black electric car in a forest green button-up shirt, tight jeans, Vans to match the shirt, and her hair in that deep side-sweep. With her smooth movements and posture, she radiates such strong energy that it takes everything in me not to drool a little.

My parents got me a tapered wool coat for Christmas, thank God, because otherwise I would be in the ski jacket she met me in when I stumbled into the vet's office—so between that, my most flattering jeans, and a tight black shirt, I'm feeling cute and confident as I walk over. I may or may not have spent an hour curling my hair and doing full makeup.

Natalie holds the passenger door open for me, and my knees weaken at the gesture. As I get in, her dark eyes trace over me and she smooths the front of her shirt, making my stomach swoop. Am I imagining the way her gaze is lingering?

It smells like her in here—warm, herbal, with a hint of sweetness. As she shuts the door and walks around to the driver's side, I take a deep breath to get ahold of myself, which is a terrible idea because now my whole body is full of her scent.

I put on my seatbelt. "So, are you taking me to the Temple of Zacharias where all cursed items are stored?"

Her cheeks lift, giving me a peek of her dimples. "Not exactly."

"But you'll tell me what's going on?"

"I'll answer some of your questions in exchange for meeting up with me like this."

Ha. She says it as if meeting up with her is a burden.

We drive through Vancouver, heading north. The sun's long rays glint off patches of lingering snow, and Natalie puts on a pair of dark sunglasses.

Ugh, those cheekbones.

"You're right that you've been finding curses." Her words come out terse, like she's struggling with the confession. "It's my job to get rid of them."

Everything inside me erupts into a victory dance. *Ho-ly crap.*

All my questions fight their way to my lips. The one that comes out is, "When you say *get rid of them*—"

"I didn't murder a kitten, Katie."

"Good."

When she doesn't elaborate on what happened to Lucy, I move onto my next question. "*Why* are all these things cursed?"

Her jaw works. "That's one question I can't answer. I shouldn't be telling you any of this, but I'm breaking the rules for a reason." Behind her sunglasses, she gives me a sidelong glance. "There's something about you that I can't figure out."

"Okay..." It's funny to think she can't figure me out when I'm not the one running around with mysterious vials in my jacket.

She turns down West Broadway, making me wonder how far we're going. A ripple of nerves flows through me. She's not taking me to the highway, is she? Oh God, did I just get into a car with a stranger without thinking twice?

Natalie taps her fingers on the wheel and shifts in her seat. "When I asked you what attracted you to that kitten—"

"Lucy." I'm determined not to reduce her to *that kitten*, no matter what Natalie says about her not being what I think she was.

"Lucy." She glances sideways at me again, a flash of concern. "I wanted to know whether you picked up on the curse or if it was a fluke. Then you came to me with a second item, and..." She huffs. "It's rare for me to see someone more than once. People end up with curses by accident. It's happened before that I've seen the same person two or three times, but only because they themselves were cursed."

I look sharply at her. "The *person* was...?"

"Yeah." She rolls to a stop at a light and turns to me. Her expression is steady. "But I don't think you are. I think, somehow, you can sense curses. You sensed it in Lucy and in the doll."

I nod. She's not wrong. "And that's rare?"

"I've never heard of it before."

I blink, astonished. A special ability? *Me*?

I'd be honored, except I still don't get what's going on. This ability seems to concern her—or at least interest her. I search the side of her face. "What do you think this means?"

The light turns green, and we start moving again.

"I have no idea. Maybe your family history includes some—" She breaks off as if to concentrate on changing lanes.

"What?" I press, filled with a sensation like teetering on the edge of a cliff.

"I'm taking you thrift shopping."

The change of topic ignites a spark of annoyance, but I'm too intrigued by where we're going. "Why?"

"I want to see if you can find a cursed item. We can test if you have an ability or if it was a fluke that you found the other two."

My pulse picks up. This feels like a weird job interview. She's testing my skills. "And if I find one? Then what?"

"Then..." She scowls at the road, as unreadable as ever. "I'll worry about what this all means if we're successful."

My heart misses a beat. If her job is to find curses, and I can find curses... It's only logical that I help her, isn't it?

"And if we fail?" I ask, unsure I want the answer.

Her expression turns solemn. "Then I'm making a pretty huge mistake right now."

A pause. The way her face falls, I have to wonder *who* might discover that she's told me stuff. Who does she report to, and whose rules is she breaking? Will she have to cut me out of her life if I don't have an ability?

Cold trickles through me at the thought of her disappearing from my life. She's been the most exciting thing to happen to me—possibly ever.

"Is a thrift store the best place to find a curse?" I ask into the tense silence. That news article about Natalie working at one suddenly checks out. She probably pretended to be a piano tuner at one time too, if a piano was cursed.

"You'd be surprised," she says. "An item isn't sitting right with someone—they get a bad vibe from it, or don't love it anymore, or it isn't working the way it's supposed to—and they ditch it. Our other option is to go to the dump."

I pretend to consider. "Tempting, but thrifting sounds nice. I could use some kitchen stuff, anyway."

"Waffle maker?" she murmurs.

I laugh, which makes her cheeks lift.

I like this side of her. The side that jokes a little and teases me with half smiles.

Mission: Accepted. Though Natalie claims she's not sure what comes next, I think I know, and it sends my heart racing. This skill I have would be an asset to her. We could work together, get to know each other... and take it from there.

She parallel parks and turns off the car. With a firm nod, she opens the door. "Time to see what you can do, Miss Alexander."

CHAPTER 10

Just Call Me a Sniffer Dog

READY TO PICK UP on the slightest hint of a curse, I ground myself as if meditating, checking in with all my senses. The thrift store buffets me with a kaleidoscope of household items and clothes, the smell of old books and dust, and a radio ad playing over the PA.

This is my chance. If this goes well, Natalie will have to accept my help—and the possibility of her *needing* me sends a thrill through my veins from head to toe.

Behind the till, a guy and a girl about my age pause mid-conversation, their gazes locking onto Natalie.

"H-hi," the girl stammers, a hand shooting up to smooth her curls. "Welcome."

The guy wears the same starstruck expression. "Our—um—New Year sale is on now."

Natalie nods politely. "Thank you."

I smile at the floor. Good to know I'm not the only one who forgets how to use words around her.

We start at a section of dishes. I scan them, waiting for that sense of anticipation to overcome me like before. But nothing remotely close happens, especially not with Natalie at my side. My pulse is racing for an entirely different reason, a warm, exhilarating rush tingling through my body.

Focus. We're here to prove my ability.

"Did you celebrate the holidays?" I ask, hoping it's okay to talk about other things while I search.

She nods. "My sister and I went to a Christmas thing with some friends."

"That's nice." Interesting she didn't mention parents. "Just the two of you?"

"My dad's in Turkey right now. He travels a lot."

No mention of her mom. I don't pry.

Nothing in the dishes section catches my attention, so we move on to lamps and furniture. I freeze as a chill sweeps over me—only to realize I'm standing under a vent. *Dammit.*

I keep moving, studying an oil painting of a meadow.

"How old is your sister?" I ask.

She paces half a step behind, hands in pockets, as if to avoid distracting me. "Eighteen. Three years younger."

"Same age as me," I say. "That makes you twenty-one, which is definitely too young to have a doctorate."

Her mouth tightens as if she's fighting a smile. "Not necessarily."

"Does your sister also do what you do?"

"No. I mean, it's a similar line of work, but no." Before I can ask her to elaborate, she says, "Did you have a good Christmas with your family?"

"I did."

"That jacket looks nice on you."

The compliment makes me want to skip, but I stay calm. "Thanks."

"Tell me about your holiday traditions."

It's a specific, pointed request. Maybe she and her sister don't have much in the way of traditions.

I meander through the furniture, grazing my fingers along the wood and upholstery in the hopes that touching a curse will help me sense it. "We have a feast on Christmas Eve, usually a roast and lumpia—they're like spring rolls. We open one present each, which is always pajamas. In the morning, we do the whole stocking and tree thing, and my dad makes crepes. We ordinarily have another feast with my extended family in the evening, but this year, we went to a restaurant since it was just us."

She watches me closely, hanging on each word. "Sounds perfect," she murmurs.

I nod. "Holidays have always been fun... ever since we were little kids staying up late in our unicorn nightgowns, watching for Santa's sleigh out the living room window. Our poor parents had to put up with a lot of screaming."

When I meet her eye, she's smiling. It catches me off-guard, tingling all the way to my toes. It's the first time I've seen a real smile on her—and it's as stunning as the rest of her. It crinkles her eyes and dimples her cheeks, brightening her whole face.

"What about y—"

"Does this shelf have anything suspicious?" She motions to a miscellany of decor and appliances.

I narrow my eyes. *Master of topic changes.*

Maybe she doesn't want to talk about her family. That's fine. I can save those questions for another day.

I bend to examine the shelf she's pointing to. Trinkets, a toaster, a mustard-yellow rotary phone. "I feel like a sniffer dog searching for drugs."

She huffs out a laugh and pats my hair. "Good girl."

I freeze. So does she.

Oh. My. God. The effect of those words is *embarrassing.*

She steps back and clears her throat. "Sorry. I meant—the dog thing—that wasn't—"

She's so awkward and mortified that I can't help bursting into laughter. "Stop it, Natalie."

At my reaction, she relaxes into a bashful smile.

But I can't unhear it. My head tingles where her hand touched me, and the fluttering in my chest is traveling lower, intensifying.

I reach for the rotary phone and dial a couple of numbers, watching it spin back with a whirr. "Do you have a vague idea of what kind of object I'm looking for?"

I can't meet her eyes. My face is hot. I'm tingling in places I shouldn't be tingling.

"It can be anything," she says. "Like you saw, it can range from a kitten to a doll."

"If you can't tell me why these things are cursed, can you tell me *who* is cursing them?"

"That's not something you need to know."

I shoot her a glare. "You promised you'd answer my questions."

"Some, not all."

"Why?"

Her brow pinches. "Some are too dangerous to be answered. Others would get me in trouble."

"Intriguing." I peek inside a slow cooker, pick it up, and examine it from all angles. Only minor blemishes.

Natalie checks over her shoulder and steps closer. "Do you feel something?"

"I might buy it. I've been thinking I should get one of these so I can come home to comfort food after class."

She sighs and keeps walking.

I grin. "So if we find something cursed, will you destroy it again by unleashing a vial of goo on it?"

"More smoothly than last time, I hope."

"You're carrying a vial now?"

"Yes."

I leave the slow cooker, intending to come back for it, and keep walking. We move onto used books, the scent of old paper wafting at us from four overflowing bookcases. Their colorful spines, worn and cracked, span a range of genres. Still, no sense of anticipation creeps in, and worry settles over me. What if I can't find one? Will she drop me off at home and that's it?

"How does a person end up in the business of destroying curses?" I ask.

"The word you're looking for is neutralize. I neutralize curses."

"Cool." I drag a hand along the books, feeling for anything weird. My fingers bump from spine to spine. "Are the staff at the vet clinics in on it?"

She shakes her head. "All they know is to call me if something inexplicable comes up."

At least there's that. I'd be furious if the random employees at Helping Paws knew the secrets I've been agonizing over. "So how did you get into this line of work?"

"That's also something I can't tell you."

I round on her, annoyed. "Natalie!"

She steps in close. Really close. I lean back against the bookshelf, the wooden edges pressing into my back. Looking up at her, every fiber in my body is begging her to keep going.

"Katie." Her breath hits my cheeks, cool and fresh. She reaches up to tug one of my curls, studying it, and heat ripples through my scalp and down my neck. "Stop trying to understand all this. I'm protecting you from something you don't *want* to understand."

She meets my gaze with her intense, dark eyes, pausing for long enough for me to dip my chin in the smallest of nods.

"This life comes with a price," she murmurs. Then she turns away, leaving me breathless against the bookshelf.

My lips tingle, my body aching. I've never wanted to lean in and close the distance more. Does she realize how hot that was? Was that supposed to be threatening?

I shake my head and force my legs to move, hurrying to catch up. Something life-changing is dangling just out of reach, and I'm not ready to drop the subject. "What if I *do* want to understand, despite whatever cost? What if I can be helpful? Let me be your penguin."

She faces me. "My what?"

"Penguin. Like the way penguins bring pebbles to each other. I can bring you curses. I can help you do your job." It's hard to keep the desperation out of my tone. This strange and unique ability feels like a calling, a purpose. I can't ignore it.

She scans me up and down, a flicker of something in her eyes. Regret? Whatever it is, she seems to consider my offer, and my heart jumps.

But she frowns and walks toward the door. "Buy the slow cooker if you want it, and let's try another thrift shop."

I scowl after her.

She waits outside while I take my purchase to the cash register in a huff. The more time I spend with her, the more frustrated I get, both with her lack of answers and in other—um—biological ways.

As I pay, something snags my attention in a vintage mirror behind the till. Someone is looking at me—a man in his twenties with fair skin and blond hair. His gaze is intentional, like he's studying me or waiting for me.

I look over my shoulder, but he's focused on the rack of clothes in front of him. Hangers squeak as he riffles through shirts.

Weird. His stare lingers on the back of my neck like a physical touch.

"Do you want a receipt?" the girl at the till asks.

I face her again. "No, thanks."

I cradle the slow cooker in my arms and head for the door, ready to persevere. I *have* to find a curse for Natalie.

But an hour later, after scouring two more shops, defeat weighs heavy in the air. Either I failed or there were no curses to be found. The possibility of failing stings—an intense, burning disappointment in myself, like when I get anything less than an A on an exam. But even worse is the thought of this being the end of our time together... that she's going to drop me off and say a last goodbye soon.

We drive back, and as Natalie turns down my street, I lean against the headrest and break the long silence. "Sorry that was a waste of time."

She parks out front and angles her body to face me. "Katie. That was not a waste of time. If anything, I wasted your time by taking you on a goose chase."

"It was a fun goose chase. I liked it." *I liked being with you.*

The unspoken words hang between us.

Her expression softens, her eyebrows pulling down. I want her to say something like "same," but she says nothing.

My pulse speeds up. The way we're facing each other in her car, sitting outside my place, feels like the end of a date.

Headlights illuminate the street from behind us, casting moving shadows over her face before the car parks and plunges us back into darkness.

Natalie breaks our gaze and takes off her seatbelt. She gets out, and by the time I'm done fumbling with my own seatbelt, she's opening the passenger door and extending a hand to help me.

I take it, sparks shooting up my arm at her gentle grip. For a moment, it's easy to forget about curses and mysteries and everything but the way her touch makes me feel.

She takes the slow cooker from my arms. "I'll walk you to your door."

"It's okay. I can manage the ten steps." I motion to the blue house on the other side of the picket fence. The stone walkway leads around back to the basement suite.

She strides ahead and opens the gate, letting me through. "I'll walk you to here, then."

"Thanks." I slip past her into the yard.

As she passes me my purchase, our hands brush, and I swear she lingers for longer than she has to. I let her warmth tingle through me as her slender fingers fit between mine... and then the moment is over, and we step apart. Is the air thick, or am I just hopelessly crushing?

"Thank you for coming with me. I'm sorry we didn't have any luck today." Her words are disappointingly formal considering the amount of time we just spent together.

Dipping her chin, she steps toward her car.

A sudden panic overcomes me, my breath hitching. My last seconds with her are slipping away. After all we've faced, all our conversations, and the swoop in my belly every time she looks at me... This *can't* be it.

"Natalie?" I blurt.

She turns, a perfect vision in the dark street.

My mouth goes dry, my nerves twisting, but I have to ask. I can't let her leave without knowing. "Did you only want to spend time with me today because you wanted to know if I have some kind of curse-finding ability, or...?"

Her lips twist, teasing me with a shadow of the smile I got to see earlier. "It's complicated. I admit I find you intriguing."

"Oh." A balloon inflates inside me, making me light.

"I like how persistent you were about a kitten you'd only had for four days. You have..." She squints into the distance as if interested in something down the street. "You have the ability to love deeply. It's an admirable quality."

"So..." I shift, my heart beating so hard it's like I'm sprinting. If she doesn't want me to pry into who she is and what all this is about, fine—but I think there's chemistry between us, and maybe we can still get to know each other. I draw a breath and summon every ounce of bravery I possess. My next words come out in a rush. "Do you want to come to a New Year's thing with me?"

Natalie freezes. After an excruciating pause, she combs her fingers through her hair, not meeting my eye. "I don't think we should spend time together, Katie."

Her words puncture the balloon inside me, taking all the air out of my body. "Why not?"

She turns toward her car. Hesitates. "Because you don't want to be involved with someone who deals with exploding dolls."

She walks away, each footstep a nail in my heart.

And yet...

I can't help noticing she didn't say "because I'm not interested in you" or any iteration of that. Her rejection is about the curses—and when it comes to that, who is she to tell me what I want?

I mean, sure, curses seem dangerous, but that doesn't make me want to back away and pretend none of this happened. Apart from solving a mystery, I *like* her. In the span of today, I graduated from having a giddy crush to a deep, aching desire.

"What if I'm meant to be involved?" I step closer, my hips pressed against the picket fence. "*I* stumbled on Lucy. We met because I found a curse."

Natalie opens her car door and pauses. I bite my lip, waiting.

But she shakes her head firmly. "I'm putting you in danger just by being around you."

"I don't care!" For the first time since arriving in Vancouver, I've found somewhere I want to be—a person I want to know. "Natalie, I'm not afraid of curses."

Her brow furrows. She studies me, one leg in her car. "Well, you should be."

She gets in before I can argue, the sound of the slamming door carry-ing down the quiet street. Her words hang in the chilly night air—a final warning.

It feels like someone stomped on my chest. It's over, then. A brief, exciting spell of curse-hunting with Natalie, done in the span of an afternoon.

But why? What's so dangerous, and who is she afraid of?

As she drives away, I'm left standing in the fading glow of her tail lights, the slow cooker's cold metal pressed between my hands, my mind swirling with more questions than when she picked me up.

CHAPTER 11

Auld Lang Syne

On New Year's Eve, I meet Clayton and my other university friends to celebrate, still bitter about Natalie's rejection.

The group chose a restaurant that serves pitchers of beer and sangria, which means the others who are nineteen can order alcohol, and those of us who are eighteen can pour some into our cups when the servers aren't looking. It's terrible and probably a flaw that'll end in the restaurant being shut down, but nobody cares. They're all just happy to be allowed to drink together in a place that isn't a dorm.

I haven't texted Natalie since our thrift shopping day, and she hasn't texted me either. She doesn't want to be involved with me, so fine. I won't force my company onto her—and I guess she doesn't care that my ability to sense curses could be useful. Totally her loss.

Instead, I'm seated at the end of a long row of four tables pushed together, bristling as Clayton leans too close, trying to avert my gaze from Mo and a girl named Laura groping each other in the booth seat across from us.

It's not even nine. Can I make it to midnight?

"Those two need to get a room," Clayton shouts in my ear.

"Yeah," I say automatically. I sip my sangria, the bittersweet taste prickling my tongue.

"They were talking about kissing at midnight." He looks at me as if hoping this will suddenly give me an idea.

"I guess that is a thing," I say. I've never done it because my relationship with Crystal only lasted the fall of Grade 10, and my relationship with Mansplainy Matt spanned from last February until June—basically from when he asked me to grad until grad was over and we both realized we didn't like each other all that much. "I normally just sing Auld Lang Syne and call it a night."

"What's that?"

"Auld Lang Syne? The song to bid farewell to the old year?"

"Oh." He gives a lopsided smile. "Well, both traditions are good."

I tug my cardigan closed over my top, which is low cut, tight, and mostly black lace. If I'd known Clayton's flirting would become more shameless with each drink, I would've dressed frumpy tonight.

I pretend to focus on the conversation Johnny, Andrea, and the rest of the group are having. Clayton stays in my periphery, his expression soft, like he's trying to look sweet and romantic.

"So, Laura, what are you studying?" I ask. The restaurant is so loud that I have to yell.

She peels away from Mo. She's pale and curvy with raven hair and goth makeup, wearing a tiny black corset that pushes up her breasts so they brush the table. A turquoise pendant catches the light in her cleavage. "It's Aura, actually."

Heat burns in my cheeks. Why can't I make it through the most basic conversation without doing something awkward? "Sorry."

"It's okay, you're not the first. And I'm studying Wicca."

Any standard response dies on my lips. "What?"

Even Clayton pries his gaze away from me to look at her. "Isn't that witchcraft?"

Aura's blue eyes dart between us, taking in our reactions, and a smile spreads across her face. "Yes. I own a shop."

I try to picture Mo with his preppy polo shirt and well-groomed facial hair walking into a Wiccan shop. "How did you two meet?"

"At a rave," Mo says, making gooey eyes at her. I've never seen him like this. I've watched girls flirt with him several times since we met, but he's never shown interest in anyone until now. Apparently, goths are his type.

"What do you sell at the shop?" I ask.

"Crystals, candles, herbs, books, potions..."

"Ouija Boards," Mo says darkly, shooting her a glare. "Never—fuck-ing—again."

She cackles, leaning into him. "I had it under control."

"I think my soul left my body."

I smile. Not only is Aura a welcome distraction from Clayton, but her words spark a deep curiosity. "What are the potions?"

She leans closer, resting her chin on her hand. "They serve different purposes. Luck, love, health, prosperity—" She pauses while a police siren whips past the restaurant and drowns out her voice. "They're in-fused teas and juices. All safe to drink." Her smile falters as she glances at each of us, making me wonder how often people question her potions.

"That's so cool!" I say.

Her smile returns. "You should come by for a sample. I'll give you a vial of good luck."

Her words swirl in my head. *Luck. Love. Vials.*

A cog shifts in the back of my mind, creaking as it struggles to click into place.

Another siren passes. Several people in the restaurant turn their heads.

"We could go together," Clayton says, taking the opportunity to look at me again.

I ignore him, my heart pounding. Was the vial in Natalie's blazer a *potion*? Not an infused tea, but an actual, real potion created by an actual, real—

My belly swoops.

Is she an alchemist?

No. But did I witness magic?

No, that's ridiculous. Magic is performed by wizards, who are fictional bearded men with wands.

I'm so close, teetering on the edge of figuring her out.

Three more police cars whip past us, yanking me out of my thoughts. Everyone in the restaurant turns toward the windows.

"Something crazy's going on," Mo says.

Aura grabs his collar and presses her breasts into him. "They're coming after a *bad boy*."

They kiss. Mo slides a hand around her corset, and hers come up to his face, and we've lost them.

I avert my gaze from their making out only to meet Clayton's eyes.

"So, where were we?" He leans closer, a hopeful glint in his eyes. "What are your midnight plans?"

God, this guy doesn't take a hint.

"Sorry, Clayton, I'm not..." I don't know how to end that sentence. How do you let someone down lightly?

As Clayton stares at me, waiting, Natalie's voice echoes in my memory, telling me she finds me intriguing only to follow up by saying I don't want to be involved with her.

I won't do the same thing and give mixed messages. I have to be direct.

"I—I'm not interested." The words feel terrible as they pass my lips. I hate this. I don't like being the cause of that sad-puppy expression on Clayton's face.

Did Natalie have the same guilt as she let me down? Did she look pityingly at my reaction?

Humiliation burns inside me.

As Clayton sits back, looking suddenly sober, I slide my chair back and stand. "Back in a sec. I just have to call home. It's past midnight there."

I grab my coat and speed-walk to the door, leaving behind Clayton's palpable disappointment, Mo and Aura's makeout session—they really should get a room—and all the other people we came with, who are getting drunker and noisier by the minute.

Outside, the sirens are louder. It's threatening to snow, and I dodge a frozen puddle before I can slip. I put on my coat, leaving it unbuttoned so I can cool off from that stuffy restaurant.

It wasn't a lie when I said midnight has already struck in Toronto, so I pull out my phone. I text Hazel first—New Year's is a huge deal on the Japanese side of her family, so they'll be partying all night—and then I send an obnoxious confetti gif to my family's group chat.

I pause, staring at Natalie's name. I want to ask her if the vial was a potion.

But her rejection was clear, and the fact she hasn't reached out since that night is even clearer. I'm acting no better than Clayton, refusing to take a hint.

It's time to let her go.

Tapping the screen aggressively, I delete our text exchange.

Next, her contact. It'll be easier if there's no temptation to message her again. Like she said, I should move on and pretend none of this happened.

Holding my breath, I tap Delete, watching her disappear from my phone completely.

A sinking, deflating feeling pulls my shoulders toward the ground. I liked having her in my life, however strange and temporary our connection was. But the mystery will go unsolved, my questions left unanswered.

I put my phone away, a hollow ache behind my ribs. Going home and crawling into bed would be really good right now. *Home* home—not the basement suite.

Someone swears, and I look up. A shift in the atmosphere surges to my attention. The street buzzes with nervous energy, so palpable that it prickles my skin. I rub my arms, surprised I didn't notice it the second I stepped out of the restaurant. Car doors slam. People shout and talk urgently, leaning out the open doors of nearby establishments. Everybody faces the same direction, looking down the block, clutching each other.

Something serious is going on.

The police cruisers that blew past are parked a block away, forming a barricade to wall off a section of the street. Their sirens are off, but the lights flash, staining the inky sky red and blue.

"...think it's a bomb," a woman behind me tells her friends. "Maybe a gas leak. There was an explosion."

I whirl around. "An explosion?"

She meets my eye, fear tightening her expression, and nods.

My skin tingles. As I face forward again, a hook sinks into my core, tugging.

Maybe it's because I was thinking about Natalie, but my brain jumps to the doll and the crater in my bed.

She said curses could be anywhere.

I may be wrong... but even if I'm right—*especially* if I'm right—the smart thing would be to walk away.

My feet stay rooted, questions swarming in my mind like bees. What if this is another curse? What if Natalie is here?

I shift my weight from foot to foot, curiosity burning. I just want to check. I'll be thirty seconds, tops.

I walk toward the barricade of police cars, the red and blue lights leaving spots in my vision. People are being ushered out the doors of a nightclub, most of them drunk and swaying, some shouting at those trying to get them to safety.

Smoke curls inside my nostrils and dries the back of my throat. A haze drifts out the open doors—I can't tell if it's from the explosion or smoke machines from the club.

I edge as close as I can to the scene, trying to stay inconspicuous. I step over a dead rat and onto the sidewalk, my pulse accelerating.

Something small perches on the hood of a cop car, illuminated by the flashing lights. My breath hitches. My imagination could just be desperately trying to fit pieces together... but it looks like one of the purple butterflies that appeared when Natalie melted the doll.

"Hey, do you know what's going on?" a gentle voice asks behind me.

I startle, spinning around, and I have to look up to meet his eyes. He's in his twenties, fair-skinned with blue eyes and blond hair. His cheeks and ears are rosy from the cold, and he shuffles his feet and ducks his chin into the collar of his black down jacket.

I motion back to where I came from. "Someone said something about a bomb threat."

He raises an eyebrow. "You heard that and decided to come closer?"

"I'm a curious person?" I say hesitantly.

His lips curve into a handsome smile. Between his tousled golden hair, ice-blue eyes, and his broad chest filling out his fur-lined jacket, he looks like he just stepped off a Viking longship.

"Sit," he murmurs, and I follow his gaze to the German Shepherd at his side. The dog was so quiet that I didn't even notice him. He sits obediently at the end of a short black leash, looking up and waiting for the next command.

I melt a little. "Oh, cute! What's his name?"

"Wyatt," the guy says, and the animal perks up on hearing his name. "Working dog. Don't pet him."

It's my turn to perk up. I love learning about working dogs. It's my dream to have a therapy dog at my practice when I start my career as a psychologist. "What does he do?"

"He's got a nose for dangerous items."

"Sounds like they could use him in there." I nod toward the nightclub.

"Maybe one day." He studies me, a crease between his thick eyebrows. "You look familiar. Hey, were you at the thrift store the other day with Nat?"

"Nat?" Something clicks into place, and my heart flips over. "Oh, Natalie—yeah. That was you in the shop! I saw you in the mirror when I was paying."

He casts me a crooked smile. "Sorry if I was staring." He looks down, the color in his rosy cheeks deepening.

"All good." I tug my jacket closed and cross my arms, hunching against the wintry wind. "How do you know Natalie?"

He tilts his head. "We're in similar lines of work."

A bolt of excitement zaps through me. Wait, this mysterious Viking man knows about curses and everything?

I try not to look too excited, offering what I hope is a casual smile. "Well, it's nice to meet you. I'm Katie."

"Freddie. Freddie Madsen." He takes a step closer. Wyatt inches over to stay heeling, still watching his handler. That is a *very* well trained dog

"Is this what I think it is?" I ask, jerking my chin toward the building.

Freddie smiles. "I'm sure you know the answer. Nat's got you on the hunt, huh?"

Disappointment and frustration twist in my gut again. "If you can call it that. It was only once."

"Any luck?"

"No," I say tightly.

He leans in, giving me a playful nudge. "But it wasn't your first rodeo?"

I hesitate. Should I be talking to him about this? He seems to already know everything, but Natalie did ask me not to tell anyone what happened.

A spark of defiance flares in me. If Natalie had given me a proper explanation, I wouldn't be standing here in confusion, wondering how much to say.

Letting spite win, I nod. "Twice."

Freddie searches me curiously, a sort of hunger passing over his expression and parting his lips.

A sharp whistle sounds beside us, and an officer waves to catch our attention. She's unrolling a line of yellow tape. "Move away, please! This is a crime scene."

"Sorry," I call back, the guilt of being caught snooping heating up my face.

"Let's step over here." Freddie motions behind me toward an alley. We walk further from the commotion and into the quiet darkness, until the flashing lights and shouts fade around the corner of a brick building. Wyatt heels with his snout pointed upward, his gaze never leaving his handler's face.

When we're two steps into the alley, Freddie faces me. "You working with Nat now?"

The twisting inside me intensifies, hot and acidic. "No."

His mouth falls open. "She's letting that kind of talent go to waste?"

I lift a shoulder, my teeth clenched. Freddie's incredulity sparks my anger all over again.

Around the corner, shouts erupt. It sounds like someone tried to cross the yellow tape and is getting yelled at for it. The argument spikes my pulse, making me want to back away.

Freddie doesn't seem to notice the chaos. His wide eyes are on me, half his face cast into shadow, the other half lit by the distant red-and-blue lights. "You know, a person with your gift shouldn't be sitting on the sidelines. We could use you."

My heart skips, his offer catching me by surprise. I glance around, the alley's shadows clinging thickly, the pulsing lights failing to penetrate the darkness. Between the chaotic scene we left behind and the smothering isolation of the alley, it's hard to think. "Um…"

He steps closer. "Your ability is unique, Katie. I'm sure you know that."

A warning bell goes off in the back of my mind, telling me to say no. I don't know why, and maybe it's this whole situation making me uneasy, but something feels off.

"I'll think about it. I'm going to school and don't really have time for much else." I shuffle sideways, nearer to the street we came from.

"I get it. Totally." He moves with me. "Can I give you my business card so you can call me when you come to a decision?"

Relief trickles through me as this conversation heads toward a close. I should go back to the restaurant and away from here. "Sure."

He pats his pockets. "Shoot. I left them in the car. Come with me and I'll get one for you. I'm just at the other end of this alley."

The warning bell gets louder. I don't care how nice this guy is or what he claims about knowing Natalie. He's a stranger inviting me down a dark alley to his car.

I pull out my phone. "It's okay. Why don't you tell me your number and I'll type it in?"

He waves a hand. "It's our office number. Family business—I run it with my parents and little sister. I can't remember it off the top of my head. Come on, we'll be fast."

I back up. No, this is definitely weird. "Thanks for the offer, but I'm not interested."

He tilts his head, his smile less warm. "Katie."

An iciness fills me, threatening to freeze me in place.

The dog turns his focus away from Freddie for the first time, his sharp eyes piercing through me. And while I've always loved dogs... something about this one sends a shiver right down to my toes.

I glance at the street, hoping to spot an officer who I can edge toward for safety. But we've turned the corner, and we're out of sight of the nightclub and cop cars.

As I step away, Freddie follows, Wyatt heeling so closely that he's leaning against his thigh. Claws click on the pavement.

Freddie's lips curve upward again, but it's not a friendly smile anymore. "Katie, stop."

Wyatt snarls at me, exposing a glint of deadly canines.

My muscles freeze, the fear of being bitten by a hundred-pound dog bringing me to a halt. Cold sweat prickles under my jacket.

"Good." Freddie grabs my arm, his grip as firm as an iron shackle. "Come with me, and we'll keep this simple."

Pain jolts through me. I gasp, panic surging. "No!"

The dog looks from me to Freddie, tense, his teeth chattering—waiting for the release command.

Freddie leans his head down to search my face. "I can see why Nat likes you. You're smart. Intuitive."

Adrenaline shoots through me. I grit my teeth, jerking back. "What do you want?"

His grip burns. How hard do I fight? Do I kick and scream despite the risk of being bitten?

"To get you to change your mind," he says evenly, forcing me closer.

My heart is beating out of my chest, trying to escape while the rest of me is trapped.

I pull back. "I said I'm not interested!"

Freddie stumbles. Hisses in frustration. Shakes his hair back from his face and keeps holding tightly. "You're causing a scene—"

"Let go!" My lungs constrict. I can't breathe. Can't think.

The dog growls, the noise vibrating through the air and crawling under my skin.

My arm tingles, my fingers going numb.

"Katie—" Freddie says through his teeth.

"Help!" My voice tears through the haze closing in around me.

I'm trapped. Suffocating. He's on me like a leech, refusing to let go until I follow him to wherever he wants to take me.

"Madsen!" someone roars from the far end of the alley, the sound slicing through the haze.

Freddie and I freeze, and he snaps his head around, keeping a painful hold.

A dark figure storms toward us, backlit by the distant street lamps. Her tall frame is an impressive sight, her ankle-length trench coat billowing open, her hair lifting in the wintry wind.

Natalie.

Chapter 12

The Madsens

A s Natalie advances on us, the dog leaps forward with a snarl, hitting the end of his short leash. Freddie lets go of me to hold onto Wyatt with both hands.

"Get the hell away from her," Natalie shouts, waving an arm. Her green trench coat is open over an olive sweater and jeans, items glinting in her inner pockets.

Relief washes over me so intensely that my knees weaken. Breathing fast, I back away from Freddie, moving deeper into the alley and closer to Natalie. My arm throbs where he grabbed me.

Freddie sneers, not bothering to tell his dog to back down. "Why? Who's she to you?"

"Does it matter? You were grabbing her."

Each time I've met Natalie, she's been calm, cool, her voice a purr—but now, she swells with anger, her expression contorts, and her voice is hoarse. I guess I do have every reason to fear Freddie Madsen.

Freddie leans back against his dog's pull, still holding on with both hands, as if to show that all he needs to do is let go. "We were just talking."

"Like hell," I snap.

A nasty smile curls Freddie's lips.

Natalie clenches her fists at her sides as she stops beside me, a few steps away from Freddie and the snarling dog. Her nostrils flare, her chest heaving. "I know what you're here for, and you're too late—"

Freddie lets go of Wyatt. "Get 'em!"

Icy adrenaline surges through my body, slowing down time as the animal rockets toward us.

Before I can put my hands up in self-defense, Natalie pushes me behind her with one hand and swipes the other through the air.

My arms prickle like I'm walking under a powerline. A gust of wind lifts my hair. The ground shudders beneath my feet.

With a deep crack that rattles through me, the pavement splits, a fissure snaking across the alley to draw a line between us and them. Asphalt crumbles into the chasm. Gasping, I stumble for balance as the shifting earth rumbles through me—but most of the quake is on the other side. Beneath Freddie and the dog, the ground swells and heaves like a living thing, jolting them so they're forced to crouch. Wyatt scrambles forward with a scrape of nails on pavement, but it keeps rising, the slope forcing him to slide back to his handler.

I take a shaky step back. I don't understand what I'm seeing. How is this happening?

Freddie's desperate roars tear through me. "Get 'em! Get 'em!"

Wyatt snarls and snaps in frustration. He regains his balance amid a cloud of dust, and then I lose sight of them. The earth keeps climbing until it forms a vertical wall blocking their path.

Natalie is still holding up a hand, palm out. She looks back at me, breathing hard, a sheen of sweat on her brow. Something flashes in her eyes—a purple glow passing through her brown irises. "Katie, in my car, now! We need to go."

I take another step back, gulping down air, my legs like jelly. My brain is sluggish as I try to understand what's going on.

Natalie's outstretched hand. The wall of pavement. *Is she…?*

No. Impossible.

My skin still prickles with that staticky feeling, a strange wind tugging my hair and clothes. "Where'd you park—"

"End of the alley."

My legs can't move fast enough. I race away, the shadows pressing in on me. My open jacket catches the wind, the wintry air raising goosebumps on my clammy skin.

I slam into her car with my palms, anchoring myself against it. She's parked on an angle in the alley, the wheels cranked as if she got out in a rush.

Over my shoulder, Natalie backs toward me, glimpses of Freddie and Wyatt visible through crumbling gaps in the wall of pavement.

My insides are numb. I must be in a dream—a nightmare.

Natalie spins around and runs at me, pumping her arms. "Go!"

Behind her, Wyatt darts through a gap and charges after her with long, powerful strides, his teeth glistening in the street lights.

"Natalie!" I shriek, pointing.

"I know!" she shouts without looking back. "Open the doors!"

While the dog gains on her in a rush of thundering paws and huffing breaths, I whip open the passenger door. I dive in and slam it, and as I lean over to open the driver's side for Natalie, she leaps onto the hood and slides across on her butt.

Wyatt catches up, snapping at her feet as his front paws scramble for purchase on the hood. He barks furiously, claws screeching on metal.

I scream, pushing the door wider. Natalie grabs it and gets in, slamming the door just in time for Wyatt to throw himself at the window. His claws and teeth scrape the glass as he tries to break through.

"Drive!" I yell over the snarling.

Natalie starts the car and stomps down, accelerating so fast that I suck back against the seat. Tires squeal, the car jerking left and right before we gain traction.

Behind us, Wyatt stops running and looks at his handler, who stumbles out of the alley and watches us go, his fury palpable even from a distance.

"Put your seatbelt on." Natalie's raspy voice fills the car.

I obey, my hands shaking, as she flies through a red light. "Will he follow us?"

"He won't make it to his car in time." She glances quickly at me, like she's trying not to take her eyes off the road but can't help it. "Are you okay?"

"Yes."

She slows a little and studies me for longer. "Look at me. Are you sure?"

The concern in her eyes melts me. I exhale, feeling safer in her presence. "I'm fine, Natalie. Thank you for—" I choke on the words. I don't know what, exactly, she's saved me from, but that icy terror is still gripping me, making me shiver.

She shakes her head, accelerating around a turn.

"He set his dog on us out of nowhere," I grumble. "Poor thing is going to get seized by the SPCA because of a reckless owner."

Natalie's lips twitch, and then she goes back to grinding her teeth. "He knew what he was doing."

"What do you mean?"

"He was forcing me to show you what—" She closes her mouth, deliberating her next words. "What I can do. Now you know. Now you'll always know, and there's no going back."

"Know *what*? Why were you there?"

"Why were *you* there?" Her gaze travels down my body—my curled hair, makeup, the low-cut lace shirt peeking out of my open jacket—and despite everything, a tingle rushes through me at the way she looks at me.

"New Year's party. I heard there was a bomb, and I thought of the doll and…"

She doesn't scoff or get angry at me for going closer. Instead, she exhales slowly, dropping her shoulders. "You're right. It wasn't a bomb."

"You were neutralizing a curse."

She nods curtly. Sweat glistens on her face, and she tries to shimmy out of her coat while weaving through traffic.

"Here." I grab the end of the sleeve.

Her hand brushes my fingers as she pulls her arm out, shedding the jacket and leaving the olive cable-knit sweater. She wipes her brow. "Thanks."

Her delicious, warm scent fills the car more than ever, making me want to lean over and see if she tastes as good as she smells. It doesn't help that her sweater looks cozy enough to curl up against.

I fold my hands in my lap, numb shock rolling over me at what just happened.

The city lights flicker over us, highlighting the sharp angles of her face. She scowls, her jaw working.

"What are you, Natalie?" My words come out tired.

She doesn't answer. I study the way her fingers caress the steering wheel before forcing myself to look forward.

"Are—" What I'm about to say is ridiculous, but everything fits, doesn't it? "Are you a magician?"

"What, like I do card tricks at birthday parties?" she grumbles. "Hang on, let me get my top hat."

I scowl, ready to persist until she cracks. "An alchemist? A shaman? A witc—"

"Stop." She puts a hand out toward me, a flash of panic in her expression.

A jolt of victory shoots through me. She's scared. Either I've guessed correctly or I'm dangerously close to the truth.

She lowers her hand, and my heart flips as she nearly rests it on my thigh.

She diverts at the last moment, grabbing the gear stick. "Katie, I really can't tell you. This is something you were never meant to stumble on."

"Freddie was about to tell me more."

"Freddie is a reckless asshole. He was trying to exploit you."

"Exploit me how? Don't you think I have the right to know what my *ability* means?"

"Doesn't today prove this is all very dangerous?" Natalie snaps, her voice filling the car.

"I don't know who Freddie Madsen is and why he's dangerous!" I wave a hand. "But he sure as hell knew who I was."

Natalie looks at me sharply. "About that. How much did he know?"

"He knew I can sense curses. He saw us in the thrift store. I remember him looking at me."

"You *saw* him that day? Why didn't you tell me?"

"What, that a stranger looked at me? I didn't think it mattered!"

Natalie groans, leaning back against the headrest. "He must have followed us—followed *me*—to the thrift store. I should never have gone out in public with you. That was so..."

"Well it's too late to regret spending time with me. What's done is done."

"That's not what I meant."

There's a pause as Natalie switches lanes.

Abruptly, she growls and slams her palms against the steering wheel. I jump.

"If he followed me that day, there's a chance he knows where you live," she says.

"I'm sure it's fine—"

"No. You have no idea..." She grips the wheel tightly, her knuckles straining. Her gaze keeps flicking to the rearview mirror.

"What? Tell me what you're thinking."

She scoots in front of a bus to avoid a left-turning car, earning a prolonged, angry honk from the bus driver.

"I don't know if you're safe at home," she says stiffly, like each word is difficult to get out. "They've probably already been watching you since..."

"Who's *they*?"

"You've been seen with me by people who shouldn't have seen us together. The Madsen family knows what you can do. This is what I meant when I told you it's dangerous to spend time with me."

Fear seeps from her pores and into my skin, making my face numb. Part of me believes her and trusts that she's trying to protect me. The other part of me is screaming to open the door, tuck and roll out of this moving car, and run as far away from this whole situation as fast as possible.

But if I run, will Freddie Madsen's dog just sniff me out? Will the Madsens come after me no matter what I do or where I go?

I feel tainted, dirty. Everything familiar is suddenly unstable, my sense of home and comfort upended all over again.

"What do I do?" I ask, a tremor in my voice.

"I have somewhere you can stay," Natalie says. "It's the safest place, especially where the Madsens are involved. Would you be comfortable with that?"

"Wait. You want me to..." My brain reels, this turn of events making me dizzy. "I can't move out of my place! How do I know you're telling the truth?"

"Katie, if you go home, he will come for you again. He'll try to take you like he did tonight." She glances sideways at me, her eyebrows pulled down. "I'm sorry. I don't want to scare you. But it's the truth."

My breaths come faster. I rub my face, smothering myself. The sensation of Freddie's hand on my arm hasn't left, tingling down to my fingers. And though I'm not sure what to believe or whether Natalie can be trusted... I can say with certainty that I'm more afraid of Freddie Madsen than I am of Natalie Zacharias. And I refuse to risk him finding me again.

I drop my hands into my lap. "What about Ethel?"

"I know." Her tone is extra calm as if to balance out my panic. "We'll go now, get your kitten, and pack as many of your belongings as we can. We have to be in and out as fast as possible, okay?"

"But—" Can I just abandon my place? It's not like my roommate will notice, but I have a life to live. "What about school? Term starts in a couple of days! I have a full timetable!"

Natalie casts me quick glances between concentrating on the road. "I'll go to class with you. This is my fault, and I don't want to put your career in jeopardy because of it."

We turn onto my street, and I blink at her, a struggle happening inside me. "Natalie, you're telling me I'll be in danger if I sleep in my own bed tonight, and now I need an escort to bring me to class. Will you please tell me what's going on?"

Her scowl softens, and she suddenly looks younger, like a teenager getting in trouble.

We screech to a stop in front of my place, and she shuts off the car. She draws a breath, drops her hands into her lap, and clenches her fists as if bracing herself. "I'm a witch."

CHAPTER 13

The Secret Life of Natalie Zacharias

FINALLY, THE TRUTH. WHILE I dump socks and underwear into my suitcase, Natalie gathers my textbooks and laptop, and my brain frantically works in the background to process this bombshell.

"That was magic you were doing?" My words come out sharp as urgency tightens my throat.

"Yes. I'm sorry you had to see it."

"I'm not. It saved both our asses." I grab all my clothes, hangers included, and throw them into the open suitcase. Reality crumbles around me, leaving everything cracked and distorted. *She's a witch. I just witnessed magic.*

But it all fits. When she opened the vial to get rid of Rebecca, the amber goo floated out without her touching it. The utter weirdness was overshadowed by everything else going on, but the way her palm hovered over the substance to draw it out...

She was controlling it with magic.

While we race around, Ethel watches from the bed, her tail swishing.

"Freddie can do magic too?" I ask.

"No. But the Madsen family has been trying to get their hands on curses for decades." The floodgates have opened, information spilling out of her lips. *About time.* All it took was me nearly getting abducted.

"That's why he was there?" I ask.

"His family has a knack for showing up to sites where we've been called to neutralize one."

I sit on my luggage to close it, my heart pounding hard. "When you say *we*... How many witches are there?"

She stuffs Ethel's food, bowls, and toys into a cloth shopping bag, stalling. It's like her instinct to deflect my questions is fighting for dominance. "Known? A few thousand around the world. The real number is higher because some choose to live in secrecy."

"Unlike what you're doing, living like an open book?" I say sarcastically.

"Keeping ourselves hidden from the public is another matter. My career is dedicated to regulating and controlling dangerous forms of magic. Same goes for everyone I work with."

I gather my plants, which I refuse to leave here to die. I can't believe I'm abandoning my place. But after what I saw, what I felt, I can't stay here alone. My arm throbs where Freddie grabbed it, my cheeks tingling where Wyatt's hot breath washed over me.

I want to be skeptical. Witches aren't real. But nothing can explain the way Natalie made the ground quake and split. And it was clear Freddie couldn't retaliate the same way.

"If the Madsens have been trying to get their hands on cursed items for so long, have they ever succeeded?" I ask.

"Enough to keep us on our toes," Natalie says tightly.

"But..." I shake my head, bewildered. The memory of the boils all over my skin hasn't faded, along with the scorpion, snake, hatching spiders... "Why would anyone *want* that?"

She takes a moment to answer. "Magic has its temptations."

"How vague of you." I dump the basket from the top shelf of my closet, where I keep scarves, mittens, and hats, and race to the bathroom. Filling the basket with toiletries and makeup, I shout, "It just doesn't make sense that they would want something that brings bad luck and like... health problems."

Natalie pauses. "You've only seen the start of a curse. They're a force in themselves, and the Madsens don't have anything good planned with that power."

I guess I can buy that wherever there is something harmful or powerful or both, there are people plotting how to use it for their own agendas.

I return to find that Natalie's gathered the photos from my shelf and placed them on top of the stack of textbooks.

"We can leave those," I say, scanning the overflowing luggage and shopping bags. How on earth did I manage to move everything to Vancouver on one flight?

"No, you should take them," she says firmly. No room for argument. "Anything else we need?"

My throat tightens as I look around the room. I'm leaving a lot behind, but I can survive without it. I think. It might just be covered in a layer of dust by the time I return... If it's *ever* safe to return. How long will I have to stay in hiding?

Jitters rise inside me. "No. Let's go."

Natalie grabs the heaviest items, including my textbooks, grunting under the weight of it all. *Chivalrous as ever.*

I wonder if she'd normally use magic to make this kind of thing easier.

Her admission has me wondering a lot of things.

I grab Ethel. With a quick kiss to the top of her head, I stuff her into her kennel, where she meows.

We fumble out the door and onto the back porch, moving my whole life to Natalie's car in one trip. The cold night air nips at my face and neck, sending shivers down my spine.

"Did you see the way Freddie looked at you? Like you were a prize to be won? That's how they see curses—power to be exploited, no matter the cost." Natalie looks cautiously around the empty street. There suddenly aren't enough street lamps, and too many shadows lurk on all sides.

"What if you just let them have one?" I say, pressing closer to her. "Let the curse finish them off."

The side of Natalie's face tightens into a deep scowl. She waves a foot under her car's bumper, and the trunk opens. She puts her armful inside and lifts my overstuffed luggage with a grunt. "It's not that simple. There are dangers beyond anything you've seen... Beyond what the Madsens understand. I can't explain right now." She glances over her shoulder, tense.

Maybe a small part of me gets it. Twice, curses have lured me in like promises, making me want to adopt Lucy and buy the doll. Are the Madsens victims of this allure, unaware of how dangerous it would be to keep a curse on them?

I strap Ethel's kennel into the back seat with a seatbelt. Too much information is swirling around in my brain, and at the same time, not enough. I don't know what to think about all this—the dangers she's not telling me about, the fact there are witches living in secrecy, and the world of magic I've only just glimpsed.

Again, part of me just wants to abandon my belongings and run—away from Natalie, away from the Madsens, away from all the curses and dangerous magic I don't understand. I could go all the way back home to Toronto, where I don't have to worry about any of this.

But if the Madsens have been after curses for years and Freddie knows I can sense them... then something tells me it won't be so easy to walk away. I've waded into quicksand, and there's no getting out.

An engine roars, and headlights shine into my eyes. An SUV peels around the corner, going way too fast to be a neighbor returning home for the night.

A stone drops into my stomach.

"Get in!" Natalie shouts.

Spots burst in my vision. I jump into the passenger seat and slam the door. The SUV doesn't brake, heading straight for us.

Holy shit, he's going to rear-end Natalie's car.

"Go!" I yell.

Natalie slams a foot down on the accelerator, tires squealing. A puddle hisses as we splash through it, the SUV revs behind us, and a deep *thump* rings out as it clips the bumper. Gripping the seat, I don't even get a last glimpse of the house before we round the corner.

"I knew it," Natalie says through her teeth, clutching the wheel. Her anger is white-hot, radiating into my bones. "They know where you live. Dammit, we're lucky they didn't get to you sooner."

I shudder, imagining Freddie biding his time, waiting for the right opportunity to talk to me—to corner me. Did he follow us back from the thrift store that night? Watch Natalie walk me to my door with the slow cooker?

Natalie turns sharply, opening a gap between us and the headlights swaying in the side mirror. God, she's going through so much to save me.

"How dangerous are the Madsens, exactly?" I ask, not sure I want the answer. Freddie's desperate shouts echo in my mind, making me shudder. *Get 'em! Get 'em!*

The muscles in Natalie's face tighten. Street lights flash across her face as she blows through a red light. Honks and squealing tires rise all around us, directed both at Natalie and the car in pursuit. "Let's just say they're willing to sacrifice for the cause."

Nausea bubbles in my gut. "They've killed?"

Her silence tells me all I need to know.

"Take tonight," she finally says, weaving through traffic. "They're smart enough not to get their hands dirty, so Freddie sent some guy in to get the curse. Paid him. Guy almost got to it before I did—I had to knock him out, and he's *lucky* that was the outcome."

I stare. "What would've happened otherwise?"

"Those curses you ended up with? Imagine being stuck with one for days."

My mouth goes dry. "It... it kills them?"

Natalie says nothing, her jaw tightening.

My insides twist. First, curses are more serious than I thought. Second, I can't believe I came face-to-face with a killer tonight.

Natalie drives us toward downtown, glancing repeatedly at her mirrors. I look behind us too, but none of the headlights are in frantic pursuit. Did she shake Freddie off?

"So I'd just be another lackey," I say, wiping sweat off my temples.

Natalie's brow furrows. "You'd be more than that. With your ability..." She shakes her head.

A pull inside me grows stronger, leading me closer to a sense of purpose. If witches need to track down curses in order to keep the public safe, I can help them. I can use this unique gift to make a difference. "Why don't you use me instead? Let me help you."

Her gaze darts sideways to me. "Nobody should be *using* you. You have no idea what you're asking for."

"I'll work for you, then. Or volunteer. Whatever."

She doesn't answer.

The sobering truth settles over me. This is why Natalie is saving me. She has a duty, and she can't let the Madsens get a hold of my ability to sense curses.

In my pocket, my phone vibrates. I pull it out.

Clayton

Hey, just checking if you got home okay. I'm sorry for making you uncomfortable. I didn't mean to make you leave.

I stare at the text. It feels like the normal part of the evening happened weeks ago.

If he only knew the extent to which I *didn't* make it home okay.

Actually, Clayton, I bumped into someone who tried to kidnap me, witnessed some kind of magical duel, and now I'm on the run with a girl who claims to be a witch.

I let out a breath, softening. It's nice of him to check in and apologize.

Katie

I did. Thanks. Don't worry, we're good.

Natalie's gaze flicks to me, but she doesn't ask who I'm texting.

The city lights blur past, and her erratic driving calms a little as we pull further ahead of Freddie. My heartbeat slows, the adrenaline leaving my body—and in its place, numb shock at how my life has managed to completely flip over in the last couple hours.

After a few minutes, Natalie pulls over in a loading zone. "We're here. Leave everything but the cat. I'll send someone to get all of it."

"Where's *here*?" I fumble with my seatbelt and open the door, my pulse picking up again.

The streets are rowdy, everyone spilling in and out of the nearby pubs as they get ready to celebrate midnight. The cold, crisp air threatens snow, sending a shiver through me. I grab the kennel and hug it to my chest, holding Ethel like she's my last tether to reality.

"Somewhere safe." Natalie puts an arm across my shoulders, scanning our surroundings as she guides me along the red brick sidewalk. "Know what part of town this is?"

My insides flip over at her hand on my shoulder and her warm, solid body at my side. I take in the brick buildings, Victorian street lamps, glass storefronts, and cobblestones. It's all familiar, but my brain isn't working well enough to place us. "No."

"Gastown. The famous steam clock is just up here." Her tone is calm and reassuring, even as she looks around vigilantly.

"Oh, right. I—I came here with my family over Christmas." Everything spins, disorienting. Is this a panic attack?

I inhale deeply, steadying myself.

"The clock is the main entrance." Natalie's voice distorts, hollow, as if coming from underwater.

"Okay." I'm too busy forcing my legs to work to ask how a clock can be an entrance. I press closer to Natalie, needing her strength. She tightens her arm around me.

The clock is visible over the smattering of people, as tall as a one-story house, its glass body revealing the engine, chains, and pendulum inside. Above the roman numeral face, steam billows out the top.

The world blurs. Lights expand and distort, and the buildings tilt.

I lean into her. "Natalie, I—I think I'm—"

The sensation of being smothered overcomes me, and I gasp. My skin prickles.

Ethel meows, the tiny sound coming from far away.

Brightness stings my eyes. An earthy scent engulfs me.

Our surroundings have changed. I'm still on my feet, leaning into Natalie, but a Victorian street lamp now stands beside me, black with a cluster of white globes casting a warm glow. Red brick walls bound us on three sides, and overhead is an arched brick ceiling. Light and dark cobblestones under my shoes form a path down a hallway.

The dizziness fades, and my ears ring in the abrupt quiet. I lower the kennel, keeping a tight grip on the handle.

"Wh-where are we?" My voice is too loud, a slight echo coming off the surrounding bricks.

"The Coven of Shadows and Alchemists for Managing Magic. It's where I live and work. Are you okay?" Natalie stoops to meet my eye. She puts a finger under my chin, inclining my face.

Her dark eyes search me, a frown pulling at her lips. As our gazes lock, a totally different kind of dizziness overcomes me. Heat spreads from where her fingers brush my face, trickling through my body.

"I'm fine," I say, barely a whisper. It's this sort of touch, the glint of concern in her eyes, that has me wondering whether she's protecting me out of duty or something else.

"Good." Her breath fans across my cheeks. She moves her hand to my neck and holds it there, her fingers warm and tantalizing beneath my ear. "There wasn't time to explain. We had to get down here as fast as possible."

Down here?

Above, through a square of hazy glass in the ceiling, a gold pendulum swings back and forth.

It's the underside of the steam clock.

Natalie has taken me underneath downtown Vancouver.

CHAPTER 14

À la C.S.A.M.M.

NATALIE STEPS BACK, LEAVING space between us.

I blink, her words drifting at the edges of my brain. "Sorry, the Coven of...?"

"Just call it C.S.A.M.M." She pronounces the acronym like *kazam*.

"Really? Like..." I wave my hand as if I'm holding a wand. "Alakazam?"

She grimaces. "Anyway, Freddie can't come down here, so you're safe. I'll have my sister park the car and get your stuff."

My chest tightens. The claustrophobia of being underground doesn't help. "How long will I have to stay?"

Her eyebrows pull down. "I promise we'll deal with him as fast as we can. I'm sorry I dragged you into this, Katie."

"No, it's—" I hate what my words did to her expression. "I'm grateful you brought me here. It's just a lot to take in."

Her shoulders slump, and she leans in as if about to step closer again. Instead, she turns and waves me onward. "Come on."

We walk down a hallway illuminated by more street lamps, our footsteps hollow, Ethel staying very quiet in her kennel. Disbelief washes over me that Natalie has taken me to her home.

"How big is this place?" Every footstep and swish of clothing is amplified in the brick corridor.

"It runs beneath the downtown core from Gastown to Robson Square, up Robson Street to Broughton, and along the harbor on the northeast side."

A blurry map of Vancouver forms in my brain from my limited knowledge, which I mostly gained last week when I took Hazel and my family on a tour. "That's... enormous. How many people live here?"

"About a hundred."

"Since when?"

"Late 1800s."

Good lord, witches have been living underneath Vancouver since the city was incorporated.

Ivy snakes across the walls, expanding until there's more greenery than brick. We pass an actual tree, an oak that grows right out of the cobblestones and curves with the ceiling. There's one explanation for a tree flourishing underground.

"The coven's whole purpose is to keep magic regulated and monitored." Natalie meets my gaze, a hint of uncertainty in her eyes. "That includes keeping it a secret. I'm going to have a lot to answer for."

Ahead, the hallway bends, a bright glow coming from around the corner.

"Natalie? How'd it go?" a deep voice calls, making me jump.

She stops, putting out an arm to stop me too. "Shit," she whispers.

Her reaction sets my heart pounding. Are we about to get in trouble?

"The explosion is all over the news, dumbass," someone else shouts. "Way to be subtle."

She looks at the ceiling and draws a breath as if steeling herself. "It didn't go down easily. Hey, listen, I need you not to freak out when I step around the corner."

Silence.

"Are you hurt?" the second voice asks sharply, footsteps coming closer.

There's a lot of scraping, like several chairs being pushed back.

Natalie seizes my shoulder and steps in front of me.

Ahead, at the end of the hallway, a girl strides into view and crosses her arms. She's athletic, about my age, with a shaved head, fair skin, and smokey eye makeup, wearing a cropped green sweater and joggers. "What are you doing? Who is this?"

Footsteps scuff, and five others join her, three women and two men.

Huh, so there are male witches, too.

Everyone is dressed casually, and their expressions change to surprise when they see me.

Natalie stays resolutely between me and them. "I didn't think you'd all still be up. I was going to—"

"It's New Year's Eve, dumbass," the girl says.

"Right. Uh, this is Katie. Katie, this is my sister, Sky, and that's Will, Hayley—"

Sky steps closer, dropping her arms with her fists clenched. "Skip the introductions and explain before I knock you out."

I shut my mouth, letting "nice to meet you" die on my tongue. This is not how I would've wanted to meet Natalie's sister.

Under everyone's glares, guilt and shame churn in my stomach. I'm getting her in trouble. "I can stay somewhere el—"

"No," Natalie says. "You're staying here."

Heels click, and they all turn as a tall Asian woman comes around the corner in a black suit and long traveling cloak. Her eyes widen and her nostrils flare when she sees me—and between the formal wear and her murderous expression, I shrink back.

"Natalie, you'd better—"

She puts her hands out to calm everyone. "It was the Madsens."

An intake of breath passes over the group, and their frowns deepen. Sky's expression turns into a full-on glower.

"They found out about the curse." Natalie drops her hands. "Fiona, we have to look into this. Freddie Madsen showed up at the site, and the curse wasn't the only thing he tried to nab. I brought Katie with me because he tried to recruit her."

The woman in the cloak, Fiona, turns her gaze to me with narrowed eyes. "And? They hire lackeys all the time. What's so special about this one?"

I bristle at the way she refers to me like I'm disposable.

"Katie can pick up on curses," Natalie says. "She's brought me two already. The Madsens are after her ability, and if we don't keep her safe, they'll get to her."

Everyone stares at me, a mixture of wide-eyed surprise and skeptical frowns. I want to say something to get them off Natalie's back—and mine too, I guess—but I don't understand enough about what's going on.

"Prove it," Will says.

"What?" Natalie asks.

Will paces closer, raising an eyebrow, until he's right in Natalie's face. She stands taller, making it clear she's got at least two inches of height on him.

"Prove she can sniff out curses," Will growls, "and you're not making this up so you can bring home a booty call."

A couple of people gasp. A flame of hot embarrassment burns inside me.

Natalie seizes Will by the collar. "Don't you dare."

Will stumbles and grabs Natalie's wrists, ready to fight back. Around us, the ivy on the walls hisses and twitches like snakes ready to strike. My skin prickles.

"Natalie, don't," I whisper, but my voice comes out so softly that I'm not sure she hears me.

"Let him go," Fiona says sharply, and they step apart, fuming. "How do you know it wasn't luck that she brought you two curses?"

"We'll take her thrifting," Sky says, a hand on her hip. "See what she can do. Maybe she'll be useful."

My breath catches. Finally, someone gets it.

Natalie forces her gaze away from Will, her chest heaving. "I know. I've tr—I'll try a test or two to see if my hunch is right."

The way she changed her words is interesting. She doesn't want them to know we already tried and failed. She's giving me another chance.

A spark of hope ignites within me. I won't fail her this time. She's going to realize how helpful I could be in tracking down curses.

"If I am right about Katie's ability," Natalie says, "then you understand how important it is to keep her away from the Madsens?"

Fiona crosses her arms. "It's worth investigating. Any magic in your past, girl?"

Oh God, she's addressing me.

I sidestep around Natalie to see her better. "Not that I know of."

I could explain the feeling I get when I see something cursed, but it's hard to put into words. Also, all the stares on me are making my tongue clumsy.

"I thought she could take one of the empty rooms down Granville hall," Natalie says. "Keep her safe until we get Freddie into custody."

Will snorts. "Good luck."

"He tried to abduct a civilian. That's enough for a warrant." Natalie looks at each of them, and when nobody protests, she says, "Time to move in. Sky?"

Sky squares her stance, and after a confirming glance to Fiona, she nods.

Fiona strides closer, searching Natalie's face. Though Fiona's a head shorter, Natalie shifts under her glare.

"I want a debrief before you turn in," Fiona says. "If you're lying, I won't be merciful."

Natalie dips her chin. "Of course."

"Everyone, as you were." Fiona waves the crowd away before turning back to me, a threatening glint in her eyes. "I'll be watching you closely. You are not to tell a soul about this place or what we do here, understand? We have our own justice system, and no lawyer can save you from it."

I nod, my mouth dry. "Yes, ma'am."

She looks me up and down, then addresses Natalie again. "Just until we catch Freddie. In the meantime, you'd better prove this isn't a big, dangerous mistake."

With a final, piercing glare at both of us, she marches back the way she came, the click of her heels fading.

Me, a dangerous mistake?

I would argue, but maybe she doesn't mean I'm the dangerous one. After what I experienced tonight in that alley, I don't know what's safe and what's not, what's impossible and what's beyond my understanding.

Sky and Will are left, standing at the end of the hall.

"Get Katie's stuff," Natalie says. "It's in my car. Watch out for Freddie."

Sky nods and brushes past us, her gaze lingering on me. It's not a glare—more like cautious intrigue. After a hesitation, Will follows, not looking at either of us.

Natalie strides ahead, leaving me to hurry in her wake. Over my shoulder, I try to see what happens when the others get to the clock, but they're already gone.

We enter a lounge with a square fireplace in the middle and a stone chimney rising into the domed ceiling. Along the brick walls, iron light fixtures give the place a warm glow, and more ivy turns the wall into green patchwork. Wooden tables, chairs, and cushy booths fill the space. A willow tree in the corner forms a canopy over a circle of bean bags, a bookshelf, and a cabinet overflowing with board games.

The people who dispersed are seated at a long table with drinks, playing cards, and poker chips scattered around. Their eyes follow us, speculating, judging.

"Happy New Year, all," Natalie says.

They murmur back, a jumble of "yeah," "cheers," and "New Year" meeting my ears.

On the other side of the lounge, archways lead to half a dozen corridors, which are marked with iron letters reading *Chambers*, *Library*, *Training*, and others I can't read from here. We enter the Chambers wing and turn left at a fork, where a brass plaque reads *Granville*.

"This hallway runs underneath Granville street?" I ask.

"Yep. Your room's under a coffee shop. You'll probably hear their pipes and see their wifi. Which reminds me, our wifi password is ChimeraTown666, capital C, capital T."

"You... have wifi down here?" I ask, bewildered.

"Well, yeah." She pulls out her phone as if to remind me she has it. "We haven't time traveled."

She takes me past arched wooden doors, each one marked with an iron number.

"So." I check over my shoulder. "Will seems like an ass."

Natalie purses her lips, looking abashed. "Sorry about him. He's not, actually. He's a good Alchemist and a dedicated coven member."

"Coworkers shouldn't get in your face like that."

"His anger was... misdirected. He was suspended for six months once for bringing his girlfriend to the lounge. He obviously thought I was making up a story to sneak you in."

My brain wants to jump right into analyzing this—does this confirm that Natalie is into girls? But I force that aside for later. "Is Fiona your boss?"

"One of several. Here we are." She motions ahead to an arched wooden door with the number 133 and an old-fashioned keyhole. "Put your palm on it to set the lock. That's all you'll need to do to access it in the future. It only opens for you and the cleaner, Elizabeth."

I do what she says and press my palm flat to the lock. It clicks, and I push the door open.

The room is all brick, stone, and greenery like the rest of the building, with a queen bed, kitchenette and mini fridge, bathroom, and wooden desk and chair. The bedding is forest green, and instead of a bedside table, there's a bonsai tree with a notebook and an alarm clock on its branches.

Natalie shuts the door, sealing us from the world—along with the judgmental glares and comments. The tension in my shoulders eases. It's just the two of us again.

She must feel the same because her expression softens.

Ethel meows, and I put the kennel on the bed and let her out. She scrambles into my arms, digging into me with her sharp claws.

"I'm so sorry about that," Natalie murmurs. "As if you haven't been through enough tonight without my colleagues breathing down your neck."

"It's okay."

"It's not."

A tingle goes through me as I look up at her, every cell in my body wishing for her to step in and wrap me in a hug.

Water whooshes beyond the walls—the pipes Natalie was talking about. I don't mind it. In this unfamiliar place, it's nice remembering ordinary people are around.

"So, um..." I hesitate, unsure how to word this. "I can leave here if I want, right? I'm not, like, trapped?"

Natalie nods. "I can take you home right now. But I hope you understand why I brought you here, and if you still want to leave, I hope you'll let me or someone else come along as a bodyguard in case..." She lowers her gaze.

"In case I get jumped by a Madsen." I nudge the bed with my toe, pretending a chill didn't just run down my spine. The reality of the danger I'm in hits me all over again. "How many of them are there?"

"Three. Freddie, his sister Oaklyn, and their mom Sophia." She hesitates. "Four, if you include the dog."

I hug Ethel tighter, suppressing a shudder. "I will definitely be including the dog."

So, three people and a German Shepherd want to kidnap me. Awesome.

Natalie steps closer. "Anything I can do to make you comfortable?"

I look around the thoughtfully furnished suite. "It's already cozier than the basement."

"Tomorrow, I'll show you the courtyard. It opens up to the sky, and there are trees and a pond and a track." She presses her lips together. "I don't want you to think I've taken you to an underground dungeon."

I crack a smile, wishing she'd brought me here under different circumstances. "It doesn't feel like a dungeon. But the courtyard sounds nice."

She nods. "Let me know if you need anything. Whatever you want."

Ugh, she's so apologetic it's melting me.

We hold each other's gaze, the silence charged. My pulse quickens and my lips tingle, as if my body is anticipating something my brain is unaware of.

"I guess we'd better hurry and find another curse before Fiona kicks me out." I try to sound determined, but it comes out breathless. "Thrifting tomorrow?"

She shakes her head. "I'll talk to her. You need to stay here where it's safe."

I blink, taken aback. Disappointment trickles over me. "Then how are we going to prove I can see curses?"

"It won't come to that. The plan is to put Freddie Madsen away so you'll be able to go home. He crossed a line tonight."

A sinking sensation pulls me downward. It's not that I want to be trapped in an underground building for the rest of my life, but I'd expected to test my ability like Fiona and Sky suggested. I don't want to sit here while Natalie handles everything.

"Your sister thinks I could be helpful," I say, my tone challenging.

She crosses the room to lean against the desk, folding her arms. "My sister plays with fire by profession."

I open my mouth to argue, but curiosity gets the better of me, and instead I ask, "What does she do?"

She hesitates—back to her default response.

I sigh. "Natalie. I'm fine with being here, but I deserve some information about where I am and who I'm with."

She scowls and stuffs her hands into her jeans pockets. "Okay. Yeah, you're right."

Anticipation skips in my chest. I sit on the bed, letting Ethel flop onto the duvet.

Natalie paces as if unable to stand still for this conversation. "She's a Shadow. They take out dangerous witches or people misusing magic."

"Like an assassin?"

"More like a SWAT team."

I nod, unsurprised that this is Sky's job description. She looked ready to take out Natalie a few minutes ago. "That's why you looked at her when you mentioned going after Freddie."

"She'll lead the operation. The Shadows have been waiting for a warrant to move against the Madsens for years—decades, even."

"If they've been trying to steal cursed items for years, why would you need a warrant?"

"Bureaucracy. We can't touch non-witches—which is a good law except where the Madsens are involved. Freddie targeting you tonight gives us cause to move in."

"You're welcome," I say flatly.

She doesn't smile, her gaze on the floor.

"So she's a Shadow, and you find and neutralize curses," I say. "Is there a name for witches like you?"

"Guardians."

"Fitting."

She tilts her head, but I don't elaborate. Maybe she doesn't realize how protective she's been all night.

"How do you know where curses are?" I ask.

"We have ears all over so we know about strange happenings. Fiona and a few others are in charge of relaying that to the rest of us and triaging assignments."

"I see. And... what magic can you do, exactly?"

She looks to the door, and I remember she promised to debrief Fiona. But instead of telling me she has to go, she comes to sit beside me on the bed.

My heart skips as the mattress depresses, forcing my hips to angle toward her.

I guess my guilt trip about deserving information worked.

Ethel crawls over to her, reaching a little paw as if to test whether Natalie will indulge her with pets. She does, stroking Ethel's back. Ethel immediately starts purring.

"It's called earth magic," Natalie says. "We can move solid elements by telekinesis. Objects, soil, plants, metals…"

"And pavement, apparently. Is it harder to move heavy things?"

Natalie grimaces, like she was hoping I wouldn't bring up what I saw in the alley. "It's more about composition than weight. Pure elements are easier to manipulate. We can also shift particles to let us pass through earth."

I look at her in alarm. "We sank into the ground at the steam clock?"

She nods. "Engulfed us like quicksand."

A shiver crawls through me as the world I thought I knew dissolves. "How did nobody notice? That street was full of tourists."

"The clock's been enchanted so the moving particles camouflage us. They take on the appearance of whatever's behind us. To onlookers, we just vanished into the crowd."

I furrow my brow, trying to understand all the details of earth magic. "You can enchant things too?"

She shakes her head once. "That's Alchemy. Not my area of expertise. It involves binding magic to an object."

I let out a slow breath, my head starting to hurt. And here I thought my statistics lectures were a lot to take in.

While Natalie pets Ethel, her other hand rests on the duvet between us. I could easily reach out and place mine over hers. We both clearly need the comfort. It's easy to imagine holding her hand, letting my fingers be engulfed in her strong grasp.

But I might be misreading the responsibility she has to protect the public from magic. She saved me because of that, not because of some feelings she may or may not have. So I keep my hands where they are, palms flat by my thighs.

"Thank you for bringing me here," I murmur.

She says nothing.

When I look at the side of her face, her gaze is on our hands too.

Maybe sensing me watching, she meets my eye. Her irises pull me in, such a gorgeous, rich shade of brown. I watch, breathless, as they travel down my face and linger on my lips.

A knock rings out, and we startle.

"That'll be Sky." Natalie crosses the room to open the door, revealing my stuff piled outside. Sky and Will didn't stay.

We drag it in. I guess I'll be unpacking tonight—or in the morning. Exhaustion weighs me down, making my eyelids heavy.

Natalie looks at her phone, then shows me the time.

12:02 A.M.

"Happy New Year," she murmurs.

"Happy New Year."

She rocks on her feet, the stroke of midnight suspended between us.

The silence is a harsh reminder that I shouldn't be here. I should be back at the restaurant, shouting and cheering with a big group of friends. Instead, I'm in an unfamiliar place with a woman I barely know. But strangely, I wouldn't want to be anywhere else.

She turns around, and my chest tightens. I don't want her to go. After learning magic is real, the Madsens want to kidnap me, and there are witches among us who can split the earth open with their minds, the thought of sleeping alone tonight sends goosebumps up my arms.

Natalie opens the door. "Get some sleep. I'll have my phone on me if you need anything."

Before she can step into the hall, I blurt, "Wait!"

She stops.

"I—I deleted you from my phone." I study the brick wall, unable to meet her eye as I admit my petty moment of anger. "Can you text me so I have your number again?"

There's a short, inscrutable pause. "Sure."

She does, and my phone beeps.

As she leaves me holding Ethel in this unfamiliar bedroom, the events of this evening whirl around inside me like a tornado. Aside from my life changing forever, it hasn't slipped past me that tonight has changed something significant for the coven. *C.S.A.M.M.* The way they all looked at me when Natalie mentioned my ability to sense curses... The way Sky suggested testing me... Even Fiona's agreement, however reluctant, hints at the potential value of what I can do.

I might not be a witch, but the fact I'm here proves I have something to offer. I *knew* it.

A decision solidifies inside me. Natalie might want me to stay in this room where I'm safely out of the Madsens' grasp—but I know I can do more than hide. I'm going to prove to her and to everyone here that I have an ability they can put to use.

CHAPTER 15

The Difference Between a Traffic Cone and Bagpipes

"**B**REAKFAST IS ANYTHING YOU want," Natalie says as we enter the lounge at eight the next morning. "Eggs, oatmeal, pancakes..."

She motions for me to take the lead to any table. Only two others are occupied, so I head for a booth on the other side of the crackling fireplace—out of sight of the hallways and prying eyes.

"Do you use magic to cook?" I ask as I plunk into the cushy seat.

"Yes and no." She puts a hand on the table and slides in across from me, drawing my gaze to the way her toned arms fill out the sleeves of her black t-shirt. "Controlling earth elements means we can cook anything plant-based in seconds, but with animal proteins, we can go as far as heating the skillet with magic. Either way, it won't take long."

Eating food cooked by magic sounds like an experience I need in my life—and after the night I had, a plate of warm, fluffy carbs is in order. "Pancakes would be nice. With maple syrup."

A tablet at the far end of the table shows the menu, and she pulls it toward her. She taps buttons for two orders of pancakes. "Coffee?"

"Yes, please. Black."

She taps that too. "And here you're witnessing a new and exciting form of magic called the internet and an app."

I laugh.

Her cheeks dimple as she slides the tablet back to its place. "Technology has become better than magic in a few areas, to be honest."

Her tone is brighter this morning, her posture less guarded. Maybe a weight has been lifted now that I know her secret.

I put my elbows on the table and lean forward. "So, have you decided how we're going to test my ability?"

She slings an arm across the back of the booth, cocking an eyebrow. "Persistent."

I return my own sassy eyebrow. "We don't have long. How quickly will the Shadows catch Freddie Madsen?"

Her lips twist. "Could be a couple days, could be a week, could be longer. But it turns out we are, in fact, going to test you this morning."

I sit taller, her words sending a shock through me. "Seriously? How? Where?"

The tablet flashes green and pings, snagging our attention.

Natalie removes her hand from the table. "Lean back and tuck in your feet."

I do, pulling in my arms and legs.

The surface warps and turns hazy, blurring the space between us. When the haze dissipates, I'm left with a steaming stack of four pancakes and a mug of coffee.

Natalie casts me a lopsided smile that makes my heart miss a beat.

Ugh, she's cute.

"You can't tell me *that* was the internet and an app," I say.

The crinkles around her eyes and dimples in her cheeks make an appearance as her smile widens. "The kitchen is below us. They send orders through the floor. You just have to be careful with your limbs, or you'll get an elbow full of syrup."

I cradle my mug, letting the warmth seep into my palms. The dishes are porcelain with flowers and the cutlery is gold, reminiscent of the vintage tableware at my Nana's place. The coziness and familiarity is a funny contrast to this exciting new world where I get to learn about magic and have breakfast with Natalie.

"So, the test?" I take a sip and let the rich brew trickle through me. That is a *good* roast.

Natalie pours a shot of cream into her coffee and stirs, the spoon tinkling pleasantly. "We've agreed to do it in a safe environment here in the C.S.A.M.M. labs. The Alchemists are collecting a bunch of objects and cursing one of them. Fiona and I don't know which item holds the curse."

"A double-blind study." The aspiring psychologist in me jumps like an excited puppy. "So if I prove I can pick out the curse, you'll let me help you?"

"One step at a time." Her response comes readily, like she knew what I would say. "Anyway, I thought your purpose was to be a psychologist."

"I can do both." It's easy to imagine living here with Natalie, sitting in this lounge, enjoying this food, playing games under that willow tree... basking in her smile. I have no intention of abandoning my career plans and the people I love, but I like what this place promises—the community, the chance to learn about magic, the sense of purpose. I want this life, even if I'm not a witch. Even if my role can't be anything more than Natalie's assistant.

A knot forms in my stomach as I take a bite. I can't screw up this test.

"Why is Greg in the dining area again?" A shrill voice shatters the peaceful air.

I turn to see a woman stomping after a fawn-colored French bulldog, who waddles between the tables sniffing for dropped food. The woman looks a bit like a French bulldog herself, with a stout build, fawn hair in high pigtails, wide-set eyes, and her face scrunched around her upturned nose.

"Greg, get out!" She shoos the bulldog, who continues sniffing without acknowledging her flapping hands.

A woman at a nearby booth stands. "Agnes, he's allowed to be here."

"It's against the *law* to have dogs in a restaurant!"

The other woman mumbles something I can't hear, putting the dog in her lap and feeding him a bit of egg off her plate.

Natalie's expression falls in exasperation.

"I wish she'd give it a rest," she murmurs while the women argue. "Familiars are free to roam the building, as long as they have a tag and are registered. We've had strict rules about keeping animals accounted for ever since a cat got into an Alchemy lab and aggravated some cursed birds."

I laugh, which makes her lopsided smile reappear.

The longing to stay turns into an ache. If I lived in C.S.A.M.M., Ethel could roam with the other pets. She would love exploring, climbing the willow tree in the corner, and making friends with other cats.

"You're not doing a good job of making me hate it here," I say.

She folds her forearms across the table, leaning in. "Who said I want you to hate it here?"

I frown. "You've made it clear you don't want me to stay."

"There's a difference," she says, her voice low, "between that and wanting what's best for you. Trust me, I very much want you to stay."

The way her dark eyes penetrate my skin sends a lick of heat through me. It travels downward, tingling, and I cross my legs. I drop my gaze to my plate so I can get a hold of myself.

I want to believe her. I want to think my feelings are reciprocated. But as long as she lets 'what's best for me' get in the way, nothing's going to happen between us.

"Who are *you*?" Agnes's shrill voice moves closer, and a flash of pain crosses Natalie's expression before she smiles up at our guest.

Irritation spikes as Agnes severs whatever tension had been pulling taut between us.

"Hi, Agnes," Natalie says politely. "This is Katie. You must have heard the gossip."

"Of course I— Well, not yet, but—" she snaps. Pink spots bloom in her cheeks. "I haven't met with Fiona yet this morning, but I'm sure this matter was first on the agenda."

"I'm sure," Natalie says.

Up close, Agnes's flustered air hits me like a gust of wind, making my shoulders tight. It's not clear whether this mood is from Greg or the fact that no one's thought to tell her about me—or maybe both, alongside a list of other stuff.

She crosses her arms, glaring at me through beady eyes. "You'd better be a witch, or else I'll have to report Natalie for breaking—"

"We've gone through the proper channels," Natalie says with an edge to her voice. She checks her phone. "Fiona's expecting us. Shall we, Katie?"

Though she's not done her food, she drops her cutlery and slides out of the booth in a hurry.

"Okay." Nerves jumping, I gulp the rest of my coffee, needing all the mental alertness I can get. I rush after her.

Agnes follows. "Expecting you? Why?"

Natalie doesn't answer, stepping closer to me until I can feel the heat of her body.

As she takes me down a corridor marked with a sign reading *Alchemy*, Agnes gasps. "Does this have to do with the items the Alchemists have collected?"

My gut twists. How many people are involved in setting up this test? Does the whole building know about it?

"Could be," Natalie says vaguely, walking faster.

I speed-walk to keep up.

Agnes picks up a trot. "As a Director, I should've been informed about this. I was the one to implement our new screening protocols last year to prevent *leaks*." She fishes into her pocket and pulls out a memo book and pen. "What are your qualifications, Katie? Your magical lineage?"

None, and none. My nerves twist tighter, threatening to eject everything I just ate.

"I'll need your name, phone number, and medical records for the logbook," Agnes continues. "Are you romantically involved with Natalie?"

"Um—" God help me.

"Later, Agnes," Natalie snaps.

We pass iron wall sconces and planters overflowing with ferns. Arched wooden doors bear iron letters: Alchemy 4, Alchemy 5, Alchemy 6... In other circumstances, I'd be dying to peek at what's behind every one of them. But I just want to get away from this woman and her prying questions. I need to focus on what's about to happen, and she's making me even more nervous.

Natalie stops outside Alchemy 8 and faces Agnes, a muscle in her jaw flexing. "This is a closed test."

Agnes puffs up, her nostrils flaring. "As a *Director*, I—"

"You'll receive a debrief from Fiona." Natalie opens the door and yanks me inside by the elbow. "Excuse us."

I get a last glimpse of Agnes's crumpled face before Natalie shuts the door on her and her memo pad.

We both let out a sharp breath.

Jesus Christ. Her busybody energy is prickling my skin like an itchy wool sweater. Do I seriously need to provide her with all that info, or was she just taking it upon herself to do an interrogation? And was that the sort of treatment I should expect to get here as an outsider?

I meet Natalie's eye, who grimaces apologetically.

"Ah, you're early," Fiona says behind us, her voice filling the room.

Jitters roll through me. I draw a deep breath. 'Frazzled' is *not* the state of mind I wanted to be in before this test.

We turn around to find Fiona, Will, and a man I haven't met standing at a long, wooden table. The latter must be in his twenties, with wild red hair and a beard that gives him a sort of mad-scientist look. Fiona is in an elegant blue suit, and the men are in dark green cloaks.

"Well, let's get started, then," Fiona says brusquely.

I twist my fingers together. *Breathe. Forget Agnes. You can do this.*

Natalie gives me a look as if to silently ask if I'm okay.

I nod curtly and step forward, ready.

The room is circular, its stone walls rising into a domed ceiling with a hole in the middle to let in daylight and fresh air. Bookshelves and cabinets line the perimeter, and on the left, an oak tree has a bench swing hanging from its largest branch.

"I've asked Sebastian and his team to gather seven objects," Fiona says, her heels clicking as she goes to stand against the wall. "Katie, tell me which one is cursed."

I swallow hard. Right to business, then.

"I know you asked for unremarkable items, but I took the liberty of bending the rules a little," the red-haired guy, Sebastian, says with a flourishing gesture to the table. "I think some of the team put a little more effort into the challenge than others. I'll be taking this into consideration in their performance reviews." He winks at me conspiratorially.

"This will do just fine, Sebastian," Fiona says.

Natalie and I approach the table, where a row of items awaits: a succulent plant in a green teapot, an antique black typewriter, a bamboo tiki torch, a grimy orange traffic cone, a pink feather boa, tartan bagpipes, and a katana with a red handle and scabbard.

Given the fate of Rebecca the doll, I hope the traffic cone is the cursed item. I don't want them to have to melt a plant or a valuable-looking sword because of me.

Will and Sebastian join Fiona at the wall. Will's arms are crossed, his expression skeptical as he watches me like I'm a lab rat. Sebastian, on the other hand, meets my eye and smiles. He bounces on the balls of his feet like he can't wait to see what happens.

Other than Natalie, he's the first person to smile at me since I've arrived, so I'll gladly accept the encouragement.

I pull my focus back, trying to ignore everyone's attention.

"Just look. Don't touch anything," Natalie murmurs in my ear.

I nod, the tickle of her breath on my neck making it hard to concentrate.

With her constant warnings, I should probably start taking curses seriously. More and more, it seems completely reckless that I picked up that doll at the flea market. No wonder she freaked out.

As I study the row of items, a chill settles over me, starting in my face and traveling down to my belly, my legs, my feet. My heart beats harder as if in fight-or-flight mode—and it's not just the pressure of the test. An invisible force tugs me closer to the table.

There's a curse here. I can feel it.

A crinkling sound comes from along the wall, and I look up to see Sebastian unwrapping a KitKat. When he sees us all staring, he winces and raises a hand in apology.

"Sorry," he mouths. He takes a slow bite, the crunch echoing through the quiet room, and Will smirks.

Annoyance flares. Is this just a fun little experiment to these people?

Natalie shifts, and I turn my attention back to studying each item.

Traffic cone. Feather boa. Bagpipes.

The curse's pull returns, and anticipation surges through me, a familiar sensation now that it's hitting me for the third time. It's a feeling like reaching the front of a roller coaster line—a bit of fear, a bit of excitement, a long wait coming to an end.

It's here. Grab it.

But which one?

With Natalie at my back and Fiona, Will, and Sebastian watching, my heart rate stays elevated no matter which object I look at.

Agnes's shrill voice echoes in the back of my mind. *You'd better be a witch, or else I'll have to report Natalie...*

My fate aside, what happens to Natalie if I fail? Will she get in trouble for bringing me here?

I study the bagpipes, a shiver rolling through me. Okay, this is it. I need it.

Or is it the katana?

My face tingles as I lay eyes on the sharp blade. I step closer, invisible hands wrapping around me and pulling me in.

It's one of these two. My pulse throbs in my fingers, like they're itching to reach for the curse.

Natalie is right behind me, a warm, solid presence.

Will whispers something to Sebastian, who shrugs and chews his chocolate bar. Fiona huffs impatiently, her heels scuffing as she adjusts her stance. The sounds grate my eardrums, making my shoulders tense.

"Th-this is all distracting," I tell Natalie, sweat prickling under my shirt.

"It's okay. Ignore us. Focus on what your gut is telling you."

I look back at the items, paralyzed. I can't tell. Maybe it's the pressure or all the magic swirling around, but I can't pinpoint where the sensation is coming from.

"Trust your instincts, Katie," Natalie says.

"I'm trying!"

"If it's going to take this long every time," Fiona says, "then it's not worth—"

"It's the katana," I blurt, my mouth dry.

Oh God, *please* be the katana.

I don't know why that word was the one to come out. Was that trusting my instincts, or was that a random, panicked decision?

Everyone turns to Sebastian.

My heart seems to stop beating.

Sebastian's shoulders sag. He shakes his head. "Shit. I was rooting for ya." A flicker of genuine disappointment crosses his face before he puts on a smile. "'Twas the bagpipes, lass!" he says in a Scottish accent.

A boulder drops into my stomach. *No, no, it can't be...*

Natalie gives a tiny intake of breath. Will scoffs, almost inaudible, but the room is so quiet that it carries.

"That was my second..." I shut my mouth. Why would they believe me? I'm just some outsider trying to convince them I'm special.

Shame burns my face, hot and suffocating. I really thought I could do this. But all I've done is let Natalie down. After everything she risked to bring me here, I failed her.

Sebastian pockets the remainder of his KitKat and pulls out a vial. "A tragedy, really, to reduce such a noble instrument to this..."

He uncorks it and moves his open palm over the vial, using magic to lift out the amber contents. The blob contorts in the air, shimmering, before he flicks his fingers to throw it at the bagpipes. It stretches and wraps around the instrument like it's alive, little fingers reaching until it completely covers its victim.

And as the curse pulses beneath it, I feel it more strongly than ever, beating against my skin. Frustration with myself singes me like a flame.

The answer should've been obvious. I was just so distracted by everyone openly doubting me.

As fizzing prickles my ears, Natalie closes a hand over my arm and pulls me back a few steps.

The bagpipes make a pathetic, squeaky, drawn-out moan—which, honestly, is exactly what I'd expect dying bagpipes to sound like.

The lights flicker.

I cover my ears, ready for the explosion.

BOOM!

Where the bagpipes were, a plume of smoke dissipates, and a butterfly remains. Its violet wings twitch as it walks across the table. There's no purple gemstone this time, but I'm too numb to analyze why.

I drop my hands, my frustration morphing into anger. This can't be it! They didn't give me a proper chance.

Sebastian claps Will on the back and turns around. "Well, that was a nice coffee break. Back to work, eh?"

Fiona lifts her chin, addressing Natalie. "After you've brought Katie back to her room, come see me. We have four new cases this morning."

"No!" My voice comes out loud, and all eyes snap to me. "That wasn't a fair test. My intuition got muddled from all the magic in here, and the pressure—"

"Don't bother with excuses," Fiona says, her tone cold and sharp. "I was kind enough to give you a chance."

"But I know I can do this!" My voice breaks, desperation tightening my throat.

Fiona's eyes flash menacingly. "You'll stay here until we catch Freddie Madsen, and then you'll be escorted home."

"If you just give me another—"

"That's my final decision. Agnes will draft up a secrecy agreement."

Dread washes over me. I *can't* go back to reality. Not after learning about magic and this hidden side of Natalie's exciting life.

Natalie steps closer to Fiona, holding herself together much better than I am. "Even if we don't use her to find curses, we can't just send her back out there. We have to let her stay."

"Your judgment is compromised," Fiona snaps, her eyes widening in outrage. "We can't keep an outsider around—especially with the recent information leaks. She hasn't sworn the oath, and she's not one of us. She's a security risk."

Shame flares so hot inside me that my face feels sunburned.

Natalie's voice rises. "But even if we catch Freddie, the other Madsens will still come for her—"

"So we'll send her home with a bodyguard, and if the Madsens come, we'll get more warrants and catch them too. But her ability is either weak or unpredictable, which means she can't stay here."

I clench my fists, swallowing down the shame. She's wrong about my ability. But I had my chance to prove it to her, and I blew it. What am I supposed to do?

Before Natalie or I can argue further, Fiona storms out of the room, her heels clicking on the stone floor.

My gaze falls to the butterfly, its wings a blur of violet as it takes flight. My eyes sting as I watch it spiral up, up, and out through the hole in the ceiling—leaving me with the hollow, empty truth.

My test is over, and the result is simple: I failed.

CHAPTER 16

An Internship in Curses

ALONE IN MY SUITE, I poke listlessly at Ethel's toe beans, their charm lost on me. Her purring fills the silence as I lay curled on the bed.

Natalie has gone to talk to Fiona, but what's the point? She's clearly closed-minded about 'outsiders' and won't be swayed. Which means I'll have to go home and wait for the Madsens to find me.

I shudder. My arm twinges where Freddie's bruising grip wrapped around it. If the other Madsens are anything like him and his blood-thirsty dog, I don't want to think of how that will go.

What do I do if they come for me? Try to convince them that my ability to see curses is unreliable, and they're better off leaving me to live my sad, ordinary life?

I roll onto my back.

No. I can't leave. More than the fear of the Madsens, I can't return to my empty basement suite and normal life. I've had a glimpse of what living here with Natalie would be like—witnessing magic, living in these halls, surrounded by mysterious rooms and corridors begging to be explored—and the threat of leaving punches a hole in my heart. I don't want to ignore the part of myself that's somehow connected to curses, even if it's scary, and even if logic tells me I'd be safer pretending all this doesn't exist. I can't recall ever having a sense of purpose like this—the feeling that I have something important to offer. The feeling of being *needed*. The community I've wanted since landing in Vancouver is within reach, if only I can figure out how to show them I'm worthy enough to stay.

And, yes, I've never felt like this about a girl before. Natalie's cute smile, her warm and protective touch, the way my heart flips every time she looks at me...

Now I'm about to leave this all behind. Because of bagpipes.

My phone rings, and I sit up. Ethel scurries between my pillows.

It's Hazel—and she wants to video chat.

"Crap," I whisper.

She's going to notice this isn't my room.

I could reject her call, but I desperately need the comfort of talking to my best friend right now.

I frantically scan for a backdrop. The exposed brick is nothing like the soulless white paint in the basement suite, the bedding is green, and not even the inside of the closet or the bathroom would pass. It's all too damn cute and cozy.

Resigned, I prop my phone against the plush, silky pillows. I'll have to make something up to hide the truth.

Putting on a smile, I answer. "Happy New Year, bestie!"

Hazel's hair is a mess and she's in an oversized t-shirt. She probably just woke up.

"Akemashite omedetō gozaimasu!" She waves mochi at me, a sticky rice cake we gorge on at her house every January. The familiar blue shade of her bedroom wall is at her back. A pang of homesickness hits me—it's the first time I'm not there to eat mochi and celebrate the New Year with her.

She takes a bite and says through a mouthful, "I'm eating twice as much on your behalf."

"Aww, thanks."

Her brow furrows. "Where are you?"

"It's..." Though I want to spill everything that's happened, Fiona's warning to tell no one has a chokehold on me. Panicked, I spew the first plausible story that comes to mind. "A vacation rental. There was a leak and the basement flooded, so I'm here until they fix it."

Hazel groans. "What a way to kick off the year. Is your stuff okay?"

"Everything important." I hold up Ethel. She squirms and bites my fingers.

"Aww, hi, sweetie," Hazel coos. "Did you get ripped away from your home?"

Ethel meows in protest, and I put her down.

"Things good with Sean?" If we linger on this topic, my feeble lie will crumble.

Hazel gives a mushy, bashful smile. "Yeah. We're both at home this week, so we haven't seen much of each other, but we're back on campus tomorrow."

I grab Ethel's feather toy from the foot of my bed for something to do with my hands, dragging it around so she chases it. "I can't believe classes are already starting. I still haven't recovered from finals."

"I know. But I decided I'm going to apply for the co-op program this term," she says, the words gushing out, "which means I'll get a summer job at an actual software company!"

I grin. "That's amazing! No more cinnamon bun baking."

Hazel bounces in her desk chair. "I want to get on board with a renewable energy company."

A knock rings out. "Katie?"

I freeze. Cold panic shoots through me at the sound of Natalie's voice. So much for concealing the truth.

Hazel's mouth falls open, and her voice rises an octave. "Oh—my—God. Are you at a girl's place? You big liar!"

"I'm—it's not like—"

"I can't believe you didn't tell me!" She jumps to her feet and paces like this is all too exciting for her to stay still.

I consider telling Natalie to come back later, but I'm doomed to answer Hazel's questions either way, so I bring my phone with me to the door.

She's standing there with that damn black t-shirt clinging to her in all the right places, her hands in the pockets of her tight jeans, her hair cascading over her left shoulder... and that smoldering gaze.

My heart launches into a frenzy, and I swallow hard. "Hey, I'm just video chatting with my friend. Um, this is Hazel. Hazel, Natalie."

Natalie leans in so she's in the frame with me.

Hazel's mouth opens. Some kind of implosion is happening inside her.

Yes, Hazel, this is Doctor Natalie Zacharias. Except she isn't really a doctor, or a vet, or a normal human being.

"Hiii! Nice to finally meet you, Natalie." Hazel's word choice and that teasing tone make heat rush into my cheeks.

"You too." Natalie lifts a hand, smiling politely, then turns to me. Since she's leaned closer to see the phone, our faces are inches apart, and there's a second where all cohesive thoughts leak out of my head.

"When you're ready, meet me...?" She points in the direction of the lounge, obviously not wanting to say much in front of Hazel.

"You got it," I say, breathless.

She leaves, shutting the door softly. When I look back at the phone, Hazel's face is so gleeful that I can't help letting out an embarrassed laugh. She definitely thinks I'm at Natalie's place because we hooked up last night—and I'm going to have to roll with it if I want to avoid spilling the truth.

Hazel claps her hands to her face, pulling her cheeks down like she's absolutely dying. "I can't believe you're hooking up with a *doctor*! This is amazing. You two are adorable together, and she's *so* into you."

I don't know what to say to that, but she's clearly misreading Natalie's body language.

Still, I can't help the flutter at her reaction.

As I flop onto the bed, Hazel's tone shifts to something more critical. "What's the deal with her, then? Did she un-dump you and take you on another thrifting date?"

I grimace. She wasn't impressed when I told her Natalie took me curse-hunting and then dropped me off at home and didn't speak to me again. Which is fair.

But after last night, I get why Natalie did it. She didn't want to bring me into a world that has the Madsens in it.

"I think there's a lot we don't understand," I say vaguely.

"Curses? Exploding dolls?"

To avoid looking at her, I run my palm over the duvet, smoothing it out. Although Fiona told me not to share anything about this place, Hazel already knows about curses, so I can't exactly backtrack. Maybe I can share *some* information. "Don't repeat this to anyone, but there was a... situation last night."

"Uh-oh."

"I ran into a guy who's..." I glance at the door and drop my voice. "...looking for cursed objects too. He knows what I can do and tried to get my help. He and Natalie got into a fight."

Hazel gasps. "Are you serious?"

"Natalie thinks he's going to be persistent about trying to contact me again."

"Um, that sounds stalker-ish. Have you reported him?"

Her suggestion is so startlingly normal that it takes me a second to process it. Do Shadows count as authorities? For the purposes of this conversation, I'm thinking yes. "Yeah. They're on it."

She sits back in her chair. "God, that's so creepy. I'm sorry you have to go through that. I'm here if you need me, okay? I'll fly out and stay with you."

I smile. "Thanks."

At the thought of her flying out, homesickness wells up all over again.

Hazel finishes her mochi slowly, deep in thought. "So some random guy wants your help looking for curses, but Natalie doesn't?"

"I know!" My voice pitches higher, a little too loud, earning a disapproving glare from Ethel. I huff. "She's concerned about my safety, but if she can work with curses, why can't I? I can handle it."

Talking about this, the secrets loosen around me, light and freeing, like peeling out of a tight dress.

"Maybe you need to prove to her how useful you could be," Hazel says.

The crushing failure returns like a boulder on my chest. I rub my face and say into my hands, "She made a test to see if I could pick out a curse again. It sucked. I picked the wrong object."

There's a pause. I drop my hands to find Hazel's mouth hanging open.

"She made—wow—I have so many questions." Her gaze darts around, her mind clearly whirring. "You probably just have to hone your skills. I bet this sort of thing takes practice."

I shake my head. "It doesn't matter. There was one test, and I failed it."

She raises an eyebrow. "Giving up? That doesn't sound like you."

I glare at her, the accusation igniting a spark of defiance.

She returns a cheeky smile before reaching out of the frame and coming back with another mochi. "There are other ways to test a person's abilities."

I chew my lip, her faith in me inflating my shriveled sense of hope. Her co-op application comes to mind. "Like the real world? Working in the field is more valuable than writing exams, right?"

She grins, a glint of excitement in her brown eyes. "You should go with her to find a curse again. Next time she gets a call-in."

I want to share her enthusiasm, but the realist in me wins. "She won't let me."

"Insist on it. Follow her. Whatever it takes. You know what I plan to do if my co-op application is rejected? Apply for internships anyway." Her voice rises passionately like it does when she talks about career plans. Her mochi sits forgotten between her fingers, her face pressed close to the camera.

I let out a breath of laughter. "Inspirational as ever."

She leans forward. "For my app project last term, I needed access to corporate emissions data that wasn't available online. I knew the government had it, and I wanted to use it. The prof told me not to reach out because I had no business contacting them as a student. But I did anyway. They gave me the data *and* asked if they could see the final app. So, was it worth going around the prof and proving my idea? Yeah. It was."

A nervous tremor goes through me. Hazel has always been bold when it comes to academia, doing whatever necessary to achieve her goals. In high school, teachers loved her and were exasperated by her in equal measure. I was never that bold—but I've seen what it's gotten her.

If Fiona won't let me use my ability, should I go around her and the others to prove I could be useful?

Hazel's story is inspiring, but this is different. This is about something more perilous than academic ambition.

Security risk... Dangerous mistake... Fiona's doubts about me hiss in the back of my mind.

But she's wrong, and I can't let her decide my fate. It's time to find my version of an internship and show these witches what I can do in the real world.

I have to tag along with Natalie to the site of a curse.

My pulse quickens at the potential danger. This could backfire spectacularly. If I fail again, that's it. I'll have to accept that I'm meant to stay hidden while more capable people protect me from the Madsens.

But I'm going to do everything in my power to be more than that.

I'm just sorry it had to come to this. Sorry I have to take such drastic measures to prove myself. But if I don't, I'll have to leave Natalie and the coven behind. And the threat of that is worse than what any curse could do to me.

CHAPTER 17

More Important than a Sociology Lecture

"A BSOLUTELY NOT," NATALIE SAYS firmly, her knuckles tightening over the steering wheel.

"Come on!" I turn in the passenger seat to face her, disappointment cinching my stomach. "This is a perfect opportunity. Libraries are huge, and there are tens of thousands of items that could be carrying the curse. Let me help you narrow it down."

The morning is chilly and overcast, and we're headed to UBC, where she'll come to all three of my lectures in case the Madsens decide to stalk me. That's what she and Fiona decided—that she'll guard me while I continue everyday life until they can be sure the Madsens won't come after me.

"We have an idea of where it is," Natalie says. "Mostly because the librarian keeps stubbing her toe in one corner."

"But my help pinpointing it would save you a lot of time."

She hesitates—either realizing I'm right or regretting telling me her assignment is in one of the university libraries. She shakes her head. "You're not coming."

I scoff and face forward, watching students pass by out the window. I should've kept my mouth shut and followed her without asking. *Better to ask for forgiveness than permission*, or however the saying goes.

Anyway, I've got time. I'll seize my opportunity when it comes.

I direct Natalie to a parking lot, and we walk through a light drizzle to my first class: sociology.

"Did you and Sky grow up in C.S.A.M.M., or is there a special school somewhere?" I ask as we enter the warm lecture hall.

I lead us past the scattered students to the empty back corner. Gazes snag on us, a level of attention that makes me fidget. Apparently, whether we're in a thrift store or a lecture hall, Natalie has a way of turning heads. She's got her hair in a high bun today, rocking a masc look that weakens my knees.

I bite my lip and dip my chin, fighting a smile. The thrill of her escorting me to class far overpowers the guilt of taking her away from her responsibilities. For the day, she's mine, and I'll relish every moment.

"We went to a normal school until Sky was seven and I was ten," she murmurs, oblivious to the stares. "Then we moved into the coven and were homeschooled from there." She sheds her bomber jacket, her scent beckoning me, and hangs it over the back of the seat. At the sight of the black button-up shirt hugging her waist, heat flares inside me that has nothing to do with the lecture hall's stuffy air.

I sit beside her in the hard plastic chair. "That must've been rough, going to a normal school and keeping a secret at a young age."

She hesitates. "The hardest part was letting go of the friends I made when I had to start homeschooling. I resisted for the first year. Just wanted to be like them so I could stay."

I nod, imagining little Natalie having to leave her friends behind. "I guess we're all desperate to fit in as kids—to be like our friends. Even if it means ignoring part of who we are."

There's a flicker of intrigue in her eyes. "You too?"

Forced together by the cramped seats, she's so close that our arms touch, and her minty breath caresses my cheeks. Her undivided attention is like a flame against my skin.

"Yeah." My hands are clumsy as I take out my notebook and pen. "I know it's not the same, but I felt that with my cultural identity. In elementary school, all my friends were white, and the more I noticed our differences, the more I tried to mold myself to be like them. It wasn't until I met Hazel that I realized I'd been neglecting half of who I was. I was trying to be like my friends, but I lost a part of me in the process."

She nods, searching my face with a furrowed brow.

The prof arrives and gets settled, plugging in her laptop and opening a slideshow.

"It's good you recognized that," Natalie murmurs. "I think some people lose part of who they are and don't realize it."

I look at her sharply. "You feel like you are?"

Her brows arch, and she runs a finger over her bottom lip, like she's debating how to answer. "Being in the coven... it's like our whole identity. I don't know who I am outside it, and I don't think anyone else does, either." She drops her hand. "I've never talked about this with anyone but Sky. She feels the same... Like we're missing part of who we are because our life is just about our duty to the cause."

This glimpse of vulnerability is intriguing. Natalie's life and family feel more mysterious than ever—even to her, it seems.

It's like invisible threads are stitching us together. I want to know her, to understand her.

"Well, it's important to express every part of yourself," I say. "The parts that make you similar to your peers... and the parts that make you unique."

She holds my gaze, a wistful smile on her lips.

The prof starts talking, going through a list of what we'll cover this term. I look at the slide, but what's on it doesn't matter.

Natalie shifts, her chair creaking, her arm brushing distractingly against mine. "Do you feel like you found belonging?"

"I did. But now..." I hesitate. My family's always been my belonging—being an Alexander. "Moving away from home didn't help. It's like starting over."

"You haven't found your people at university?"

A strand came loose from her bun while we were outside, and I grip my pen harder to stop myself from reaching up and tucking it back. "Not really. I've found people who I might call friends, but no sense of home yet."

"I think that's normal for someone who's a little bit introverted."

I nudge her, a pleasant jolt shooting up my arm. "Who says I'm introverted?"

"Just a hunch I had when we packed up your cat, plants, and impressive array of loungewear. Not to mention all the pillows, essential oils, and novels we had to leave behind."

I stifle a laugh, heat blooming in my cheeks as she recounts the details of my personal space. My heart flutters uncontrollably at her cute half-smile, her closeness and warmth, her searching gaze.

My phone lights up with a text.

Clayton

Hey, we're studying at the cafe over lunch if you want to join.

His blunt, exclamation-mark free message hints that he's still feeling awkward about his advances on New Year's Eve.

In my periphery, Natalie looks sideways at my phone.

"Classmate," I explain.

She says nothing.

"Are you jealous?" I tease, shamelessly hoping for a specific answer.

"Do you *want* me to be jealous?" she asks.

I narrow my eyes.

"You should be taking notes," she adds.

"Yeah, yeah." I grab my pen again and try to pay attention—but the invisible threads between us continue to pull tight, more questions fighting their way forward. "How did you and Sky get into your lines of work? Is it because you can do earth magic?"

The corner of her mouth quirks, pulling my attention to her lips. They're the perfect shape, so smooth and full.

She glances at the prof, like she's considering telling me we can talk about this later—but to my delight, she leans in, dipping her head closer to mine. "All witches can do the same magic. Our roles are more like career paths, and we're sorted into them as teenagers based on our personalities and strengths. For Shadows, they have to be physically fit, fearless, and have strong morals. Like, you can't hesitate to take someone down when the time comes, but you need to keep a level head."

Makes sense, from what I saw of Sky. "And your job?"

"Guardians have to be ready to do whatever it takes to track down a curse. You can't be afraid to come face-to-face with a dangerous one. You've also got to be a little outgoing because it can be a social career."

I hum. I could summon bravery, but the 'outgoing and social' part would be my downfall.

"The goal is to nab items before they fall into the wrong hands," she says, "which is why I'm on call as a vet. My first job was at a recycling depot. Found a couple of cursed electronics in my time there."

I try to picture a teenage Natalie. Was she lanky and pimply like I was? At what age did she grow into this absolute goddess?

"I guess odd jobs like piano tuning and working at a thrift shop would also be appropriate?" I venture.

Her eyebrows shoot up.

I smile. "I may have done a bit of research after we met."

She studies me, a glint of amusement in her eyes. She hasn't leaned away, and the closeness makes my insides simmer.

"Were you happy when they made you a Guardian, or would you have wanted to be something else?" I ask.

She frowns. The prof's words drift somewhere in the distance, an incomprehensible murmur. Finally, she says, "Nobody's asked me that before."

Her arms are pinned to her sides, like she would be more comfortable if she could spread them out—maybe sling one over the back of my chair.

The silence stretches on, and when it's clear she's not going to answer my question, I ask, "What other careers are there?"

"Well, the original two guilds were Shadows and Alchemists, hence C.S.A.M.M.'s name. But since its inception, more specialties have been added." Her shoulders relax, and she seems grateful for the change of topic. "Alchemists do a few different things, like create the compounds that neutralize curses. They're the brainiest, the meticulous ones who don't mess up numbers or instructions. They spend a lot of time thinking, exploring, and creating."

Sounds like a career for Hazel.

I open my mouth to ask what else Alchemists do—the mysterious work that falls under 'a few different things'—but she continues before I can speak.

"We've also got Trackers, who search for curses in less obvious places. They're like... archaeologists, kind of. They have to be okay with leaving for months at a time, sometimes venturing alone, other times in groups.

My dad is one. He doesn't care where he's going, as long as it's somewhere new."

"Which is why he's in Turkey right now?"

She fidgets with a bent corner of my notebook, trying to smooth it. "Yep."

Finally, information about her family. But it's all still hazy, everything about her life and the world of witches a big mystery.

"Are you close with him?" I ask.

"We text a lot. Updates on work, mostly. But I hear from him almost every day." She reaches toward her pocket as if to hold onto the device that keeps them in touch, then crosses her arms. "Anyway, then there's our government, which is made up of Directors like Fiona and Agnes—"

"Agnes is in *government*?" I blurt, then duck down a little as a guy a few rows down glances back at us.

"She's junior, but yeah," Natalie says with a sigh. "She wasn't always this intense. I think the power got to her head."

I wrinkle my nose. "Their meetings must be a blast."

Natalie chuckles. "So, those are the coven's five guilds—Shadows, Alchemists, Guardians, Trackers, and Directors. There are other professions in the building, of course, like cleaners, cooks…"

"Would I be a Tracker?" I ask. "Because I can sense curses? I think that'd be useful."

Her expression clouds over. "No. You'd be none of them. And that's the beautiful thing."

Disappointment flickers inside me.

The energy between us thickens. Her shoulders are tense, her brow pinched. She's back to the protective mode I saw when she stormed after Freddie in that alley—dead serious about not wanting me to be a part of any of this.

It hurts as much as it warms me. I should be grateful that she's concerned about my safety, but gratitude is tough when it means she has to keep me at arm's length.

"You really should be paying attention," she murmurs, her breath tickling my lips.

I swallow hard and look ahead. She's right, but how can I pay attention to a sociology lecture when the alternative is talking about magic with Natalie?

I manage to take three lines of notes before the lecture ends.

When we leave, we walk a little closer together this time. Though I hope it's because she's feeling more comfortable, it could also just be a protective thing.

My second class is English Literature. It's in a classroom setting instead of a hall, with enough desks and seats for about thirty students.

Natalie pauses at the door. "Think the prof will notice I'm not registered?"

I grimace, recalling a small class I took last term where the prof took attendance. "It's possible."

"I can wait for you here."

I picture her standing outside the door like a bouncer while I sit inside the classroom for the next hour. "Or you can go grab a coffee or something instead of lurking like a weirdo."

She shoves me playfully, sending a pleasant tingle through my midsection.

I grin. "Natalie, I don't think a Madsen is going to barge into this room and abduct me in front of all these people. Go get a Starbucks. My treat."

"I'm fine, thanks." She shifts on her feet. "Listen, the curse I need to neutralize is in Woodward Library. If I go take care of that quickly, you promise you'll wait for me when class is done?"

"Yeah, for sure," I say casually, averting my gaze so she won't see the flash of victory in my eyes. *Woodward Library.*

She squints suspiciously. "You'd better."

I cock an eyebrow. "Or what?"

She steps in, her body heat radiating. "Or you'll be in *big* trouble."

I open my mouth, but no sound comes out. Is it inappropriate to tell her that's more of an invitation than a threat?

She backs up, the hint of playfulness vanishing. "Seriously. See you soon."

As she leaves me melting into a puddle, I drag my feet into the classroom and settle into a plastic seat.

My knee bounces. My window of opportunity is here.

At the front of the room, the prof settles in and checks his watch.

I need to follow Natalie. As pissed off as she'll be when I show up in the library, how else am I supposed to prove I can be helpful? She's being stubborn, and I have to take this into my own hands.

Before I lose my nerve—and before the prof can start talking—I grab my bag and bolt. A few people curiously watch me leave.

My heart slams into my ribs as I walk down the hallway. Natalie is going to be furious. But I tried to ask for a fair trial, and she wouldn't listen. A single test in a lab with a bunch of people watching wasn't good enough.

I push through the doors, the chilly January air biting my cheeks... and my steps falter. Guilt crushes me, slowing my feet until I come to a stop beneath an overhang.

This is shitty of me. Natalie clearly wants to keep me safe.

"Dammit," I whisper. A ball of frustration forms as I stand on the paved walkway. What am I supposed to do? Yes, Natalie is being overprotective by refusing to let me help, but she's going out of her way for me, and I don't want to be ungrateful.

Do fighting for myself and betraying Natalie really have to be the same thing? Isn't there another way?

I bite my lip. My inner moral compass spins around and around before stopping, pointing firmly back inside.

Ugh. My annoying guilty conscience.

I growl and spin—and smack into someone in a leather jacket.

"Oops!" She puts her hands on my shoulders before either of us can fall over. "Watch out, sweetheart."

Heat rushes up my neck. "I'm so sorry."

I look up into the face of a girl my age with snow-white skin and black hair worn in a short shag. Between her muscular build, black lipstick and eyeshadow, septum piercing, and the razor lines notched into her eyebrows, there's an intensity about her that dares anyone to mess with her.

I make a sound like an awkward laugh and step back.

It's then that I realize her hands haven't left my shoulders.

Her grip tightens as she sets her dark lips into a knowing smile. "Nice to finally meet you. I'm Oaklyn Madsen."

CHAPTER 18

An Earth-Shattering Situation

T HE BLOOD DRAINS FROM my head in a dizzying rush.

Oh—shit.

"You're going to turn and walk with me," Oaklyn says slowly and clearly, her expression not inviting me to fuck around. "I'm going to keep my arm over your shoulders so you don't get any ideas."

My feet move on pure survival instinct, walking with her away from the building and in the opposite direction of where Natalie would have gone to get to Woodward.

My heart beats in my throat. How far did she get? Will she hear me if I scream?

As we descend a set of stairs and turn onto a paved walkway, students walk between classes all around us, absorbed in their headphones and conversations. The thought of screaming and drawing everyone's attention is humiliating.

Even as the thought comes, I internally kick myself. How can I be concerned about being humiliated right now?

"If you try anything, you're going to get a fun lesson in earth magic," Oaklyn murmurs in my ear, her breath warm on my neck.

A chill runs through me. I'm trapped.

Or am I?

Didn't Natalie tell me the Madsens aren't witches? Oaklyn might be lying to get me to cooperate.

Then again, she looks strong enough to pick me up and slam me down like a wrestling move, so earth magic or not, I'm not sure about my chances.

I close my fingers over my phone in my jacket pocket. I have to get a hold of Natalie.

"Before you do this," I say, a quaver in my voice, "you should know that we tested my ability, and it's useless. You're going to be disappointed."

She hesitates for the briefest moment. "Maybe your ability just needs to be coaxed out of you."

I don't like the sound of that. What does she mean by coax?

Brown plants line the walkway beside us, bald and dormant with lingering patches of snow between them. She guides me to a row of parked cars—and nausea rises inside me. I'm running out of time.

Ahead, a street sign says *Wrong Way*.

My inner voice shouts, *I know!*

I need a weapon, a plan, anything. Empty concrete planters with the ghosts of flowers sit too heavy to move. Classes have started, and nobody else is in sight. Why don't I carry pepper spray?

"Silver Toyota," Oaklyn says. "Back seat."

She points me toward an FJ Cruiser, the kind of SUV where you have to open the front door in order to get into the back. I think they call that a suicide door. *Fitting.*

Worse, there's a grate between the front and back, the type used to keep a dog contained. Once I'm in, there'll be no hope of jumping out.

I am absolutely not getting in that car.

Adrenaline floods my veins. Time seems to slow as I make my move. I wrench away, twisting out of Oaklyn's grasp. The straps of my backpack dig into my shoulders, a sharp tug as she tries to hold on, but I drop my arms and shrug out of it.

Free, I take off. One step, two, and no grabbing fingers haul me back. I race around a white sedan, yanking my phone out of my pocket and holding down the side button.

I raise it to my lips, shouting. "Call Natalie! Call Na—oof!"

Oaklyn's arms encircle my waist. The pavement slams into me, sending shockwaves of pain up my wrists and knees. Air whooshes from my lungs. My phone clatters away. She's freakishly strong, and with the fluid way she's moving, she might be trained in martial arts.

Crap.

I kick wildly, my heels thumping against her. Her grip doesn't loosen.

I suck in a breath to scream for help—but a sharp, cold point digs into my neck.

"Get up and stop struggling," Oaklyn hisses.

My brain disconnects from my body. A *blade* is pressed to my skin. More than that, something is coiling around my neck like a noose.

"Okay, okay." I stop thrashing, grabbing the tightening noose. My hands meet something cool, rough, and too uneven to be a rope. It smells like damp earth. *What's happening?*

Distantly, Natalie's voice comes out of my phone, which slid across the ground and bumped into the sedan's tire. "Katie? Hello?"

"Shit," Oaklyn whispers, looking at the phone.

Hope surging, I yank whatever is around my throat. It snaps at the back of my neck, coming free. I grab Oaklyn's hand holding the blade and use all my strength to keep it away from me. "Natalie! It's Oakl—"

Her knee hits my ribs, and I splutter, the wind knocked out of me. Everything spins as she wraps an arm around my neck and drags me toward the FJ. I gasp for air, choking in the crook of her elbow.

Dizzy, I fight back instinctively, kicking her shins, clawing, biting. Nothing works. She opens the car door and shoves me, my hip hitting the back seat.

"No!" I roar, bracing myself against it, refusing to go an inch further.

"Hey, what's going on here?" someone shouts. A young Black man with a backpack rushes toward us, his eyes wide in alarm. "Let her go—"

Oaklyn releases me and punches him in the jaw. Hard. He crumples, unconscious before he hits the ground.

I shriek, using the seat for leverage to kick her in the gut with both feet. Maybe it's adrenaline combined with fury over her knocking out someone who was trying to help, but my kick lands harder than expected.

Oaklyn slams into the sedan behind her, the breath knocked out of her. The car alarm erupts.

I leap out of the FJ and run.

I make it two strides when something trips me. My hands and knees crack against the pavement again. I cry out, pain and frustration bursting from my lips. How did she trip me from two steps back?

Then, above the car alarm, a groan reverberates through my bones. The ground rumbles.

Crrrack! The pavement splits in the middle of the parking lot, and dread grips me. What's she doing now?

But Oaklyn screeches. She tries to stand as the ground shakes, only to fall back to her knees.

My skin prickles like a static charge has filled the air. My hair lifts, dancing in a sudden wind.

Hope crashes over me. This quake isn't from her.

"Natalie!" I gasp.

At the end of the line of parked cars, Natalie stands with her fists clenched, her stance wide. Even from a distance, her eyes flash dangerously.

Awe fills me as she charges toward us. *She* made the earthquake. Now, as the tremors subside, she raises her hands, summoning a swirl of dust and pebbles that circles us like a tornado.

I scramble to my feet, backing away from the cars.

Natalie's eyes narrow, focusing on Oaklyn. "You've graduated from theft to kidnapping, I see."

"Whatever it takes to make you share." Oaklyn slashes her dagger, and dark, fibrous ropes erupt from the tip, twisting through the air like snakes.

Roots. That's what she wrapped around my neck. But... how?

A chill sweeps over me. I thought Oaklyn was lying about using earth magic.

Natalie's face hardens. She swings her arm, and a boulder soars through the air, knocking the roots aside with a *crack* before they can reach her. The boulder slams into the pavement, shattering it. The roots smack against the sedan and leave dirty streaks.

I drop to my knees beside the guy who tried to help me, tapping his face. "Hey. Come on, you need to get out of here," I whisper, checking over my shoulder.

Oaklyn swipes her dagger again, unleashing a knot of roots. Natalie counters with a chunk of pavement. They collide in an explosion of dust and dirt.

My mind is hazy, my balance unsteady. Grit stings my eyes and coats my throat.

A groan makes me jump. The young man's eyelids flutter open, and he looks groggily past me. He can't be any older than I am—a teenager in his first year of university.

"You need to run," I tell him. "There's something bad going on, and you can't be here."

Blinking, he takes in the cracked pavement, the roots, the boulders, and the two women facing off. Cracks, booms, and the whoosh of dirt and pebbles fill the air.

He stumbles to his feet, swaying. Mouthing in wordless terror, he covers his head and disappears through the swirling debris.

Nausea churns inside me. Did I compromise Natalie's secrets? What if this guy tells someone what he saw?

This is all my fault. I should've listened to Natalie and stayed in class.

"Get behind me, Katie!" Natalie roars.

She swipes her arm, pelting Oaklyn with pebbles to block her from advancing. Oaklyn throws her arms up, and I leap over the fissure in the ground and run to Natalie.

With another swipe, she pulls a boulder in front of Oaklyn's path. Oaklyn wraps roots around it, hauls it aside with a deep grinding noise, and advances, the roots undulating above her head like Medusa's snakes.

Natalie waves her hand again, and a concrete planter grinds across the pavement. Oaklyn flicks her wrist, the roots tossing that aside too. She's like a puppeteer, manipulating everything Natalie throws at her.

Only a car's length separates them now. They're both breathing hard, faces clammy, nostrils flaring. I'm two steps behind Natalie, unable to do anything useful. My skin prickles as her power intensifies.

"You've made a mistake, Oaklyn," Natalie barks. "The Shadows have no choice but to come for you now."

Oaklyn rolls her eyes. "Not the threat you think it is, sweetheart. Your junior spy club already caught up with us."

Wait—the Shadows already found the Madsens? If Oaklyn is here, then where are they?

Natalie is quiet, maybe wondering the same thing.

Oaklyn sneers. She slashes the dagger, and the roots strike. Natalie reacts in a blink, sending a wave of pavement and dirt that lifts Oaklyn into the air before dropping her back to her knees.

Dust fills my mouth and nose, making me cough.

"Get in my car," Natalie says, panting. Sweat glistens on her face, her hair coming loose from her bun. Her irises are purple like when she used magic in the alley.

Behind us, a gap opens in the swirling dust and pebbles, revealing her black car.

I back up a step. "M-my bag and phone are..."

She follows my gaze to where my belongings are scattered on the ground.

Oaklyn strikes, and Natalie slams the planter into her without mercy. Oaklyn screams in pain as she flies backward and hits the ground.

Fear grips me, tightening my chest. I thought I wanted to see everything Natalie could do, but this is beyond anything I imagined.

Natalie curls her fingers, and pieces of rubble nudge my bag and phone toward us. I force my legs to move and grab my stuff with numb, trembling hands.

Before Oaklyn can stand, Natalie hurls the boulder back at her, pinning her legs. Oaklyn's shriek is a cry of genuine pain as the weight crushes her.

"Katie, go!" Natalie shouts, sprinting toward me.

We race to her car. Around us, the swirling dust dissipates.

As we get in and slam the doors, a heavy thud reverberates, and everything darkens. I scream. A mass of roots slides down the windshield and off the hood.

Even injured and with her legs pinned, Oaklyn is still fighting.

Natalie switches on the windshield wipers to clear the dirt and mud, and we speed away.

Our breaths roar from our lungs, the sound filling the vehicle.

I'm trembling all over. My back tingles where Oaklyn's car pushed against it, a reminder of how close I was to getting forced inside. Even when I press the heels of my hands to my eyelids, I can still see the dark roots erupting from her dagger, and Natalie's face twisting with rage as she sent boulders and concrete flying with a flick of her fingers.

"Katie?"

I flinch, sucking in a breath as I look at her. Icy fear floods my veins, cold sweat prickling under my clothes.

Natalie's expression shatters me. Her brown eyes are wide with concern, her eyebrows arched. This is worse than making her angry—she's scared, sad, a mix of everything I don't want her to feel. And this is my fault for trying to follow her.

"You okay?" she murmurs beneath my ringing ears.

I nod automatically, but I'm not sure if I am. With shaking hands, I rub my neck where the roots wrapped around it, grit clinging to my fingers. "Y-you said the Madsens aren't witches."

"They aren't." Natalie's knuckles tighten over the steering wheel, the leather groaning under her palms. "I have to talk to Fiona."

"Oaklyn got a hold of a magical object?" I draw deep breaths to steady my shaky voice. Away from her, it was clear she wasn't doing magic the same way as Natalie was. I recall the wild look in her eyes—dark eyes, not purple. Her power came from the dagger alone.

Natalie nods curtly, her jaw working. The silence rings as we weave through cars.

"Did she come into the classroom?" she asks.

I hesitate—and the pause says everything. She looks at me sharply, her nostrils flaring.

"I told you to stay there!" Her anger bursts from her lips.

I flinch. "I—I knew the second I left that I made the wrong decision." My voice breaks as hot shame washes over me. "I was going to turn around and go back inside, but she was right there on the other side of the door, waiting for me."

Natalie jerks her head, her brow furrowed. She weaves between cars and passes recklessly, taking us back to Gastown. "I never should have left you."

"This isn't on you. It's not your job to keep me safe."

"It is! I brought you into this messed-up world." Her voice cracks, like she hates herself for this, and my heart breaks a little more. "Now I have to protect you from it—the Madsens, magic, curses—"

"Why, though?" I've stopped trembling, a spark of frustration igniting amid everything else. "Why are you so determined to stop me from helping you find curses?"

"Because they're dangerous!"

"And? *You* work with them. Everyone you know works with them. I'm prepared to take the risk—"

"I don't want someone I care about to get hurt!" Her voice fills the car, reverberating off every surface.

My insides flip over, like I've done a somersault off a high dive. "You care about me?"

She casts me a sidelong glance, and if I'm not mistaken, there's panic in her eyes.

I don't know what to make of this. Does she care about me in the way that I hope, or does she care about me the same way she would care about anyone who nearly got hurt by magic?

"Natalie... I don't want to go back to my normal life." My mouth is dry. I have to tell her what this all means to me—why I so badly want to help her find curses. Even if I have to open my heart and pour out all my insecurities. "I feel like I've finally found belonging, a purpose, something I'm good at. You asked if I'm an empath. I've always felt like I am, and it would make me good at helping people. I... I think this somehow relates to my ability to see curses. I sense things that other people can't. Energy. Auras. Whatever you want to call it. I'm meant to do this."

My throat seals up before I can go on—before I can tell her that I don't want to go back to a life without her in it.

Natalie twists her grip on the wheel, restless. "I get it. I know you want to help, and I think you could. But you've seen what dark magic can do and how curses can escalate."

"I understand what I would be getting into. My dad's a firefighter. My mom's a nurse. It's kind of a family trait to do whatever it takes to help others."

She falls quiet, taking us to her parking spot in Gastown. My memory tingles with the last time this happened, when we fled the other Madsen sibling. She's determined to protect me, and I'm missing the real reason.

I don't want someone I care about to get hurt.

Her confession lingers over us. A hunch drifts into my awareness like fog rolling in.

"Has someone you care about been hurt before?" I venture, my voice barely above a whisper.

She doesn't answer right away. She shuts off the car, stares ahead, and speaks without meeting my eye. "My mom was a Guardian too. She was killed by a curse."

CHAPTER 19

A "Career" in Psychology

A COLD WAVE OF realization crashes over me. This is why Natalie is afraid to expose me to curses. Her own mother was a victim of one.

From the recesses of my memory, her concerned voice drifts forward. *"Can you breathe okay?"*

I had no idea how bad the truth was.

We get out of the car, my limbs moving automatically.

"How old were you?" I ask through numb lips.

"Seventeen." Natalie guides me toward the steam clock with a firm hand on my lower back, keeping me half a step in front of her. We sink through the ground, and I'm ready for the sensation this time, exhaling through the nauseating dizziness.

As we walk down the ivy-lined hallway, she continues. "She was on an assignment in the suburbs. We caught wind of a curse—a musician who asphyxiated. He'd bought a second-hand guitar and was holding it when they found his body."

She drops her hand from my back and falls quiet as we cross the lounge, where several people are having lunch. Thankfully, Fiona isn't there to ask how her mission went at the library.

Walking toward my room, Natalie continues in undertones. "My mom went to get the guitar, and Sophia Madsen showed up." She spits the name, her hatred simmering. "Mom fought her off. She was always incredible with magic. But Sophia's just... so twisted."

My heart breaks into more pieces with each word.

We arrive at my suite, and I let us in and close the door softly. Ethel meows in greeting from my pillow, flashing her claws as she stretches. I distantly register the made bed—the cleaner, Elizabeth, must have come while I was out.

"She caught Mom with a bear trap and took her vials." Natalie crosses her arms, and her scowl deepens, like she's walled her grief behind anger. "Left her with a mangled leg and a cursed guitar with no way to neutralize it. She called my dad in a panic, tried to get someone to meet her halfway, but the curse was already working against her. Traffic accidents, a storm, a power outage..."

A shiver rolls through me as she lists the curse's familiar effects. My stomach roils, and I sink onto the bed.

She sits beside me, her eyes narrowed as the dark memory spills out. "She started to asphyxiate while she was still on the phone with my dad. He didn't find her body until the next day, an hour from home."

Sympathy wells up as I imagine the panic they must have felt. My voice quakes. "Natalie... I'm so sorry."

She gives me a tight-lipped attempt at a smile, her brave face so fragile that my eyes prickle. I take her hand—soft, smooth, and warm. She doesn't pull away.

"How's your family doing?" I ask. "Your dad and Sky?"

She studies our entwined hands with her brow pinched. "We're coping in our own ways. Sky's hellbent on avenging her. I feel sorry for any Madsen she catches. My dad is... running from it, I guess. He's never home, always keeping busy as if he hopes to distract himself from reality."

"And you?"

"I'm..." She lifts a shoulder.

It's obvious. She's afraid of losing someone she cares about, so she's not letting herself care about anyone.

"Do you worry about Sky?" I ask.

"All the time. Even now, I keep waiting to hear from her. I didn't want to send her after the Madsens, but I learned long ago that I can't stop her from doing her job. She'll be okay."

Seething hatred for the Madsens simmers inside me, intensifying with each piece of information I learn about them. "How do they know to show up wherever there are curses?"

"That's what we've been asking ourselves. Lately, the Madsens have been getting a lot of the same news as we do about potential curse locations."

"You think there's a traitor in the coven?"

"We launched an investigation the first time it happened. That was weeks ago. Everyone turned up clean. So we've either got a really good liar or the Madsens have a secret means of figuring out where we're going. Today was..."

I study the side of her face. Her steady breaths calm me, her warm scent giving me a cozy feeling. But her brow is furrowed, her lips turned downward, as if she's dwelling on what happened with Oaklyn—regretting it, even.

"I don't want you to blame yourself for bringing me into this," I say. "I brought myself into it. I'm making my own choices."

"They're not very smart choices," she says with a hint of a smile.

"Bad decisions are my thing. I should tell you about when Alyssa taught me to drive when I was thirteen."

Natalie sighs and looks at the ceiling, which makes me laugh.

"You're infuriatingly stubborn, Katie."

"And you like that about me. Admit it."

She smiles and doesn't deny it. My heart thrums.

We're still holding hands.

"Thank you for telling me this," I say. The reality that a capable witch was killed by a curse hits hard. It's possible that Natalie is never going to let me help her, no matter how much I insist I'm okay with the risks.

Her fingers tighten infinitesimally over mine. "Thanks for listening."

"And thanks for answering my questions earlier—telling me about the different career paths in the coven and stuff. I... I liked that you came to class with me. It was nice." Sociology feels like days ago, but the thrill of having her there with me lingers, a glimmer of happiness beneath everything else.

Natalie's expression softens. "All of this is going to be detrimental to your degree. You didn't learn a thing today. You didn't even attend more than one class."

I shrug.

The heat of her body beckons me closer, making me want to lean my head on her shoulder and stay like this for a while.

"You know, I've never brought anyone into the coven before," she murmurs, the low purr of her voice resonating in my core.

"I figured as much, given everyone's reaction when we walked in on New Year's." Still, it's nice hearing it.

"I've never..." Her throat seems to close, and she tries again. "I don't typically feel this way. About people."

My heart skips. What is *this way*? Is she saying what I think she's saying?

Her breaths shorten, and she lowers her gaze to our entwined fingers. Her lips are parted, smooth and full, and I want nothing more than to feel them against mine.

With nothing to lose, I let the words tumble out. "I like you, Natalie."

Her dark eyes lock onto me, pulling me in. A falling sensation sweeps through me. I've never been drawn to anyone like this before, never been so attracted with every cell in my body.

She moves decisively, lifting her hand to my cheek. I stay still as her thumb brushes my lip, sending a tantalizing, molten surge through me. Her palm is soft as it slides around to the back of my neck. Heat pools in my middle, desire building until I can't take it anymore.

Her scent fills me. I lean closer, needing to taste her.

"This isn't..." she trails off, her fingers tightening on my neck. Her lips part.

It's finally going to happen!

But then I see it—a widening in her eyes. A sharp inhale. A flicker of doubt.

"Natalie," I whisper, pleading.

She pulls back and winces as if in pain, regret flashing in her eyes. "We can't."

No!

The warmth in my belly turns cold. My lips tingle, yearning for what they nearly had. I reach up to lay a palm over her hand, holding it to my neck. "Why not? I know everything now. I've been exposed to curses and magic, and I'm still here."

She traces a thumb along my jawline, soft and tender, before dropping our hands to her lap. "You've only seen the surface. It's not that simple."

I squeeze her fingers. "Tell me, then."

A pause.

She stands abruptly, putting distance between us, and combs her hair back. It's a mess from the fight with Oaklyn, her bun barely hanging on. "Shit," she whispers.

As she fights with the elastic and shakes her mane free, letting it cascade over her shoulders like a shampoo commercial, my brain stalls.

I didn't think it was possible for her to look any more sexy, but *God*. A primal urge to jump on her flares to life inside me.

She wrestles her hair into a high ponytail, which is worse because now I can see the full breadth of her toned arms.

Get it together, Katie. Jesus.

I avert my gaze, drawing a breath to control my urges.

When she's done, she huffs, stepping away from me. "This can't be anything." She motions between us. "This is strictly forbidden. *Punishable,* and for good reason. There are things you don't know—things you should *never* know."

I can't fathom what she's referring to, and the mystery feeds the ball of frustration in my stomach. I thought I figured her out—curses, earth magic, her coven. Apparently, that isn't enough, and I'll always be a world apart from her.

"Fine." I can't mask the hurt, and my tone comes out cold and flat.

I have every right to be pissed off. She led me on, let me believe she was going to kiss me, and then rejected me again.

There's a heavy pause.

At least Natalie has the grace to look uncomfortable.

"I promised to show you the courtyard," she says, all emotion gone from her voice. "Grab your laptop, and you can catch up on the classes you missed this afternoon. I have to go back to UBC to repair the damage."

Ah, the damage. After seeing what she can do, I'm sure she'll have the parking lot smoother than ever in about sixty seconds—like none of it happened.

Sitting in a mesh hammock under the open sky, I'm at a loss for what to do next. Following Natalie to the site of a curse was a terrible idea, and I like her too much to keep fighting her. But I can't ignore my ability—my calling to help find curses. Should I be afraid of whatever Natalie doesn't want me to know? Is she right to resist how she feels about me, or are we missing out on something amazing?

I rest a foot on the grass and swing the hammock, the ropes creaking on the willow tree's thick branch. Around me, the courtyard is an oasis nestled between brick walls, so lush and perfect that it must have been crafted by magic. Warm, humid air embraces me, ivy spills down every surface, the trees are as green and leafy as springtime, and a koi pond burbles in the center—which Ethel would love. Longing fills me as I picture her happily watching the fish and birds... and me, making friends with the witches who are currently ignoring me.

Witches walk along a gravel path that winds through everything, while others sit at picnic tables. A pair of older women play mahjong without touching the tiles. On a bench, a slender blonde woman cuddles up next to Sebastian, knitting needles hovering in the air before her, clicking as they create a green scarf. A few teenagers who must be in high school sprawl in the grass with laptops and textbooks, laughing as their pens and highlighters skate over the pages of their own accord.

Surrounded by all these friends and families who've known magic all their lives only adds to my loneliness—the sense that I'm an 'other.' It doesn't help that I'm drawing stares but nobody is coming to say hi.

I settle deeper into the hammock and fold my legs under me, opening my laptop. Time to get advice and support from people who have my back. My family, my friends... my community. The people who love me unconditionally.

I video call Mom. My parents have helped me through everything from friendship drama to deciding what to bring to university, and they'll be able to give me perspective on whether I'm fighting for the wrong goal. I'll just have to find a roundabout way to ask for their input without bringing up curses, magic, or witches.

Mom answers with a blurry view of her forehead. "Hi, Katie!"

I smile, lighter at the sound of her voice. "Hey!"

She props her tablet on the table and sits. The kitchen behind her is the familiar, eclectic blend of both sides of the family, from Mom's wooden fork and spoon on the wall to Dad's moose painting from the prairies. Between the glimpse of home and Mom's smile, my heart squeezes—especially after the ordeal today. Being safely surrounded by loved ones would be pretty comforting right now.

Dad appears in the frame, cut off at the neck. "Who're you videoing?"

"Who do you think?" Mom asks with a bit of irritation.

He leans down, squinting at me. "Hey, kiddo! Wow, looks nice there. How was class?"

"Um..." The memory of Oaklyn trying to stuff me into the back of her car flashes across my mind—and Natalie coming to save me, and the two of them hurling bits of earth at each other. "Fine."

Mom angles her head back so she's looking down at the screen through her reading glasses. "You look skinny and pale. Have you been eating your vegetables?"

I sigh. Okay, maybe I'm not *that* homesick.

"I'm eating well, Mom. I'm just a little tired from..." I trail off. From what, the holiday break? One day of class? Time to get into what's on my mind. "Anyway, I was wondering something."

Dad sits beside Mom, both of them leaning in with interest.

A flutter of anticipation fills me. First, I want to find out if there's a reason behind my ability—a connection to magic somehow. "Do we have anything weird or interesting in our lineage? Anyone who can do or see... supernatural things...?"

Dad's brow furrows. "What the hell are you talking about?"

His blunt words yank me back to reality. Do I think I'm going to suddenly learn that Dad's great-great-grandma comes from Salem? Heat floods my cheeks.

Feeling like an airhead, I mumble, "Never mind."

Mom hums and puts a finger to her lips. "We did have shamans on my mother's side."

My eyes widen. "Are you serious?"

She breaks out into laughter. "No. Is this for a project or something?"

Dad joins her in chuckling, nudging her playfully.

I scowl at them. "Yeah, a project."

"Sorry to disappoint you." Mom tilts her head. "We're farmers through and through."

"Except for your ol' Uncle Bill," Dad says. "He could talk to the dead. Every Thursday was graveyard night."

"Okay, okay." I roll my eyes as they burst into laughter again. They've always had the same infuriating sense of humor. "Sorry I asked."

A scuffle comes from off-camera, and they turn.

"We're talking to Katie," Mom says. "Come say hi."

"Hi," Nicky says, deadpan.

"Hey dude!" Pearl calls.

They come over with their backpacks on, home from school. Pearl is in a pair of my overalls I left behind, and Nicky is in a cute argyle sweater and jeans—going for a preppy look this term, I guess. She changes her style every few months, depending on who she's friends with.

"How was—" Mom starts, but they're already talking over each other.

"I'm not in any of the same classes as Angela," Nicky says, dumping her bag and going to raid the fridge.

"I have the *worst* French teacher," Pearl says. "Most of us can speak French better than she can, and she's the *teacher*. Also, she has bad breath. I don't even want to take French."

"You might need it," Dad says. "Being bilingual is a requirement for a lot of government jobs."

"I don't want a government job."

While Pearl plunks down so she fits in the frame with my parents, Nicky flits in and out of the background, making a snack.

Mom turns her attention to me. "Pearl has to decide whether to apply to university within the next couple of weeks. She doesn't know what she wants to do."

"It's hard to pick a career path when you're only seventeen," I say sympathetically.

Pearl huffs. "I took an online quiz to figure it out, and the website crashed."

I purse my lips. "Why don't you take general studies and see what subjects you like best?"

"But every career sucks."

I don't blame her for saying so, but agreeing wouldn't be helpful. "They've all got pros and cons."

Mom and Dad nod.

An idea sparks—a way I can ask some questions without telling the whole truth. "Even a dream job has crappy parts, right?"

"Of course," Mom says. "Nothing in life is perfect."

Dad squints. "Why?"

"I'm learning about the different fields I can study within psychology." I stretch out a leg and rock the hammock again. "Some fields are more... intense than others."

Dad nods knowingly. "Forensic psychology?"

Pearl draws back, her gaze darting between our parents and the camera. "You want to work with serial killers?"

A decent metaphor for curses. I'll roll with it. "Maybe. It's important to do whatever it takes to help, right?"

Mom and Dad exchange a look.

"You've always been compassionate," Mom says. "I think you're meant to go down the path of altruism."

I stop rocking the hammock. "So you believe it's worth taking risks for the greater good."

Dad chuckles and rubs a hand over his thinning hair. "Your mom and I both built our careers on doing just that, so you might be asking the wrong people."

Or the right people. They get it. If they knew the truth about why I'm asking, they would probably agree that helping to prevent curses from getting into innocent hands—or dangerous hands—is important.

"I don't think you should get into forensic psychology," Pearl says matter-of-factly. "Working with criminals would affect you. You're so in tune with other people's energy that you'd pick up on all the darkness."

My heart leaps. It's exactly what I said to Natalie about being an empath. Far from dissuading me, her comment makes certainty trickle through my veins.

"True," I say. "Thanks."

Between this and my parents' belief that I'm destined to help people, what more do I need? I'm meant to stay here and use my ability—even if it's dangerous.

Nicky comes over with a sandwich and peers down between Pearl and Mom, her brow pinched. "Where are you?"

"Um—" Before I can come up with an answer, activity stirs around me. People get up and walk toward one of the courtyard exits, their movements purposeful, like they've been called.

I sit up, rigid. Something's going on.

"I have to go," I say quickly. "I'm studying with... people."

"Oh, are these your *friends*?" Nicky makes air quotes. "Can we see them?"

"Bye! Love you all!" I end the call and shut the laptop, looking for some indication as to what's happening.

Ahead, a woman in her thirties rushes to a group of people at a picnic table, her urgent words drifting toward me. "The Shadows are back."

CHAPTER 20

The Curse of the Pet Emporium

HUGGING MY LAPTOP, I shuffle into the lounge with the crowd, finding dozens of people gathered. Murmurs ripple, low and urgent. The high schoolers studying in the grass are now standing in a booth, craning their necks.

I take their lead and stand in another booth to see over everyone's heads. The Shadows are unmistakable—six people wearing floor-length black traveling cloaks with hoods, utility belts around their waists. God, did they walk through downtown like this?

They're tightly clustered, moving as a unit. One turns her face toward the crowd, and relief crashes over me upon seeing the familiar features of Natalie's sister. Sky looks unharmed, but her shoulders sag and her steps are slow.

Questions roar through me. I assume they didn't catch Freddie, or else he'd be with them, right? So where is he? Why is everyone so tense?

"Move, people," a deep voice orders. "Don't block the halls."

At the front, onlookers shuffle out of the way, and the Shadows break apart. I suck in a breath. A ghostly pale man is being supported by two others, his arms over their shoulders, his head lolling. A blood-soaked bandage covers his neck, dirty and crimson, the sight churning my stomach. Their shouts spike my adrenaline as they order people to step aside, and they split off, rushing him down a corridor.

A tall Black girl with sharp cheekbones and a scar down the side of her face addresses someone at the front of the crowd. Natalie introduced her when I first arrived, along with Sky and Will. *Hayley.*

A wave of shushing noises ripples through the room.

"...seem to have acquired more..." Hayley murmurs. "...nasty security system... Trevor got the worst of it..."

A few gazes turn to me, burning hot. This is my fault. I'm the reason they had to go after Freddie Madsen. And based on the gawking audience, this sort of thing isn't a regular occurrence.

"So the Madsens are still out there?" Agnes's shrill voice cuts through the hum, dripping with accusation. She's pushed her way to the front, too short to see but loud enough to be heard from the back.

Hayley narrows her eyes. "Feel free to head out there if you want to give it a shot. I'll lend you my belt."

"I'm just saying," Agnes snaps, "you came back a little early."

Hayley looks murderous, and I have to admire Agnes's bravery in the face of a Shadow who could easily knock her unconscious.

Sky touches Hayley's arm and holds her gaze, some kind of wordless conversation passing between them.

"That's enough," Fiona says, her tone casting a hush over everyone. "It was the right call to bring Trevor back and regroup before anything worse happened. And I have an update for you regarding Oaklyn's whereabouts."

Discomfort settles over me, and I shuffle my feet. The update is definitely about my being attacked by her an hour ago.

I grab my phone and text Natalie, my fingers trembling.

I stare at the screen until it goes black. She's probably busy with damage control.

A tiny part of me, a part worthy of being scolded, is relieved they didn't find Freddie yet. It means I have more time to prove to Fiona that I should stay.

As I slip my phone into my pocket, Sky scans the crowd with narrowed eyes. Probably looking for Natalie.

Her gaze locks onto me, and she jerks her chin, motioning for me to step aside with her.

My heart jumps. *Me?*

She taps Hayley's back and says something I can't hear before heading in the opposite direction of the other Shadows, toward the corridors. Hayley watches her go with a pinched brow, casting me a suspicious glance.

I force my legs to move, holding my laptop to my chest like some kind of shield or emotional support device.

A thousand questions and possibilities zip through my mind like cars on a highway. Did Natalie get a hold of her? Is this about Oaklyn?

I stop in front of her beneath the archway leading to the Library wing. "Welcome back," I say, trying for casual.

Sky's face is clammy, her eyes puffy. But she hasn't lost her fire, and I feel X-rayed as she scrutinizes me. She has the same dark eyes as Natalie, which should put me at ease, but it doesn't. I shift my weight, waiting for her to speak.

"What room are you staying in?" she asks.

"133."

She nods, her expression neutral. "I'll have a long debrief tonight, but I'll be by in the morning. I want to talk about something."

A wave of unease rolls through me. It's 'we need to talk,' except it's coming from Natalie's sister who is a witch assassin. What could go wrong?

I nod, and she turns on her heel and walks away, leaving me under the stares of everyone in the vicinity—Agnes, Will, and the group of high schoolers among them—and a lot of questions roaring through my mind.

At nine the next morning, I'm in the passenger seat of Sky's SUV, a nervous tremor racing up and down my spine. She hasn't said much since she knocked on my door, just handed me a parka and scarf as a disguise and invited me to leave the building to talk in private.

"It's about your ability," she said, and that was all it took.

Now, as we drive away from Gastown, she graces me with a smile, the warmth in her eyes putting me at ease.

"Do you believe me?" I ask. "That I can pick up on curses?"

Her jaw works in a way that reminds me of Natalie. "Nat told me about the lab test and the thrift store."

The knot in my stomach tightens at the memory of my failures.

"But she also told me about the kitten and the doll." Sky stops at a red light and turns to study me. She looks less tired today, even energetic. Her smokey eye makeup is flawless, her cheeks rosy, her shaved head freshly trimmed. "I want to see what you can do, and not in a lab setting."

Her words erupt through me like fireworks. Finally, somebody agrees that a real-world test would be more valuable. "Are you serious?"

She presses her lips together and faces forward as the light changes, her cheeks dimpling.

"Sky, thank you!"

"Well, we'll see." She shoulder-checks and switches lanes, heading toward the Cambie Street bridge. "There's this pet store. It's been oozing signs of a curse for a year, but nobody's been able to pinpoint what, exactly, is cursed. Could be anything—a budgie, fish food, a squeaky toy, a hat for a guinea pig..." She shrugs. "Figured you might crack the case. It's driving us nuts."

"I'm in," I say at once, tamping down the urge to do a victory dance.

"Thought you might be."

This is all I wanted—one person to have faith in me. "It's lucky Natalie got a callout this morning so we could—oh."

I flush as Sky raises her eyebrows mischievously. I should've guessed when we left unimpeded that the urgent call from a vet's office was a decoy.

"Will Fiona be okay with this?" I ask, my nerves cranked tight as I imagine her fury over us going behind her back. It's one thing if I get myself in trouble, but now I'm dragging Sky down with me.

Sky grins. She has the same dimpled smile as Natalie. "She will be once we get back with the good news."

I grimace. *No pressure, then.*

"I hope she doesn't scare you," Sky says with a glance at my expression. "She's only a hardass because of the oath."

It's the second time someone's mentioned that word. "Oath?" I ask.

"Nat hasn't told you? Witches have to swear an oath to be in the coven. It's not like a normal job where you just get fired if you mess up. Directors are pretty much guaranteed prison time for breaking it."

Holy hell. "What's the oath about? Keeping magic a secret?"

"Something like that. Which is why I can't tell you. But I just want you to understand that Fiona's life mission is to make sure it stays under strict control. Nat was ballsy to bring you to us."

That's becoming clearer by the day.

Sky pulls over at a parking meter and uses her phone to pay. "How long will this take? A half hour?"

I lift a shoulder. How should I know?

She must see this on my face because she says, "Right. Yeah, half an hour will be fine."

We get out and head down the sidewalk, Sky's traveling cloak catching the wind. Traffic whooshes by, a crosswalk beeps, and four crows bicker noisily over a spilled takeout meal. The cold air bites my cheeks, and I zip my jacket up to my chin.

"Has anyone broken the oath?" I ask.

"A few times. Magic has its temptations."

Her words echo Natalie's from not long ago. I guess I understand what they mean, given that I'm still trying to go after curses despite every indication that I should walk away.

We head to the glass door of a nondescript pet store. *Barbara's Pet Emporium* is painted on the windows in colorful letters.

"Nat and I don't spend a lot of time talking about our feelings, but..." Sky opens the door and motions for me to go ahead. "The way she's acting around you? It's weird. Like, good weird."

My insides do a jump and twist. "What? Really?"

"Let's just say she's never flown to Ohio to get a kitten for anyone before."

"That was..." I splutter, my heartbeat quickening. "She needed one that looked like Lucy so I wouldn't... Are you sure?"

She raises an eyebrow. "You don't think so?"

The memory of that almost-kiss floods back, making my lips tingle. "Whatever she's feeling, I don't think she's going to let herself act on it."

Sky sighs. "No. She's not allowed to, for one. But the rules don't stop some people from… carrying on with things under the radar…"

Hope zaps me like a bolt of lightning. I wait for her to offer more—maybe a promise to talk to her sister about what a fool she's been, and she should obviously run up to me and apologize and give me the passionate kiss I've been waiting for.

Is that a flush in Sky's cheeks? Wait, is *she* one of those people who's carrying on a relationship in secret?

Before I can find a way to strategically ask, she says, "So, bird feed aisle or cat food?"

I turn my focus to the surrounding clutter. Hay and critters blend to make it smell a bit like a barnyard in here. Céline Dion croons from the overhead speakers, the music competing with some chirping birds at the back of the store.

"Let's start with the cat food," I say.

We walk slowly past the bags and cans, and I scan everything, waiting for the familiar anticipation to grip me. A bag of tuna treats snags my attention, but this isn't the time to shop for Ethel.

"Natalie won't tell me why all these things are cursed," I say casually, watching Sky for a reaction.

She doesn't meet my eye. "Well, here's a fun fact. Superstitions actually come from real curses throughout history."

This isn't what I was getting at, and I'm sure she knows it, but I'm curious anyway. "So you're saying at one time, a broken mirror really did bring bad luck?"

She smiles. "Oh, that one's good. A king had a cracked mirror that held a curse. Everyone thought the bad luck came when it broke. But no, the mirror itself was imbued with a curse."

"Huh."

We reach the end of the cat food aisle and move onto dog toys.

We weave through two more aisles, and the prospect of failing again closes around me, suffocating. What if my ability went away and I can't find the curse? This will definitely be it. Three strikes, I'm out.

Sweat prickles under my jacket, and I unzip it to let some air in.

We walk through the section with aquarium supplies—and there, at last, my breath catches. A chill runs through me like an icy finger tracing up my spine.

I stop. "Oh my God."

It's here.

Invisible ropes tug me to the right. When I turn my head in that direction, my heart skips.

I follow the sensation, brushing my fingers along the rows of fish food.

"Feel something?" Sky asks, her words tinged with disbelief.

I nod, scanning each item on the shelves. A thrill pulls me onward, desperate, like I'm about to miss a deadline. *Hurry. Take it.*

"Somewhere..." I bend down. My pulse races, rushing in my ears as my body responds to the curse.

"It's an aquarium decoration." My voice comes out urgent, my movements frantic.

I rummage in a metal basket of items, fingers poking through synthetic coral, grass, hollow logs, shipwrecks...

My gaze lands on a figurine, and I suck in a breath, not touching it. "This is it. This thing is cursed."

Sky bends closer to peer at it. Her lips flatten into a grim line. "In more ways than one. What is that, an astronaut?"

"A scuba diver." And a hideous one at that, with its plastic sheen, chipped orange paint, and dented helmet.

"Oh. Right." She straightens up. "Well, I can see why it's been here a while."

She moves to take it, and I grab her wrist, stopping her.

"What if the curse is strong?" I ask.

"It probably is. But we have to touch it to make sure this really is the object." She reaches into her utility belt. "As soon as something weird happens, we'll nuke it."

I nod, glaring at the little figurine. "I'll do it. You just focus on using the vial."

There's a tense pause as I meet her gaze.

She pulls out a vial and nods firmly. "Ready."

My heart is beating out of my chest, both from the curse's effects and the thrill that I might have finally proven myself.

I can't wait to see Natalie's face when we tell her.

Steeling my nerves, I reach into the basket. I hesitate, take a breath, and pick up the scuba diver.

The moment my fingers close around it, the lights flicker as if there was a power surge. Birds squawk.

"*They're heeere*," someone says.

Sky and I freeze, staring at each other with wide eyes.

Then the same voice says, "Hello, pretty bird. Pretty bird."

I let out a huff of laughter. It's just a parrot—one who can perfectly mimic a line from *Poltergeist*, apparently.

"Well, you did it, Katie," Sky says, shaking out her arms as if to get rid of a chill. "This thing is cursed as hell. Let's—Jesus Christ!"

She grabs my arm and pulls me away from the shelves. A furry wave surges out from beneath them, dozens of beady eyes glinting in the fluorescent lights. Rats, a writhing mass of them, skitter past—whether escaped from cages or feral, I don't know.

As we dance out of the way, the speakers overhead crackle, and "Stayin' Alive" by the Bee Gees blares throughout the store.

"Sky, quick!" I shout, holding out the scuba diver.

"Yup." Sky pops the cork off the vial—and at the same moment, a dark shape detaches itself from the shelf over her head.

Before either of us can react, a black cat lands on Sky's head, claws out, hissing furiously. Sky roars and flings her arms upward.

"D-don't spill it!" I splutter, reaching for the vial.

A pop rings out at the far end of the aisle, pulling my attention. A crack opens in a fish tank, spilling water onto the beige floor. The guppies inside swim in frantic circles.

"The fish!" I cry.

Sky is busy. Yelling in pain, she grabs the attacking cat with her free hand and throws it aside. It lands on its feet and bolts, leaving Sky gasping with lines of blood oozing down her cheeks. "Motherf…"

Shouts and footsteps come from the front of the store. "Oy! What's going on back there?"

Shit. We're about to have a lot of explaining to do.

"Quick, fix the tank!" I tell Sky.

"What? Oh?" She wipes her bloody face, looking stunned, and extends a trembling hand toward it.

Immediately, the waterfall slows. The glass welds back together, sealing the crack from bottom to top as if her palm is a soldering iron.

But another crack rings out. A jagged line runs down the tank beside it, sending more water onto the floor.

I'm powerless to help, standing there with a tight hold on the tiny scuba diver.

The footsteps get closer. I check over my shoulder, and my stomach drops. A horde of mice and hamsters bounds toward us. They scurry up the shelves to escape the river of aquarium water, getting unsettlingly close to face-level.

I whimper, stepping back so I don't get a pile of rodents on my head.

"Brad, the lizards are out!" someone shouts from the next aisle over.

Okay, this stops *now.* I dash to Sky, panic constricting my throat. "Sky, the vial—"

A strange sensation freezes me in place. My throat keeps tightening, as if the muscles and tendons are swelling. I inhale—and not enough air passes through.

My heart lurches, a tingle running through my head and neck.

No.

I try to gulp down air but can't get any. My chest spasms, a jolt of pain shooting through my ribs. Spots erupt in my vision, blackness obscuring everything but a few patches of vinyl floor and swirling fish.

The scuba diver clatters to the ground.

I reach for my throat, my fingers working as if to massage my airway back open.

Can't breathe.

Dizziness overcomes me, making me sway. The Bee Gees keep singing "Stayin' Alive," the words warping as if coming from underwater.

Glass shatters. Birds squawk.

"Katie!" Sky's voice mingles with everything else, faint and distorted.

Pain shoots up my legs from my knees. I'm on the ground, clutching my throat, trying to pull air into my lungs in short, desperate gasps. Sharp little claws dig into my thighs through my jeans.

There's a distant fizzing sound. Smoke obscures what little patches of light remain.

BOOM!

An explosion shakes the shelves, sending bottles and containers rolling across the vinyl floor. Water sloshes out of tanks.

A gasp rattles my body, and my ears ring. I'm on all fours, coughing, panting hard as oxygen returns to my brain. My jeans are soaked to the knees, my fingers cold where they're splayed in a puddle.

The dizziness wanes, and for a moment, I can't move.

A crater blackens the beige vinyl. A purple butterfly sits on top of a gemstone. It flaps its wings, then takes off, soaring over the bird seed aisle and out of sight.

Sky's hands close over my shoulders, her face swimming into my vision. "Hey. You did it. You got through it."

Slowly, I register her words. *I did it.* I helped Sky locate the curse that nobody's been able to find for a year.

Sky turns her attention to the crater in the floor, pocketing the gemstone and moving her hands to fix the damage while glancing over her shoulder.

Footsteps pound closer, the staff finally having found us among the aquariums. "What the hell is going on?" a man shouts. "Get out before I call the police."

Sky meets my gaze, a mischievous smile on her lips. There's apparently no protocol for how to deal with the aftermath of neutralizing a curse because she seizes my hand and hauls me to my feet. "Run."

We sprint out of the pet store, and my shock falls behind me like I'm shedding a heavy jacket. It gives way to elation—warm, rising, free, like being in a hot air balloon.

"Cursed aquarium decor is no match for me!" I shout, and Sky laughs with me.

We jump into her car, and she taps the clock. "Two minutes to spare."

I grin as she peels away, taking us into the flow of traffic. "I did it!" I squee, stomping my feet.

She reaches over and squeezes my shoulder. "Impressive, Katie."

The buzz stays with us all the way back to C.S.A.M.M., where Sky throws open the door of an Alchemy lab to reveal a group of people that includes Fiona, Will, and—God help me—Natalie.

"Fiona!" Sky shouts, interrupting their conversation.

Everyone falls quiet. Fiona faces us with an eyebrow raised.

Sky motions to me with a flourish, giving a little bow. "Guess who just solved the Curse of the Pet Emporium?"

CHAPTER 21

Please Make the Right Choice

"**Y**OU DID NOT," FIONA blurts, a flash of childlike elation in her expression that I haven't seen before. Then her gaze darts to everyone around her, and she lifts her chin and smooths her blazer, composing herself. "You're telling me you neutralized whatever was in the pet store?"

Sky walks forward, taking the purple gemstone out of her pocket, and slaps it onto a stone table. "Aquarium decorations, aisle six."

I hold my breath while Fiona stares at it.

She turns to me. "You're lucky I trust Skylar."

I raise my eyebrows. Is she implying she wouldn't believe me otherwise? "And I'm lucky she gave me a proper chance to test my ability," I say before I can stop myself.

Maybe it was snarky, but the adrenaline made me do it.

Fiona's nostrils flare.

Everyone around us is quiet, looking on with expressions of surprise. I can't meet Natalie's eye, afraid of what I'll see. Her tension is palpable, her arms crossed over her navy blue t-shirt. Her gaze burns the side of my face like a torch.

"You have to admit, it's impressive," Will says, and Fiona shoots him a glare.

I suppress a smile. Maybe Will's not so bad.

"How long did it take?" Fiona asks Sky.

"Twenty-eight minutes from the time we stepped out of my car. Seconds, once we hit the right aisle."

There's a pause. Nobody has anything dismissive to say, which is... wow. Three others I haven't met stand behind Will, exchanging meaningful looks and silent conversations.

Fiona scans me up and down with narrowed eyes. "You want to do this as a career, then?"

I blink, her question catching me by surprise. I hadn't thought about it like a career, only an opportunity to help. "I just want to put my ability to good use."

"Well, that means working for us," Fiona says impatiently. "We expect part-time availability, and you'll get laid off if you aren't up to par. Got it?"

Her words hit me like a drop on a roller coaster. *Holy – crap.* "Yes, ma'am."

"I'll need you to fill out an employment agreement, and we'll get you onto the payroll. As far as the government is concerned, you're working for a research lab. Unless you want to be a veterinary assistant. Do you want to be a vet?"

"I—no," I stammer. "A lab sounds good."

Really good, actually. Much like Hazel applying to software companies, 'research' is exactly what I need on my resume for my psychology degree. I'll just have to tell future employers the work was classified.

I shake my head a little, pulling myself back to the present. I'm being offered a job in C.S.A.M.M.!

"You'll be a Junior Guardian," Fiona says, checking her phone, "but your documented title will be Research Assistant. You'll be earning minimum wage, and you'll report to me."

"Can—can I keep living in room 133?" I ask, a tremor in my voice.

She pockets her phone and turns to a bookshelf, preoccupied. "I don't see why not."

I could kiss her.

"One last thing. Do *not* go on assignment without my knowledge again." The sharp edge in her voice tells me she definitely doesn't share my affection. "Same goes for you, Skylar. This is your one and only warning."

Sky nods solemnly. "Yes, ma'am."

The job offer rockets through me, and I have to suppress the squeak of excitement that wants to burst out.

I get to stay.

I'm a Guardian.

I'll be working alongside Natalie.

I risk a glance at her, and my excitement deflates like someone letting the air out of a balloon. She's glaring at Sky, her expression murderous—jaw tight, brow furrowed, fists clenched so hard that veins pop in her forearms. A jolt of fear shoots through me to see her looking the same as she did both times she had to save me from the Madsen siblings.

But she's not saving me from a Madsen now. This time, she's directing that rage toward her own sister. And maybe Sky and I both deserve that look. We went behind her back, after all.

A pang of guilt hits me, but I keep my stance confident. It worked out, so it was worth the small betrayal. A curse needed destroying, and I knew I could help, so I went after it. Big deal.

"We'll leave you to it, then," Sky says, touching my arm and backing up a step. "Sorry for the interruption."

Fiona waves her off—but Natalie steps forward. "Sky. Can I talk to you?"

At her sharp tone, Will turns on his heel and walks away, and the others follow as if called to the other side of the room. Even Fiona. Will grabs a book at random and buries his nose in it.

Apprehension pulses through me. I was so worried about Fiona that I forgot to consider how Natalie would react.

I swallow down the looming sense that Sky and I are in big trouble.

Sky smiles as if oblivious. "What's up?"

"What is wrong with you?" Natalie growls, getting right in her face. "Did you even think about the implications?"

Sky plants her feet and crosses her arms, clearly unafraid of her older sister. "You weren't giving her a chance. She's got a skill we can put to use, and you know it. Don't let your anxieties get in the way of—"

"Don't." Natalie's rage is palpable, lingering over the three of us like a storm cloud ready to unleash its worst. "This isn't about anxieties. It's about being smart."

"Isn't it? Nat, you haven't let yourself process losing Mom, and now you're letting it stop you from living your life."

My heart squeezes. Of course Natalie's reaction is about more than just keeping me away from magic and curses.

Chest heaving, she points at Sky, her finger an inch from her sister's face. "If you endanger Katie again, I won't be so nice next time."

Sky slaps Natalie's hand out of her face and turns toward the door. "You're welcome for finding a way to let her stay. I'm going to have a beer and a nap."

Natalie glares after her as she leaves the room.

Sky's comment about Natalie liking me drifts forward. That's what this is about? Sky wants me to stay for her sister's sake?

That, or I'm reading too much into her words. It's like Sky said—I have an ability they can put to use, and she didn't want that to go to waste.

I shift my balance from foot to foot, my stomach twisting. Do I follow her? I definitely shouldn't be in this lab right now, interrupting whatever meeting was going on.

I motion toward the door, afraid to meet Natalie's eye. "I'll just—"

She grabs my upper arm, sending a jolt through me, and calls over her shoulder. "Back soon, Fiona."

Fiona waves us away, engrossed in conversation with the others.

Natalie's strong grip sends my heart fluttering with a confusing mixture of emotions. First, it's hard to suppress how I feel about her and the way her hand sparks pleasant tingles through me... even when she looks like she's ready to rip a door off its hinges.

Second, there's fear over how angry she is. Fear that I've lost her trust and messed up what slim chance I had with her.

"We need to have a talk," she growls as we leave the room.

Shit.

Fear wins out, making my mouth dry. I try to think of something to say to ease the tension.

But I won't apologize for going after what I wanted. I understand she's trying to keep me safe, but she can't stop me from living my purpose.

"You could've been killed." Her voice is clipped as if she's ready to explode. She's still holding on as if she thinks I'm going to flee.

"But I wasn't," I say, defiant. "In fact, I got through the risks you were talking about, and it turns out, I can handle it."

We stop at my door, and she lets go of my arm, facing me with a dangerous flash in her eyes. "What do you mean?"

I press a trembling hand to the lock and let us into my room. "There were cracking fish tanks, asphyxiation, the Bee Gees—"

"What?" she roars.

I purse my lips, stepping around her. I slid in asphyxiation between the other things in the hopes that she'd let me gloss over it, but no such luck.

"It was no big—" Before I can shut the door, a furry white blur darts past and out into the corridor. I gasp. "Ethel!"

My kitten skitters down the hall with her tail up, apparently wanting to get far away from our argument.

Seeing her go, a strange lightness fills me. She's *allowed* to roam these halls now, and so am I. She'll probably find the courtyard in a few minutes and spend the afternoon watching the koi pond.

But how can I be happy about that when Natalie looks like I've slapped her in the face?

I shut the door, plunging us into silence. Dread builds over what she's going to say. How much have I hurt her?

"I'm sorry I went behind your back," I say, my throat tightening around the apology. "I know you just want to keep me safe."

"Exactly."

"And I promise I'm fine," I say, trying to sound gentle. "Sky came to the rescue, and we succeeded. Now no one else will stumble on the curse, including the Madsens. This is precisely why I can be useful."

Natalie paces my room, running her fingers through her hair. "Katie, I don't want this for you."

I cross my arms. "What *do* you want for me? To drop me off at my basement suite and never see me again?"

She stops pacing, turning toward me with slumped shoulders.

I stay still, waiting. It's time for her to make a choice. She can continue fighting, or she can accept where I've ended up.

She rubs her hands down her face and lets out a frustrated growl. "I don't know."

The silence stretches on. She really can't figure it out.

"You keep telling me I don't want to be involved in all this," I say quietly. "But you don't get to make that decision for me. I feel like I belong here, which I never thought I'd hear myself say about anywhere but home. So, my choice is to stay and use my ability to help find curses. What's yours? Are you going to keep trying to stop me from following this path, or are you going to accept that I've been offered a job and a room in your coven?"

Her fists are clenched at her sides. Her chest rises and falls as she stares at me, her anger flickering like a dying candle.

Something else takes its place—something more intense, so blazing hot that I feel it sizzle in my lips, my neck, my core.

She walks forward, her long strides closing the distance between us.

My breath hitches as her warm hands slide around my waist and into the small of my back. I incline my head, and in the next beat of my heart, her lips crash into mine.

Sparks skitter across my skin. A molten rush of pleasure swells inside me. Her taste is so sweet that I let out a moan, melting into her strong body. I cup her face, her soft hair tickling my fingers, her ears cool against my palms, her cheeks smooth beneath the heels of my hands.

My reaction seems to charge her, and she presses into me so I'm forced back a step. Her lips move urgently, parting mine. Her hands are unyielding, holding me against her.

I arch into her, wanting to feel her against every part of me. Each shift and flex of her toned body sizzles through my belly. Her intoxicating scent fills me, making me open my mouth to taste more of her.

She guides me backward, and I'm too dazed to track where we're going. Everything around us dissolves until the world is nothing but her soft lips and tongue, her warm hands, the curves of her body.

The wild sensations coursing through me reach my brain, and my inner voice screams in victory.

She's kissing me. Natalie – is – kissing me!

My back hits the door, and I exhale sharply into her mouth.

A groan rumbles through her, making me quiver. She runs her palms down either side of my waist, tugging my shirt up so she's touching bare skin. The cool air raises goosebumps over my abdomen.

Oh-God-oh-God...

It's like I'm rolling down a grassy hill, dizzy, out of control, my body reacting without my conscious decision. Pinned between her and the door, I lift my knee up, using my leg to pull her hips against me.

She hisses out a breath and laces her fingers through mine. The backs of my hands press against the cool door by my head, her palms hot, our fingers interlocked.

Our lips and breaths grow frantic, her body pressing harder against me. Her breasts, her hips, her thighs... I close my grip, my fingertips brushing her knuckles.

"Katie—" She pulls back and rests her forehead on mine, breathing hard. "I want you to stay here. Of course I do. But you're making it impossible for me to resist you."

"Then stop resisting."

I look past her to the bed. My desire builds to an unbearable ache between my legs. I need her to touch me, devour me, slide her naked body over mine...

Anguish flashes across her face. She releases my hands and flattens her palms against the door on either side of my head. She pushes back, her flexing triceps drawing my gaze. "You don't know how badly I want you. But if anyone finds out—"

I run my fingers over the swell of her breasts and down her abs, my breaths coming fast and shallow. "We won't tell anyone."

She grits her teeth, closing her eyes for a moment as if to summon self-control. When she opens them again, her pupils are still dilated, her expression still wild. "Listen. There are witches so determined to keep our secrets that if they think I'm sharing things I shouldn't be, we could both lose everything."

"So everyone in the coven is supposed to just stay single forever? Devoted to nothing but the cause?" My voice comes out snappy over how ridiculous this is. "What is this, a cult?"

"No. But there are strict rules around relationships, and dating non-magical people is especially complicated."

"Forbidden? Illegal?" I challenge. "Why are they controlling who people can date?"

"Because there's a lot of confidential information in here, and if they think you're trying to squeeze it out of me or use me in some way, we'll both get in shit. I'm talking probation, suspension, even a trial by jury if they think I've shared too much."

"But—" Okay, it's true that I'm trying to get information out of her, and they have good reason to suspect I'm using my closeness to Natalie to learn their secrets. I huff, refusing to be intimidated. "Are we really going to let the coven stop us from being together?"

She falls quiet, her jaw working. Our faces are close, the tickle of her breath teasing me.

"You're just too afraid to let yourself have me," I murmur, giving her my best sultry look.

She holds my gaze, her eyes glinting in a way that tells me a million thoughts are swirling around in her brain.

She exhales sharply, putting her hands on either side of my neck. "The things I want to do to you right now..."

Her words and the placement of her hands light a fire inside me, weakening my knees. I'm about to lose control.

I grip her shoulders and push her toward the bed, bolder than I've ever been. "Show me."

She takes my wrists and stops me. "I can't... It's the middle of a workday. I have to return to Fiona and the others."

Frustration cinches my insides. I forgot about that part.

"Come back tonight," I say, and it's not a question.

Who *am* I? I'm acting like I'm confident and experienced in the ways of sex, when in reality I've only done it with a girl once, and it was mildly awkward. But Natalie is unleashing a new part of me—a shamelessly horny one that desperately needs to be stripped naked.

She steps in, bending her head down, and brushes her perfect, heart-shaped lips softly against mine. Her kiss isn't urgent this time. She's lingering, slowing down, savoring the way the air crackles between us.

I could melt into a puddle.

"That'll give me the time I need with you." Her murmur travels through my core like a ripple in a pond. "Meet you here at eight tonight."

CHAPTER 22

A Guardian's Oath

"**N**OTHING IS MORE IMPORTANT than keeping magic safe and regulated," Fiona says, her sharp voice pulling me out of my fantasies.

I blink and focus on her stern face. I'm going to have to say an oath in a minute, and I need to pay attention.

Even if all I can think about is Natalie's mouth on mine, her hands under my shirt, and her body pinning me to the door. I'm aching to feel her bare skin beneath my palms, her breath on my neck... and a whole lot more.

Amid our kissing earlier, she forgot to mention that being inducted into the coven would mean partaking in a ceremony tonight. So it was with a little confusion that I let a couple of witches whisk me into an office after dinner.

Now, I'm standing in a high-ceilinged chamber, the brick walls cloaked in thorny roses, sconces casting flickering shadows over everyone present. It's my first time in the Library wing, and magic crackles in the air, as tangible as if I've been plunged into hot water.

Fiona stands in front of me holding a leather-bound book, which she's opened to a page with beautiful hand-written calligraphy.

I shift under everyone's stares. Beneath jeans and a soft pink blouse, I'm wearing my sexiest bra and underwear set made of barely-there red lace.

Natalie and Sky are seated at a long wooden table, along with Will, Sebastian, Agnes, Hayley, and three others I haven't met. If I'm right in guessing all their jobs, that's two witches from each of the five guilds to witness my oath. Natalie and Sky smile encouragingly, steadying me as I battle stage fright. The rest wear deep frowns, probably wondering why I'm doing a rite meant for witches.

And yeah, I'm not so naive as to think I belong. I'm the only non-magical person who's ever sworn this oath. But my ability is enough to have earned Fiona's acceptance, so it'll have to be enough for the rest.

"You've shown a dedication to our cause," Fiona says, fixing me with her stern gaze. "But to be a member of the coven is to walk the path of secrecy. *All* of what we do must remain hidden from the world. Understood?"

"Yes, ma'am." Guilt twists in my gut. Natalie risked a lot by telling me she's a witch. I guess she trusted me more than I thought. Would she have been punished if I turned out not to have an ability and she'd spilled their secrets for nothing?

"As a non-magical member, you will only be given knowledge about our operations on a need-to-know basis," Fiona says. "Accessing information beyond your station will result in punishment for all involved."

I nod solemnly. I'm getting a rising feeling that I'm going to have to work extra hard to prove myself.

"This means," she continues sharply, "you are not to try and *coerce* information out of anybody here. You are not to *accept* information should somebody offer it. You are not to *mingle* with others in any way that could compromise their oath."

I nod again, discomfort writhing in my stomach. Okay, Natalie really did tell me more than she was supposed to—about the coven, the guilds, earth magic... And my repeatedly asking her to spill confidential information *might* qualify as coercion...

Agnes gives a very audible, "Hmph!"

Fiona raises her eyebrows.

Agnes flushes. "Suffice it to say she's been mingling already. A *non-magical member*... What's next, inviting the Madsens for coffee? Honestly, she's not even wearing ceremonial robes. This is a mockery of our practices."

Nausea rises as she confirms what a total outsider I am.

"Interrupting a ceremony," Sky snaps, "is a mockery of our practices."

"Quiet, everyone." Fiona's eyes widen in stern warning, and Agnes and Sky sink back in their seats.

Fiona returns her attention to the book, and I catch Natalie's eye. She gives a reassuring half-smile and eye roll, a silent dismissal of Agnes's grievances, and the tension in my shoulders melts away.

After spending so long wanting nothing more than to join the coven, I just want this rite to be over so Natalie and I can head back to my room and pick up where we left off. My skin tingles where her hands were all over me, my heart flipping as I recall how she felt pressed up against me. Her taste lingers on my tongue.

Dammit, focus, I tell myself. *This ceremony is important, and you've been wanting this for ages.*

It doesn't help that Natalie's gaze is traveling hungrily up and down me, a flirty look for me alone.

Her thoughts, like mine, are clearly elsewhere.

"Objections?" Fiona asks.

My heart lurches. *Of course there are objections. Look at all the frowns.*

Sure enough, Agnes's hand shoots up, followed by Will and Hayley. Nausea bubbles again at all the hands in the air—at the disapproving atmosphere penetrating my skin.

Before Fiona can call on one of them, Agnes lifts her chin. "Why do we need someone to help detect curses when we've been doing fine for all these years?"

"Because fine isn't good enough," Natalie says coolly, peeling her gaze away from me. "We have to move faster. Oaklyn Madsen has already gotten her hands on a dagger because we didn't get there first, and God knows what they've got in place around their house that fucked up Trevor like that. The last thing we need is them obtaining something even more serious."

Agnes shrinks a little under her sharp tone.

The others put down their hands.

Natalie's faith in me is like a supportive hand squeeze from across the room. After all the time she spent trying to keep me safe, she's making it clear whose side she's on. And her assertiveness is... super hot.

Let's get a move-on, I think, shifting impatiently.

"Yeah, look at the Pet Emporium," Sky adds. "We couldn't find that one at all until Katie came along."

My fondness for her grows. I catch her eye, hoping she can read my gratitude.

Hayley nods and drums her fingers on the table, looking thoughtful. "You raise a good point. She might be the advantage we've been waiting for."

Will scoffs. He won't look at me or Natalie, his lips puckered like he's eaten something sour. Beside him, Sebastian's eyes are bright as he studies me, fidgeting with his beard.

Fiona waits for any other arguments or objections. Everyone stares at me, making sweat prickle beneath my shirt—but nobody else speaks. Agnes's face is so scrunched up that it looks like she's bracing for a punch.

One thing's clear: several people still need convincing that I am who I say I am, and that I'm not about to sell the coven's secrets.

My ability had better be up to snuff. Fiona made it plain that I can get fired, so I have to take my assignments seriously.

"The oath, then," Fiona says, turning the book around and presenting it to me.

I place my hands under the worn leather book to bring it closer. I lick my lips, willing my mouth to cooperate and read the words without stumbling. "I, Katherine Medina Alexander, hereby swear upon my induction into the Coven of Shadows and Alchemists for Managing Magic to uphold and defend their mission of protecting the world from the dangers of magic. I vow to do everything in my power to keep magic classified, secure, monitored, and regulated. I understand that the consequences of breaching this oath are severe, and I accept that if I am found to have violated this oath, I will be subject to punishment as determined by a jury of my peers."

Damn, Natalie and I are getting off easy. She must be thinking the same because I sense her shift in her seat. I'd also better put a lid on the details I'm sharing with Hazel, if I want to avoid a trial by jury.

I draw a breath and continue. "As a Guardian, I pledge to use my knowledge and skills to protect the public, to work in harmony with other members of the coven, and to never use magic for personal gain or to harm others. May my commitment to this oath be unyielding, and may my loyalty to the coven be unwavering, for as long as I shall live."

I look up, my heart pounding. The parts about using magic don't apply to me, but I've definitely just sworn to something I have to take seriously. No hinting at magic to Pearl in the hopes that she guesses it, and no chickening out when it comes time to grab hold of a curse. I have a responsibility—to the coven and to the world.

I hope this doesn't make it difficult to be normal around family and friends. I'll have to watch what I say and come up with a plausible story.

Anyway, no going back now.

Fiona shuts the book with a muffled *thwap*. "The ash ritual. Sebastian?"

The what? Hearing the word *ritual* from a literal witch isn't exactly comforting.

"Coming right up, m'lady!" Sebastian stands, his chair scraping on the stone floor. He takes a tray off a small table in the darkest corner of the room and brings it to us with a pompous air, as if delivering a crown on a velvet cushion. "The elixir of ash, distilled from the essence of a thousand twilight blooms and infused with the tears of a unicorn."

Fiona looks at the ceiling and sighs.

Sebastian sets the tray on the edge of the long table and offers an elaborate bow, trotting backward and sweeping out his arms. On it is a mortar and pestle filled with fine ash, a potted lily with beautiful pink-and-white petals, and a small metal watering can.

What will they have me do? Am I about to have some magical charm placed on me to make sure I don't break my oath?

I glance to Natalie, who shifts, her chair creaking. "It's just a tradition," she says, the words blurting out. Everyone turns to look at her. She taps her fingers on the table and clears her throat. "It's symbolic. It won't do anything to you."

Fiona shoots her a glare. "Yes. As Natalie boldly interjected, this is an age-old rite that signifies your rebirth as a member of the coven. Please nurture both ash and flower with life-giving water, then mark the inside of your left wrist with ash and your right with the flower's pollen."

"Okay." I step up to the tray. My hand trembles as I pick up the watering can and splash its contents on the ash and soil. I mix the water into the ash, forming a paste, then dip two fingers in and smear parallel lines over the inside of my left wrist.

My skin tingles and burns. I know it's in my head—I trust Natalie when she says it's only symbolic—but it feels like something real is happening. I'm leaving my old life behind, reducing it to ash.

I lift my right arm and brush my wrist over the lily's pollen, drawing an orange line. It, too, leaves a tingling sensation that spreads to my palm and fingers. I can't help thinking of earth magic, and the way Natalie and Sky can manipulate their surroundings just by opening their palms.

A deep longing fills me—a wish that I could manipulate earth's elements too. But I should be grateful I have any ability at all.

I drop my arms to my sides and look up, ready for whatever comes next.

Fiona nods, and I get a glimpse of something rarer than a cursed doll at a flea market. It's a small smile. "Welcome to the coven, Katie."

The words wrap around me like a warm embrace.

Sky whoops and claps, and to my relief, Sebastian and Hayley join the applause. A genuine smile dimples Natalie's cheeks, crinkling her eyes. I grin back, joy filling me to the brim. The others don't clap, but screw them. I'll prove them wrong.

I'm officially a member of C.S.A.M.M. This is the first day of living my calling—to use my unique ability to protect the world from dangerous magic. What'll my first assignment be? Where will this new path take me? An excited flutter builds inside me, making me want to skip.

What's more, this means I get to stay with Natalie. And I'm desperate to act on this, fighting the urge to ask if we're done here so she and I can race back to my room. It's nearly eight, and my whole body is tight with anticipation.

Fiona has me sign some papers—a more detailed, documented oath and an employment agreement among them—but I'm in too much of a hurry to read them in detail. I skim and sign with a trembling hand, and then the witches around the table stand up to shake my hand and welcome me. Warmth floods my veins.

"Well, this should be interesting," Agnes says loudly, doubt dripping from her tone.

Natalie steps close to me, clasping both my hands in hers. "Congrats," she murmurs. "Welcome aboard."

Her words are neutral, but her eyes are a fiery promise of what she's going to do to me as soon as we can get out of here. Between that and her scent, my knees nearly buckle.

I'm ready to sprint out the door now, but everybody else has other ideas. Sky comes over to talk to me, telling me about the clubs I should join, while Natalie is swarmed by Sebastian, Will, and several others.

"Lucky that all worked out for you," Will grumbles to Natalie.

"Oh, knock it off," Sebastian says, cuffing him on the arm. "You know she's going to be useful..."

"...there's a great gym here," Sky says, pulling my attention back. "It's attached to a practice room, so you can watch the Shadows train if you want. It's kind of cool."

"Awesome. Thanks."

Natalie catches my eye, her expression betraying her frustration.

"Feel free to head back to your room," Fiona tells me as she walks past with the leather-bound book in her arms.

"Oh. Okay." I glance longingly at Natalie. "Thanks."

Sky claps me on the shoulder and heads for the door. "Night. Hope we get to work together on something."

"Yeah, same."

She leaves, and I linger, pretending to admire the roses on the wall.

"I'll be off," Agnes says loudly. "I have some very high-priority matters to attend to before turning in tonight."

Nobody's listening.

"Natalie," Fiona says, pulling out her phone. "We got a call in Surrey that I'd like you to address. Not urgent, but very strange..."

"Send over the details," Natalie says.

Fiona shows her the phone. "Have a look at this…"

A knot of frustration tightens in my stomach. Dammit, she's never going to make it to my room if people keep talking to her.

With nothing left to do but leave, I brush past her on my way out the door.

Please tell these people you've got to go, I think.

The air between us crackles with tension, heat spreading through me. I feel her posture shift, but she keeps talking to the others, nodding as if fully engrossed.

Silence closes around me as I walk back to my room, my heart pounding in anticipation. The magic in the hall thickens with each step, as tangible as when I'm near a curse—maybe more.

Do others feel this when they're near magic, or is this my ability again? And what is it about the Library wing, exactly? I look over my shoulder, but all I see is the empty corridor.

In my room, with something more important on my mind, I race to get ready. Makeup, perfume, hair, the works. I turn off every light except for the soft reading lamp on the desk, casting just enough to see.

What if she's pulled away to other priorities? What if she's hours late—or can't come at all because she has to head out to the curse Fiona showed her? I can't handle waiting. I need her like I've never needed anyone.

I check my reflection—my hair in loose curls, my eye makeup dark and sultry, my blouse low-cut—and I can't help smiling a little. No wonder she had that hungry look in her eyes.

I pop open a button, making the shirt more risqué than I'd ever wear in public. A tease of red lace makes an appearance.

My inner wrists are still striped with gray and orange—the ash and pollen symbolizing my rebirth. I don't wash it off, staring at the lines, craving everything they represent.

Knock knock.

I freeze. In the mirror, my pupils dilate.

She's here.

Somehow, my feet carry me to the door, even as my mind dissolves into a giddy haze.

But as I seize the door knob, panic closes around my chest, making my breath catch.

What if it's not her? What if it's Fiona telling me I missed a signature on those papers, or Sky coming to tell me something she forgot to mention about the book club, or—

I swing the door open.

Flames lick through me, searing hot.

Natalie stands there with her hands in her pockets, her hair cascading over her shoulder, her lips parted. Her dark gaze melts me until I'm ready to yield to her every need.

CHAPTER 23

How to Get a Witch Naked

NATALIE CLOSES THE DISTANCE between us in two strides, her hands sliding around my waist with an urgency that steals my breath. Her mouth finds mine as she kicks the door shut, the sound reverberating in the silence.

I kiss her back hungrily, my fingers exploring the angles and curves of her body—her arms, her shoulders, her back, her breasts. My every sense is tingling, her body crackling beneath my palms.

"I was—worried you'd get sent on an assignment tonight," I whisper into her mouth.

"You underestimate how high priority you are," she murmurs.

I don't know if it's a bad thing to take her away from her work—and maybe this is part of the reason our relationship is forbidden—but I'm not about to argue.

Natalie's fingers deftly trace the curve of my waist, making me shiver as she draws a path under my shirt. This time, she doesn't stop. She runs her hands up and over my bra, palming my breasts before tugging my blouse upward. In one swift motion, she pulls it over my head and tosses it aside.

A purr rumbles deep inside her as her gaze flicks up and down my body. "Gorgeous…"

She dips her head, her lips finding the sensitive hollow of my collar bone.

A shockwave travels through me, making me moan as she leaves a trail of kisses over my clavicle and down my arm. I thread my fingers through her hair, the soft strands and rough little braids adding to the pleasure coursing through me.

She doesn't stop until she reaches my hand, pressing my palm against her lips. She lingers, holding my gaze, the gesture so intimate that it awakens butterflies inside me.

"Can I take you to bed?" she murmurs into my palm.

I dip my chin. "You can do anything you want."

I've been wanting this for too long to give any other response, evident by the molten heat pooling inside me.

Our mouths crash into each other again, all restraint vanishing as she walks me backward. Stumbling toward the bed, I part her lips with my tongue and deepen the kiss, needing to show her how much I want her—how much she's been missing out on because she was too stubborn to let this happen sooner.

She pushes me, and I land on the mattress, leaning back on my hands.

My breaths quicken as I take in the wild look in her eyes, her full, parted lips, and her tousled hair. She grabs the hem of her shirt and tugs it upward—and the smallest whimper escapes me.

I finally get to see the contours that were teasing my fingers a moment ago. I drink in her strong shoulders, sculpted abs, and the cleavage peeking out of her black sports bra, sitting up so I can run my hands over her bare skin.

Before I can touch her, she's on me, pushing me back down. With one hand in the small of my back, she lifts me and positions me beneath her. Her hair forms a curtain around our faces, her arms on either side of my head as she hangs suspended over me.

I palm her breasts, the reality of the moment hanging somewhere at the edge of disbelief. I can't believe Natalie Zacharias is shirtless on top of me.

Maybe she's having a similar thought because the tiniest of smiles tugs her lips.

"This doesn't change that you'd be better off away from all this," she says.

"Something must have changed, or else we wouldn't be in this position."

An adorable scowl creases her brow.

I touch her bottom lip, relishing the cushiony softness against my fingertips.

"I've accepted that you're going to be stuck here," she says. "Helping us. Staying safe from the Madsens. And I know that while you're here, alone in your room every night, it's going to be impossible for me to resist you. No matter how forbidden."

I bite my lip, liking the sound of *every night*.

As she bends down and kisses me deeply, I bring my knees up to her hips, pulling her closer. She hisses out a breath, grinding against me. I let out a moan that gets lost in her mouth.

"Natalie..." I whisper, my voice strained with impatient desire. I reach down between her legs, rubbing her through her jeans.

She grabs my wrists and pins them above my head. "First," she purrs, "I need to taste you."

Her words send me to another planet. Speechless, I whimper.

She kisses my chest, her warm lips leaving a trail of fire that makes me squirm. She lets go of my wrists to hold my waist, tracing her tongue over my abdomen. Her fingers find the button of my jeans, and the slow tease of the zipper being undone is too much to handle.

She reaches behind me and unclasps my bra, and I free my arms and toss it aside.

A rush of vulnerability sweeps over me as I lay bare beneath her—but when she moans and takes my nipple in her mouth, swirling her tongue, any insecurity dissolves.

I gasp, arching into her. I'm so focused on her mouth on my breasts that it takes me a moment to realize she's also tugging my jeans down. I lift my hips to help her slide them off.

She wraps her hands around my midsection, kissing my abdomen, working her way down.

"I've wanted to do this for so long," she murmurs.

"R-really?" I stammer, dazed.

"Katie..." she says like this is obvious. "In other circumstances, I would've asked you out the day we met. Well, maybe after the doll, when you gave me that damn sexy pout and asked for my number *in case you found another curse.*"

I laugh as her words light a flame inside me. I guess I knew she liked me, but she was so good at resisting it and following the rules that I couldn't be sure when it started. I definitely wouldn't have guessed that her interest sparked the day we met, given the balaclava and skin boils.

She removes my underwear, and I'm completely naked, the cool air raising goosebumps all over.

The brush of her hair against my inner thighs makes me quiver with anticipation.

She kisses her way inward, and by the time she rewards me with an exhilarating slide of her tongue, I cry out. For all her forcefulness, grabbing me, pushing me onto the bed, she's torturously gentle with her mouth.

"Careful, or the neighbors will hear," she warns.

"O-okay." I run my fingers through her hair, urging her on breathless-ly. I bend my knees and open my legs wider. "God, you feel so good..."

I'm dizzy, unraveling as she devours me.

She wraps her arms around my thighs, groaning, the vibrations mak-ing me tremble.

"Natalie," I say, her name a gasp.

"Is this okay?" she murmurs. "You're comfortable?"

"Y-yes. Keep going exactly like that." I'm more than okay. Naked with her, I feel safe, cared for, like there's nowhere else I want to be.

She does as I say, and I struggle to lower my voice as I guide her. I completely dissolve as she responds in all the right ways, running her tongue over places that make my thighs quake.

As I tangle my fingers in her hair, the inside of my wrist catches my eye. Distantly, I register that I've smudged the lines of ash and pollen from the induction ceremony. But the world beyond this room feels impossibly unimportant.

After torturously long minutes at the mercy of Natalie's tongue, I reach the top of the roller coaster, and there's nothing left to do but freefall.

"Natalie," I whimper, heat building low inside me.

She hums, and her warm breath pushes me past the point of no return.

"Oh, God—" My words pour out incoherently, mingled yeses and curses rising in volume.

I hold her head in my hands and stifle my cries as the pleasure comes to a peak. My body moves of its own accord as wave after wave hits me. Hips bucking. Legs writhing. Fingers clutching. From my lips to my toes, everything tingles.

I've pushed myself halfway up the bed by the time the waves finally release me.

Natalie sits up, grinning, and unbuckles her belt.

I'm disoriented as I watch her, gasping for breath. Every cell in my body is throbbing, concentrated between my legs.

"That was unbelievable," I say weakly. Never in my life has anything felt so good.

She unbuttons her jeans and opens the zipper, looking down at me with an expression I've never seen on her—a feral craving, blazing with intensity.

Desire stirs in my belly.

I sit up and put my hand on her shoulder to push her down. But before I can flip us over, she stops me, taking my hand and lifting my fingers to her mouth. "Stay there," she murmurs, running her tongue between my index and middle finger, then sucking on them. The sensation ripples through me, making my breath hitch.

She guides my fingers down between her legs, rubbing her over her unzipped jeans. "I want to kiss you while you touch me," she whispers.

I nod, too dazed to speak.

"Good girl," she says with a playful quirk of her lips.

I return her smirk, even as there's an explosion inside me—and then I'm treated to the full view of her as she takes off her sports bra.

Help.

She strips down completely and climbs back on top of me, her mouth finding mine again.

Our bodies slide against each other, arching, writhing. I'm lost in her smooth skin, her hard nipples, her tongue, her lips. The whole world is just her—her warm, herbal scent, her hot skin, the taste on my tongue.

Her mouth finds my neck, nipping a trail from my earlobe to my breasts.

Panting, I reach between her legs, savoring the process of slowing down and teasing her. I draw a trail over her hips and inner thighs, moving slowly inward. Her skin feels so unbearably good under my fingers that I want to prolong this as much as possible.

When I finally reach her center, she gasps into my mouth, a shiver sweeping over her. I bite back a grin, satisfied by how ready she is.

As I massage her, she moans, rocking her hips against my hand.

With her knees, she pushes my legs apart, bringing a hand down to touch me too.

Oh, fuck. Oh-fuck-oh—

I gasp, spiraling out of control as she enters me.

"This okay?" she murmurs against my neck.

"Y-yes," I manage. "Very, very okay."

As sensitive as I am, this feels too good to make her stop.

She pulls out to massage me, and then in again, moving slowly.

I moan, sucking on her lip, and move my own fingers faster.

"Katie," she gasps.

I fight to stay coordinated as she toys with me. I smother my cries in her mouth, unable to stop the noises I'm making. Time loses meaning, everything measured in hitched breaths, rocking hips, and sliding fingers.

When she pulls back to meet my gaze, I see something new in her eyes—something so vulnerable that my heart misses a beat. The walls she normally hides behind are down, and the stubborn adherence to the rules has vanished. It's just the two of us, desire guiding our actions, and nothing else in the world matters.

She leans down to kiss me again, and I open my mouth, letting the kiss deepen until she fully claims me with her tongue. I'm at her mercy, her deft fingers pushing me to the brink, her tongue tracing the inside of my mouth, my legs held apart by her thighs.

She stops kissing me to bury her face in my neck. "Fuck," she whispers.

Her body grows clammy. Her fingers move faster, her breaths sharp in my ear. Each stroke brings me closer to the top of the roller coaster again.

Our breaths mingle. I respond to her soft noises, changing what I'm doing every few seconds.

"Katie..." she groans.

The urgency in her tone tells me she's close, which sends me over the edge.

"Yes, yes…" I whimper. "Oh God…"

I gasp as she hits just the right spot, arching into her—and she shudders, biting the pillow as our muffled cries blend together.

CHAPTER 24

Sophia Madsen's Legacy

WE CATCH OUR BREATH under the covers, Natalie on her back, me pressed against her side and using her as a pillow, our legs entwined. Her scent envelops me, and though we're both sweaty, I don't want to move.

My pulse races and my skin tingles from her touch, as if my body is reveling in what happened. Thrill mingles with disbelief—I was beginning to think hooking up with her would never happen. I mean, she's a solid ten in all departments... and she's a *witch*.

Her breaths become deep and rhythmic, her belly rising and falling like a gentle tide beneath my palm.

I chew my lip, a question burning. I have to ask, even though I'm dreading the answer. "Now that I'm a member of the coven, is this thing between us any less forbidden?"

She peers down at me. "Not really."

"Why?"

"Because the coven's secrets are layered. There's a lot you don't know—even a lot I don't know. The Directors will think you're trying to lure it out of me, which isn't good for either of us."

I scoff. "Come on. I'm not some femme fatale flirting my way to your darkest secrets."

She kisses my temple, her lips soft. "Everyone insists they won't tell their partners about magic, but it's hard to be in a relationship and not let things slip. Like I said, Will got suspended once. His ex-girlfriend now has to spend the rest of her life having signed a secrecy agreement, and the Shadows check in on her once in a while. It stresses the hell out of her, knowing that if she slips up and mentions anything to do with C.S.A.M.M., she could go to prison."

God, that poor girl.

I scowl. "I think someone's partner finding out about magic is the least of the coven's worries."

Her brow furrows. "Why do you say that?"

"How'd the Madsens find out about magic if they aren't witches? Who told them?"

She huffs out a breath of laughter. "Sophia dated a coven member, and he spilled everything."

Ah. That's not the answer I was banking on. In fact, it probably impacted this whole *no-dating-outsiders* rule.

Natalie must see my disappointment. "Yeah. Sophia became hellbent on collecting magical objects. She's brilliant and comes from a wealthy family, so she always got whatever she wanted. She wouldn't accept *no*, and she did what it took to get answers."

I blow out a breath. "They tightened up the rules about dating outsiders after that?"

She nods stiffly.

"What happened?"

She hesitates. "This was before I was born, so I only know the stories. There was a series of trials for the man she dated... He was stripped of his rank and went to jail. Took his own life in there when he found out Sophia had moved on."

I shiver. "That was a pretty drastic punishment. Can't you modify a person's memory if they find out about magic?"

"No." There's a sharpness in her tone, like I've crossed a line. "And we wouldn't do that sort of invasion of someone's mind even if we could."

There's a pause. I listen to her breaths, rocked by the soothing rising and falling.

"So to sum up," I say, "we can fuck, but we can't let anyone know we're together."

Her eyebrows pinch, her lips turning downward. "I hope you know you mean more than that."

I rest my chin on her shoulder, studying her profile. My heart thrums. "How would this play out if we could openly date?"

She brushes her fingers lightly up and down my arm. "I'd have taken you out several times by now. Tonight, we would go to a fancy restaurant... and I probably would've researched *fun and unique date ideas in Vancouver*, which means we would end up ice skating at Robson Square or playing glow-in-the-dark mini golf."

I laugh. "Sounds nice."

"Instead," she says with a sigh, "we'll have to call our curse-hunting assignments dates."

"Which would be the most interesting dates I've ever been on, actually."

She presses her lips into a thin line, unamused.

I reach up and squeeze her cheeks. "Stop worrying about me."

"As soon as you stop getting into trouble," she says through puckered lips, which makes me laugh.

A rap on the door splits the air.

Natalie sucks in a sharp breath and sits up, the sudden movement sending me tumbling onto the pillow.

The cozy warmth leeches away, dread creeping over my skin.

"*Ohmygod,*" I blurt, the blood draining from my head.

We stare at the door, a pair of guilty statues.

Natalie springs out of bed and rips open my dresser drawer, pulling out the first pajama top—my moon-phases t-shirt—and throwing it at me.

With wide, panicked eyes, she retreats into the bathroom, easing the door shut with a soft, nearly inaudible click.

"Coming!" I shout. My hands tremble as I pull the shirt over my head. It's long enough to cover my nakedness, and after shoving our discarded clothes under the bed, I don't have time to put on pants.

Humiliation floods my veins, prickling my skin. Is it obvious what just happened in here?

I rake my fingers through my tousled hair, taming my brown locks as best I can in the few steps it takes me to get to the door.

With a deep, steadying breath, I smooth my face into an approximation of sleepiness and open the door.

My stomach drops when I see Fiona, her eyes immediately raking over my disheveled state—hair, pajama shirt, bare legs. Her scrutiny is agonizing.

Of all people, why her?

"Katie, I'm sorry to bother you at this hour," she says, her sharp gaze returning to my face.

"No worries," I respond automatically, then suppress a wince. Was that too casual for addressing a Director?

"I was trying to reach you." Fiona waves her phone. "I need you on your first assignment at four in the morning. I know it's early, but there are signs of a curse at Waterfront Station, and it's going to pose a danger to commuters. I'll want you to help Natalie pinpoint it."

"Y-yeah, sure," I stammer, caught off guard. *Right, I have the responsibilities of a part-time job now.* "Four o'clock, Waterfront with Natalie. Got it."

She nods curtly. "Do you know where she is, by the way? I can't reach her."

"No," I say quickly, then clear my throat. "I haven't seen her since I left the ceremony."

I cross my arms, the ravaged lines of ash and pollen hidden against my shirt. My mouth is dry as I avert my gaze to the door on the opposite side of the hall.

Fiona huffs. "She'd better pick up soon, or I'll send you pounding on her door at four in the morning whether she's ready or—"

"Excuse me?" A shrill voice cuts through our conversation, coming from the end of the corridor. "Fiona, are you talking to Katie?"

Fiona dips her chin. "Yes. Is that hers?"

My chest constricts at the sound of Agnes's voice. Just when I thought this couldn't get worse.

She stops beside Fiona with Ethel squirming in her arms. "Katie, you can't let your cat roam around without being registered. We need to be able to trace all familiars."

She holds out Ethel, who reaches for me like a child reaching for her mom, desperate to get away from Agnes's grip. I take her gently, her body light and soft, and she purrs and nuzzles into my neck.

"Right," I mumble.

"I called the number on her tag and got Katie's voicemail," Agnes tells Fiona as if this was some impressive detective work.

"I see," Fiona says flatly.

Agnes scans me up and down, sucking back so her chin disappears into her neck. "Good God, were you already asleep? Well, early to bed, early to rise, I guess."

"It's been an eventful day," I say, focused on petting Ethel. I resist the urge to tug my shirt lower. All it would take is a simple lift of my arms to give everyone a show.

I can feel Agnes scrutinizing me, and when she not-so-subtly leans over to peer into my room, I put a hand on the door to close it. "Thanks for returning Ethel. I'll register her tomorrow after I get back from my assignment."

Ethel snaps her gaze around, staring intently at the closed bathroom door beside me.

Shit.

"Have a good night." I offer a strained smile as I shut the door.

The moment it's locked, I set Ethel down and cover my mouth, letting out a mortified noise comparable to dying bagpipes.

That was a dangerous near-miss. They're probably suspicious. Could they tell I just finished having the best sex of my life on the bed behind me?

Ugh, end my suffering.

I swing the bathroom door open, and my heart somersaults at the sight of Natalie standing there naked. But all the earlier heat is gone—her face is ashen, her eyes wide with fear.

"I guess you should go—"

There's a double tap on the door.

I groan softly.

Slumping, Natalie shuts herself in the bathroom again, and I pick up Ethel and answer it.

Sky stands there holding a small cardboard box. "Just wanted to drop off a congratulatory gift!" Her gaze lands on my shirt and bare legs, and her bright tone falters. "I woke you up. I'm sorry. I won't stay—I just wanted to say a proper congrats and welcome."

I take the box, warmth spreading through my chest. "That's really nice of you. Thanks."

She bounces on the balls of her feet. "Open it."

I fumble Ethel and the box, not wanting to put her down in case she runs away again—or worse, draws attention to the bathroom door. Sky takes pity on me and reaches out to open it, revealing a dark green leaf inside with a vaguely triangular shape. She swaps the box for it in my free hand.

It's light and firm. I brush my thumb over the smooth, glossy surface. "It's beautiful."

"It's a fingerless gauntlet made from an enchanted fig leaf. You use it like a shield." Sky lifts her fist in front of her face as if deflecting bullets.

I gape at the gift. "Are you serious?"

I see it now—it's meant to wrap around the base of my hand, the bottom of the triangle latching together at my wrist, and the top point looping over my middle finger to hold it in place.

"This is... the most badass gift anybody has ever given me." My throat tightens with emotion. This means more than she knows.

She waves it off and backs up a step. "Just want to keep you safe, with everything going on right now."

I'm speechless, staring at the gauntlet in my hand.

Enchanted.

Oaklyn's dagger comes to mind, and the way roots erupted from it. That must have been enchanted too.

How will Natalie feel about me having a magical object?

"Get some sleep," Sky says, backing away. "Oh, hey, do you know where Nat went? I've been trying to text her."

I shake my head, hoping she can't tell that her question hit me like an ice cube on the back of the neck.

Sky sighs. "Well, I'll keep blowing up her phone 'til she answers. Night."

With my hands full of Ethel and the gift, I lift my chin. "Night. Thanks again."

With a nudge of my hip, I close the door, then set Ethel down.

After a pause, I murmur, "All clear."

The bathroom door opens.

"Jesus Christ, you're popular tonight," Natalie whispers.

My heart is in my throat. "How are you going to slip out of here without someone seeing you?"

She saunters over and leans down to plant a kiss on my lips, which loosens the tension in my shoulders. "Things quiet down around here by eleven. We'll just have to find some activity to occupy us until then."

I smile coyly.

She looks down at the gauntlet, her brow pinching. She lifts a hand as if about to touch it, but drops it at the last moment. "Sky's right to give this to you."

As the room's warm light hits the leaf's glossy texture, it shimmers with a gentle purple hue, as if hinting at the magic woven into its filaments.

"How common are enchanted objects?" I ask.

"They're rare and valuable. Sky must think..." Natalie hesitates, then shrugs. "Well, I'm glad you have it."

A tremor creeps through me. My first assignment looms over our heads, mere hours away. In a race against the Madsens, I'm going to head out into the world and do my part to neutralize curses.

The gauntlet comes to me in a new light—an extraordinary piece of armor that can help me survive what's coming my way. Whatever its story and origins, Sky and Natalie think I'm the best person to have it.

Maybe Sky knows how Natalie feels about me and wants to protect me for her sake... or maybe she thinks I'll need all the help I can get.

CHAPTER 25

Some Might Call this a Double Life

"**H**AZEL, YOU SHOULD'VE SEEN me. My senses were tingling, my intuition was rock solid..." I pace my suite rapidly, filling her in on my first assignment. Despite my vow to rein in what I tell her, it's impossible to resist sharing *some* of it. We always call each other first after something big happens, and it'd be too weird not to. I need to maintain some semblance of normalcy. "We got to the Skytrain station, and I could feel it right away, you know? It took like ten minutes for me to pinpoint it—a bag of ketchup chips inside a vending machine."

"Cursed chips?" she cries, leaning closer to her laptop. Her jaw is slack, her eyes gleaming. She's in her dorm at her desk; behind her, fairy lights cast a warm glow over the stark white walls.

"I know!" I punch my fist into my palm, adrenaline still pumping. "Natalie nuked it, and we were out of there in seconds. God, that was good."

I didn't have to use the gauntlet from Sky, which was a tad disappointing but for the best. It felt badass to wear it, anyway.

Hazel claps. "Yes! So did you have to buy a bunch of chips before you could get to the cursed bag?"

I hesitate. Natalie used magic to pull the chips right through the glass, and it was mind-bogglingly cool. But this is a detail too far. With a pang of guilt, I say, "Yeah."

There's a pause. Hazel's eyebrows shoot up.

Ugh, I'm a bad liar.

It feels unnatural to keep things from her—like I'm putting up a wall that's never been there before. We've always told each other everything in intimate detail. And keeping with tradition, the first thing I did when she answered was give her a graphic play-by-play of last night with Natalie. But the induction ceremony, my oath, the gauntlet, and other details about magic and the coven? Though I want to spill it all, fear and responsibility silence me.

Fiona would be furious that I've told Hazel this much, but I can't backtrack on what I spilled weeks ago, and I'd probably combust if I had to keep *everything* from her. So, I've made the executive decision to continue filling her in on what she already knows—that curses exist and I can detect them.

"Did you figure out what's up with her?" Hazel asks. "Is she really a vet?"

My heart lurches at the question. "I'm still working on figuring her out."

Another pause. Hazel's shoulders sag almost imperceptibly.

"You can tell me things," she says, a strange note in her voice. "I promise I'll keep your secrets. I don't have to share any more info with Sean."

Ouch, my heart. She thinks I don't trust her.

"You're the first person I tell about anything and everything," I say, stepping closer to the laptop. I hope she can read my sincerity.

She casts me a small smile. It's almost sad, like she's hoping for more.

But I can't give her more. Not only would it violate my oath, but there's also a real chance it would put her in danger. The less she knows about witches and magic—and the Madsens—the safer she'll be from all this.

"Looks like a nice room you're in..." Hazel leans back in her chair. "Tell me this, at least. Is your basement really flooded, or have you been staying with Natalie?"

I purse my lips. Her assumption isn't entirely wrong. Anyway, it's probably safer to let her think I've been living at Natalie's because we're hooking up.

Her smile turns smug. "Wow. You warned me girls move fast."

I laugh. "It's not like that. It's complicated."

"I gathered. Are you spending more time at her place or yours?"

"Hers." I chew my lip. She'll think I'm nuts if I tell her I don't intend to go back to mine at all. I plan to give my landlord notice and pick up the rest of my stuff eventually, but for now, it isn't safe to return. Not when Freddie Madsen knows where I live.

"And Ethel?" Hazel asks.

"She goes where I go." I pick up my precious baby off the bed and kiss her soft head. I'll figure out how to register her as soon as we're done talking so she can go back to exploring her new home.

"You brought the furbaby and everything..." Hazel shakes her head, her cheeks dimpling. "This girl has a firm hold on your heart, Katie."

My face heats up. Again, she's not wrong. "It's—"

"Complicated, I know."

When I don't elaborate, her smile fades.

It hurts to hide things from her. And I can't fix this.

She sighs, fidgeting with something off-screen. "You've always been good at reading people, so I trust your decisions. But... guard your heart a little, okay? You met through a weird circumstance, and I feel like there's still a *lot* you don't know about her."

I try to see this from her perspective. I suppose watching your best friend fall for a mysterious woman who has something to do with curses would be a little concerning.

And she has a point. Natalie was shrouded in secrets when we met, and that hasn't changed.

I nod. "I will. Thanks."

She nods back, as if we've come to an agreement.

"Why don't I spare you from blushing any deeper and fill you in on my co-op job applications?" she asks—a peace offering.

"Please," I say desperately, both to avoid how much I'm blushing over Natalie and to skirt more questions I can't answer.

Hazel's eyes crinkle as she laughs at my awkwardness, and I relax, returning the smile.

While I rub Ethel's chin, Hazel tells me about her upcoming co-op interviews and her latest dates with Sean—but with each forced laugh and excessive bubbliness in our tones, I can't shake the feeling that the last thread of normalcy is fraying between us. Living across the country was hard enough on our relationship, and now I've added secrets into the mix.

Guilt bubbles up in me, leaving a bitter taste. When I said my oath, I didn't consider what it would mean for every other aspect of my life—most of all, friendships and family. How many lies and half-truths will I have to tell them? Will I ever be able to have a normal conversation without watching my words?

Knowing about magic and curses is a level of responsibility I'm not used to, and it's quite possibly going to change my relationships with everyone I love. But it *must* be possible to balance these parts of my life. No matter what, I refuse to let the coven take away my most important relationships. Guardian or not, I'm still Katie Alexander, and no threat from any witch is going to make me shift my priorities.

I kiss Natalie urgently, running my fingers through her hair. Her lips are warm against mine, her hands clamped around my waist beneath my unzipped jacket. My back presses into the wooden wall, pinned by her body.

We're in a dressing room in a historic theater, stealing these few minutes before we have to return to C.S.A.M.M. Red ambient light bathes us, making Natalie's features unbearably sexy. A crater smolders in the floor where a cursed fog machine once sat emitting soap bubbles in the shape of crude words. Now, the word 'wanker' floats through the room.

I bring my knee up to Natalie's hips, holding her to me. No matter how close she is, it isn't enough—my stomach twists, desperate to feel her body against every part of mine.

Slowing down our kiss, she traces her fingers over my bare thigh, teasing me by moving higher.

My heart skips. She's about to find out why I wore a dress on an assignment.

As she gets to the spot where my underwear should be, she freezes, pulling back to gape at me. "Are you serious?"

I flash her a flirty smile.

She slides her hand around to my butt, groaning hungrily, and leans in to kiss my neck.

I shiver, massaging between her legs over her jeans. "Want to?"

She pulls back again. She checks over her shoulder at the open door, though it's midnight and we're the only ones here. For now, anyway. Explosions often result in filed complaints, which means law enforcement might pop in any minute to check on the place.

"Come on," I whisper, undoing her belt. "It's been days, and I need you."

She doesn't stop me, letting out a breathy, "Katie…"

Fire licks through me as she grins and slips her fingers back under my dress.

As much as I relish these stolen moments to make out—and more—while we're on assignment, frustration simmers beneath the desire. We can only meet strategically. We can't be seen together too often, which means I usually take meals alone. I still haven't been to her room because she lives in a corner unit at a busy intersection. Any time we have together is quick and frantic. But while the secrecy was once exciting, now, it's confining.

I slide my hand into her jeans, and her eyelids flutter closed, a shaky breath escaping.

She grips the back of my knee and lifts my leg, giving her better access. I clutch the back of her neck and whimper.

All that heated kissing made me so ready for her, and as her fingers glide along my center, hunger passes over her expression. "I can never get enough of you."

"Same," I whisper.

As she touches me, I bite back a moan. Everything in me melts in a rush of pleasure, and it's a good thing I'm being held up between her and the wall. I surrender to the rhythm of her fingers, letting out tiny gasps.

She feels excruciatingly amazing, making me question why we don't throw caution to the wind and do this every day. Multiple times a day, even.

"We'll have to—figure out how to sneak me into your room," I murmur between hitched breaths.

She hesitates for the briefest moment. "Maybe on a holiday—when people leave to see their extended families. But then…"

Then I would be with my family, too. Are we ever going to get a chance to be in a normal relationship? One where we can go on dates, hold hands in public, and spend unlimited time together?

She claims my mouth again, distracting me from that train of thought.

Our rhythm quickens as we get lost in each other, our breaths coming faster.

With my knee on her hip, the purple gemstone in the pocket of her trench coat thumps against my outer thigh, our trophy from neutralizing the curse. A reminder of how much I don't understand about magic.

I try to ignore it, but a spark of frustration returns. Despite our assignments, despite taking the oath, I still don't know the coven's secrets—or Natalie's. What are they keeping from me?

Natalie pauses, sensing my distraction. She meets my gaze with a soft, concerned expression. "You okay?"

I nod quickly. "Yeah. Keep going."

Pushing down my doubts, I sink back into the present. We don't have long, and I'm ruining this fleeting moment by overthinking.

I should be grateful for each second with her, whether we're in a dressing room or a train station. Because between the coven and the Madsens, there are too many reasons it could all come to an abrupt end.

Balancing my life doesn't get any easier. One minute I'm pressed against Natalie, frantically kissing her while a curse blows up whatever room we're in, and the next, I'm in the calm C.S.A.M.M. courtyard with my laptop, pretending to be a normal university student. It's a dizzying double life, but I keep afloat through sheer stubbornness, refusing to let any part of my life sink.

On the first day of February, as I'm catching up on sociology lectures in the courtyard, a Director named Amir strides toward a group of Shadows at another picnic table. His brow is pinched, his face lined and solemn.

I tuck my hair behind my ear, straining to hear the conversation.

His low voice barely reaches me. "...Freddie and Oaklyn...cemetery..."

"Looking for a curse?" Hayley asks.

"Seems so."

A shiver runs down my spine.

Natalie and Sky enter the courtyard too, both wearing black trench coats. Their expressions are grave, a palpable tension raising the hairs on the back of my neck.

I catch Natalie's eye and glance pointedly at the group, a silent question.

She nods and says something to Sky, motioning in my direction.

While Sky goes and slides in next to Hayley, Natalie comes to my table—which is as unoccupied and lonely as ever—and sits across from me.

"An Alchemist, Jaques, took his kids to Fort Langley today," she murmurs. The place name is familiar—a little historical village an hour east. "We just got a call from him. They spotted the Madsen siblings skulking around by the cemetery. He's keeping an eye until we can get there."

I sit taller, my heart pounding. "We?"

Natalie nods grimly. "They're searching for something."

"Someone tipped them off about a curse in the area?" I venture.

"Seems like it. Fiona just told me about a curse there last night, and now, here they are." Her scowl deepens. "Can you be ready to go in five minutes?"

I slap my laptop shut and scoop my textbooks, phone, notebook, and pens into my backpack. "I'm ready now."

We head to my room to drop off my bag, where I put on a jacket and the gauntlet—which I still haven't had to use.

"Just a pit stop in the Alchemy wing to get a vial." Natalie guides me with her hand hovering near the small of my back, hesitating before making contact. Her feather-light touch sears through my layers, sending a flutter through me.

I want her to keep it there, but she drops her hand before anyone can round the corner and see.

I'll take what I can get, I guess.

I study each door we pass, curiosity about the unexplored rooms eating away at me. "In the Library wing, I felt magic in the air. Is that normal?"

Natalie arches an eyebrow. "It's... rare."

"Do you feel it when you walk down that hall?"

A pause. "No."

I suppress a self-satisfied smile.

But when I look up, she's frowning.

"What's wrong?" I ask.

She glances sideways at me. "I'm taking you away from studying again."

Somehow, I don't think that's what she was frowning about. But I wave a hand. "I'll catch up later."

"Don't you have midterms? What about that sociology essay?"

I resist the urge to kiss that concerned look right off her face—Alchemists trickle through the hall all around us.

"I'm keeping up just fine, Natalie. Don't worry, school is important to me, and I'm not letting anything slip." It's the truth, even if I'm a little more stressed than I otherwise would be. "Anyway, I don't need you to oversee my studying."

She stops at a locked door, Alchemy 13. "You're missing out on the university experience because of me. You should be going to class in person and seeing your friends."

"It's not *because* of you," I tell her firmly. "Stop blaming yourself for the fact that *I* stumbled on a cursed kitten."

Attending lectures is too dangerous after what happened with Oaklyn, but I don't mind studying remotely. Sure, some aspects suck—I'm still in a group chat with Clayton and the others, which means I watch their plans fly by without participating in any. And I care about this more than I thought I would. I guess I was starting to consider them friends, after all.

But it's hard to feel sad about missing out on study groups and beer gardens when I get to help track down curses with Natalie every couple of days—we found fourteen in January. Not to mention I get to have her naked in my bed.

I bite my lip, hyper-aware of the way her arm brushes mine as we stand a little closer than necessary.

She puts her palm on the lock of Alchemy 13. It clicks. When she pushes open the door, icy air blasts out, prickling my cheeks and the tip of my nose. I recoil as white vapor curls before us, my breath misting in the doorway. The dark room is a walk-in freezer, the frosty walls lined with dozens of shelves of glass vials—all tubular, thumb-sized, and full of that shimmering amber substance.

Natalie sees my awe and smiles. "The Alchemists make it in large batches. Saves time."

She steps inside, takes two off the wall, and drops them into an inner pocket.

I watch closely, distracted by her fingers and the memory of what they can do.

"What're you thinking about?" she murmurs, stepping close. Her cocked eyebrow tells me she's correctly reading my expression.

I smile mischievously, leaning back against the door frame. "About what we'll do when we get back later."

"Oh?" She's right in front of me, the heat of her body warming my cheeks as I incline my head. She touches my bottom lip, a gentle tease.

"If I had it my way, I'd take you right here up against—uh, we should go."

Her sudden change in tone from sexy-as-hell to blandly professional leads me to believe someone is approaching.

"Yep," I say, turning around.

Will strides past with a cart of empty vials wheeling in front of him on its own. He shoots us a glare. "Playing a dangerous game, Zacharias," he mumbles.

Natalie does a double-take. "Come again?"

Will jerks his chin toward the room. "Shut the door before you let all the cold air out."

She frowns but lets it drop, closing the door.

Shit. Did Will see us in the door frame, or were we out of sight? Does it matter when he seems to have a strong suspicion about the two of us already?

Natalie casts me a guilty grimace, which I return. We rush back to the lounge, neither of us willing to discuss what just happened when there could be listening ears.

In the lounge, Sky, Hayley, and four other Shadows have assembled, their terse murmurs breaking up the charged silence. They're ready for action in their black traveling cloaks and utility belts.

Sky pulls her hood up. "Listen up, everyone. We're going to split up and close in on their location from six points. We'll get an update from Jaques on their exact whereabouts before moving in. While Nat and Katie find the curse and neutralize it, the rest of us will focus on trapping those assholes."

Natalie shifts infinitesimally closer to me, her arm brushing mine in a subtle but supportive gesture—a reminder that she and I are a team.

Sky waits for everyone to nod, then jabs a thumb toward the exit. "Let's move."

As we head to the steam clock, Natalie seizes the excuse to put an arm around me—I need a witch to bring me back out to the real world, after all. But the others don't miss it, every gaze lingering a tad too long. Brows pinch and lips tighten in the few seconds Natalie's arm is across my shoulders, and she removes it quickly, the discomfort palpable. She and Sky exchange a look I can't interpret.

We might be worse than I thought at keeping our situation a secret. Does everyone see the familiar way we melt into each other's bodies? Has someone even seen Natalie leaving my room or returning to hers in the midnight hours?

We have to be more cautious. I care too much about her to mess up everything she's worked for.

As we drive to Fort Langley in the back of a dark cargo van, I clench my fists in my lap, wishing I could reach over and take her hand. The danger of working with curses hits harder now that I've experienced how deadly they can be—knowing all this could come to an end if we can't neutralize one in time. Knowing the Madsens are willing to do anything to get their hands on one.

It's scary how I feel about Natalie—how much is at risk. I've never spent so much time thinking about a girl, never been so giddy about one... and never been so afraid of losing someone.

CHAPTER 26

Shadows in the Graveyard

I WONDER IF THE people milling around Fort Langley realize there are a couple of killers in their midst.

In the back of the SUV, I press my nose against the window as Sky drives us past the village, which is a fusion of colorful heritage buildings and trendy shops and restaurants. In any other circumstance, I'd be racing through every door, geeking out over the history of the trading post, and taking pictures of the Fraser River. Instead, we turn down a quiet street and roll to a stop in an empty parking lot at the back of the cemetery.

We get out, breaths misting, a chill rippling through my body. I adjust the gauntlet before stuffing my hands in my pockets to keep warm. At our backs is a deserted playground. An icy wind makes the swings creak and bare branches scrape against each other. Ahead, past a tall row of hedges growing over a chain-link fence, the cemetery stretches across several acres.

"Why couldn't the curse be hiding somewhere fun, like a donut shop?" I mumble.

Natalie scans the misty scene that awaits us, solemn. The gray clouds sit low, threatening snow or sleet.

Hayley studies our surroundings with a practiced eye. "We need to lure them somewhere they'll be easy to trap. Let's get Katie to walk—"

Natalie rounds on her. "We are *not* using Katie as bait."

My heart skips a beat as I become the subject of the conversation.

"Why not?" Hayley asks, unintimidated. "We won't let anything happen to her."

Sky's eyes dart from Natalie to Hayley, a hint of nervousness as tension simmers between them.

Neil, a muscular Asian guy with a shaved head, shrugs. "It's not a bad idea."

The cold has already seeped through my layers, and I shuffle my feet to keep warm, my boots crunching on the salted pavement. Given all the witches here, I don't think I'd be in danger, and it'd be nice to be useful. Even if it's in the sort of way a live worm is useful to a fisher. "I don't mind—"

"No." Natalie glares at the others in a way that could melt steel. "I'm sure you can all manage to apprehend Freddie and Oaklyn without endangering an innocent life."

Something about her word choice feels like being called helpless. And something about her phrasing must have pissed off the others too, because suddenly we're all scowling at each other. The air between us seems to have congealed.

Sky's phone buzzes. She answers with a curt, "Yeah."

Natalie turns to everyone else. "Look, I need Katie's help finding the curse. You'll have to catch them the usual way, all right?"

They shift uncomfortably. A couple of them nod.

Sky hangs up. "Jaques is taking the kids home. The Madsens are near the cenotaph at the front."

"The what?" Hayley asks.

"It's a monument. You'll know it when you see it."

Hayley hesitates, then nods. "Okay. Let's hit it."

The Shadows split up to check the area on all sides, which leaves Natalie and me to do our part finding the curse.

I roll my shoulders and let out a slow breath, focusing. The sooner I find it, the quicker we can get out of here—and hopefully avoid a run-in with the Madsens.

My pulse picks up as we pass through a gap in the hedge and enter the cemetery. Gravel paths break up the cut grass, crossing through the middle and running down the left side. Ahead, mature cedars and chestnut trees are scattered across the field, blocking our view of the monument.

I lead Natalie to the right, planning to weave through the tombstones and trees until something hits my senses.

Though the village is bustling with pedestrians a block away, it's eerily still among the graves, the frosty grass groaning beneath our boots as we walk. I concentrate on my heartbeat and any strange sensations. Another shiver rolls over me as I try not to think about what's under our feet. God, I'm glad it's daytime.

Natalie's fingers brush my arm. "Stay close."

I ignore the heat blooming beneath her touch. "I am."

"You keep darting ahead."

"Well, I can't focus on finding the curse when you're literally breathing on my neck." I cross my arms and hunch against the cold, ready to get away from these heavy gray clouds and back to the coziness of the enchanted courtyard.

"I'll breathe in the other direction, then," Natalie says doggedly.

I face her. "Natalie, I'm not going to get abducted."

Past her, Hayley strides down the sidewalk on the other side of the cemetery's iron fence, and her eyebrows shoot up as we argue. We're drawing attention to ourselves.

"You're being overprotective," I whisper to Natalie. "Never mind trying to find a curse, you're making your feelings obvious. You don't see any of them panicking over my safety."

She says nothing. My heart swells knowing this is true.

We keep walking through the graves, Natalie putting exactly one foot of space between us. My nose and chin are numb, and I cup my face to try and warm up. We pass headstones of all shapes and sizes, from evenly-spaced plaques to large crosses with benches. Many are weathered and mossy, their inscriptions barely visible in the weak daylight. Others have personal adornments, like artificial or real flowers, wreaths, trinkets, and flags with poems.

"I still don't get why the Madsens want to steal a curse," I murmur. "Like, the second a person touches one, it starts trying to kill them. What are they planning to do once they get one?"

Natalie stays quiet. When I look at her, her gaze is on everything but me.

Frustration churns in my gut. "You're going to keep withholding information from me?" I ask flatly.

"It's for your own safety."

I press my lips together to avoid spitting out an argument. This need-to-know arrangement blows. I get that Natalie is just following the rules and keeping me safe, but it's forcing me to be less than everyone else in the coven. What'll it take to truly belong with them?

The hairs on the back of my neck lift, and my feet move faster before I process what's happening.

"It's close," I whisper, letting instinct guide me.

Natalie hurries to keep up.

I cross to the next row of graves, nearly breaking into a run. *This* is why I'm here. This is the power none of them have, and I'm going to use it to the fullest.

My breaths quicken. Anticipation tugs me onward like a magnetic force.

Near the center of the cemetery, hidden from public view by trees, a headstone with a square top sits darkened by moss. A bouquet of artificial white roses rests against its base, frost clinging to the faded green stems and weathered petals.

I stop, my heart beating out of my chest. Icy wind curls around us, making branches groan.

"The flowers?" Natalie murmurs.

I nod.

She crouches and studies the headstone. Her brow pinches.

"Familiar name?" I ask. *Have we found a witch's grave?*

"Not sure."

I roll my eyes in frustration. *Vague and secretive as ever.*

She checks over her shoulder and reaches into her inner pocket for the vial. "Don't touch it. We'll neutralize it right here."

Suddenly, something grabs my ankles, yanking so hard that I fall forward. I catch myself with my hands, crying out as pain shoots up my arms.

"Katie!" Natalie shouts, jumping to her feet.

The grass slides under me, icy and wet. I grab onto anything I can, trying to stop, coming away with fistfuls of mud. I kick to free my ankles, but they're bound together.

What's happening? What's dragging me?

An image of zombies rising in the graveyard flashes through my mind's eye before reason takes over. This must be related to the curse, or...

A deep bark reverberates through the tombstones, sending a shiver through my core.

The Madsens.

My heart jumps into action as it becomes clear we're in danger. How did they find us so quickly?

Paws thunder closer. I wince, bracing myself for Wyatt's jaws. But the dog leaps over me, darkening the sky, and continues barreling toward Natalie.

"No!" I cry, thrashing as panic closes around me. A thick root binds my ankles, dragging me further from her with every frantic beat of my heart.

Natalie sweeps her arm, and a patch of grass raises like a shield, a *rrrip* filling the air as it tears away from the dirt. The dog bursts through, jaws snapping.

She raises another shield, but again, it isn't enough—and a cold realization crashes over me. She can't pull up big chunks of earth to fend off the attack because we're in a graveyard. To pull up the earth would be to pull up corpses.

"Someone, help!" I shriek, kicking. We need the Shadows over here. *Now.*

Everything darkens as the root pulls me into the shade of a tree. It stops, and I get my hands under me and sit up, gulping down air. My palms and fingertips sting from grabbing at the ground.

"Hey, sweetheart," a low voice says.

A chill ripples through me. I lift my gaze to a pair of tight jeans, a black leather jacket, and a snow-white face with black makeup. Oaklyn's lips curve into a smile.

She's pulled me into a copse of four yew trees, their dense branches shielding us from the others.

"All this for a curse?" I ask, my voice rough.

She cocks an eyebrow, a flash of bewilderment crossing her face. Before she can respond—and before I can figure out what the hell that expression was about—branches groan. She sucks in a breath and flicks her dagger upward so the root releases my ankles.

Sky sprints toward us, a hand extended to manipulate the yew trees. The branches reach for us as fluidly as arms, the needles grabbing Oaklyn like thousands of fingers. I seize the chance to scramble to my feet. *Thank God.*

"Ow!" Oaklyn stumbles back and slashes her dagger like a whip, blocking the attack.

I back up, my legs shaking and my hands throbbing. Mud is smeared all down my front, the icy dampness seeping through my jeans.

Through the trees and back where I came from, furious barking fills the air. Natalie has formed a wall with gravel from a nearby path, forcing Wyatt back. And behind her... the cursed flowers are out in the open, a white beacon under the dark clouds.

Urgency constricts my chest. I have to get to the curse before Freddie does—wherever he is. Even if that means touching it.

I take a single step when an arm wraps around my neck, pulling me back.

"No, you don't," Oaklyn hisses in my ear, her other arm still fending off Sky's attack.

I roar in frustration, elbowing her and stomping on her foot. She grunts but holds on. Her arm is like a metal band across my throat, pressing against my airway as she pins me to her. I wheeze, my head clouding with panic.

Shouts break out nearby. Finally, more Shadows are here. Oaklyn spins us, and I try to stay standing, my feet clumsy.

Snap! The iron fence surrounding the graveyard groans, bending around the dog as if made of rubber. Hayley and two others control it, racing to Natalie's aid.

Neil, meanwhile, comes to help Sky. Oaklyn's arm tightens, her breaths labored as she fends them off.

A deep groan fills the world. With a jolt, the earth beneath our feet splits. It knocks Oaklyn off balance, and she stumbles. But the quake wasn't enough, and she drags me back with her.

A branch whips across my face, a sharp sting. I hiss. Warmth trickles down my cheek.

Oaklyn barks out a laugh. "Careful you don't damage your biggest asset."

"Neil, watch it!" Sky snaps.

"I'm trying to help!" he growls, slipping in the icy mud.

We're losing control. The Madsens are holding nothing back.

In a desperate bid for freedom, I kick hard, my heel glancing off Oaklyn's shin. She grunts, but her grip stays firm. Frustration writhes inside me.

"Get—the curse!" I choke out. "That's—the priority!"

Neil hesitates and checks over his shoulder toward the others, but Sky cries, "Like hell we're leaving you here!"

A sharp whistle pierces the air.

Shouts break out.

Wyatt has changed focus—he's coming for us, his paws leaving prints on the frosty grass.

"Shit," I whisper, writhing in Oaklyn's grasp.

She forces me backward, abandoning the copse of trees and taking me further from everyone else.

"Let go of me!" I roar. "You can't force me to find curses for you—"

Pain erupts in my ankle, and I scream. Wyatt clamps down, the agony of his jaws on tender bone paralyzing me.

"Good pupper," Oaklyn croons. She releases my neck, and I fall, landing hard on my back.

I cough, gulping down air.

Sky lunges, grabbing for the dog, but Oaklyn stops her with a massive root. It catches Sky in the chest, sending her flying back with the force of being hit by a car.

I try to shout after her, but no sound comes, my throat spasming. The dog is dragging me by the ankle, and struggling only makes his teeth sink deeper.

Neil, still in the trees, summons a chunk of grass to cushion Sky's fall.

"Katie, don't let them take you!" Natalie roars from somewhere past the trees—growing further away.

"Obviously!" I grit out. My eyes water as the dog tugs, pulling me by inches.

A wall of pebbles rises up from the nearest footpath, arcing toward Oaklyn like a tidal wave. She ducks and throws up her arms, blocking the brunt of it with a tangle of roots.

The dog tugs again, and incoherent sounds spill from my lips. The world spins around me, a blur of frosty grass and gray sky and tombstones. Nausea floods me.

"Here! Here!" Freddie roars from behind me.

Wyatt drags me in bursts like I'm prey he's captured. His breaths come in short *huff-huffs*.

Panic mixes with excruciating pain, drawing sharp gasps and cries from my throat. Where is he taking me? I try to kick him with my other foot, but it's impossible to be coordinated when pain lances through me with every tug.

My breaths escape in frantic whimpers. My limbs are moving of their own accord, trying to get free. Nothing else matters. The whole world is just the primal need to get away from this predator's jaws.

Cold realization floods me—I'm alone in this. Footsteps pound and shouts pierce the air, but nobody catches up.

Hands close around my upper arms, lifting me roughly to my feet. "Out!" Freddie shouts.

Wyatt lets go of my ankle, and a new stinging pain erupts—probably the punctures left behind.

The flash of relief is instantly smothered as Freddie tightens his hold. He releases one arm to gesture back to the fight. "Get 'em!"

"No!" I scream, fighting against his grip as the dog rockets away.

A cold, sharp point presses beneath my chin, and I gasp, freezing in place.

"Something a little less interesting than magic," Freddie says, "but effective enough. Follow me, and I'll be nice."

I don't move. If he wants me for my ability, he won't kill me. I'm no good to him if I'm dead. "I'd rather stay," I snarl.

The point digs deeper into my skin, and I bite my lip to keep from grunting in pain. I won't give him the satisfaction of knowing this hurts. Though with blood dripping down my cheek from the branch and a sickening warmth oozing around my ankle, my appearance probably speaks for itself.

Freddie hauls me backward, forcing me down a gravel path toward an exit at knifepoint.

My chest tightens with panic as the prospect of being abducted becomes real. What are they planning to do with me? Are they going to torture me until I agree to help them?

"Just get to Katie! Now!" Natalie roars from across the cemetery. Through rows of tombstones and scattered trees, she and the others bombard Oaklyn and Wyatt with chunks of earth, trying to reach me.

But we're losing. The iron fence is already at my shoulder, and something hits the back of my thighs. I fall, my elbows landing on hard rubber mats in the back of an SUV. It's positioned right outside the open gate, the rear door swung wide—ready for me. God, did they do this the second we parked?

The Shadows sprint toward us, Natalie in the lead. A rock fires at us like a bullet, rebounding off the vehicle with a *crack!*

The tiniest spark of hope flares inside me. If I can just fight Freddie off for long enough...

"Assholes." Freddie's hands close over my ankles, and I roar in pain as he shoves me in.

I kick him in the gut. "Let—me—go!"

Come on, stumble. Anything!

He grunts and steps back, then hisses as a second rock slams into him from behind.

My heart in my throat, I seize my chance and launch myself out—but he catches me around the waist, throwing me back in like a sack of potatoes. My head hits the back seat, and bright lights pop in my vision.

A rattling thump reverberates through my bones.

I sit up, disoriented in the sudden dimness.

He's slammed the rear door.

"No!" I kick the door and turn upright, shrieking in frustration.

Behind me, a grate separates the SUV's front and back seats. I'm trapped.

A choked sob escapes, panic closing my throat. This is the same FJ Cruiser Oaklyn tried to shove me into at UBC—and this time, Natalie is too far away to come to the rescue.

CHAPTER 27

The Method to the Madsens' Madness

THE TIRES SPIN AS Freddie stomps the gas pedal, and I grab the back seat to steady myself. The smell of wet dog and old rubber fills the back of the vehicle, nauseating.

"You think you can just force me to work for you?" I spit out. "What are you going to do, put me on a leash and take me out curse-hunting?"

"I'm not kidnapping you. I just want to talk." Through the grate, Freddie's blue eyes flick to me in the rearview mirror. His cheeks are rosy from the struggle, his breaths coming fast.

I let out a bitter laugh, feeling for a way to open the rear door from the inside. "Nothing says *friendly chat* like stuffing someone into the back of an SUV."

"I had to get you alone. Those freaks never let you out of their sight—shit!" A log slams into the passenger side, branches scraping the windows, and the vehicle wobbles.

A deep rumble fills the air, the road splitting beneath us. A bubble of hope inflates in me. Maybe they can still stop the car.

"Those witches don't know when to quit." Freddie accelerates, driving over the cracks and bumps, using the car's four-wheel drive to get through every obstacle the Shadows put in our way.

We skid around a corner into a residential area, and the car steadies. The ground has stopped shaking.

"God dammit!" I punch the wall in frustration. Why couldn't he be a terrible driver in a terrible car? The earthquake should've been enough to stop us.

There's a dent in the hard plastic where my fist hit the wall.

Wait, what?

I stare at the gauntlet on my wrist.

Another punch for good measure.

It dents the wall again.

I scowl. Why didn't Natalie tell me this thing gives me a good punch? Was this another of her secrets, trying to prevent me from knowing too much or having too much power?

"What the fuck are you doing?" Freddie cries, checking over his shoulder. He sees the damage and groans. "Oaklyn's going to kill me..."

Maybe I can smash the window and crawl through. I mean, I'll probably slice myself open in the process, and I'll break something when I fall from a moving car, and Freddie will just pull over and stuff me inside again...

I'm so screwed.

Sinking down, I dig into my jacket pockets, my hands numb from the cold and stinging from all the scrapes. An overwhelming wave of relief crashes over me as I close my fingers over my phone.

I can text Natalie.

Better yet...

Trembling, I unlock my phone and share my location with her. Then I put it on Do Not Disturb mode. I don't need a beep or a buzz to give away my only hope.

My heart pounds, desperation squeezing my chest. As long as Freddie doesn't come back here and throw my phone away, Natalie will be able to use my location to track us.

"What I find interesting," Freddie says, "is that you aren't stopping the car with your mind or chucking boulders in front of us. This tells me you can't do magic."

"Of course I can't do magic," I snap. Does he not remember how I needed Natalie to save me on New Year's?

I scan the trunk and the back seats. It's empty—rubber mats on the floors, nothing to use as a weapon. The grate is between the front and back seats, so there's nothing stopping me from crawling up to sit properly instead of on the floor... but I don't want to get any closer to this asshole than I have to, so I stay in the trunk.

Maybe I can smash the lock on the back door with this gauntlet next time we come to a stop.

Then what? Hobble away on a mangled ankle? my inner voice sneers.

"You mean to tell me you're working for them but they haven't told you the truth?" Freddie asks.

"They've told me plenty," I say defensively, though my *need-to-know* situation renders this frustratingly untrue.

We turn a sharp corner, and I brace a hand on the back of the seats, wincing at the pain in my palm. Damn, I got beat up. I don't even want to look at my ankle, which feels like it's on fire.

"Are you and Nat... you know... a thing?" Freddie asks. He lingers on me in the rearview mirror, stealing glances at my reactions.

I don't need the Madsens knowing about my personal life, so I scoff like the idea is ridiculous. "No."

I scowl out the window as if memorizing every turn will help me understand where he's taking me.

"So she hasn't explained *why* all these items are cursed?" His voice is calm and even.

I bristle. It was one of the first things I asked Natalie. Her response? *That's one question I can't answer.*

"The witches have told me everything I need to know," I say.

But that frustration lingers in the pit of my stomach. As much as I want to ignore Freddie, the answer hangs suspended in the air between us.

I tear my gaze from the rear door to meet his eyes in the mirror.

He shakes his head. "Katie, your buddies are the ones to put curses on items in the first place."

I scoff. "Is this your attempt at getting me to join your cause? The coven is trying to contain magic, not create more curses—"

"Listen. A curse is meant to deter someone, right? It makes a person want to get rid of the thing causing them harm." He's a confusing mix of hardness and softness, like his gentle tone might put me at ease if he hadn't just shoved me aboard the Kidnap Express.

"Uh-huh. So they're cursing bags of chips to stop anyone else from eating them?"

"They're cursing what's hiding underneath—the power fused to these objects." Freddie turns onto a quiet residential street, slowing down. His gaze darts from mirror to mirror as he checks whether we've been followed.

I furrow my brow, trying to grasp what he's saying. "Explain."

He pulls over in front of a blue ranch-style house. Cars are parked along the street, their windows frosted. On the opposite side, a woman in a knee-length parka walks her Golden Retriever and tows a kid in a wagon—life carrying on as normal.

"I want you to understand what's going on," Freddie says. He puts the car in park and turns around in the driver's seat to face me. "Witches curse objects to hide the real magic underneath."

I stare at him, my heart thudding. I didn't consider that curses are there to protect something, but it fits. The coven is trying to regulate magic, and what better way to stop someone from accessing it than by hiding it beneath a curse?

"What kind of magic?" I ask, skeptical.

"All of it."

When I keep staring in confusion, his thick eyebrows shoot up. "Wow, Nat hasn't told you anything, has she? Katie, witches are *made*, not born."

"That's not…" I trail off, my mouth dry. Did Natalie ever actually say she was born with magical abilities?

My pulse quickens. The urgent need to escape the vehicle fades, replaced by a burning desire to understand what Freddie brought me here to tell me.

I swallow, finding it harder to sound unconvinced as my voice trembles. "You're telling me every time I've laid hands on a cursed item, I've been holding the ability to become a witch?"

The purple gemstones flash through my mind's eye. Is that real magic appearing after a curse is neutralized?

Freddie nods, his mouth a thin line. His blue eyes are piercing against the drab, wintry sky. "They've been lying to you. They're making you do their dirty work without giving you the option to have the magic you're helping to destroy."

Doubts crash through my mind like waves in a storm. I feel small, pathetic, a tag-along on all these assignments. Is Freddie right? Have the witches ever thought of me as one of them, or am I just a workhorse?

"But why would they want to destroy magic?" I ask.

A car approaches, and Freddie snaps his gaze ahead. But it's just a red minivan. As it passes, he lets out a breath and continues. "It's in the name. The oath. The Coven of whatever for *Managing Magic*. Their whole goal and purpose is to stop anybody but themselves from using it. All that means is they're hoarding it."

"They're keeping the public safe," I say—but I'm spewing what they've told me. Do I really believe this? A knot forms in my stomach, twisting tighter with each word Freddie speaks.

"You agree with the oath, then? Do you think nobody, even yourself, should have the right to magic?" His voice is gentle, his cheeks rosy, his eyes bright, reminding me of when we met on New Year's. I thought he was nice before his intentions became clear. He's like a shapeshifter, one minute a terrifying criminal, and the next, this normal guy trying to explain his cause.

I grind my teeth, unsure how to respond. A pang shoots through my temples, like my brain is working too hard to try and sort through this information. How am I supposed to work for the coven when I don't know the full truth about what they stand for?

"You've been fighting against me and my family without understanding why," Freddie says. "We just believe the coven has had an unfair monopoly over magic for long enough. Don't you think anybody should be free to use magic? Yourself, even? This is about equality."

I don't know what to say. Yeah, I'd like to be a witch. I'd love to be able to move the earth the way Natalie can.

My brain feels like a wasp nest, and I suck in a breath, trying to calm my racing thoughts. Is the coven creating a class system by hoarding magic? Do they have the right to decide who can and can't access it?

A new kind of pain hits me, a betrayal so deep my chest aches. When I came to the witches with a skill they desperately needed, they could have granted me magic. Instead, they've kept me on the outskirts, dangling scraps of information while taking advantage of my ability.

My nails dig into my palms as the truth bubbles through me like lava.

Freddie opens his door and steps out. Through the window, he walks around to the back. He swings open the trunk door, and a blast of cold air hits me.

He stands there with his arms at his sides. I don't move.

"How do you access the magic once the curse is neutralized?" I lift my chin to look up at him, my voice trembling.

Freddie crosses his arms over his broad chest. "That's what we've been trying to answer for years. We can never do it before the curse's full power takes hold and…" He trails off, and I think of the lackeys Natalie mentioned. The people they send in to grab cursed items. Each one they acquire must be a race against time—a desperate quest to figure out what to do with it now that they have it.

"But you know how to neutralize a curse?" I ask.

"Those vials they always whip out?"

"Yeah." Between Natalie telling me nothing and the fact that the coven won't let me be on everyone else's level, rage simmers inside me, and bile creeps up my throat. "I don't know anything more than that. I'm lucky she even showed me Alchemy 13."

Freddie steps closer, his piercing eyes widening. "You have access?"

I shake my head. The exhaust from the running vehicle clouds the air, searing my nostrils.

"Where is Alchemy 13?" Freddie asks, an unsettling sharpness in his tone. There's his dark side again.

A pang of guilt cuts through my fury. I shouldn't have mentioned the room. I let anger take over and didn't consider who I was talking to.

But he can't get into C.S.A.M.M. anyway, so maybe it's fine.

"Was today all a setup?" I ask, deflecting. "You wanted to get me alone, so you brought me and Natalie to a curse in a graveyard, where she wouldn't be able to fight properly?"

His lips quirk into a smile—and there's his soft side. "Took a while for a curse to show up in one, but we got there in the end. Touché for bringing the whole SWAT team along. Didn't expect that."

"Well, you suck at being sneaky."

He chuckles, the lines in his forehead softening.

A pair of crows on a power line fill the silence. Too much information is swirling around in my head for me to really feel anything.

Freddie steps back, putting more space between us—as if to show me I'm free to step out of the car. "I just needed you to know we're on the same team. We deserve the magic the witches have been keeping from us."

I say nothing. We are definitely *not* on the same team.

But we aren't on opposite teams, either.

Dammit, why did Natalie have to keep secrets from me, while *Freddie Madsen*, of all people, is standing here telling me everything I wanted to know?

He extends a hand, offering to help me get out of the car. His palm is soft, worn, a couple of calluses and scars he no doubt acquired doing something shady.

I don't take it. I swing my feet over the edge of the trunk and hop out, avoiding putting weight on my injured ankle.

Freddie drops his hand, his lips twitching as if he's about to smile. He doesn't apologize for making his dog treat my leg like a chew toy.

We stand in the billowing exhaust, surrounded by a putrid haze that mirrors what's going on in my brain.

Freddie reaches into his coat pocket and takes out a white card. "I was serious when I said I have business cards, by the way." He holds it out cautiously as if trying not to startle me. After I take it, he puts his hands up in surrender. "Think about what you want."

The card is thin and discreet. Black ink, Times New Roman, with his name, number, and email. That's it.

"You've got your phone on you?" Freddie asks.

My heart jumps into my throat. I say nothing, unsure which answer would be in my favor.

"I'll take that as a yes," he says. "I assume the witches know where you are, which means they'll be here any second. I'm going to drive away now. I just ask that you consider what we talked about."

I nod, keeping my jaw clamped. I'm not making promises. As surprised and relieved as I am that he's letting me go... "This doesn't change that you're an asshole."

He winks.

As he gets back in the car, I cross my arms and shiver. If Natalie doesn't give me a valid explanation for everything Freddie told me, I'm going to have to decide what I really believe—and whether the Madsen family might have a point.

CHAPTER 28

The Strange Limits of Earth Magic

M Y WHOLE BODY ACHES as I let Natalie carry me into C.S.A.M .M. My ankle hurts more than my pride, so I surrender to her strong arms, my legs dangling and my head resting against her shoulder.

Before today, the thought of her bridal-carrying me would've been romantic and exciting. Now, all I feel is anger.

It's hard to give her eye contact after what Freddie told me, but she doesn't seem to notice. She's a storm cloud, intent on bringing me to safety.

"I'll take her to the medical wing," she tells the others, striding ahead.

"Go. We'll brief Fiona," Sky calls after us.

Natalie stomps down a corridor like a raging bull, and we descend into silence except for her rapid breaths and footsteps. With each swing of my leg, the throbbing, searing pain in my ankle flares.

The comfort of being in her arms battles with bubbling anger. Maybe it'd be better to wait until later to confront her about what Freddie said, but all the lies are eating away at me.

"How old were you when you became a witch?" I murmur.

Natalie's steps falter, but she says nothing.

"Freddie told me witches are made," I say, lifting my head and staring at the side of her face. "How old were you?"

Her fingers tighten over the back of my knees and around my arm as she adjusts her hold. "Our parents gave us magic when we were seven and ten."

I try to picture little Natalie being told she's about to become a witch—how exciting it must have been, and what sort of conversation her parents would've had with her. "Is that a common age for it to happen?"

"Give or take. Old enough to keep a secret, but young enough that you go along with it."

We arrive at a set of wooden double doors, and her fingers flutter on the back of my legs. The doors swing open on their own.

"What do you mean by *go along with it*?" I ask. "Would you have chosen otherwise, if you could go back in time?"

She meets my eye. "It's hard to imagine any other life."

"Hm. Why would you want to give up this power, right?" My tone is dripping with venom.

Natalie swallows, and her jaw tightens. She's finally picked up on my mood. "We'll continue this after."

She brings me inside, where the sterile, white infirmary is at odds with the rest of the building—the only part not covered in plants and wood. Antiseptic burns my nose rather than the usual warm scent of greenery. It fills me with unease, like it isn't right to have this sort of room here.

"Doctor Sharma?" Natalie calls as she sets me down on a hard, cold bed. "The Madsen dog bit Katie's ankle."

"Oh dear." Footsteps pad closer, and a woman in her fifties in a white lab coat tugs on a pair of gloves, wiggling her fingers. Carefully, she rolls up the blood-spattered hem of my jeans. "Ouch."

"Ouch," I repeat, bristling at the understatement.

Natalie drags a chair over. She takes my hand, which earns a glance from Doctor Sharma—and despite my anger over all the secrets and half-truths, my heart softens.

The bed is the first in a row of four. A white curtain is drawn around the one at the far end, but other than that, Doctor Sharma seems to be the only one in the room.

"You're in good hands," Natalie tells me. "Doctor Sharma has been our resident physician for nearly thirty years and has seen it all."

"Then you must know more details about everyone's life than any other person here," I say, lying back and covering my eyes with my arm. Between the bright lights and the shooting pains, it's possible I have a migraine coming on.

"Mm, the emergencies I've had to deal with would shock you." And with that mysterious statement, she gets to work examining and flushing out each tear and puncture—eight, to be exact. Two require stitches.

As she pokes and prods, a cold sweat breaks out across my whole body, even my toes. The room tilts until I have to take deep breaths and count the white bricks in the ceiling.

"Nothing looks broken," she finally murmurs, "just torn up. No need for a hospital transfer."

I don't know whether to celebrate this or not, so I say nothing. Natalie, however, lets out a breath, and her shoulders relax. She stays by my side, holding my hand with a firm grip despite all her warnings about secrecy.

"Why isn't magic being used to patch me up?" I ask, my voice hollow as I fight to stay conscious.

Natalie and Doctor Sharma exchange a look. Something transpires between them that I don't understand.

"Because earth magic controls earth, not people," Natalie says.

Her answer is simple, but that meaningful look wasn't. I scowl at the too-bright ceiling, biting the inside of my cheek.

By the time Doctor Sharma peels off her gloves and gets me antibiotics and painkillers, I'm swallowing down the urge to vomit.

"Take your time sitting up," she says. "No rush."

"Thanks." I rub my clammy forehead, still lying flat. "Do I need a rabies shot?"

She shakes her head. "Your bite isn't the first we've had from dear Wyatt, and we can confirm the Madsens keep their dog up-to-date with his vaccines."

"How responsible of them," I mumble, sarcasm dripping.

When she leaves us, I swing my legs over the edge of the bed and sit up, swaying.

Natalie reaches out as if to stop me from falling.

"I'm fine," I snap.

She sits back.

There's a pause while I frown at the mess that was once my ankle.

"Are you going to tell me what's going on?" she murmurs.

I scan the sterile room. Doctor Sharma has vanished beyond the curtain on the other side.

"When were you going to tell me that the coven puts curses on objects in the first place?" I ask, my heart pounding as I dive head-first into confrontation.

Natalie stiffens.

I stare cooly back, waiting.

She glances past me at the shut curtain, then stands. She opens her hand, and a crutch soars into her palm with a *thwap*. "We should get you back to your room."

I accept the crutch and hobble toward the doors. It's too tall, but before I can say so, Natalie twirls her fingers, and I jolt as it shrinks to my height and positions itself comfortably under my armpit.

Show-off.

The crutch makes a rhythmic *clunk* as I move down the hallway. It's a relief to leave the infirmary behind, the warm brick walls and hanging plants feeling more like home.

"What else did Freddie tell you?" Natalie asks, catching up easily. She hovers close as if ready to catch me if I stumble.

I set my gaze ahead and suppress a wince with each step. "That magic is stored in cursed objects. That you're all hoarding magic and controlling who can and can't access it."

She groans, which enrages me even more. *Yeah, Natalie, I've found out about the dirty secrets you've been keeping from me.*

I try to move faster, but it just makes me wobble, so we're forced to plod along to my room.

Natalie glances around and drops her voice. "Okay, look. Magic has a time limit within the body. A witch has to replenish every few years in order to continue wielding it. So, most of us store more magic in objects to make sure we don't run out when the time comes."

I squint at her. "Like a squirrel hoarding nuts for the winter?"

A grimace flickers across her face. "I guess so."

"Is this why there are random magical objects everywhere? They're caches that people have lost or forgotten about?"

Natalie stuffs her hands deep into her jacket pockets. "Or the person who created it passed away."

"And once you've stored magic, you curse the object to stop anyone else from accessing it."

She nods, avoiding my eye.

"So, my ability to sense curses..." I say, inviting her to complete the puzzle.

"Is likely an ability to sense the underlying magic," she says. "When the Alchemists ran that lab test, it was probably hard for you to pick the correct object because they only fused it with a basic curse, not magic as well."

I scoff. I *knew* the test was unfair. "Then to become a witch, a person just has to find one of these curses and—"

"And figure out how to neutralize the curse without dying, reduce the magic to its pure form, and consume it." Natalie takes her hands out of her pockets, her fists balled. "It's not *just*. It's dangerous and complicated."

We stop outside my room, and I glare at her. She glares back.

I let us in and limp to the bed, where I sit with a groan. Shooting pains erupt in my whole body, the drugs not yet taking effect.

Natalie paces my room, agitated. "We have an entire *team* dedicated to harnessing feral magic to prevent anyone from—"

"Feral magic?" I ask.

"Magic that flows freely in the world. Its natural state isn't to be contained in dolls and vulgar fog machines, believe it or not."

I narrow my eyes at the sarcasm but push past it, more interested in learning about this free-flowing magic. "What does feral magic look like?"

"It usually takes the form of a natural feature—a Joshua tree, a pool at the base of a waterfall, a coral reef. Magic can be harnessed from these sources." She hesitates. "This is what Trackers are searching for. When they find it, they capture it, then fuse it with a curse to protect it."

I huff. "Another lie."

She faces me. "What?"

"You told me your dad was traveling to find curses, but really, he's creating them. He's scouring the globe for feral magic and going through the complex process of trapping it so nobody else can use it."

"And now I'm telling you the truth."

Too late.

"And I *would* make a good Tracker," I add, though this is beside the point. "Do others have my ability too?"

She glares, then looks past me like she's trying to figure out a way to avoid answering. Finally, she sighs. "To an extent. But I've never seen an ability as strong as yours."

My chest inflates a little. *Ha.*

Still, she's not going to admit I'd make a good Tracker. She's as determined as ever to make sure I stay ordinary.

"Why do you have the right to decide who can and can't have magic?" I ask. "Why do you want to keep me from doing what you can do?" My voice breaks, betraying how much it hurts that she's been keeping all this from me.

She rubs her hands down her face, letting out a slow breath. "Katie, we're protecting magic to keep people safe. The Madsens believe even the most dangerous forms should be a universal right."

"But why are some people allowed to have it while others aren't?"

She stares at me. "I really hope you're not considering whether the Madsens have the right idea." There's a quiet desperation in her tone—a fear that Freddie might have gotten to me.

When I say nothing, she adds sharply, "Don't mistake their cause for a noble one. They just want the money and power that would come with being the distributors of magic. They could sell it to civilians, the government, anyone who offers a high price."

"And what about those of us who want to use it for good?"

She steps closer, anger twisting her features as she looks down at me on the bed. "Magic is dangerous, and it has to be regulated the same way weapons and drugs are. The Madsens claim they're fighting for a free world, but there's no freedom in the power imbalance that would come with it."

The silence rings, each of us refusing to bend.

"I get that magic is a weapon and has to be regulated," I say, trying for calmness. "I just hoped that..." I wave a hand, unsure how to finish the sentence in a way that isn't selfish or naive. What, did I hope I was special because of my ability? Do I want to be the exception to the rule because I'm Natalie's squeeze? I huff and change topics. "Have the Madsens ever managed to steal real magic? Or just Oaklyn's dagger?"

She lifts a shoulder. "To our knowledge, they're limited to the dagger. We have our suspicions about the dog, too."

"You think he has magical properties?"

"There's something abnormal about him."

A chill ripples through me at the memory of Wyatt's sharp gaze and chattering teeth. "Freddie already knew a vial is needed to neutralize a curse, but he didn't seem to know much beyond that."

Natalie freezes. Her face slackens, her eyes widening as if she's spotted a monster. "What did you tell him?"

Oh. Shit.

"Nothing," I say quickly.

"Then what did you mean by *beyond that*?"

I open and close my mouth as her shock melts into something more dangerous. Her eyes narrow and her nostrils flare.

"I—I only mentioned Alchemy 13," I say, hot shame returning. "That's it."

She throws her arms up. "Jesus Christ, Katie. What were you think-ing?"

I try to stand, hiss at the pain in my ankle, and point to her instead. "I was thinking about how fucking angry I am that you've spent all this time lying to me about who you are and what the coven stands for!"

"So you agree with the Madsens, then?" Her voice rises, ringing through the room. "You're ready to feed them information to help their cause?"

"That's not what happened!"

My eyes burn, fury bubbling up. I'm angry at Natalie, at the Madsens, and now I can add myself to the mix for carelessly throwing around those words about the vials. What if I compromised the coven?

Natalie runs a hand through her hair and paces, her tension palpable. "Katie, what you've seen so far is magic in its most benign form."

The statement takes a moment to sink in, oozing through the cracks this conversation is opening inside me.

Did she just call the ability to throw boulders at people *benign*?

"Earth magic isn't the only type of magic," she says. "There's another that's completely forbidden—and it could bring the world to its knees if the Madsens got it. *That's* what you don't understand. *That's* why our secrets are so important and what you don't seem to grasp when you're out there throwing information around to dangerous people."

This news hits so hard that I forget to be angry. Is this what everyone's so afraid of? Not earth magic, not anything I've seen, but a power so terrifying that nobody can even talk about it? "What kind of magic is it?"

She spits out a humorless laugh. "You think I'm going to tell you? Fuck, this was a mistake."

The sting of her words is worse than anything else, hitting me like a punch to the gut. "What was? Bringing me here?"

She says nothing, pacing.

There's a sensation like ice sliding down my back. She *can't* mean it. I wait for her to soften, to apologize for saying something so hurtful.

Instead, she steps closer, her expression stern and her voice low. "You took an oath of secrecy. Amazing, really, how quickly you broke it."

Gritting my teeth, I stand successfully this time, steady despite the pain. "Natalie, I am *not* spilling secrets to the Madsens, and the fact that you don't trust me is bullshit!"

"Well, you certainly told them something they didn't know before."

Hot, furious tears prickle in my eyes. My nails dig into my palms. All this anger and she doesn't even know how much I've been telling Hazel. Is this dumpster fire of secrecy and mistrust really what I signed up for when I swore my oath? How does anyone function here?

"Get out of my room," I growl.

Natalie stares at me.

I stay strong, lifting my chin. "You've lied to me, kept secrets from me, and now you're telling me you regret bringing me here."

Her shoulders drop. "Katie—"

"Out!" I roar. I want her to feel even a fraction of the pain she's causing me. "I don't want you here. I need to be by myself."

Seeing my expression, she backs up with her hands raised in surrender.

Dropping eye contact, she leaves my room, plunging me into a ringing silence.

CHAPTER 29

The Other Kind of Magic

"**D**ID YOU REALLY GET dragged through a graveyard by Wyatt Madsen yesterday?"

Two middle schoolers have stopped at my picnic table in the courtyard, summoning the bravery to talk to me after an obvious whispered debate by the koi pond. They look so much alike that they must be brother and sister, with deep brown skin, tight ringlets that reach the boy's shoulders and fall a few inches longer on the girl, and string-bean frames like they're in the midst of growth spurts.

"Yeah," I say, shifting uncomfortably. The crutch is leaning against the table and my leg is stretched across the bench, slight relief offered by elevating my ankle.

"*Wow,*" they say together.

Wait, is that awe? Heat rises in my face. I'm not used to being admired here. Or like, ever. "It was about as fun as it sounds."

My laptop and psychology textbook are open in front of me, the textbook soaked in coffee after I spilled it while trying to juggle my drink, crutch, and bag earlier. After a painful and restless sleep, it hasn't exactly been the best morning. Not to mention the hole burning in my brain over the *other magic* Natalie hinted at, which has fear prickling at the nape of my neck.

Seriously, what could be more powerful than earth magic? Should we be worried about the Madsens getting it?

I glance at my bag on the table, where Freddie Madsen's business card lays hidden.

I bet *he* knows about it.

"Did it hurt?" the boy asks.

His sister elbows him. "What do you think, turd? Getting mauled by a dog that weighs as much as she does?"

He looks down, ashamed. "Sorry."

I smile at their innocent interest. "It's fine. Yeah, it hurt like hell." I pull up my pant leg to show them the injury, and they both gasp. It looks just as bad as yesterday, if not worse with the Frankenstein sutures pulling the skin.

"What's it like being hunted by the Madsens?" the boy asks, which earns him another elbow.

"You can't just *ask* someone a thing like that." His sister rolls her eyes. "Sorry. He has no filter."

"But it's worth asking, don't you think?" he insists. "Nobody knows what powers they have, and the more we know, the more we can be prepared."

I furrow my brow. These kids have a healthy dose of fear for the Madsens. "Be prepared for what?"

They exchange a look.

"For if they ever get their hands on magic," the girl says seriously.

Unease coils within me. Should I be concerned that even these middle schoolers are afraid of what the Madsen family might do?

Nearby, an orange cat gazes into the koi pond, his tail swishing as he debates going in for the kill. I might as well be a fish swimming around in my safe little pond, oblivious as to what's beyond it.

"So, what did the Madsens do to you?" the boy presses, scanning me from head to toe as if searching for more injuries.

They wait with rapt attention, and if I'm not mistaken, the next picnic table of witches on a coffee break has gone quiet.

Apparently, all it took was getting attacked by the Madsen dog to get people to take an interest in me around here.

"I'm not sure yet if I'm allowed to talk about that." I offer a kind smile to cover up my wariness of sharing anything I'm not supposed to. Again. "But when I find out what I can share, you'll be the first to know."

This must satisfy them because they exchange a conspiratorial grin.

Though I'd bet my laptop that if Fiona wants to talk to me about yesterday, I'll end up even more disgruntled than I am now.

Sebastian's wife, Millie, walks past and comes to an abrupt stop, her eyes widening at my exposed ankle. "God, it's true. How are you feeling?"

"Doing okay. Thanks."

A couple of days ago, I was invisible to everyone here. Now, the sudden interest—but not for reasons I'd hoped. I'm more of a curiosity than a part of their community.

Dammit, here the coven is treating me like an outsider and a spectacle, while Freddie has given me all the information I ask for and an offer to join his team—his *family*. This is backwards.

Millie turns to the kids. "Shouldn't you two be studying? Don't make me tell your mom."

The kids look at each other and bolt.

Millie must be in her mid-twenties, but there's a heaviness about her—a gauntness in her cheeks and fine lines around her blue eyes. She frowns at my injury. "Doctor Sharma will have you back to normal in no time. She's good at her job."

"I guess everybody here must know her well by this point."

"Some of us more than others." Millie sighs. "She's supported me through chemo. I have to go up to the *real world* for treatment, but there's nothing like having a doctor living a few doors down from you."

My heart squeezes for her. "I'm sorry to hear. I hope your treatment is going well."

She smiles bravely. "Time will tell."

Guilt hits me for not knowing what was going on in Sebastian's life in all the times we've interacted. He hides his pain well.

Millie frowns at my ankle, something working behind her eyes. I feel it in her presence—suffering beyond anything I understand.

"Anyway, I wish you a speedy recovery," she says.

"Thanks."

I can't help recalling the glance Natalie and Doctor Sharma exchanged when I mentioned using magic to heal me. Worse than my injured ankle, it hurts knowing Millie's illness can't be fixed. Natalie wouldn't elaborate, but maybe someone else will.

"It's too bad magic can't be used for healing," I add.

Millie looks at me sharply, then averts her eyes to the koi pond. The look was fleeting, but it's too late to change that it happened.

There's something I don't know.

"Nobody's ever tried it?" I press.

Her gaze travels over my stuff sprawled across the picnic table. She hovers her palm over my psychology textbook, and slowly, the coffee-stained pages return to normal.

"Ah, thanks," I say.

She moves her hand over my ankle as if about to fix that too, but of course, nothing happens.

"It's criminal, really, that they let us suffer," she murmurs.

My heart beats faster. "There's a way to do it?"

Millie balls her hand into a fist, letting it drop. She looks over her shoulder, her gaze skating over the people who might be eavesdropping.

She smiles and squares her shoulders. "It was nice meeting you, Katie. Get well soon."

Before I can open my mouth, she walks away, leaving me with just as many questions—and ready to do something desperate to get them answered.

I glance at my bag, where that business card might as well be fighting like an animal trying to get out of a cage.

Hazel's warning about Natalie lingers in the back of my mind. "*I feel like there's still a lot you don't know about her.*"

There's a lot I don't know about any of this. But if I'm going to continue to risk my life to keep the world safe, to uphold my oath, I need somebody to tell me what I don't know. I have to understand what I'm fighting for, why it matters, and what I'm up against. That's *not* too much to ask.

Contacting Freddie is a dangerous move and a betrayal to the coven—and more importantly, to Natalie. But...

A lack of information is worse. This isn't just about solving a mystery or satisfying my curiosity. This is about understanding people—my guiding force. I've seen how understanding can make all the difference—it improved my relationships with my sisters and countless others in my life. I've never regretted having knowledge when the alternative is ignorance.

Now, the coven is keeping something important from me. What critical mistake am I going to make by not knowing? Who is going to suffer as a result?

There must be a reason Freddie Madsen is willing to kill to obtain magic. And I might be the only person in the coven close enough to him to ask why.

As the phone rings in my ear for a fourth time, my nerve is about to snap. I crumple the business card in my clammy palm and let out a shaky breath.

Sitting on my bed, it's hard not to remember all the time Natalie and I have spent here. Murmured conversations while sharing a pillow, grappling with feelings I've never had for anyone...

A pang of guilt shoots through my gut. This is a betrayal. I should hang up before—

A voice breaks through the silence. "Hello?"

My mouth goes dry. I don't know how I expected Freddie to answer the phone, but the ordinary greeting and his soft, pleasant tone are at odds with what I know about him.

Unable to sit still, I swing my good leg, my toes brushing the floor. "It's Katie."

A pause. "You don't know how happy I am to hear those words."

His voice is deep and close, tingling down my spine.

"Yeah, well, keep it in your pants. I just have a question."

He chuckles. "One question leads to another, and another—"

A dog barks in the background, and I wince.

"Wyatt wants to know how your ankle is doing," Freddie says.

I ignore the taunt, eager to get this conversation over with. "What do you know about the other type of magic? The kind nobody can talk about."

"Ah. So you've found out about it. Is this what finally tempts you over to me?"

"I wouldn't go that far." I chuck his business card on the floor for Ethel to play with, relishing the sight of her sinking her claws into it. Petty, but satisfying.

"What do I get in exchange for answering your question?" Freddie asks.

I hesitate. I'm not about to promise my allegiance, even if he tells me everything.

"I want one of those vials from Alchemy 13," he says.

"I don't have access." *And it's a lot more complicated than getting your hands on a vial, dumbass.*

"Then figure out how to get one some other way. Slip your hand into Nat's pocket while you two are making out and take one."

I grit my teeth, my cheeks burning. "Fine, I'll get you one," I say, having no intention of following through.

"Good." He grunts and lets out a breath as if sinking into a chair. "So, earth magic and alchemy are only two-thirds of the picture. You're talking about the third pillar—biological magic."

My pulse ticks up a notch as he puts a name to the secret. "What can it do?"

"Let's discuss it over dinner. Pick you up by the steam clock at six?"

Is he fucking with me? The audacity, after everything he's done.

I hum, pretending to consider. "Given what happened last time I saw you, I'd rather keep this over the phone."

He laughs again, his mood way too light for how much I hate his guts.

"What's biological magic?" I press.

"Something your buddies are even more obsessed with hiding than earth magic. *Nobody* is allowed to use it, not even your Directors."

He pauses. I wait, ears tingling, gaze unfocused as Ethel bats the crumpled business card across the floor in blissful oblivion.

Freddie lowers his voice. "Katie, this isn't just something that lets people pass through earth and make rocks jut up from the ground. This is magic in its most powerful form, and it's completely forbidden because the people in charge of the building you're in are cowards."

I tighten my grip on the phone, my palms clammy, listening hard. "Why is it so powerful?"

Another pause.

Ugh, he's enjoying this—holding me in suspense when I'm ready to beg for information.

I keep a firm lid on the bubbling guilt, unwilling to think about how Natalie would feel if she knew I was talking to Freddie. But what choice do I have?

"Imagine bending biology to your command," Freddie says.

"They can already control plants—"

"No. I mean sentient beings. People and animals, right down to the neurons in someone's brain."

I suck in a breath. "Like mind control?"

"Among other things. Shapeshifting, to name a fun one."

My pulse quickens as the potential rockets around in my head—mind controlling political opponents, amassing armies, shapeshifting to impersonate a leader...

I squeeze my eyes shut, my insides sinking as everything fits. He's talking about immense power so casually, as if it isn't a terrifying responsibility.

Suddenly, I understand why the witches don't want anybody to take hold of this.

"Is this what your family is really chasing?" I ask.

"All magic deserves to be wielded."

As I imagine the horrifying potential of controlling living creatures, something slides into place. He already has a weird level of control over an animal, doesn't he?

I snap my eyes open. "Is Wyatt some kind of biological magic?"

"To an extent." Freddie seems to search for the right words. "I can share thoughts with him, if that makes sense. Not to downplay my dog training abilities, which are spectacular, but Wyatt and I have a connection that can only be explained by magic."

"Is he stolen, then?"

"A gift from my mother. Rescued from a kill shelter, poor thing."

I'm not sure whether to believe that these assholes went out of their way to rescue an animal, but either way, he's just admitted that he's telepathically trained an attack dog. *Super.*

But I need the full picture. What was Millie getting at?

"This magic could be used for good too, right?" I ask. "Like, a doctor could zap cancer out of a patient."

"Exactly!" His tone is eager, like I'm finally understanding what he's been trying to tell me. "How can anyone justify keeping something locked away that could cure disease and stop wars?"

But my stomach churns, acid rising. This is the complexity, then. It's a cure for cancer, but it's also an unstoppable weapon. Would releasing it do more harm than good?

"Katie, the witches are giving you the wrong idea of magic. They want you to believe it's some wild, deadly force that needs to be tamed. But we know better. It's part of nature, and its ability to change the world has to be given a chance. *Everyone* deserves the opportunity to be extraordinary."

His words are seductive, and for a moment, I let myself imagine a world where I can wield the same power as Natalie. But the reality is too dark to ignore—if even one person were to misuse it, the results could be catastrophic. The potential for abuse is too much.

"Do you ever consider that witches must have locked up biological magic for a reason?" I ask, my voice steadier than the turbulence inside me.

"Their reason is flawed. They're forgetting how many people would use it to make the world a better place."

"But would they? You honestly think everybody would be responsible?"

I can feel his smile through the phone, the confidence of a man who believes with all his heart in the cause he's fighting for. "And that's the conversation worth having, isn't it?"

"I don't know if it is, Freddie." My pulse quickens, my words coming out shaky.

He sighs, his breath hitting the phone. "All this knowledge and you think the right thing is to bury it?"

I put a hand on my forehead, burning with a realization. Natalie is right. Magic is more dangerous than I thought. I just wish she'd told me everything instead of trying to make me believe her without giving me all the information.

I lie back on the bed, and Ethel takes the opportunity to hop up and lay on my chest. I stroke her back, searching for comfort in her familiar warmth.

Freddie poses a tempting offer—freeing magic that can cure disease and eradicate suffering if used properly. But does he honestly think this power would stay in the right hands? Even the noblest hearts are corruptible, and even the most well-intentioned people would be tempted to use it for selfish reasons.

"What would you do with it?" I ask Freddie.

"Ever lose a loved one, Katie? Ever get angry at modern medicine for just not being *quite* good enough?"

My stomach drops. "You're saying you could save someone?"

"We could save a lot of people. We could, theoretically, take the dementia right out of my grandma's brain."

I swallow hard, forcing down the hint of sympathy that's trying to surface. Whether that's true, and whether saving people motivates him more than power and money, it doesn't change everything else biological magic is capable of—all the dangers and potential harm.

Natalie and the others are working to protect the world from a power too great for anyone to hold, and the more the implications unravel before me, the more convinced I am of which side of this issue I land on.

"So you wouldn't be tempted to use it to rob a bank, or sway politics in your favor, or... make someone fall in love with you?" I ask.

"Oh, Katie," he says as if he's rolling his eyes. "The coven's been wasting all this power. Think about the weapons and armies we could create to maintain peace, or how easy it would be for law enforcement to just use their minds to stop criminals. We'll be creating a better, freer world."

I shake my head, my heart beating faster. "Weapons? Armies? Cops who can do mind control? Freddie, that isn't freedom."

"You're determined not to get it, aren't you?" he snaps. Then he huffs, pausing as if to regain his composure. "Listen, Katie, I shouldn't be telling you this, but you need to know what you're leaving on the table. We're close to being able to set magic free. A plan is in motion, and change is coming whether you're with us or not. This is the last time I'm going to offer you an alliance. Will you join me in fighting for equal rights to magic? Please?"

I freeze, an icy chill rippling through me. "A plan?"

"That's not an answer."

I sit up, sending an irritated Ethel rolling onto my lap. Whatever he's planning, it can't be good. "What are you going to do, Freddie?"

He chuckles, and the sound is colder this time. "You'll find out if you give me the right answer."

My breath quickens. Should I say yes so I can go into the Madsen family as a spy? Or would that be walking into danger?

No. Natalie's warnings finally make sense, and I have to help the coven protect the world.

"Where have you been getting your information?" I ask. I know what he'll say, but I have to try. "You always swoop in just in time for a curse."

"I'd love to share, but I'm sworn to secrecy."

"Who isn't?" I mumble.

"Welcome to the world of magic. So, what'll it be?"

I grit my teeth, ready for what comes next. "I'll die before helping you track down magic, Freddie. And that's my final decision."

"Mm. Too bad." His voice is hard, cold, like the version of him that emerges when he's about to set his dog on me.

A chill races through me, and I lay my palm flat on the bed to anchor myself.

I'm safe. I'm in C.S.A.M.M. He can't hurt me.

"Then consider my offer off the table," he murmurs. "I guess we'll be seeing you again real soon. It's just a shame it'll have to be under these circumstances."

He ends the call, leaving me in a ringing silence.

I'm on my feet and out my bedroom door before I can catch my breath.

CHAPTER 30

Define "Coercion"

A FTER A FRANTIC BUT laborious hobble through C.S.A.M.M., I find someone worth telling.

I tumble through the gym door, out of breath. "Sky!"

She's facing a mirror doing kettlebell swings, wearing a black sports bra and biking shorts, frowning in concentration. Floor-to-ceiling windows look out on the courtyard and let in daylight, and as promised, half the room is empty for combat practice. Big foam blocks are scattered across the floor like it's a kids' gym—probably for hurling at each other. The faint scent of old sweat wafts under my nostrils.

She puts down the weight with a grunt. "Hey, sunshine. How're you feeling?"

"Fine." I scan the room to make sure we're alone. "I—I just remembered something Freddie told me yesterday when he stuffed me in the car."

Sky's eyebrows shoot up.

"He said a plan is in motion to set magic free. He wanted me to join him in a fight for the right to magic."

Sky stares at me, her face slack. "He told you this when he captured you?"

I nod, wincing as I catch my balance on my good leg. The physical difference between the two of us right now is a painful reminder of how vulnerable I am.

"And you're just remembering it now?" she asks.

I nod again, unable to meet her eye. "I haven't been able to think clearly since it happened."

Guilt simmers as I feed her the lie, but no way am I admitting I willingly got on the phone with a Madsen.

"Right. Of course." Her gaze darts across the floor as she absorbs the warning. "Thank you for telling me, Katie."

When she doesn't elaborate, I press. "What does it mean?"

She picks up the kettlebell again and sinks into a half-squat. "I'm not sure. I'll talk to Fiona."

She does ten reps then puts it down and walks in a circle, panting. Beads of sweat roll down her face and chest, dampening her sports bra.

"Could the Madsens be about to do something serious to try and acquire magic? Are we in danger?"

Sky doesn't meet my eye, stretching her quads. "Tough to say."

My God, the oath has everyone here by the balls. How can anything get done if we're not allowed to discuss it?

I steel myself, nerves jittering. "Can I ask you a question, then? About the history of the coven?"

She stops stretching and puts her hands on her hips, breathing hard, a bit of apprehension on her face. "Sure."

"When did witches decide to start controlling magic?"

She doesn't answer right away. A fan whirrs overhead, blowing cool air over me that raises the hairs on my arms.

Sky crosses to a bench and grabs her water bottle. She takes a big gulp and towels her face and neck. "The laws were put into place in the early

1900s. It'd become clear that some witches were using magic in dark ways, even trying to change the course of history in World War I."

Unease trickles down my back. Biological magic must have been involved—mind control, telepathy, shapeshifting.

She kicks one of the foam blocks as if needing something to do with her feet. "An early version of C.S.A.M.M. was formed to make sure magic could only be possessed by a select few. The first iteration didn't go well."

"I'm guessing only the rich and powerful were allowed to use it?" I venture.

"Exactly. Plus, it hinged on the idea that those people would use magic purely for good."

I chew my lip. It's the same conclusion I drew while talking to Freddie. "Like for every person using it to cure disease, there was another amassing an army or mind-controlling the government?"

Her water bottle slips from her hand and spills all over the rubber-matted floor. She swears and drops her towel onto it to mop it up. "Where did you hear about that?"

I bend to pick up the empty bottle and pass it to her. "I've overheard things in my time here."

"You don't just *overhear* information like that. People don't talk freely about..." She mouths the words "bio magic" as if afraid of eavesdroppers.

I lift a shoulder. "Sometimes people forget I'm there."

Good lord, I'm a bad liar.

She looks at me sideways, definitely unconvinced. "Well, the conflict escalated into a civil war—those in favor of regulation versus those against. You know who won. A new C.S.A.M.M. was founded, and the witches in charge opted to lock away all of *that type* of magic. They decided nobody is allowed to use it, ever, no matter what."

A chill ripples over me at the thought of a war among witches—the blood that must have been shed. "And earth magic? Alchemy?"

"Strictly regulated and kept a secret, as you know." She carries her wet towel to a hamper and drops it in, pausing before turning to face me again. "We haven't seen a serious abuse of magic since 1928. Stuff happens, yeah, or else I'd be out of work. But nothing as horrifying as back then."

I nod. Freddie would probably tell me 1928 was the year magic died, but Sky's haunted expression tells me the other side.

"What happened to the people who lost the civil war?" I ask. "The ones who wanted to keep magic free."

Sky kicks the foam blocks scattered around into a pile. "Killed, imprisoned, silenced. If anyone still believes in free magic, they're quiet about it."

Millie comes to mind, the way she looked at my wounded ankle and seemed to wish with every fiber of her being that her illness could be cured by magic. I can't blame her. Who wouldn't want the same?

"I'd bet money," Sky murmurs, barely audible, "that at one time or another, every witch has entertained the idea of trying to find bio magic and consume it in secret. But that doesn't mean it's right. And you'd be better off not talking to anybody else about this."

Guilt writhes inside me. "I won't."

She studies me for so long that my face heats up, and I pretend to be interested in what the people in the courtyard are doing.

She definitely doesn't believe that I happened upon this information while walking around C.S.A.M.M. But she also has no way of knowing I called Freddie.

"Thanks for explaining things to me," I say.

Sky nods, not meeting my eye.

As I back away, she extends a palm toward a green foam block. It lifts into the air, and she brings her arm back like a baseball pitcher. With a grunt, she throws, and the block whizzes across the room in a blink. It slams into a red X on the opposite wall with a *thwap* that makes my ears ring.

What a long way magic has come—from being a weapon of war to this controlled exercise in a gym. The coven has done a thorough job.

But the bloody memory of war hovers thickly throughout this building, guiding the actions of everyone in it... and I can't help wondering if history is doomed to repeat itself.

My stomach churns as I leave my room in the morning, heading toward the courtyard to study. More likely, I'm about to stare blankly at my textbook while my mind races and my knee bounces.

How many witches believe the coven is doing the right thing by locking up biological magic? How many have tried to take some for themselves—or at least considered it? And *what* was Freddie on about when he said a plan was in motion?

My thoughts are such a whirlwind as I round a corner that I nearly smack into someone. I let out a little scream and jump back.

Natalie stands there like a wall, scowling down at me. "Who told you about bio magic?"

I hug my laptop to my chest like it's a shield.

Shit. Sky must have mentioned I was asking questions.

A little spark of anger ignites, then fizzles and dies. It isn't like I asked her not to tell Natalie about our conversation.

"What do you care?" I snap, a little sharper than intended.

She looks down at me, fury twisting her beautiful features. She opens her palm to reveal a crumpled piece of paper.

I stare at it for a second before it dawns on me. Freddie's business card.

The brick walls on either side of us seem to close in, suffocating.

"You're damn lucky Elizabeth likes me," Natalie growls. "She found this while cleaning your room and decided to bring it to me instead of straight to Fiona."

My blood runs cold. "It's—it's not what you—"

Natalie steps closer, closing her fist around the card. "I'm going to ask you plainly, and I need you to be honest. Are you in contact with Freddie Madsen?"

"Wh-what do you mean, *in contact with*? I'm not a spy or some..." I wave a hand, searching for the right word. "Turncoat."

"Katie, if you're withholding critical information about the Madsens' whereabouts, do you realize how serious this is? You could face a trial by jury. You could be imprisoned."

My chest constricts at the harsh warning. I splutter. "It's not like that!"

Natalie takes another step in, and my back hits the brick wall.

"What's it like, then?" she growls. "Why do you have his contact info?"

Footsteps approach, and I turn, my hair getting caught in a fern on the wall. Amir, the Director, walks by.

I bat away the fern and wait until he's out of earshot before continuing in a low voice. "I did talk to Freddie. But it was only once, and it was only because I had no idea what was going on or what sort of danger any of us were in!"

Natalie rubs her face, walking in a little agitated circle. "Jesus. Sometimes you need to let a subject drop! There are things you can't know about."

My fingers tremble as I clutch the laptop to my chest. "You just want me to shut up and be a lamb? Go along on assignments without understanding what I'm actually doing?"

"This isn't only about following rules, and you know it." Her nostrils flare as she struggles to control her anger. "I want you to stay safe, and I want both of us to keep our oath so we don't get in shit!"

"The *oath*," I spit. "I thought you were letting me be a part of something by bringing me into the coven, but Freddie was right. You're making me do your dirty work while keeping me on the outskirts."

Her eyes widen a fraction. "You *wanted* to help!"

"And I thought you'd at least tell me what I'm helping to do. You know, I found out while talking to Freddie that they're planning something—"

"Yeah, we're on it. That doesn't make what you did right." Natalie's brow pinches as she looks past me. She can't even meet my eye.

Beneath my white-hot anger, guilt acts as kindling, bringing the flame to life. Fine, I shouldn't have talked to Freddie, and I definitely shouldn't have mentioned Alchemy 13 to him. In trying to gather all the information, I broke my oath—and I broke Natalie's trust. But it's hard to feel the full force of regret when I finally understand what I've sworn to protect.

"Natalie, I need to know what I'm doing when I'm running around finding curses." I almost reach for her but stop myself, afraid she'll pull back. Afraid of what this fight means. "I deserve to know what sort of magic I'm helping to regulate and what dangers are involved. If I'm going to work for C.S.A.M.M., I have to know what this place stands for."

She stares at me, expressionless. "And do you agree with what we stand for?"

I open my mouth to respond—but I need to understand something before I answer. I stand by what I told Freddie, about how I'd sooner die than help him, but one thing isn't sitting right.

"Would biological magic have saved your mom?" I ask quietly.

Natalie blinks, sucking back a little as if I took a swing at her. Then she regains her composure, and her face settles into a neutral mask. "Yes. It probably would have."

Another hitch in this fucked-up dilemma.

If a family member was about to die, I'd do everything in my power to save them, including breaking the law. If someone I knew had cancer and biological magic was the cure, I'd scour the earth until I found it.

"If saving one person means a million others suffer, what's the right answer?" Natalie asks.

My eyes burn. It's an impossible decision. How do you weigh lives against each other like that? "I... don't know," I say, the words barely coming out.

This is hurting my brain. What's the solution when a force can be used for both incredible good and pure evil?

Natalie steps closer, a breath away. I lean back, trapped between her and the cool brick wall.

"So don't judge me or my family for making a certain choice," she growls, her voice low and firm. "This is *not* a black-and-white issue."

I nod. A chasm seems to open between us—a breach in trust that might never be mended. Her eyes are cold, her posture tense, and any comfort I usually feel in her presence has dissolved.

Heels click, and we both turn. I have to lean away from the wall to see around the fern.

"Well, well." Fiona walks toward us down the corridor, her eyes narrowing.

Natalie steps back, leaving a draft, and it hits me how close we were standing... How this must look...

"Uh-huh," Fiona says as if unsurprised. There's a dangerous glint in her eyes, a curl in her lip. "Seeing as you're both here, this will make the conversation a little easier."

Natalie catches my eye for a fleeting second, a flash of uncertainty that sends a chill down to my toes. The air in the corridor feels thick and murky.

"It's been brought to my attention that the two of you seem to be involved," Fiona says, a slight tremor in her voice, like she's barely suppressing her anger.

A thousand outbursts rise in my head. Who told her? Why do they care? Is this really the first thing she's going to say to me after I nearly got my foot chewed off while fighting for C.S.A.M.M.'s cause?

"After *everything* you were warned about," Fiona snarls. "After your *oaths*! The fact that you're still willing to put confidential information at risk—"

"I haven't told Katie anything beyond what she's supposed to know," Natalie says. She meets my eye, the accusation hanging in the air. *But she's managed to find out anyway.*

My face heats up as I recall my induction ceremony—Fiona warning me not to try and coerce information out of anyone. Natalie has upheld their secrecy on her end, but I definitely have not followed the rules.

Fiona nods, seeming satisfied with Natalie's assurance, then turns to me with a narrowed gaze. "For both your sakes, you'd better be staying in your own lane. If you're prying into things beyond your station, suspension is the least of your worries."

I dip my chin, the word *suspension* hitting me like a punch. "Of—of course."

She smooths her blazer, her nostrils flaring. "We'll have to bring your situation to the board to evaluate whether further action is—"

"That won't be necessary," Natalie says.

My stomach plummets. It keeps falling, sinking right through the floor and into oblivion.

Fiona raises an eyebrow. "And why not?"

Natalie shoves her hands into her pockets, not meeting my eye. "Katie and I were just discussing how it's best for everyone if this stops now."

Her words carry through the empty corridor. The sense that multiple things are coming to an end looms over me like a storm cloud—a relationship, a partnership, any trust I've built with people in my short time here.

All because I was desperate for answers.

"I see. Katie, can you confirm?" Fiona's gaze burns the side of my face, but I can't bring myself to meet her eyes.

Numb, I set my jaw and nod, trying desperately not to convey how much pain is lancing through me with each beat of my heart. My mouth is dry, my next words tasting like ash. "Yes. Whatever was going on is over anyway."

CHAPTER 31

Cookies for Heartbreak

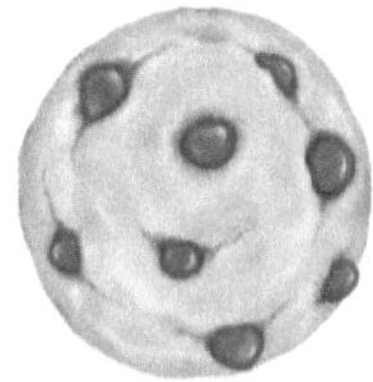

Our relationship will not be brought to the Directors. We will not have to sign anything or be put on trial or face a punishment—because there is no relationship. It's over.

Natalie walks away with forgiveness, and why wouldn't she? Everyone likes her here. She's been part of the coven since she was a kid, and she's never had to fight to prove her loyalty.

As for me?

I'm alone in my room in a ringing silence, pacing as I process this abrupt end. After a last, cold stare, Natalie and Fiona left me in the corridor, my chest so tight I thought I would suffocate, my eyes stinging until the hallway became a blur.

I can't stay here anymore. I don't know what I'm fighting for, and I don't know what I'm fighting *against*. I'm just a pawn in a game I barely understand. Is locking up bio magic really the right answer when it could stop so much suffering? Would setting it free just mean trading one type of suffering for another? I'm not the person to solve this problem. I just want to go back to normal life and normal decisions—away from magic and oaths.

Natalie has chosen her coven over me, and I can't blame her. I don't want her to sacrifice everything she's worked her life for, so it's better if I go. It'll be easier to get over each other if we aren't living in the same building.

So, that evening, I take one last look around the cozy suite that has been my home these past weeks. I touch the bonsai tree beside the bed, its soft leaves tickling my fingers, already missing it.

I place Ethel into her kennel and extend the handle of my suitcase, which is crammed with my ever-dwindling belongings. I'm only making one trip, so I'll have to leave half my stuff behind. At this rate, a few more moves and I'll have nothing left but Ethel and my laptop.

Inhaling the room's earthy scent one last time, I back up through the door and into the corridor. I use my suitcase as a crutch, limping heavily on my bad ankle. The rolling wheels and my uneven footsteps reverberate off the brick walls, a hum that fills my chest until it's ready to burst.

If the people in the lounge see me and wonder where I'm going, they don't stop me to ask. Maybe they'll come for me when they find out I've left, or maybe not. My oath didn't say I'm trapped for life. And they sure as hell don't care enough to fight to keep me here.

Passing the Library wing, that familiar sensation of nearby magic tugs at me, a hook sinking into my core and pulling me toward it. This place is a cavern of secrets—worse than an Egyptian tomb, worse than a haunted mansion, worse than a treasure chest that's been bolted shut, thrown into the ocean, and guarded by sharks. I'm not meant to know why that particular corridor beckons me to follow its winding halls so badly, and I have to accept that.

I keep going to the exit, where I stare up at the underside of the steam clock, its inner workings churning away—my first view when Natalie brought me into this world. I don't know how I'll get out without being escorted, but surely someone will pass by eventually and can bring me with them.

I wait, bitterness rising as I stand here, helpless to do so much as leave the building without magic. Like a cat needing someone with thumbs to open its crate.

Soon, quick footsteps approach, and I stiffen.

The two middle schoolers who talked to me in the courtyard come racing down the hallway, their smiles fading when they see me standing there like a runaway.

"Heading up?" I ask them.

The boy nods. "Going ice skating. Are—are you leaving?"

"I'd like to." I shift my weight, wincing. "Can you bring me out with you?"

"Where are you going?" the girl asks.

"Home. I'm not cut out for this place."

Her big eyes widen. "But the Madsens—"

"Are finished with me," I say. I made my stance clear to Freddie, and he made it clear that he's done asking me to join him.

Voices hum around the corner, and my heart jumps. I don't want to face anyone else right now.

"Come on." I wave the kids over, positioning myself beneath the clock.

They exchange a look, then nod, moving to stand on either side of me.

I let out a breath of relief, grateful I don't have to endure a confrontation.

The hall blurs, my ears popping, and they lift me into the chilly wind of an ordinary Vancouver evening. As their hands fall away, I stumble for balance on the cobblestones, the harsh street lights replacing the warm glow of C.S.A.M.M.'s halls.

There's no sign of the world I'm leaving, only the clock billowing steam into the inky sky. It begins to play a familiar tune—the Westminster Chime melody, its long, haunting whistles signaling eight o'clock.

I square my shoulders and tighten my grip on the kennel and suitcase.

Time to find out where I belong in this city... and leave the coven behind forever.

For the next two weeks, I go to class and occupy my rented suite like I was meant to do all along. I ignore Natalie's calls and instead text her to tell her I'm fine, and eventually, she stops checking. I sink back into my old life, the gutter runoff pattering on the walkway outside the window, my diffuser working to mask the musty smell, and my stack of textbooks on quick rotation on my desk as midterms approach.

But even with Ethel's company, the lifeless basement is colder and lonelier than I remember. This place isn't home—it never was.

Sitting in my lectures, surrounded by unfamiliar faces, I feel like a stranger in my own life. Despite my efforts to balance everything, I'm behind in coursework, which feels dull compared to the world of magic and curses. Any connections I made last term have withered, and I haven't talked to Hazel in weeks.

Lying awake each night, wishing for Natalie's warmth beside me, I've never felt more alone. I'd be happier if I never met Natalie or found out about witches... Or if I never moved away from home in the first place.

The Wednesday before reading week, as I'm studying at my desk with Ethel on my lap, my phone beeps with a text.

I blink at it. It's the group chat with Clayton and the others living on campus.

My heart lifts with the first glimmer of hope in a while. I assumed they'd given up on me. But maybe I'm still part of the group, even if I don't feel like it.

I hesitate. What will they think if I suddenly talk to them again after being silent for the entire month since New Year's?

Well, nothing to lose.

I stare at the chat, holding my breath for their response.

Shame fizzes in my gut. Yup, I ghosted.

I re-read the words, not believing them. A warm wave of relief hits me, and my heart thaws a little. Maybe I was too dismissive of my friendship with these people—and maybe making friends in university is easier than I thought, just like Hazel said.

As the texts fly back and forth with evening plans, I rub my forehead and let out a breath of resignation. It's time to move on—from both Natalie and the coven. I have a degree to earn and friendships to repair, and it's not too late to reclaim the normal university life I should've had.

Bolstered, I grab my laptop and video call Hazel.

She answers from her laptop, her messy bedroom behind her and a tired look on her face. "Hey, bestie."

The tension in my head eases at the sight of her. "Been a while. Surviving?"

"Yeah. Sorry. I've been..." Her voice is thick. Her face is blotchy, her eyes puffy.

Wait, is she crying?

My heart plummets. "What happened?"

She blinks a lot, making a pitiful attempt at a brave face. It crumbles instantly. "Sean and I broke up."

I gasp and grab my screen with both hands as if to reach through it and hug her. "No!"

"He said he wanted to focus on school and didn't have time for a relationship. I sh-should've n-noticed the signs..." Hazel waves a hand, drawing a shaky breath. "He obviously didn't f-feel the same w-way about..." She puts her elbows on her desk and her palms on her face, and her shoulders shake as she dissolves into tears.

My heart bursts, all the little pieces sinking like stones. I clutch the collar of my sweater as the news smothers my own problems. "Oh my God. I'm so sorry. I wish I could be there to hug you right now."

"Thanks." She rubs both hands down her face, her breath hitching. "I could picture our whole future. I know that's ridiculous when we weren't even together long... but you know me... I fall hard..."

"It's not ridiculous," I say gently. "Falling hard is a beautiful thing, and you're meant to be with someone who reciprocates."

She nods, her face twisting as she fights back tears. She grabs a tissue and aggressively wipes her eyes. "Men suck. Tell me you and Natalie are still happy and there's joy in the world."

I grimace. "Actually..."

She gasps, dropping her hands and sitting taller. "No!"

"I... sort of went behind her back for information. She's really mad at me—and I'm not sure how I feel, to be honest."

Hazel sits back in her chair, her tears stopping. "What information?"

I hesitate. "I needed to know more about what they were having me do. With the curses and all. I... don't regret finding out the details."

Her shoulders slump. "It sucks you had to go around Natalie."

"Yeah." My eyes prickle and a lump rises in my throat. I blink, forcing the tears to stay down.

We stare at each other through the video call, two heartbroken, teary-eyed girls, and homesickness wells inside me worse than ever.

"Man, this would be a really good weekend for cookies and binge-watching," I say with an attempted laugh. But it comes out hollow. It stings that we can't spend time together when we both desperately need it.

"I know." Hazel sighs. "What are you going to do during reading week?"

Ugh, that's next week already. And I'm going to spend it totally alone. I shrug.

Hazel chews her lip, then grabs her mouse, her eyes narrowing in determination. "I'm booking a flight."

"What? Where?"

She laughs. "To you, dork. I'll come for reading week."

My heart jumps. "You don't have to! I can come there."

"No, I want to come to Vancouver. It'll be fun. I loved visiting over Christmas, and you can show me the stuff we missed out on during the last visit."

Lightness tingles through my head at the prospect of not spending the break alone. I can't think of a better way to pass the time than with my bestie, getting over our breakups together, and laughing and being ridiculous like normal.

"That would be really, really nice," I admit, and the tension in my face eases as I smile for the first time in two weeks.

As reading week begins, I bus to the airport to meet Hazel, my heart lighter in anticipation of seeing her. This week will be a much-needed reminder of who I was before all this business about curses and witches—a reminder that I have people who accept me as I am, who don't need me to prove myself as a prerequisite. And really, there's nothing like a big dose of unconditional love to help a girl get over a breakup.

As Hazel bounds toward me in Arrivals, we crash together in a jumping hug. The familiar scent of her shampoo hits me, and for a moment, I feel like I'm back home.

"I know just where to go to get cookies the size of our faces," I announce, grabbing her carry-on bag.

We get cookies, visit Chinatown to keep eating, then hit up a craft brewery—a perfect, normal evening with my perfectly normal best friend. The next morning, we continue the tour, first heading to the Harbour Centre to ride the glass elevator and look over the city. I'm lighter than I've been in weeks—and while my ankle is still mangled and

I'm generous with the painkillers, I no longer need a crutch, freeing us to walk unimpeded.

"Damn, look at that view," Hazel says, pulling out her phone. It's sunny for once, the world around us bright and blue. She raises her phone—and pauses, squinting at a message she's received. She reads it, her lips parting, and turns to me with a gleam in her eyes. "I've got good news."

"What?!" I cry so dramatically that the nearest people turn. I cover my mouth.

Hazel looks ready to burst, a smile lifting her cheeks. "I accepted a co-op job offer with a renewable energy company."

I gasp. "Yes! That's amazing!"

"And," she says with the air of someone about to drop a bombshell. "It's in Vancouver."

My jaw unhinges. "Like... you'll be moving here for four months?"

She nods, grinning.

I scream and throw my arms around her. "Oh my God! Why didn't you tell me sooner?"

She waves her phone. "I wanted to wait until it was confirmed."

I scream some more and wrestle her into a tighter hug, earning more stares.

She laughs and hugs me back. "I'm nervous. It was brave of you, moving away from home. You'll have to show me how to survive here."

I scoff. "You'll be the one showing me! You fit in everywhere. I've done a terrible job adjusting and haven't stopped being homesick."

Hazel tilts her head, studying me. "Katie, you've adjusted fine. You've made friends, you know where to go for the best food, you have a favorite grocery store, a walking loop, a hairdresser... Stop denying it. You've sprouted roots."

I stare at her, the bright Vancouver metropolis sprawling around us. I've been resisting calling this city home, thinking of it as a temporary arrangement while I finish school. But in the six months I've lived here, it *has* become home. I've gotten to know bits and pieces of it—the Granville Island market, the historic town of Fort Langley, the best places for food and drink, thrift stores, pet shops... the Gastown steam clock. I've grown and changed here, made memories here, and all with people I recently met. *Friends*, if I dare to use the word.

A wave of something unexpected washes over me. It's not just relief, but a rightness I haven't felt since leaving Toronto. The future I'd pictured, the one that always had me returning home after graduation, suddenly feels blurry and uncertain. What if that's not the only option? What if the community I've been starving for is right here, waiting for me to settle into it?

I smile. "Moving away isn't so bad. Plus, we'll have each other."

We head back to my place to make lunch, planning where we'll live and how to decorate our home when she moves here. Obviously, we'll have to be roommates.

As we pass through the gate and around the side of the house, my ankle throbs with every step, begging for more painkillers. I let Hazel go ahead so she doesn't see me limping. I might've been overly ambitious with the amount of walking today.

She reaches the back porch and calls out to me. "You've got a package."

I furrow my brow. "I didn't order anything. Is it for my roommate?"

"It's got your name—and there's a note!" Excitement floods her tone, and she gasps. "Katie, is it from Natalie?"

My heart leaps, a surge of hope catching me off guard. I tamp it down and hobble to catch up, needing to see for myself.

"*See you soon, sweetheart,*" Hazel reads, squatting down in front of a paper shopping bag. "Aww!"

Cold prickling spreads across my skin. The words, the tone... It's off. Natalie has never called me *sweetheart*. In fact, the last time someone called me that was...

My ankle throbs, pulsating, heat licking up my leg. Then, as quickly as it came, the pain gives way to a different sensation—a tug inside me, a desire to step closer to whatever is in the bag.

"Look!" Hazel exclaims, pulling the gift out to show me.

It's a plush dog. A German Shepherd.

Its glassy eyes stare blankly at the sky, its fur engulfing Hazel's small fingers.

She turns it, studying it from all directions.

"Do you think she's—holy hell!" She ducks as a sparrow dive-bombs her, chirping furiously.

"Drop it!" I shriek, jolted into action by the unhinged bird.

I lunge for Hazel and bat the toy out of her grasp.

But even as it falls to the ground, I know it's too late. She's already touched it.

The sparrow circles back, chirping louder.

The curse has been unleashed.

Curse of the Canines

"**H**AZEL, THAT WAS MEANT for me!" I roar, my voice filling the covered porch. "You weren't supposed to touch it."

"I—I'm sorry, I—" Her eyes are wide, startled, as she ducks to avoid the sparrow.

There's a *pop!* as the lightbulb above us bursts, raining fragments on Hazel's head. She screams and flinches.

"It's cursed!" I yank her toward me, my chest constricting. It's like I think I can protect her, like I can stop all this if I hold her tightly enough.

Hazel brushes bits of glass out of her hair, hissing and shaking out her hands as lines of blood appear on her fingers. "What?!"

Her phone falls out of her pocket and hits the ground, the screen cracking, a web obscuring the photo of the two of us she set as her background yesterday. The music player appears, and "Who Let The Dogs Out?" bursts through the yard at full volume, drowning out the rabid sparrow chirps.

"What the *fuck*?" Hazel shouts, picking up her phone and smearing blood on the screen.

"Shit, shit…" I fumble for my own phone, dropping my purse in the process. "We need to get to C.S.A.M.M. *now.*"

"Get to *who?* Jesus, why won't this pause?" She jabs her thumb at her phone screen, getting more blood on it.

I punch Natalie's name, and she answers calmly, her voice low and breathless. "Katie, I'm glad you called. I've been—"

"The Madsens delivered a curse to my doorstep!" I shout over the chants of Baha Men. Snatching up the plush dog, I leave my purse on the ground and shove Hazel toward the street. "Maybe Oaklyn, based on the note, or Freddie, based on the dog. We're catching the first bus downtown. Meet me part way."

She hesitates for the briefest moment as she absorbs my frantic explanation. "Did you touch it? Who's *we?*"

"Hazel. She picked it up first, so the curse is attacking—gah!" I break off as she stumbles and crashes into me.

"Ow! Dammit." She groans, limping. "I rolled my ankle on a freaking pebble!"

I wrap an arm around her waist and hold her to my side, my voice quaking. "Natalie, what if we don't make it?"

There's a pause that holds an unbearable weight—her mother's death, their inability to get to her in time, the emptiness in her life since it happened.

The song reaches the first verse, a stab of annoyance pulling me out of my spiral.

"*Fuck!*" Hazel screams again, waving her arms to defend herself from the bird.

"You will," Natalie says, firm and steady. "I just left C.S.A.M.M. to head to a different curse location. I'm turning around."

I cling to her reassuring tone, gripping the phone tighter. "Thank God."

Hazel gives up on her phone and pockets it, flapping her hands in her signature *oh-my-god oh-my-god* gesture. "She's coming with the cure?"

"She's already in the car." I keep a tight hold on the plush dog, ready to throw it under the vial the second we see Natalie. It feels cheap and hard, the synthetic fur abrasive between my fingers.

"Is this the first you've heard from the Madsens since you left?" Natalie asks on the phone.

"Yes." Awkwardness curdles in my stomach at the reminder of me leaving. "Have the Shadows seen them since?"

"Funny you mention it. We had a sighting an hour ago. Sky and the others are on it."

I look around as if expecting to see the Madsens right here. "Where? Near me?"

Hazel and I make it to the bus stop, out of breath. The obnoxious music attracts the stares of everyone waiting.

"North Shore, actually," Natalie says. "And we were *also* called out to deal with a high-profile curse at the Convention Centre."

I furrow my brow. "All this at once?"

"I know."

Suspicious. Why would the Madsens be on the North Shore while delivering a curse to me in Point Grey at the same time? Not to mention the curse at the Convention Centre... Have they planted several incidents at once? And why?

"Bus, bus, bus!" Hazel cries, relief flooding her voice.

She tugs me closer to the curb as the bus pulls up.

The doors open—and it's crammed full. Through the windows, teenagers fill every square inch of space. A high school class has apparently decided to use it for field trip transportation.

Everyone ahead of us at the bus stop scoffs and groans as they're unable to get on.

I push Hazel onward before she can panic. "Keep walking. Natalie, meet us on West 10th."

A crow swoops down and drops a pine cone on Hazel's head. She cries out and throws her arms up.

"Got it," Natalie says.

Hazel and I continue hobbling down the sidewalk on two bad ankles.

"I feel sick," Hazel says, breathing hard. "I might throw up."

She's scratching the back of her hand compulsively, reddening the skin.

I slap her hand away before she can draw blood. "What are you doing?"

"I'm itchy!"

"Well, which is it? Are you itchy or nauseous?"

"Both!" she wails.

"As long as you can still breathe," I murmur.

"*Excuse me?*" she cries.

"Nothing. Keep going." My mind reels like I've snagged a whale on a fishing line. I'm scrambling to understand what this all means, ears ringing, pulse throbbing in my neck. "Natalie, don't you think it's weird that all this stuff is happening at once?"

"Yes. But we've had busy days like this before." In the background, cars honk and tires screech, and she exhales sharply.

"But a lot of witches have left the building just now, right?" I ask.

"You don't have to worry. The Madsens can't get into C.S.A.M.M. The building could be entirely empty and still perfectly secure."

"Because you need earth magic in order to pass through the steam clock?"

"Exactly."

I chew my lip, a theory rolling around in my brain like a hot potato. Freddie was hinting at something big—something to turn the tables.

What else could it be? "Natalie, I think the Madsens have gotten a hold of earth magic."

A pause. She's either in the middle of breaking a traffic law or thinking. Likely both. "Well, we know Oaklyn has her dagger—"

"No, like... fully. So they can do what you do."

"They can't. Not without the means to neutralize a curse and process the stone."

"Or capture feral magic."

More silence. I look around vigilantly, scanning for danger.

"Why *this song*?" Hazel sobs, jabbing her phone screen again to no avail. Her hands are redder than a moment ago, hives blooming across her skin like she's having an allergic reaction.

"Even if they somehow acquired pure earth magic," Natalie says, "only one of them could possess it."

"And that's all it would take," I argue, yanking Hazel out of the way of an oncoming cyclist. "Freddie mentioned the steam clock entrance when we were talking. He seemed convinced that things were about to change and he was about to set magic free. What if he can do earth magic? He'd be able to get into C.S.A.M.M., wouldn't he?"

"He would, but... There's no way. He was probably just screwing with you."

Hazel jerks to a stop, pulling me with her. "Um..."

A woman sprints toward us down the sidewalk, fear tightening her expression. As she pushes past, two more people race after her.

My blood turns to ice. This *cannot* be good.

More and more people sprint by us, heading in the opposite direction.

"What are they—" Hazel begins, and then we see it.

A pack of eight coyotes hurtles toward us, their gray-brown fur ruffling in the wind, their paws thundering over the concrete. Their jaws snap and their heads tilt back as they let out a chorus of "*yip-yip-yip!*"

"Run!" I shout, pulling Hazel by the wrist.

"What's happening?" Natalie shouts.

The plush dog swings from my hand as we follow the crowd down the sidewalk, fleeing the pack as fast as our injuries will allow.

"Coyotes!" I shout into the phone.

My heart pounds in my ears, drowning out everything else. The world blurs around me, my lungs burning. It's as if the curse is a dark shadow looming over us, breathing down our necks, plotting its next move.

"I heard the c-coyotes were aggressive here," Hazel says between breaths, "but this is—"

"It's the curse!" I shout. "Natalie, where are you?"

"Five minutes."

"Fuck."

Hazel skids to a stop and pulls at a shop door. It's locked.

I drag her along and pull at the next one. It opens, and we dive inside a packed donut shop.

The coyotes race past, yipping, the noise mingling with pedestrians' screams.

As it fades, the shop's soft piano music tingles in my ears.

"We're—fine—" I tell Natalie, wheezing.

"Just stay safe. I'm going as fast as I can."

"Question—" I wait until we're back outside before pulling the phone closer to my mouth. "When a witch curses an object, does she dictate the curse's effects?"

"What do you mean?" Natalie asks.

"Like, curses seem to have a twisted sense of humor. Playing songs on repeat, haunting the person in strange ways..."

"Oh. A curse has a mind of its own, but yes, it takes on some of the personality of the witch who created it."

There's a hole in the sidewalk ahead, and I pull Hazel closer to me so she doesn't step in it and roll her other ankle.

"So how do you explain why this curse is taunting me with the memory of being dragged by a dog?" I ask Natalie. "These *symptoms*, or whatever you call them, are very specific—more than in the past. The plush dog, the coyotes, the song... Whoever made this curse has tailored it to me and my history with Wyatt. And how did they manage to create a curse if they can't do magic?"

She's quiet. My heart beats faster, my pulse ticking in my fingers.

Beside me, Hazel gasps.

I whip my head around, dreading the next attack.

Her hand is on her throat, massaging it, her mouth open as if to cough.

The whole world grinds to a stop, a chill crashing over me like I've plunged into glacial water.

"No!" I cry, lunging for her. The phone slips, and I let it hit the ground. "Hazel!"

She sinks to her knees, wheezing like she's trying to breathe through a straw.

"Slow breaths," I say. "Stay calm. Natalie, hurry!"

Her shouts rise from my dropped phone, but I can't take my hands off Hazel. I tip her head back, trying to help her get more air.

"Oh my God—" I don't know what to do. Would CPR work? The Heimlich maneuver as if she's choking? An Epi-Pen to open her throat like in an allergic reaction? Would *anything* that isn't magic help?

Hazel meets my gaze, her eyes wide and terrified. She spasms as she tries to get oxygen.

Pedestrians gather around, asking if they can help, asking what's going on.

"Call 9-1-1!" a woman shouts.

"She's choking!" cries another.

Hazel sinks further down, her lips turning blue. I hold her head, dizzy with panic. My knees hit the hard, cold concrete, the plush dog that did this to her squashed beneath my legs.

"No, no..." Denial spills from my mouth, my hands scrambling across her face and neck, searching for a way to save her. We need a doctor, a nurse, anyone.

A stab of pain shoots through my own chest. My eyes burn. This is my fault. She's paying the price for my mistakes. I should've known the Madsens weren't done with me.

Her eyes roll back.

"Hazel!" I shriek.

I bend to give her mouth-to-mouth. It's the only thing I can think of. I pinch her nose and pull her jaw down, closing my lips over hers and blowing.

The air doesn't go anywhere. It stops like it's hit a wall, refusing to fill her lungs.

"Hazel!" My voice tears out of my throat, broken, sobs rattling my chest.

I can't lose her. Not Hazel. My best friend, my other sister, my anchor. Since high school, she's been the one person who's stopped me from descending into loneliness. Before her, I was adrift with no sense of belonging—a ship without a rudder, floating aimlessly in a sea of awkwardness. Who will I be after her? Will I ever be the same without my bestie to balance out all my weaknesses, my shyness, my lack of purpose?

Her face turns deathly gray. She's unconscious, not responding to my cries or movements.

Panicked shouts mingle together, the sky darkening as people swarm us to see what's going on. But nobody can help. Nothing can be done. Their cries only make this more real.

I'm out of ideas. The world closes in around me, a hollow, rushing noise filling my ears. Everything spins.

Distantly, footsteps pound over the concrete. A strong hand grabs my shoulder, pulling me back.

The plush dog rips out from under me.

Which can only mean...

My heart misses a beat. *Natalie?*

I don't take my eyes off Hazel. I can't. Her blue lips, her gray face...

There's a *hiss*. A spitting sound, like a rogue firework.

BOOM!

An explosion rattles the world, debris peppering my shoulder and head. Dust fills my mouth, making me cough.

Beneath my ringing ears, people scream. Footsteps scatter. Smoke billows, the tang stinging my nostrils.

Silence descends.

Not daring to let myself feel relief, I shake Hazel's shoulders and tap her cheek. "Wake up! Please!"

She doesn't move.

I bend and give her mouth-to-mouth again—and this time, the air goes down her throat. Her chest inflates, and when I sit back, it deflates again.

I watch her, my eyes burning, holding her cold face between my hands. "Come on!"

Don't be too late. Please.

Abruptly, she sucks in a rattling breath, her eyes flying open. She coughs, thrashing on the concrete. "Coyotes—Baha Men—"

"Hazel!" I choke out. I throw my arms over her, burying my face in her neck. "This was all my fault. Have I told you I love you?"

Natalie slides her arms under Hazel, picking her up. "We have to go. Get in the car."

I let go and scramble to my feet, tears flooding out as she carries Hazel to her vehicle. The people who gathered around shout protests—an ambulance is on the way, after all—but there's no time to explain, even if we could.

Weak in Natalie's arms, Hazel rubs her face with trembling hands, coughing and breathing fast. "C-can I go home now?"

"Yes. You can and you should." I open the passenger door of Natalie's car and meet her eye, making a silent request to leave Hazel out of this mess.

Natalie nods, easing her into the seat. "Katie and I have to deal with this, but I'm going to give you my keys, and I want you to drive back to Katie's place."

Her voice is calm for Hazel's sake, but I can hear the tension underneath.

Hazel blinks. "Oh. No, I can help—"

"Don't *even*." A purple butterfly flaps past my nose, and I bat it away irritably before getting into the back seat. "You're going back to my place, and you're going to put Ethel in her kennel and prepare to flee if you have to."

Hazel splutters. "Excuse me?"

"Drive, Natalie," I bark as she gets into the driver's seat.

She punches the accelerator, and we leave the confused crowd behind, whipping into traffic so fast that several cars honk.

My hands are shaking. Beads of sweat roll down my temples, and my heart is beating so hard I can feel it against my ribs.

"You both okay?" Natalie asks. Her dark eyes find mine in the rearview mirror. Her nostrils flare, a muscle working in her jaw.

I hesitate, then nod. Hazel is alive, and that's what matters.

My eyes burn as I try not to think about how that could've ended. But beneath the terror, something white-hot sizzles through me. My breaths heave in and out. I glare out the window at the passing cityscape, my nails biting into my palms. The urge to hit something is overwhelming—to inflict pain right back.

I might not have magic or a pack of coyotes, but I've got something better: the stubbornness of an Alexander and a complete lack of self-preservation. The Madsens nearly murdered my best friend, and for that, I'm going to get revenge on every one of them.

CHAPTER 33

Unwanted Guests

As Natalie speeds to C.S.A.M.M., I perch forward in the back seat, poking my head up between her and Hazel.

"Do you think I'm right?" I ask, catching my breath. "That the Madsens are going to try to infiltrate C.S.A.M.M.?"

Natalie's jaw works. "It's a theory we should take seriously. Did Freddie say anything else to make you think this?"

I sift through memories of our conversations. Nothing specific comes to mind, but this is about more than the words he said. "Look, I know it might sound weird, but sometimes, I can read people in a way that's hard to explain."

"You know I don't think it's weird," Natalie says.

"Yeah, it's useful," Hazel chimes in.

My cheeks heat up. "Right. People just don't take me seriously when I say—"

"You're an empath," Natalie says. "I believe you. What did you sense in Freddie?"

Fidgeting under her vote of confidence, I run my fingers along the coarse seam on the back of her seat. "It was scattered the couple of times we met. Like, one minute he's a normal guy, friendly even, and the next, I want to back away. All I know is he's dangerous. When we talked on the phone, he seemed genuinely convinced that something big was about to go down."

Natalie exhales slowly. "And what would give him the audacity to think he could take on a building full of witches?"

"Exactly."

"Jesus." Natalie rubs her neck. "I think you're right."

I suck in a breath. As relieved as I am that she believes me, I'd rather not be right about this.

Sweat prickles on my back. I shed my bulky jacket, leaving a green t-shirt that still feels too hot.

Natalie taps the dash display, making a call. *Skylar Zacharias* appears, and the loud ringing attacks my ears.

"Your sister is in your phone as *Skylar Zacharias*?" I ask flatly. "What am I in there as?"

She arches an eyebrow, confusion plain. "Uh, Katie Alexander?"

I scoff, thinking of the number of heart emojis and nicknames in my contacts.

Hazel turns in the passenger seat to meet my eye, a knowing smile on her lips.

The ringing stops, and Sky's voice fills the car. "What's up?"

"How's the mission?" Natalie asks.

"A bust so far. No sign of Freddie."

"Listen, I'm with Katie and her friend. They got hit with a curse."

"Oh, shit. Are they okay?"

"Yeah, but it was a close call. Sky, we think the Madsens might be trying to distract us so they can break into C.S.A.M.M."

She snorts. "Good luck to them."

"That's the thing. Katie thinks they might've gotten access to magic."

A pause. "How?" Sky asks, a sharpness in her tone.

"We don't know."

"They're after bio magic," I cut in. "I think this is what Freddie meant by a plan in motion. The sighting was a false alarm—a lure to get you to leave C.S.A.M.M."

Sky hisses. "Dammit. I *knew* something was... We're on our way back."

She hangs up.

Hazel slumps lower in her seat. "I have no idea what any of that meant, but consider me confused and terrified."

Neither Natalie nor I have any reassuring words.

She pulls over at the steam clock, and we scan the area. No signs of the Madsens or anything amiss.

We get out, and before Hazel climbs into the driver's seat, I stop her for a hug.

"Be ready to get out of here in case things go south," I say into her shoulder.

She leans back, searching my face. "Are you sure I can't help—"

"I need you to go get Ethel. You're her godmother."

She dips her chin and gets in, looking tiny and fragile in Natalie's car. As she pulls the seat all the way forward and adjusts the mirrors, Natalie steps up beside me.

"Ready?" she murmurs.

I meet her dark eyes, finding a storm that reflects everything going on inside me.

I nod.

With a last look at Hazel, I back up and lean into Natalie. She slides an arm around my waist and tugs me against her, and we walk toward the steam clock.

The world distorts, as dizzying as ever, and I press closer to her for support.

C.S.A.M.M.'s brick hallway ripples into form—and as we land, the ground jolts beneath my feet. I stumble, my heart slamming into my ribs as a quake rattles the world. The ivy on the walls twitches, bricks groaning and cracking.

I look up at the arched ceiling, grabbing Natalie's arm as the corridor threatens to cave in and bury us alive.

As the tremor settles, a cloud of dust drifts toward us from the lounge. I cough. "Wh-what was—?"

An alarm pierces my eardrums, an oscillating howl that sends a chill to my core.

Natalie's jaw is slack, her gaze unfocused, like she's in shock.

"Earthquake!" Someone's shout is all but drowned beneath the wailing alarm. "Everybody out! Let's go."

Natalie breaks into a run, and I hurry to follow, sprinting down the hall. The noise fills my head, smothering our footsteps and rasping breaths.

In the lounge, dust prickles my nose, a haze obscuring the air. Thunder rumbles through my bones that might be falling bricks. People rush through the debris toward the exit, indiscernible figures that could be anyone.

"Millie!" Sebastian shouts, his voice breaking.

"I'm here!" Millie yells.

The panicked cries spike my pulse, my every sense on edge. Natalie sweeps an arm out and pushes me behind her as people stampede past—five, ten, twenty witches heading in the opposite direction toward the steam clock.

Natalie reaches into the crowd to pull someone out. "Will. That wasn't an earthquake."

Will stares back, searching Natalie's face as he processes her words. His gaze darts to me, a flicker of blame in his furrowed brow, as if this somehow has to do with me. But then, to my surprise, he says, "Beginning to think I was wrong about you. Good to have you back."

A strange sensation trickles through my heart. Before I can think of a response, Fiona's voice rises over the din.

"Not an earthquake?" Through the haze, she lifts her hands toward the ceiling, mending a large crack in the bricks. She catches Natalie's eye and arches an eyebrow. "What was it, then?"

Natalie flicks her hand toward the corner as if to throw something, and the alarm quiets. The room descends into a ringing silence, footsteps fading down the hall as people rush to the exit.

And there—another sound. Footfall, but moving away from us, along with...

A chill sweeps through me.

A panting dog, and heavy paws thundering across the hard floor.

"Madsen!" Natalie roars. "Security breach! Every available person to the lounge!"

Screams break out. There's a flurry of movement as the remaining people gather closer.

"What do you mean?" Fiona snaps. "They can't possibly—"

Freddie's laugh echoes off every surface in the crumbling room. I grit my teeth, fury coursing through me at the sound of him—this man who almost killed my best friend.

"Freddie!" Natalie breaks into a run. "You've made a mistake coming here."

Will sprints after her, his hands raised as he summons rubble to use as a weapon.

I'm numb, my body and mind disconnecting. It's really happened. Freddie Madsen has breached C.S.A.M.M.

I race after Natalie, wishing I could do magic, wishing I could do *anything* to help.

"You all should've left when you had the chance," someone yells, and before I can process who said it and what it means, an explosion ahead rattles the world.

Shrapnel stings my face. I throw my arms up, catching the rest with my forearms. The ground jolts, and my knees crack against it, followed by a stab of pain in my wrists. The heels of my hands skid across rocky debris.

Coughing on grit, I stay down, trying to get oriented.

Someone lets out a terrible scream.

"Wh-what's going on?" I choke out, my voice faint beneath a hollow *whoosh* in my ears.

I try to stand, but my knee bumps something soft. I look over—and cry out, recoiling. It's a *person*. Someone is lying on the floor.

"Oh my God..." I crawl closer, grabbing their arm. "Are you okay?"

White skin, brown hair, short beard...

"Katie?" Natalie says, her voice distant and panicked.

I'm frozen, not comprehending what I'm seeing.

It's *Will*. His eyes are open, glassy.

I scream, letting go of him and falling back onto my hands. "Natalie! Will is— He's—"

"What? No!" Natalie drops to her knees beside me. "Will!"

The world tilts. My stomach churns, acid rising.

"Everyone, back up, or you'll be next," a high voice snaps.

"N-Natalie, he's dead," I say numbly, the words choking me.

I knew the Madsens were capable of murder, and I've seen with my own eyes how dangerous they can be, but to see Will dead on the floor...

Natalie grabs my arm, her grip painful, and pulls me to my feet. My legs threaten to give out, trembling as I lean into her.

Wyatt barks frantically, the sound reverberating through the lounge.

"The Shadows are on their way back!" Natalie shouts. "Surrender before you get hurt."

"They'll be just in time to see the end of the coven's reign," Oaklyn says, raising her dagger. "*God*, it feels good to be on a level playing field for once."

Three people come into view against the far wall—Freddie standing with Wyatt crouched between his legs, Oaklyn with her dagger, and a middle-aged woman with fair skin and white-blonde hair woven into a thick braid. She can only be Sophia.

Across from them, Fiona, Sebastian, Millie, Agnes, and Amir stand with their backs to the courtyard, breathing hard and coughing.

My heart plummets into my feet. Everyone else must have left the building. Between the curses planted to get the Guardians out, the fake sighting to lure away the Shadows, and the quake to force out the remaining witches, the Madsens have tricked the coven into clearing the way for them.

Freddie catches my eye and cocks an eyebrow as if to say, *Told you so*.

I scowl back, my teeth clenched.

Sophia Madsen steps forward, her full lips twisted into a cruel smile. Between her high cheekbones, flawless skin, and piercing blue eyes, it's easy to see where Freddie and Oaklyn got their looks. She looks like she's one musical number away from being a real-life snow queen. But there's nothing beautiful about the way she's sneering. "Show us where you store biological magic, and nobody else has to get hurt."

Wyatt's low growl ripples over my skin, raising the hairs on my arms. He flashes his gleaming fangs, his hackles rising as he waits for a command.

Fiona steps out from the witches, blood on her cheek. "You're a guest in our house, Sophia, and I don't think you're in a position to be making demands."

She twitches her fingers, and in a blink, an iron sconce rises from the rubble and rockets toward the Madsens.

Oaklyn is quick with her dagger, snatching the sconce out of the air with a long, whip-like root.

"Well done, sweetie," Sophia purrs, a purple glint in her eyes. She raises her arms, her manicured hands curled like claws. "That's no way to treat a guest."

A wooden table groans and cracks, lifting into the air.

Well, we know which Madsen is in possession of earth magic.

Natalie and several others react, and the table disintegrates into splinters before Sophia can use it as a weapon.

Sophia grins, undeterred. She's been waiting for this for decades, and she's enjoying every second of it. "All we need is a tiny hint." Her voice ripples through the lounge. "We could search each corridor, but it would be a shame to have to render the whole building into this state."

"Don't let them move," Fiona barks. "Block everything. Whatever it takes."

The witches turn their attention to the corridors, lifting rubble and furniture in the air to barricade them as quickly as possible. Plants weave into nets, and bricks stack to form new walls.

"You must be a Director," Sophia says to Fiona with a little bow of her head. "Kids, have her share where they hoard their magic supply."

Oaklyn flicks her dagger like a whip, and Freddie shouts, "Get 'em!"

Roots snap out of the dagger like tentacles. Wyatt rockets toward Fiona.

Natalie and the others respond, raising a wall of rubble to block the attack and launching pieces of it like bullets.

"Push them back to the exit!" Fiona shouts.

Sophia's lips curl into a twisted smile as the lounge explodes into chaos, debris flying. Natalie steps in front of me to shield me from it. Still, a sharp sting hits my shoulder, followed by a warm trickle of blood.

I hiss. Adrenaline surges through my veins, telling me to run, to hide, to *do* something. "Natalie, I need the gauntlet."

To my surprise, she nods and pushes me back. "Agreed."

Dust swirls, filling my nostrils and turning the air opaque, making it hard to see where the Chambers corridor is. "It's still in my room."

Natalie shakes her head. "When you left, Elizabeth had to vacate your suite. I grabbed your stuff and kept it safe." She takes my hand, tugging me with her. "Come on."

We follow the rush of people barricading the corridors. Furniture and rubble continue to pile up.

As we cross the lounge, barking erupts, the pitch higher than Wyatt's boom. The French bulldog, Greg, tears inside from the courtyard, yapping his head off. Wyatt barks back, his jaws snapping, but Greg is quick and bites at the larger dog's heels.

"Greg, get out!" Agnes yells, adding to the din.

Natalie pushes past her toward the Chambers corridor. "We need to get through."

Agnes turns her bulging eyes onto us, her pigtails in disarray, her teeth bared. "Where do you think *you're*—"

"Bring back something useful, Natalie!" Fiona shouts from nearby. "Agnes, let her through."

Ignoring Agnes's outrage, Natalie uses magic to open a hole in the barrier, just big enough for us to slip through. The ease of passing through it doesn't bode well for Sophia being able to do the same... But at least it'll impede Freddie and Oaklyn.

Beyond it, I sprint after Natalie, gritting my teeth against the throbbing pain in my ankle. The roar of the fight fades into the distance, replaced by my ringing ears and loud, frantic breaths. We follow a maze of hallways to a four-way intersection with a street lamp in the middle. There, she leads me to a corner suite with the number 52 on the door.

My heart skips. Finally, I get to see Natalie's room—and it's on the day this whole building might be destroyed.

CHAPTER 34

No More Secrets

THE WALLS IN NATALIE'S suite are exposed brick like mine, the dark wood furnishings simple and elegant, the space as organized as I expected. Books are arranged neatly on shelves beside the desk, and bonsai trees cover every surface, meticulously trimmed and nurtured. The scent of her fills the room, warm and comforting—but even that can't loosen the knot of fear in my gut.

The only clutter is a corkboard, which is swamped in photos, trimmings, and maps—maybe related to curses she has yet to find. This is the side of her that won't rest until she's freed the world from dangerous magic... Until she's fulfilled her sworn duty to the coven.

She pulls my gauntlet from her bedside drawer, pausing before holding it out to me. "It was our mom's."

A fist clenches around my stomach. Wait, Sky gave me a *family heirloom?*

I don't take it, backing up a step. "I shouldn't have it, then. This belongs with you and Sky."

She shakes her head and presses the gauntlet into my hands. "She was right to give it to you."

I hesitate, then gently close my fingers over the enchanted fig leaf, brushing a thumb across the cool, smooth surface—this connection to the mother she lost. Am I worthy enough to wear it?

Natalie steps closer, the heat of her body enveloping me. "Katie, there's something I have to tell you."

My stomach tightens. "About the gauntlet?"

"About my mom." She pauses as if unsure of what she's about to say. She swallows hard. "Your cat, Lucy... She was bio magic that my mom stored and hid."

I stare at her. Her own mother, who swore the same oath as everyone else here, had a secret supply of bio magic?

She must see the disbelief on my face because she says quickly, "I would never have thought she would do something illegal... But we never knew the extent of the magic she stored, and we kept finding it after she died. When you told me about Lucy, I knew it was her work."

I blink, struggling to absorb what she's telling me. "But how could you tell it was hers?"

"The curse's..." She waves a hand. "*Personality*, as we put it earlier. She used to tell us that when she was first learning how to do magic, she had a knack for accidentally melting everything. You said Lucy melted her food bowl, and when I took her away for treatment, the kennel door started melting before I could get her out. That isn't a typical curse symptom. That had my mom written all over it."

I exhale, my shoulders sagging. I wish I didn't have to be the cause of a painful memory for her. "Natalie, I'm so sorry—"

"Don't apologize." She steps closer. "I'm the one who needs to say sorry. Remember when you said it's not my fault that you got dragged into this world? Well, it kind of is. If I'd been able to find my mom's stored magic in time, you wouldn't have stumbled on the kitten, and none of this would have happened."

I shake my head. "You can't blame yourself. She was the one who hid bio magic, not you. Besides, I'm positive I would have stumbled on magic anyway because of my ability. Like, the doll had nothing to do with your mom, right? There are so many other ways I could have found a curse. This isn't your fault."

She says nothing, not meeting my eye.

I furrow my brow, thinking of Lucy's tiny cotton-swab tail and baby-soft fur. "But the kitten was so young. I thought your mother died years ago."

The corner of her mouth lifts in a sad half-smile. "The kitten wasn't a kitten."

"Right." I don't know why it's so hard to get that through my head. "What was she, then? Is that what bio magic looks like?"

"No, it's..." Her eyebrows arch sadly, her gaze pleading. "I'll show you one day. This isn't me keeping a secret, I just need to show you."

I nod. Not knowing doesn't bother me this time. Maybe I'm finally understanding why witches keep so many secrets.

With no time to waste, I fasten the gauntlet to my hand and flex my fingers.

Natalie opens her closet and grabs a cylindrical container from the side. It rattles as if it's full of marbles as she straps it across her back like a quiver.

"What's that?" I ask.

"The *something useful* Fiona told me to get. Bullets, sort of. Perfect spheres, pure copper. Optimized to be easier for a witch to manipulate than any other element. They're illegal except in desperate circumstances."

I nod and turn around, ready to race back out there. "Let's go."

"Wait." Natalie seizes my forearm, pulling me back to her. "Katie, I should've told you everything. I don't want to keep anything from you anymore, even if it gets us in trouble. I'm sorry I kept you in the dark—"

"I forgive you." Her words wash over me, soothing all the hard feelings. The sincerity in her eyes, the desperation in her tight grasp, it all tells me how much she wanted to protect me. Besides, she isn't the only one who has to apologize. Phoning Freddie wasn't the first time I went around her to get what I wanted, but I'll make sure it's the last. "I'm sorry, too. I shouldn't have gone behind your back and talked to Freddie. That was reckless and disrespectful, and nothing like that will ever happen again."

"But I get why you did it." She slides her hand down my arm to entwine our fingers. "I should've told you more about what sort of magic we're dealing with. Fuck the oath. You deserve to know."

I press my lips together, attempting a smile. "Thanks."

She lifts a shoulder. "We've all explored the issue at one time or another, and you had just as much a right to."

I furrow my brow. "What issue?"

"Whether magic should be locked away."

I search her face, trying to read her thoughts in the fine lines around her eyes. "I thought you'd all made up your minds on the matter."

She shifts on her feet, a hint of discomfort tightening her expression. "What are we supposed to do with a power that's so spectacular and so dangerous all at once? Is it possible to make sure magic is only used for good?"

I don't have an answer. Maybe nobody does, and that's why wars have been waged over it—why a battle is being fought as we speak.

But the fact she's telling me this, confiding something so serious and secretive, means more than anything else she's said.

I step in and take her face in my hands, standing on my toes to bring our lips together.

For a moment, she freezes, and then her hands are on me, her palms dragging up my waist, her arms pulling me close.

She kisses me with soft, insistent lips, her hair tickling my cheeks and sending fire through me. One hand glides around the back of my head and tangles in my hair, the other tugging me closer until every inch of me is pressed against her.

As she opens my lips, deepening the kiss, a ripple of pleasure runs down my core and momentarily drowns out everything else. I surrender, arching into her. Her warmth seeps through my shirt, her hips pressing into mine, and her scent transports me away from all this fear and pain. I'm lost in her taste, in the way she wraps around me as if to protect me from the danger outside.

Then her arms loosen, and we step apart, reality crashing back.

"I checked on you over these last couple of weeks." Her tone is urgent, desperate. She stoops her head to hold my gaze. "I need you to know that. I want you to know I didn't just let you wander out in the world with the Madsens on the loose—"

I kiss her again to stop her rambling. "I know," I whisper into her lips.

There's more I want to say, words that encapsulate how I feel about her and how much it would destroy me to lose her. But now's not the time, and we can't waste another moment.

I take her hand and tug her out the door, back toward the lounge. As our pounding footsteps echo off the walls, mirroring my racing heartbeat, the gauntlet warms against my skin.

Suffocating panic bubbles up, and I swallow it down, forcing all the what-ifs from my mind. The unknown outcome of the fight we're diving into... The threat that the Madsens might win...

And the possibility that I might have just kissed Natalie Zacharias for the last time.

CHAPTER 35

The Right to Magic

WE EMERGE IN THE lounge to rejoin the fight in numb shock. It's like someone took a wrecking ball to the place. Natalie pushes aside heaps of rubble littering the ground where booths and the bar once stood. We stumble through, smoke and dust burning my eyes and throat. Ahead, the fireplace and stone chimney lie in ruins, a smoldering pile that sends plumes of dark smoke curling toward the ceiling.

Resounding cracks and shouts assault my ears. In the haze, more Alchemists have arrived to help, their green robes billowing in cross-winds as magic flies to and fro. My heart lifts a little as our defenses form a wall between us and the Madsens, stopping them from reaching the corridors.

But as we join them, it's clear the Madsens are a terrifying force. Oaklyn is ruthless with her dagger, and witches yell in pain as roots slash hard enough to draw blood and knock them off their feet. Sophia blocks every brick and hunk of metal thrown her way. She fights like she's spent her whole life planning and visualizing each attack, preparing for the moment she could do magic. She shows no hesitation as she aims to kill.

Freddie, meanwhile, hangs back, scanning the blocked corridors with a calculating look. He's searching for something—and I know exactly what. The barrier to the Alchemy wing is weak, gaps visible in the pile of rubble and furniture.

"Reinforce the Alchemy wing!" I yell, pointing to it.

Millie is closest, and she's the only one to spin around. She follows my gaze. "On it!"

Wow, someone listened.

I sprint toward it, and she and Sebastian peel away to help.

Freddie breaks into a run too, his roar cutting through the din. "Get 'em!"

Ice shoots through my veins as Wyatt charges, a flash of fur and fangs. In two swift strides, he latches onto Sebastian's arm, shaking it like a rag doll. Sebastian's agonized scream pierces the air as he falls to his knees, a spray of blood hitting the floor.

"No!" Millie raises a hand to retaliate, but Freddie is on her in an instant, wrapping an arm around her neck in a chokehold. Millie claws at him, her face turning red as she struggles to breathe.

Without pausing to think, I grab a toppled chair and raise it over my head. "Let go of her!"

I slam it into the back of Freddie's legs with all my strength. He shrieks and crumples to the ground, his grip on Millie loosening.

Millie rolls away, gasping, and swipes a hand to send a fragment of stone toward her attacker's head. But Wyatt is there, leaping into the air to bat the stone away before it can strike his handler.

Sebastian roars in pain where the dog left him, cradling his bloody arm.

Freddie staggers to his feet, his face twisted in fury. He lunges at me, but I'm ready. I wind back and punch him in the stomach with every ounce of strength I have, the gauntlet glinting in the dim light.

He—goes—*flying*.

He soars the length of a car and slams into the wall beside the Alchemy wing with a sickening crunch. As he hits the ground, he sucks in a rattling breath, his body wracked with coughs.

Sebastian and Millie stare at me, frozen, their eyes wide with shock.

I look down at the gauntlet—the innocent-looking fig leaf wrapped around the back of my hand. "Holy shit!" A wild, giddy sensation overcomes me, and I point to Freddie. "You've just been served the Katie Alexander special, fucker! One knuckle sandwich with a side of—"

Something dark whips past us, and a tangle of roots bursts through the Alchemy barricade like a cannon, opening a hole big enough for a person to slip through.

"Thanks, sis," Freddie croaks, stumbling to his feet and darting through the opening. He's unsteady, his breath coming in ragged gasps, but he manages to find his balance and escape.

Wyatt barrels after him, leaping through the hole in the barricade and charging out of sight.

I growl in frustration, knowing where that asshole is headed. Do I go after him?

Over my shoulder, Natalie is absorbed in the fight. She reaches back for her quiver and fires a copper bullet at Sophia so fast I can't even see it.

Sophia shrieks as it catches her upper arm, a crimson stain blossoming where it hit.

I turn back to Sebastian and Millie, breathing hard. "Freddie is heading to Alchemy 13."

Millie, bent over her husband and cradling his mangled arm, nods. "Go. I'll send someone after you."

"Give him—a kick in the nuts for me," Sebastian grunts.

I charge after Freddie, my steps uneven as my ankle sears mercilessly.

I sprint down the corridor and around the corner toward Alchemy 13—but before I can get there, Wyatt's tail disappears through the open door of Alchemy 8. It's the room that held my failed test when I first came here.

Checking my speed, I take careful, quiet steps.

Freddie scans the bookshelves and flings open cabinet doors while Wyatt sniffs around with the focus of a bloodhound.

Heart pounding, fists clenched at my sides, I step through the doorway. "Wrong room, buddy."

Freddie and Wyatt spin around. Wyatt snarls, his hackles rising.

"Katie!" Freddie looks past me, and his surprise melts into a sneer. "Here all alone with nobody to protect you?"

Wyatt creeps forward like a wolf stalking his prey. His claws click on the stone floor.

Fear prickles up my spine, but I stand my ground, trying for a taunting grin. "Not the threat you think it is, when all you've done is tried to recruit me over and over... and over."

He drops his chin. "Well, you made your allegiance clear. I think I've given you enough chances."

I edge sideways along the wall. The items from my failed test are still piled on a wooden table—the antique typewriter, traffic cone, feather boa, and the katana with a red handle and scabbard.

"I should've taken that thing from you while I had the chance." Freddie's gaze falls to the gauntlet on my hand. "That'll teach me to be nice."

"Yeah, you've been a real peach."

He tilts his head. "You still owe me a vial, by the way. We had an agreement."

Wyatt stalks too close for comfort, his fangs glinting in the glow from the skylight.

"Considering the circumstances, I hope you understand why I've changed my mind." I lunge for the table of items and grab the katana—my mark of failure when I first came here. Now, I hope it's about to redeem me. I hold it in front of me with both hands, trying not to let the heavy blade waver.

Dog and handler tense, but they stay put.

I cock an eyebrow, challenging Freddie to try me.

"Did you like our gift?" he asks, mockingly casual.

"A bit on-the-nose." I adjust my grip. My first time holding a sword, and it's heavier than expected. "I gotta say, your mom's already pretty good with earth magic. The curse was strong."

"Helps when the magic is fresh." He walks closer, coming to stand beside Wyatt. They're a step away from the sword tip.

Sweat prickles on the back of my neck. "How'd she get it?"

Freddie smirks. "You have your secrets; we have ours."

Dammit, where's the help Millie promised to send? I strain my ears to listen for approaching footsteps, but none come.

"I have a hard time believing you figured out how to neutralize a curse *and* turn the gemstone into magic," I say. "Which makes me wonder... How did you find feral magic?"

He inclines his head, a gleam in his eyes.

He steps sideways, and Wyatt steps in the opposite direction.

Shit. If they come at me from two sides, I'll have to choose where to swing the sword. I flick my gaze between him and the dog, ready to defend myself.

"We had some help," Freddie says.

"Someone in the coven?" Cold realization trickles through me. "Same person who's telling you about curse locations?"

A little smirk appears on his lips, like he's sharing a private joke. "In a way. He's not exactly *keen* on helping us, but when your next meal is on the line, it's a little easier to talk."

Disgust rises in my throat, bitter and acidic. "You're holding someone captive like a prisoner of war?"

"That's a harsh way to put it," Freddie says casually. "But I suppose."

I try to fit the pieces together. "How does he find out about all the new curse locations if he's imprisoned?"

Slowly, Freddie's lips curl into a grin. "Nat is in close contact with her dad. It's sweet. Texts him to tell him every detail."

My heart plummets into my feet. My chest constricts, panic closing in. *Natalie's dad?*

No, it can't be. He's traveling.

Or, he *was*.

"Y-you've been forcing him to feed you intel?" I stammer, my mouth dry.

"No, no, it was much easier just to take his phone. I've been the one texting Nat back for the last few months, pretending to be Daddy."

I grip the katana tighter, trembling with barely contained rage. *Natalie's* unknowingly been the one leaking information to the Madsens? *She's* how they're finding out about the locations of new curses?

White-hot anger courses through me.

"I already knew I wanted to kill you," I snarl. "This only makes me want it even more."

Freddie sighs, disappointment flickering across his face. Calmly, almost inaudibly, he murmurs, "Finish her, Wyatt."

The dog lunges, and I swing the sword. "Get back!"

My pulse picks up. Freddie wasn't bluffing when he said he'd given me enough chances. He's done going easy on me.

Wyatt crouches, threatening to pounce but not so reckless as to lunge at someone brandishing a sword. He stalks back and forth, holding my gaze, waiting for me to show weakness so he can get past the blade.

"Freddie, I *really* don't want to have to hurt a dog," I say with a tremor in my voice.

Wyatt snarls.

Freddie laughs, stepping sideways, positioning himself to swoop in. "He says he has no qualms with hurting you."

I edge around the cluttered wooden table, my heart pounding out of my chest. I've got one idea, and if it doesn't work, I'm a goner.

I lower the sword, making myself vulnerable—and Wyatt wastes no time. He leaps onto the table to get at me, and I duck beneath it, rolling to the other side. He barks and snaps. Claws scramble over my head. The typewriter hits the floor with a heavy thud, the tiki torch clattering after it.

I straighten up as the dog lands where I was standing. With a roar, I grab the edge of the table and flip it over.

The table pins him to the floor, everything else falling around him. He barks furiously, nails scratching stone as he tries to get out from under the pile.

An arm wraps around my neck, pulling me back. "Good effort," Freddie hisses in my ear, his breath hot on my skin. "But you're going to wish you just let Wyatt tear you apart."

I choke from the pressure, swinging the sword backward at him. But my movements are frantic, uncoordinated, and he grabs my wrist easily and squeezes until I'm forced to open my fingers and drop it. The pressure rises into my head. My lungs beg for air.

"I should've killed you in the graveyard," he growls. "I was too soft—hoping you'd see you've been fighting for the wrong side. But you're just as brainwashed as the rest of them. Why should an ordinary guy like me have the right to magic, eh?"

A small part of me wants to reason with him, wants him to know it's not like that. It's so much more complicated. But my throat is too crushed to speak, and even if I could, he'd never listen.

My head swims. *Air. Need air.*

In the distance, footsteps echo off the walls. "Katie!"

Relief jolts through my chest at the sound of Natalie's voice.

I buckle my knees and let my weight drop, driving my fist as hard as I can into Freddie's groin. The gauntlet slams into him, and he makes a pitiful whimper and curls in on himself. His grip loosens enough that I can duck out of the crook of his elbow.

I gasp for breath and try to shout for Natalie. I can't make a sound—can't do anything but cough.

"Katie?" Natalie shouts again, maybe hearing the commotion. Wyatt is barking, scrambling, nearly out from under the table.

Natalie's shouts continue, growing more panicked with each call of my name. It transports me to all the other times she had to save me from Freddie—the graveyard, the dark alley on New Year's, and even today, saving me and Hazel from that curse.

No more. This is the last time Freddie Madsen endangers my life, and the last time I'm going to need rescuing.

A shadow crosses overhead as he looms behind me, obscuring the skylight.

With a roar, I lunge for the katana and seize the handle. I roll onto my butt and swing it, and Freddie doesn't recoil fast enough. A gash opens in his thighs, tearing a clean line through his jeans and flesh.

"Fuck!" he spits, stumbling. His red face contorts with rage, a more terrifying sight than any snarling dog. "I'll kill you!"

He kicks at my head, and I swing my fist, a sickening *crack* ringing out as the gauntlet hits Freddie's shin. He stumbles, clenching his teeth to stifle his roar of pain.

I push myself back with my heels, trying to put distance between us so I can stand up. "Natalie!" I yell. "Room 8!"

"Too bad she won't be quick enough to save you this time." Freddie stoops to pick up the antique typewriter, his muscles flexing as he lifts it with one hand.

A jolt shoots through my chest. He's going to club me with it.

He steps toward me, raising it.

I roll onto my knees. I have a second to act—a second to come to terms with the fact that only one of us is making it out of this alive.

Holding the katana so firmly that my knuckles protest, I lunge, driving the blade as hard as I can at him.

It sinks into his belly. A strangled gasp escapes him.

I roar as adrenaline shoots through me.

Rocking back, I yank the blade free, opening the wound.

His blood cascades over the stone floor. The typewriter crashes down.

Numbness overtakes me as Freddie drops to his knees, his mouth open and his eyes bulging. A gurgle from deep in his throat prickles my eardrums.

He locks me with his gaze—those piercing blue eyes. How is it that I once looked into those eyes and thought he seemed friendly... just a normal guy standing in the streets? How did the lure of magic bring us to this?

He falls, slumping onto his side in his own pooling blood. A wave of nausea hits me as I watch his life drain away. In the next beat of my heart, his eyes become glassy and lifeless.

"Oh my God," I murmur, my grip weakening.

What did I do?

My breaths rasp in and out, my chest heaving as I fight a surge of dizziness. I've taken a life. A strange disconnect opens inside me, like I'm watching this happen to someone else. Like these shaking, red-splattered hands are not my own.

Behind me, there's a clatter of objects and a scramble of paws.

I jerk my head around to see Wyatt rise to all fours. His eyes gleam with a vengeance that sends a chill through my core.

As I bend to pick up the katana once more, he lunges, ready to tear my throat out.

I swing the weapon to keep him at bay, and he leaps sideways to avoid it.

My hands shake, my palms too sweaty and my muscles too weak to hold on much longer.

"Wyatt, stop," I beg, hoping the dog can understand me—hoping that whatever magic tethered him to Freddie can dissolve.

Footsteps pound, and Natalie's voice reverberates through the high ceilings. "Katie—Jesus Christ!"

The door is behind me, but I feel her presence in the room, wrapping around me like a supportive embrace.

"N-Natalie," I stammer, keeping the blade pointed at the snarling dog.

"Back up toward me," she says, sharp and commanding.

I take one, shaky step back.

Wyatt barks and lunges, no less ready to kill than he was a minute ago.

A bookshelf flies across the room and stops between the dog and me, forcing him to back up. He snarls and snaps at it. Books lift from the tipped-over shelves like birds, flapping above him, and he snatches one out of the air and shakes it, sending pages flying. The sounds he's making send a deep, primal fear through my veins, urging me to get away.

As hard as I try to avoid looking at Freddie, my gaze pulls to his lifeless body, to the scarlet pool spreading around him. My eyes sting, tears rendering the room into splotches of brown and red, and my throat tightens until it hurts.

I killed someone.

"It's okay, baby. Keep coming." Natalie's voice is soft and reassuring.

The books still fly, distracting Wyatt, giving me precious seconds.

A sob escapes as I force my feet toward the door, following the soothing sound of Natalie's voice.

At last, I hit a warm, sturdy body, and I could sink to my knees in relief. Her strong hands close around my shoulders and tug me hard, forcing me out the door with her in two stumbling steps.

I trip over my feet and fall into her.

Wyatt leaps over the bookshelf, racing toward us.

Natalie's arm shoots out beside me, her palm open, and the door to Alchemy 8 slams shut, trapping Wyatt inside.

We lose our balance and topple backward. The katana clatters to the floor. I land on Natalie, her body cushioning my fall.

The dog barks frantically, his claws scratching at the door with enough force to rattle it.

"Are you okay?" Natalie's voice is loud, urgent.

"I—I'm fine," I stammer, my tongue barely working.

The katana lays beside me, soaked in blood, and the spray has covered the front of my shirt and jeans.

Natalie slides me off her so she can roll onto her side. She crushes me to her chest, burying her face in my hair and inhaling deeply. She plants a line of frantic kisses before pulling back to look at me. "Did they hurt you?"

"No. I don't think so." Resting my head on the cold, stone floor, I meet her dark eyes. Her expression is so terrified and vulnerable that the crushing reality of what I've done reaches a peak.

I cover my face, trying to smother my panicked breaths and the sobs that want to escape. "I didn't mean to..." I say into my hands. "He was coming at me..."

But I *did* mean to, didn't I? After what they did to Hazel, I was out for blood. I wanted Freddie Madsen dead. What kind of monster am I?

Natalie's fingers lace through mine and pull my hands down from my face. She caresses my cheek and pushes my sweaty hair back. "You had to. It was him or you. Him or *all* of us."

I nod, wanting to believe her, but guilt and horror wrap around me like a noose. I blink back the sting in my eyes, trying to calm my breathing. Am I doomed to see Freddie's lifeless body every time I close my eyes from now on? Will I forever wonder whether that was really necessary, or if there was another way to stop him?

A clamor in the distance reaches my ears, and we both turn toward it.

"The Shadows are here," Natalie says.

My heart leaps. "Thank God."

"We'll see." She frowns, a deep crease appearing between her eyebrows. "They might be too late."

CHAPTER 36

C.S.A.M.M.'s Darkest Corners

"How are Sophia and Oaklyn still standing?" I shout as we race back to the lobby, fear turning my voice raw. "We outnumber them, and only *one* has full magical abilities!"

"Sophia's power is... concerning," Natalie replies, her mouth turned down. "But people with brains like hers tend to become powerful witches, so I guess we shouldn't be surprised. More importantly, they're fighting dirty."

As we burst through the crumbling barricade and back into the lounge, it's clear what she means. Everything from the stone chimney to the willow tree in the corner is in shambles, smoke rising into the air. I cover my mouth, my eyes burning. Something about the broken, splintered tree, with its beautiful green leaves sprawled across the bookshelves and bean bags, puts a lump in my throat. That the Madsens would destroy so much in the name of getting to magic...

But more people have arrived, and it's the glimmer of hope we need. Sky, Hayley, Neil, and the other Shadows stand with the others, fists clenched, expressions fierce. My heart lifts to see them all.

I scan the crowd, a chill sweeping over me. "Where are the Madsens? And Sebastian and Millie?"

Natalie shakes her head slowly. The room is a haze, debris obscuring the air like fog.

They're nowhere to be found.

My stomach churns at the memory of Sebastian's mangled arm. *Please be okay.*

Sky shouts orders. "Hayley, take four people down the Alchemy wing. Neil, Chambers..."

Group by group, the Shadows and Alchemists take off down the corridors.

And once again, our team breaks apart. A chill ripples down my spine as the crowd in the lounge dwindles, leaving only Fiona, Agnes, Amir, and Sky. "I don't like this," I murmur. C.S.A.M.M.'s vastness, the maze of halls... It all feels like a giant security problem.

As we approach, Fiona addresses Natalie, her face smeared with dirt and blood. "They scattered. Did you lose Freddie?"

My breath catches, his name already haunting me. The image of his body is right there as if imprinted on my eyelids, his blood splattered across the stone floor, his eyes glassy.

"He's dead," Natalie says.

Sky's mouth falls open.

"It was an act of self-defense," Natalie adds firmly.

Through the brain fog, I recall her explaining how complex laws prevent coven members from harming ordinary people. She's protecting me from their justice system—from the consequences of my actions. I won't get a thank-you for what I've done, nor do I deserve it. I shudder and fold my arms over my stomach as if to hold myself together.

"Well, we've lost the others," Fiona says, her voice tight with frustration. "Sophia raised a cloud of dust, and they vanished behind it. They've likely split up in the corridors in search of you-know-what."

"Or they're waiting for the chance to capture Fiona," Sky says. "They clearly want to question her, and—"

"And what about the *other* Directors?" Agnes snaps. "Are we not important too?"

Sky rolls her eyes. "They don't seem to know who else is a Director. So unless you're willing to volunteer yourself as someone who has the information they're after, I suggest you shut up."

I step forward, my heart pounding. Enough beating around the bush. "We should be focusing our efforts. Forming a defensive barrier in front of the bio magic. Fiona, where's it kept?"

Fiona and Amir stiffen. Sky grimaces.

Agnes's face turns a blotchy pink, and her eyes narrow to slits. "That is *classified*!"

"This isn't the time for secrets," I argue. "We have to know where it is if we want to protect it!"

Agnes steps closer. "How do we know you don't want to help them get it? *Someone's* been feeding them information, in case you didn't realiz—"

Abruptly, she's launched backward, her cry echoing beneath the cavernous ceiling. Roots wrap around her throat, midsection, and limbs, yanking her away from us. She roars and thrashes, but with her hands engulfed, she can't do magic.

The dust and debris clears, revealing Sophia and Oaklyn. Every inch of their skin is scratched and bruised, Sophia's hair is tangled and singed, and their clothes are torn and covered in blood. This fight has taken its toll, but they aren't giving up.

Natalie, Sky, Amir, and Fiona launch attacks, but the Madsens are quick to retaliate, blocking anything from hitting them.

"Tell me you're lying," Oaklyn snarls. "Tell me Freddie isn't dead."

Fiona looks my way, inviting all eyes to fall onto me. I shiver, my throat too tight to let me speak. If I tell the truth, will they snap and kill Agnes?

I've already got one person's blood on my hands today. I can't handle another.

"He is," Natalie says, palms up, ready to fight. "And it's no one's fault but your own."

Oaklyn trembles, a glint of tears in her eyes. She turns to her mother, her chest heaving. "We can still save him. The bio magic."

I don't know enough about magic to know whether this is true—whether they can bring him back to life. But if they're mistaken, nobody corrects them.

"We just—need—directions to it," Sophia says through gritted teeth.

Agnes whimpers, suspended upside down beside Oaklyn, all her earlier bravado evaporating.

"Care to share where you hoard your magic, Miss *Director*?" Sophia yells, her eyes wild. "Or would anyone in the audience like to step forward and spare her life?"

"D-don't kill me," Agnes squeaks.

"Talk, then," Oaklyn snaps, and Agnes squeaks as the roots groan and tighten around her.

Fiona swears under her breath.

"Don't say a thing, Agnes!" Amir shouts—and there's no mistaking the panic in his tone.

They're afraid Agnes is going to crack.

Natalie's eyes reflect the fear rocketing through my chest. If Agnes tells them, will we be able to stop them from getting it? They'll gain access to mind control, telepathy, shapeshifting, and God knows what else. And while there might be some good people who would only use this power for saving lives, for acts of charity, for world peace... I know with absolute certainty that the Madsens are not those people.

As if reading my thoughts, Oaklyn's eyes find mine, and her expression is so icy that I shiver.

"You and I," she says, her voice just loud enough to hear over the din, "are going to have so much fun once I take some bio magic."

Nausea fills me, my mouth going dry. I don't want to think of what sort of torture is possible with that power—how she'll be able to control me, to hurt me, to make me beg for her to stop and wish I'd never killed Freddie. And she'll probably do the same to Natalie.

We need to stop them from seizing bio magic, no matter what it takes.

"Natalie," I whisper, "what do we do if Agnes tells them where it is?"

No answer. Her brow is pinched, her breaths heaving. She doesn't know.

Nobody around me seems willing to admit how close the Madsens are to taking bio magic. Maybe they're overconfident in their abilities, or maybe they're underestimating what the Madsens can do. Maybe they just haven't been attacked by the Madsens like I have—all the kidnapping attempts, the curse delivered to my door, the conversations with Freddie. Could I be the only one who fully comprehends how sinister these people are? The only one who understands how dangerously close they are to getting what they came for?

Call it instinct or intuition, but I feel it deep within me that I need to get to the bio magic first. And though the Directors won't share where magic is stored, that doesn't mean I can't find it on my own.

Trusting my gut, I let my gaze pull like a magnet toward the corridor marked *Library*. It's needled me since I arrived, that strange, beckoning call from the depths of the building.

That *has* to be it.

I clench my fists, a plan forming.

"Natalie," I whisper, my voice barely a breath. "Distract them."

Her eyes snap to me, wide with alarm. "Don't. Whatever you're about to do—"

"We don't have a choice. They're going to find it, and you know it."

She opens her mouth, but no sound comes out.

Agnes's pleading drifts through the room, a reminder that we can't afford to waste another second.

I back up, preparing to break into a run. I give Natalie a look that says, *I'm going whether you help me or not.*

She swears under her breath and extends a hand, raising a cloud of dust. Shattered brick, wood splinters, and upholstery swirl like a tornado, obscuring my view of the Madsens.

I seize my chance and take off, hurtling toward the Library corridor. My pulse throbs in my ears, adrenaline surging through my veins like fire.

Thumps and crashes rise as a fight breaks out behind me.

Agnes's desperate voice rises above the rest. "Stop! I'll talk!"

My stomach clenches with dread. She's going to crack. We're out of time.

Footsteps pound at my back, and my heart jolts with fear before a familiar voice calls out.

"Keep going!" Natalie shouts. "I'm coming with."

Relief floods through me. The fact that she's following and trusting my plan instead of forcing me to stop is the vote of confidence I need.

As we race deeper into the corridor, the tug inside me grows stronger, urging me onward. Magic shifts around me like enormous lungs expanding and contracting.

At a four-way intersection, I pause and close my eyes, reaching out with my other senses.

Come on. Tell me which way.

Natalie's heaving breaths are the only sound as she waits for my decision, her steady presence acting as my anchor.

I walk a circle, paying attention to the static-like prickle on my arms and the urgency constricting my chest.

Thunder roars through the hall, shouts growing closer. People are following.

"You can do it," Natalie says. "Listen to your intuition."

I nod, slowing my breath and concentrating on the sensations in my body. The magic is right there, a whisper I can barely hear.

"Left," I say, the word coming to my lips automatically.

I follow the pull around a curve. More intersections take me right, then straight, then straight again, each decision easier than the last. I'm deeper into the building than ever before, the labyrinth disorienting me until I don't know which way is out.

Finally, the pull gets so strong that a tremor passes through me.

"It's here. Right around this corner."

We arrive at an arched metal door, and I stop, my breath catching. Criss-crossed and swirling designs cover the door from top to bottom, gleaming in the corridor's dim lamplight. Vines and small purple flowers creep along the wall and surround the frame, threatening to overtake the door. The iron handle serpentines like the letter S, its 45-degree angle suggesting it needs to be twisted upright to disengage the lock.

This is it. This is where bio magic is stored.

Before I can approach it, footsteps echo in the corridor behind Natalie, and we whirl around.

No. Already?

Natalie moves in front of me, her shoulders tensing, her hands up and ready to fight. Her body is a shield, protecting me as resolutely as ever from whatever danger is approaching.

Two people round the corner and stop, breathing hard.

Relief floods through me at the familiar faces.

"Sebastian! Millie!" I cry. "I was worried—"

"Open the door," Millie says sharply. She steps closer, a wild glint in her eyes. "Did you get access, Natalie?"

Sebastian reaches for her and rests a hand on her shoulder, his expression grim. His arm is mangled and bloody from Wyatt's attack, and he's severed his robe at the bottom to make a bandage.

Natalie drops her hands, furrowing her brow at the pair of them. "No. What are you doing here?"

"We were searching the wing and saw you run past," Sebastian says.

I study the lock. "We came here because the Madsens are about to find this room. We have one last chance to stop them from taking what's ins—"

"Look, I don't give a shit what you do and who gets access to it," Millie snaps. "Just open the door. It's why you came here, isn't it?"

Sebastian tightens his grip on her shoulder and addresses me, his brow furrowed. "Do what she says."

I blink, bewildered. "I don't—I can't—"

"What's going on?" Natalie demands.

"You have the gall to ask me that?" Millie hisses. She swipes a hand over her head and rips off her blonde wig, revealing her bald scalp—the reminder of her chemotherapy treatments. "I've suffered for long enough when the cure is right here in the goddamned building. Health and happiness are on the other side of that door, Natalie. Now will you please *open it*." Her voice breaks, and she clenches her fists, her eyes reddening as tears threaten to spill.

My eyes prickle. I don't know what to say. The cure *is* on the other side of the door—bio magic, the means to restore her health, to mend the bite on Sebastian's arm, even to stop the searing pain in my ankle. I can't imagine the suffering Millie has endured, knowing what's hiding within the walls of this building. And Sebastian, knowing he could fix his wife's pain if he threw aside his oath and duties in order to break into this room.

Shouts mingle in the distance. A thunder of footsteps drifts closer. The walls rumble with earth magic.

They're coming.

I clench my fists, and the gauntlet presses against my knuckles—like a message from Natalie's mother beyond the grave.

"Natalie," I say, my words sharp. "When bio magic is free—feral—is it hard to capture?"

She hesitates, eyeing me warily. "Nearly impossible. That's why we have Trackers. They spend their whole lives hunting it down all over the world."

I nod firmly. "Good."

The next step in my plan illuminates, as clear and bright as a bolt of lightning.

There are two evils ahead: one in which the Madsens corner us, break into the room, and get what they came for... and the other in which bio magic is set loose, feral once more, where *nobody* can catch it.

Before Natalie can stop me, I spin and raise my fist, lining up the gauntlet with the serpentine door handle. With a grunt, I smash it as hard as I can, the impact reverberating up my arm.

CRACK!

A fissure appears in the handle, the iron splintering under the force of the blow.

"Katie!" Natalie shouts.

I hit it again. The handle clatters to the floor, the sound echoing.

Millie's breath hitches. She leans forward as if ready to kick the door open and seize the power that's been denied to her for so long.

I meet Natalie's eyes, more certain than I've been all day. "They're not going to give up until they've taken what's in this room. We have to set it loose so they can't steal it."

She looks past me at the door, panic crossing her face. "It took over a *century* to contain all this!"

"Exactly. If it's feral, they won't catch it—but if it's here, it's easy to take, and you know how this will end."

Natalie, Sebastian, and Millie exchange a look, their chests heaving as this monumental decision hangs between us.

Natalie says nothing. She has no argument.

My heart skips a beat. I'm doing this, then. I'm going to undo a century of work in order to prevent deadly power from falling into the Madsens' hands.

"And you'll give me some before freeing it," Millie says—a statement, not a question. "Just to heal myself. I swear."

I look at Natalie, knowing what I want but unsure what this would mean.

"I'm not going to stop you," she says, her words stilted.

Millie nods, satisfied.

"And we set the rest free?" I ask.

Natalie says nothing, breathing hard, holding my gaze.

"Think of what the power in this room can do in the wrong hands," I say, stepping closer, begging her to see reason.

Her dark eyes narrow, and she clenches her fists at her sides. "Set it free."

CHAPTER 37

ChimeraTown666

A S WE ENTER THE room, darkness swallows us whole. My heart slams into my ribs, reacting to unseen forces.

Natalie's hand slides around my waist, firm and reassuring. She side-steps behind me, and a torch on the wall roars to life, bathing the room in a flickering glow. It triggers a chain of torches, each one illuminating a moment after the last.

The light reveals a walkway stretching down a long, narrow room, bounded on either side by iron bars. *Cages.* Left and right, their doors are padlocked shut, the iron gleaming. The walkway stretches into the distance, fading to blackness, giving no hint of how many there are. The cages reach the top of my head and are big enough to house livestock—but inside...

My brain churns like rusty cogs. Even after staring for several seconds, I can't put a name to what's inside. I can't put a *shape* to them. In the nearest cage, something lies on the floor—an animal? It expands and contracts, breathing, its form in continuous flux. My mind tries to label it a lion, a goat, a snake. It has every feature of every animal, and at the same time, it has none of them.

A pang shoots through my head like I've stared at the sun for too long, and I blink, looking away.

"I don't understand," I whisper, a tremor in my voice.

"Pure bio magic doesn't have a form," Natalie murmurs, her presence sturdy at my side.

"It's beautiful," Millie whispers, taking Sebastian's hand and stepping closer to the nearest cage.

I squint at the creature inside. "Is it an animal?"

"It's..." Natalie tilts her head, deliberating her words. "You know how our brains fill in gaps in an ambiguous image? It's one explanation for paranormal sightings. Like, someone sees a vaguely human shape in a graveyard at night and interprets it as a ghost, or—"

"Some burn marks in a piece of toast look like a face?" I supply.

"Exactly. With bio magic, our brains try to fill in what we're seeing, but it doesn't quite work... leaving us with a mishmash that we call a chimera."

"Chimera," I repeat. Of course—the hybrid creature.

Past the first cage, every other one within sight is occupied. Millie lets go of Sebastian's hand and walks down the aisle, looking left and right, her footsteps filling the silence.

"Are they asleep?" I ask. They're all breathing, and the room is very much alive. I run my hands over my bare arms to soothe the prickling sweeping across my skin.

"In a way. The cages are enchanted to subdue the magic," Natalie says.

Hesitantly, I touch one of the large iron bars. Magic crackles up my arm and into my core, and I take my hand away quickly, shaking out the discomfort. "And if I break the locks?"

"They'll be free."

A sharp voice behind us makes us all whirl around. "*No—they—won't.*"

Adrenaline spikes, and I clench my fists, ready to fight.

Fiona stands in the doorway with her chest heaving and her palms up. She's even filthier than before, and there's a wild, furious look in her eye.

"Fiona," Natalie says, her words clipped with urgency, "the Madsens only need *one* instance of bio magic in order to put the whole world in danger."

"And your answer is to set it all free?" she snarls. "To release magic that's taken generations to contain?"

"It's better free than in the wrong hands," I say.

"Don't you dare talk about magic like you understand it," Fiona snaps. "The last thing I'm going to do is let some outsider make the biggest mistake the coven has ever—"

"Enough, Fiona," Natalie barks, her voice cracking like a whip. "Katie isn't *some outsider*, and she's got a point. The Madsens will never be able to capture it if it's feral."

Fiona's eyes bulge, her mouth hanging open. Natalie has probably never taken such a harsh tone with her, and the tension between them grows thick.

Something squeezes in my chest. Natalie is really going against Fiona and her oath as she stands at my side.

"Fiona, listen," she says, softening. "Between Sophia and Oaklyn, they have enough power to steal any of the magic in here. By holding it in cages, we're as good as handing it to them."

Fiona scoffs. "And what'll they do once they have it? They don't know the ritual."

"They've—" I start, then hesitate. This isn't how I wanted to share what Freddie told me, but I have to. "They've captured Natalie's dad. That's how they've been getting information about curses, and that's how they got earth magic. It's possible they'll torture him for instructions on how to embody bio magic—or that they've done so already."

Natalie stumbles backward as if punched. "Wh-what? No. I just texted him yesterday!"

My heart aches for her. Hot tears prickle in my eyes, and I blink, forcing them back. "You've been texting Freddie," I say, barely a whisper. "He told me before he died."

Natalie's chest heaves, her expression twisting with rage. She looks past me, her eyes distant, vacant. "I'll kill them both."

"And in the meantime..." Fiona lifts her chin, her palms steady in front of her. "All four of you have five seconds to get out of this room."

"Fiona—" Natalie starts.

"Now!" she barks, her shout carrying strangely through the dimly lit room. "And you can be sure you'll all face suspension after this. Never have I seen such an oath violation—"

"Would you shut up about the oath for once?" Natalie shouts, stepping forward. "My dad is being held captive. Will is *dead*. All because someone wanted the magic in this room so badly that they were willing to kill for it. If we don't get rid of what's in here, any one of us could be next."

"*What's in here* is a century of scouring the earth—"

"Oh, for fuck's sake," Millie growls from the depths of the room, and a flaming torch rips off the wall and hurtles toward Fiona.

Fiona screeches and ducks, the torch soaring past her and out into the corridor, where it clatters to the floor and extinguishes. There's a split second where she seems to process the attack, and then her face contorts with rage. She raises the broken door handle off the floor and fires it back at Millie.

Sebastian swipes the air, stopping it before it gets there.

The look on Fiona's face is murderous, her eyes gleaming behind the loose locks that were once pulled back into an elegant bun. It's quite possible that she's ready to kill all four of us in order to keep bio magic contained.

She launches another attack, her movements wild and desperate. While Sebastian and Millie retaliate, Natalie grabs my shoulders and pulls me in.

"We'll hold her off," she murmurs in my ear. "Do what you need to do. These padlocks won't break open under ordinary earth magic."

I nod and clench my fist, feeling the tug of the gauntlet around my finger. A tremor passes over me.

"The magic will be able to get out of here?" I ask, glancing up toward ground level. "You're sure the Madsens won't catch it?"

Natalie nods. "Magic always finds a way to get where it needs to go."

She steps back, leaving a cool draft where her hands were.

While she, Sebastian, and Millie keep Fiona at the door, I spin around and race for the row of cages, my footsteps pounding on the stone floor and echoing through the room. The magic in the air is thick and heavy, pressing down on me like a weighted blanket.

I reach the first cage, my hands shaking as I grasp the bars. The iron is cold beneath my fingers. With a grunt, I raise my hand and smash the gauntlet against the lock, the impact reverberating up my arm.

The lock cracks like breaking porcelain, crumbling into pieces.

Sucking in a breath to steel myself for whatever is about to happen, I yank the door open.

I don't know what I expected—that the magic inside would stretch like a dog waking from a nap, or that it would drift into freedom like a gust of wind? Instead, in a blink, I'm face-to-face with an enormous cat—thick, gray fur dotted with black rosettes, and fangs the size of my hand. A snow leopard. Its purple eyes glint hungrily, and I instinctively step back.

With a snarl, it bounds past me, its powerful muscles taking it toward the others.

"No!" Fiona screeches, and it's not just anger in her voice, but fear. She really doesn't understand that this is the only way.

She aims her palms at the creature, but before she can do anything to stop it, it leaps into the air and shifts into a crow, letting out a loud "caw!" as it rockets by her head.

My heart slams into my ribs. One down... How many to go?

Suddenly, a blast rocks the room, sending dust and debris raining down on me. I cough and cover my mouth.

Yells erupt in the doorway.

"What's going on?"

"The magic's escaping! Stop it!"

More people have caught up.

"It's *supposed* to be escaping!" Natalie shouts. "Hold back the Madsens!"

Sophia shrieks, her voice rising above all else. "No!"

"What the fuck?" Hayley cries. "What's wrong with you?"

"They're traitors!" Fiona yells.

A frenzy of accusations rises.

Great, now we have a civil war happening among the witches too.

This is going to weaken our defenses even further. I'm out of time.

I turn to the next cage, frantic. I smash the lock and throw the door wide. A bay stallion pushes past me and gallops for freedom, its hooves pounding the stone, its dark mane and tail streaming.

Someone screams. Shouts and crashes escalate, but I can't afford to stall. I have to keep going, to free every chimera before the Madsens plow through our feeble defenses.

I race to the next cage, and the next, and the next. There must be dozens, and every lock takes several seconds to break. Sweat trickles down my temples and back, my lungs aching as I wheeze in each breath. My hand throbs, the muscles in my arms screaming, my bones tender beneath the gauntlet. But with each instance of bio magic I set free, the air pulses with it, fueling me with enough energy to push on.

I smash the next lock, but before I can open the door, Millie appears beside me, making me gasp.

Her face is pale, beads of sweat glistening on her forehead. "Let me take this one," she whispers.

I hesitate, searching her desperate expression. I want to let her, but I'm afraid of what this means. If we do this, we aren't just letting bio magic go feral again—we're allowing someone to embody it. This is exactly what we didn't want. This is what Fiona's petrified of.

"C-can you use it to—force the Madsens back?" I ask, my words coming in short, sharp gasps. "Capture them or something?"

If this would help us stop the attack, it would be easier to defend what I'm about to do. Every second the fight continues, someone is in danger of being hurt or killed. Beyond Millie, the clashing grows louder than ever, and the torches on the wall thrash as they threaten to extinguish.

But Millie shakes her head. "Magic takes weeks to figure out. I won't know how to use it right away."

I chew my lip, wishing she had a different answer. "Promise me you won't use it for anything but your health," I say, touching her wrist. "Please promise me."

She nods. No hesitation, nothing but a desperate plea in her eyes. "Only my health. Nothing more. I swear on my life, Katie. On Sebastian's life."

It'll have to be enough.

I step back, letting her swing the door open.

There's no time to stand and watch... but as I race to the next cage, fear for what she's about to do gets the better of me, and I can't resist glancing back.

The magic takes the form of a dark gray wolf, its fur shimmering with an otherworldly light. It crouches in the center, its muscles coiled and ready to spring, its piercing purple eyes fixed on Millie as she slips inside with a palm up—as if that's enough to make this enormous beast stop.

Shutting the door behind her, Millie stands with both hands up in a gesture of peace, looking tiny in the face of the massive wolf. The wolf's lips curl back into a snarl, and its ears twitch.

Terror seizes me, freezing me in place. This is a bad idea. One bite with those jaws and she's done.

But Millie stands strong, keeping her hands in front of her—and it's then that I see the blood dripping from her palms. It splatters onto the stone floor like crimson rain drops. She's etched a symbol into each palm, the cuts deep and jagged, and is presenting them to the wolf.

The beast's muscles bunch, ready to pounce, but neither of them makes a move. My breaths heave in and out, a nervous tremor passing through me. I'm witnessing something beyond my understanding—a negotiation between a witch and feral magic.

Forcing myself to move, I smash the next lock with a shaking fist.

A snarl rips through the air, and I snap my attention back to Millie.

The wolf leaps at her, a rush of glinting teeth and ruffling fur.

"No!" I cry, lurching back toward Millie as if I can save her.

But then, in mid-air, the wolf begins to dissolve, its shimmering violet particles drifting to Millie like floating pollen. They enter her body through the cuts in her palms, and she lets out a blood-curdling scream, dropping to her knees.

"Millie!" I stop at the entrance to her cage, afraid to step inside.

She doesn't answer, stifling her shouts through clenched teeth. But she keeps her hands up, even as she trembles and writhes under the magic pouring into her bloodstream.

"What's happening?" Sebastian shouts. "Millie!"

Outside us, the sounds of the fight draw closer, panicked yells rising over each other.

Natalie's yells hit my ears, her words jumbled and frantic. "Amir! Shit! Someone help him!"

Keep moving! my inner voice shouts—but shock has my feet rooted to the floor as Millie absorbs the bio magic.

I watch, numb, as the wolf dissolves completely. It's gone—finished fusing with her.

She falls forward on all fours, gasping for breath.

"Are you okay?" I ask, my voice thin as fear grips my throat.

No answer.

Dammit. Do I go to her or continue opening cages? I rock from foot to foot, torn between priorities.

Another explosion rocks the room, and I duck as debris hits my head and shoulders.

"Katie—we can't hold them back any longer!" Natalie shouts from much too close.

Millie stirs. With jerky movements, she crawls backward, then gets her feet under her and stands. She turns her head to meet my gaze, a purple gleam in her eyes that sends a jolt of adrenaline through me. "Go," she says, her voice raspy.

She's done it. Whatever ritual that was, it's over, and that wolf is part of her.

I turn on my heel. The fight is drawing closer, shouts following us down the aisle, and I can't afford to waste more time.

Pain slams my leg, and I yell as I stumble, reaching automatically for the source.

Iron shrapnel is embedded in my thigh.

As Sophia barks out a victorious laugh, I stare at the protruding iron, fighting the urge to vomit.

Don't think. Get it out.

I clench my teeth and grab it. I roar as I yank it out, the hot swell of blood trickling down my leg.

Adrenaline dulls the pain, letting me push onward. I can't stop now. My breaths ragged, I limp to the next cage.

Footsteps pound closer. "Stop her!" Sophia shrieks.

A clump of roots slams into the cage beside me, sending a haunting chime through the room as it hits the bars.

"Katie, hurry!" Natalie shouts.

My head is spinning like I'm on a fairground ride, threatening to knock me off my feet. Every muscle and bone in my body screams for relief as I reach the final chimera. With a grunt of effort, I bring the gauntlet down on the lock.

Something wraps around my ankle and tugs, and I cry out as I hit the unforgiving floor on my stomach. A jolt of pain shoots up my wrists.

A hand grabs my shoulder and roughly turns me on my back. A weight presses down on my thighs, and Oaklyn's face swims into my vision through the dim lighting.

"What did you do with Freddie?" she asks, her voice rough with exhaustion.

She's straddling my hips, holding me down, her dagger ready to pierce my throat.

I open my mouth but choke on the words. There's a vulnerable glint of fear in her eyes, and I can't help putting myself in her shoes for a moment—the shock and terror that must come with knowing a loved one is dead. Her *sibling*. The emptiness, the refusal to believe it until you hear it spoken aloud.

I might feel sorry for her if she wasn't in the middle of a murderous rampage. I raise my arms in front of me, a sickening uncertainty as this feeble gauntlet becomes my only hope.

Her dagger glints in the dancing flames, her chest heaving.

I swallow hard and force the truth out. "His body's in Alchemy 8."

Oaklyn's shriek of rage fills the room, and her eyes turn wild.

Then she lurches as something slams into her.

Natalie has landed on her, scrambling to put her in a chokehold. Oaklyn roars and elbows her, and they scrabble for each other's faces, throats, hair, holding nothing back.

I tamp down the instinct to jump in and help. *Not yet.* I flip over, clambering, reaching for the final cage with my last drop of strength.

As I wrap my fingers around one of the cold bars, Oaklyn's hand closes over my calf.

She pulls me back, but I keep a firm hold, letting the momentum wrench the door open.

A fox bounds into freedom and leaps over my head, its delicate paws quiet on the stone floor.

"Grab it!" Oaklyn shouts.

Sophia shrieks.

I bark out a triumphant laugh, relief flooding my veins. Shaking, I get my hands and knees under me. Empty cages surround me, their doors swung wide, their shattered locks on the ground.

"It's done!" I shout, my voice ringing beneath the cavernous ceiling as the fox transforms into a dove and flies away.

CHAPTER 38

Welcome to our Freaky Zoo

A STORM OF DUST, smoke, and debris batters us as we race through the crumbling remains of C.S.A.M.M., following the Madsens and the last of the chimeras.

Keep going, keep going, I think, praying that the chimeras will continue fleeing until they're well away from the Madsens and anyone else who wants to abuse their power. The world doesn't need this sort of dangerous magic locked in cages—it needs to be far away and out of reach.

My heart hammers like it's trying to escape my chest as I struggle to keep up, pushing through the pain spiking in every cell of my body. Blood oozes from my thigh where the iron shrapnel got me, and my mauled ankle is sending stabbing pains all the way up my leg and into my abdomen. My only hope that this is all going to be okay is Natalie's warm hand in mine.

But as we rise through the steam clock and into the world, roars and otherworldly shrieks erupt in my ears. A blur of movement swirls before me, and I've barely registered what's going on when Natalie yanks me back. Steps away, a black panther the size of a Thoroughbred leaps onto a parked minivan, teeth bared, hissing at all the screaming people. The car's suspension groans under its weight, and its claws leave deep gashes in the metal. Above it, a massive vulture stretches out its wings, casting a shadow over the street. It lands on top of the four-story building across the intersection, its cries echoing through the city.

"Oh my God," I whisper, the words lost beneath the din. "Natalie, we have to get them out of here!"

"The chimeras or the innocent bystanders?" she asks, tugging me further back.

"Um—"

People scream in terror all around us, their faces twisted in fear as they run for their lives. They scoop children into their arms and stand guard to herd others to safety. Dogs bark furiously at the end of their leashes, their instincts torn between fighting and fleeing. A block away, an SUV has driven off the road and has its nose buried in a storefront. Its doors hang open, the seats empty, the airbags deployed and the horn blaring incessantly. Other cars honk and try to turn around, clipping each other.

"All of the above?" I squeak.

The responsibility to fix this crushes me, taking my breath away. This is out of control, and not at all what I had in mind when I envisioned setting magic free. I thought the chimeras would disappear into the sky, never to be seen again. Someone is going to get hurt or killed.

"We have to make sure the Madsens can't get any of—" I begin, breaking off with a surprised shout. At our feet, worms and insects are emerging from the ground beneath the steam clock. A wood bug crawling toward my toes shapeshifts into a fluffy brown hare, takes one hop, then shifts again, growing larger.

Natalie and I stumble back, and before my next breath, we're face-to-face with a grizzly bear.

It growls, which I can only interpret as a promise to eat us as an appetizer.

What—did—I—do?

"N-Natalie?" I say, hoping for a solution.

"Run." She tugs me by the hand, and we sprint in the other direction.

The bear huffs in agitation, and I *swear* the ground rumbles beneath its enormous paws as it follows. My lungs are on fire and my legs are agony as we race past storefronts, Natalie using magic to hurl objects across the bear's path—a newspaper stand, a garbage can, a Victorian street lamp.

I risk a glance back, relief trickling through my head as the bear navigates the obstacles. "It's working."

Someone steps out of an alcove in front of us. "I wouldn't be so sure."

I gasp, jerking to a stop.

"Sky!" Natalie shouts.

Sky raises both hands. "Move."

Natalie yanks me out of the way. The ground jolts as cobblestones rise behind us, forcing the bear back. As it roars, Sky seizes our arms and pulls us into the alcove.

We flatten against the wall, breathing hard. There's a rumble and an explosion of dust. A second later, an enormous flying creature rockets past, stretching out its wings and disappearing from view.

"What was that?" I ask, not sure I want the answer.

"Doesn't matter," Sky says, out of breath. "Listen, these things are clearly pissed off, and we have to push them out of the city. Try to get them to transform into birds and fly away. Got it?"

Natalie nods.

Before I can ask what I can do to help, Fiona races past and skids to a stop. She snarls. "You—brainless—fools. You can't just set magic free without consequences! It's been held captive, and it knows it."

Agnes crashes into her from behind. "Why did you—oh."

She sees us and straightens up, baring her teeth at me like an angry dog. "Do you have any idea what you've done? You've unleashed feral magic!

Bio magic! It's just—" She flaps her arms. "Running amok in the world now!"

"So we'll push it back into nature," Natalie snaps.

I open my mouth to defend my decision, but no words come. Guilt squeezes my airway until I can't speak, can't even breathe.

"You have to admit this was the only way," Sky says, drawing everyone's gaze. "Imagine what would've happened if Sophia got into that room while the magic was still caged. We might as well have handed it to her on a platter."

Fiona points at her. "Don't you— That's not what—" she splutters, but no argument forms.

I swallow hard. Sky's words mean more than she knows. Standing in the middle of this mess, I could easily regret what we did—but she's willing to argue with two Directors to defend our actions, and that counts for something.

Though as a hippopotamus lumbers down the street, getting in trouble with C.S.A.M.M. authorities is the least of anyone's worries. Right now is about dealing with the consequences of what we've done—and staying alive amid a stampede of pissed-off magical forces.

"We can finish this conversation later," Fiona hisses.

She, Agnes, and Sky dash into the mayhem, raising barricades to try and force the chimeras into the clouds and away from civilians.

I scan for Millie and Sebastian, but they're nowhere to be found. I have to assume they made it out okay—that they're on their way somewhere safe.

Natalie faces me, hooking a finger under my chin so I have no choice but to turn my attention to her. "Katie, I have to help drive the chimeras off before they hurt someone. I didn't think it would be this..." She looks around, her eyes wide. "We have to get to safety. Figure out what to do about—about all of this."

I nod, wishing I could help. My whole body is trembling with exhaustion.

She holds my gaze, hesitating like she wants to say more—and then her mouth is on mine, her lips moving feverishly, her soft hands cupping my face.

I kiss her back, responding on autopilot, holding her against me. Through the haze of fear clouding my brain, something else beats stronger, a burning rush pulsing through my veins. I pour that into her—everything I want to tell her when we reach the other side of all this.

Too soon, she breaks away, spinning around in time to launch a parking meter at a tiger chasing a meal delivery guy on a bike.

As the tiger morphs into a duck and flies away with an angry "quack!", Natalie freezes, going rigid as she spots something back the way we came.

I jump out of my hiding spot to follow her gaze, a chill sweeping over me.

Back at the steam clock, Sophia and Oaklyn Madsen have appeared—and my stomach gives a sickening lurch as I see Oaklyn carrying her brother's lifeless body. Wyatt stalks between them, looking around vigilantly, his teeth glinting as he snarls at the chaos. Sophia uses magic to yank an abandoned car toward them with a screech, and they all pile inside.

Natalie sets her jaw, a dangerous gleam in her eye.

"Natalie, don't," I say, because as much as I want to go after them and stop them, now is not the time. We need an army and a rock-solid plan to fight against the Madsens.

But she's already advancing, fists clenched, shoulders tight.

I race after her. "Natalie!"

Sky is there in a blink, grabbing her arm and forcing her to stop.

"Not now, dumbass," she says sharply. "You'll get killed."

Natalie rounds on her. "Sky, they've captured Dad. They took his phone. Forced him to get earth magic for them."

Sky freezes, turning pale. "Wh-what?"

A bellowing sound interrupts them, a harsh reminder that there isn't time to discuss this. There's no time to do anything but run.

A bull the color of flames gallops toward us down the sidewalk, as big as a car, its horns the size of my legs.

Natalie's hand finds mine, and she tugs me behind a delivery truck in time for the bull to charge past, grunting angrily. I lean against it and press a hand to the still-oozing hole in my thigh, unable to get enough air into my lungs.

We watch, helpless, as the Madsens peel away in the stolen vehicle.

"We have to find him! Like, *immediately*," Sky says, her voice high.

"I know," Natalie says, clutching her side.

Around us, witches fight tirelessly to keep civilians safe, and it's working—there are no bodies on the ground, no injuries to tend to other than our own. They're upholding their oath to protect the non-magical public even in the midst of pandemonium. The hippopotamus transforms into a seagull and takes flight, rising above the buildings and retreating over the ocean. The bull shifts into a rat, scurrying into a storm drain. A trickle of relief dares to course through me.

Then, a shriek fills the world like nothing I've ever heard. I snap my gaze toward the sound, looking skyward.

The Harbour Centre building is across the intersection, its round lookout tower visible from here—and a strange feeling overcomes me as my brain fights to comprehend what I'm seeing.

Hazel and I were just there this morning, gazing over the peaceful city, giddy about spending the summer together. Now, a massive creature clings to the lookout tower, its wings wrapped around the circular structure, its claws shattering windows and sending large chunks of rubble crashing to the street below.

"By the way," Natalie says, still clutching her side, "I can finally answer your question."

I stare blankly at her as I staunch the wound on my leg. "What question?"

She points at the thing clinging to the Harbor Centre. "*That*," she says, "is Lucy."

I straighten up, my jaw unhinging.

Lucy. My precious kitten. Feral magic, a shapeshifting monster beyond my worst nightmares. And she's in the process of destroying downtown Vancouver.

She soars overhead, her wings blotting out the sun, and the name for this sort of creature hovers just out of reach. It's like someone smooshed together an eagle and a lion and called it nightmare fuel.

Numb, I trace my gaze over her beak and wings, down her mane, to the talons on her front legs, and to her large paws.

There's a smudge on her left back paw.

The griffin—Lucy—opens her beak, and a deafening roar fills the air, raising the hairs on my arms and sending a tremor through my bones. She swoops down, and every witch in the street dives out of the way, sprawling flat on the ground.

Lucy lands on the steam clock, making it look puny. Her talons click against its face as she scrambles for grip.

The historic clock cracks beneath her monstrous weight, crumbling. She sinks her beak into the whistles on top, and with a final groan, the clock gives way, its gears shattering to pieces over the brick sidewalk.

Seeing Lucy in this form—her *true* form—reminds me that there is still so much I don't understand about magic. "So, this is what you meant when you said she wasn't a cat," I say, barely a whisper.

Lucy turns her feathery head—and I swear to God she looks right at me. For a moment, she doesn't move, a gleam in her purple eyes. A shiver rolls down to my toes.

Then she aims her beak skyward and stretches out her wings, taking flight once more.

I meet Natalie's eye in numb surprise. She must know what I'm thinking because she grimaces.

The Madsens might have driven away without capturing bio magic, but we've set an unparalleled force loose on the world.

We have a big mess to clean up.

CHAPTER 39

New Promises and Old-Fashioned Threats

As the last chimera takes flight, its wings casting a shadow over the devastation that was once Gastown, the piercing wail of sirens fills the air. Witches, injured and smeared with dirt, vanish into the ground beneath the crumbled remains of the steam clock.

My eyes prickle as I take in the city I've come to call home—the ruined storefronts with shattered windows, broken bricks and cobblestones, toppled structures... Not to mention the people who had to flee in terror. My heart clenches, guilt gnawing at my insides like a hungry rat.

A black car navigates the disaster, coming to a stop in front of us. The window rolls down, and it hits me that I'm looking at Natalie's car. Hazel's behind the wheel with Ethel's kennel riding shotgun.

"I... packed up as much as I could from your place..." Hazel says weakly, her eyes wide with shock as she takes in the apocalyptic surroundings.

A tiny meow emits from the car's clean interior.

"Good timing." Natalie's hand closes over my arm, and she guides me to the vehicle. She cranes her neck, glancing around. "Get in."

I startle, rooting my feet. "What? Why?"

She opens the back door. "Because you and I are going to have a lot to answer for."

Sky appears beside us, her mouth pulled into a deep frown. "Fiona wants you down below," she tells Natalie, her eyes flicking nervously to me. "She's asked everyone to be in the courtyard. Now."

I wrench out of Natalie's grasp, my heart skipping. "Then I should go too."

She takes my arm again, her touch firm. "You don't understand the seriousness of what we've done. I think I can talk Fiona down, but I don't want you there for this. Go somewhere safe, and I'll come get you when this blows over."

I set my jaw, defiant. "I don't want to leave you!"

"It's not a question," she says harshly.

Typical Natalie, trying to protect me from something I have to face.

I open my mouth to argue, but Sky interrupts. "Natalie's right. You're both in *shit*."

"The others are wrong—" I start.

"I know." Sky grips my shoulders, holding my gaze. "I know you did the right thing, and this would've been a hell of a lot worse for all of us if the Madsens had stolen what was in that room. But Fiona doesn't see that. She only sees how you broke our laws."

My eyes get infuriatingly wet. A tornado of emotions swirls inside me—anger at the injustice of it all, sadness for the destruction, fear for what Natalie will have to deal with.

Sky drops her hands, scanning the empty street. "Related note, either of you know where Sebastian and Millie are?"

I shake my head, not meeting either of their gazes. I don't think anyone needs to know that Millie's in possession of bio magic. As long as she and Sebastian stay hidden, there's no reason the coven has to find out.

I say a silent prayer for her, hoping she quickly figures out how to use it to ease her pain and heal her illness.

"Will Fiona want all the freed bio magic recaptured?" I ask.

Sky and Natalie exchange a look, like they're each checking if the other has an answer.

"We're not done with it," Natalie says carefully. "I know that much."

"Why can't bio magic just be allowed to roam free?" I ask, a strange tightness in my ribcage at the memory of the chimeras trapped in cages. "Seeing it locked up like that... It felt wrong. Cruel."

"The problem is that bio magic does whatever it wants," Sky says, her tone somber. "Some of it might end up in forests, mountains, oceans... But some of it will end up near people. Cities, parks, places where it can do harm and where it might land in the wrong hands."

"Then I'll help find it and push it out. We all know I can sense magic, so let me help track down the chimeras that are hanging out where they shouldn't be." My words come out strong and certain. It might be a reckless offer, but all this feral bio magic is my doing, and I need to see it through. I have the ability to keep the world safe, and I refuse to let it go to waste when I could be helping.

Sky searches my face, her brow pinched. I hold her gaze, letting my determination show on my face. She must like what she sees because her expression relaxes, and she nods firmly. "Deal."

Warmth ignites inside me, a sense of purpose sparking back to life.

I turn to Natalie, who nods as well. "I think you'd be particularly good at that. But first, you need to get away from here and let some of this fizzle out."

"Fine."

As Sky strides toward the steam clock, ready to sink into the earth, Natalie calls after her. "What are we going to do about Dad?"

Sky scowls, balling her hands into fists. "We'll find him—and we'll give the rest of the Madsens the same treatment as Katie gave Freddie."

A chill ripples through me, and I wrap my arms around myself as if to ward off the memory.

But something occurs to me, a glimmer of hope beneath all the darkness. "If Sophia Madsen's a witch now, then she's not outside the coven's laws anymore, right?"

Sky and Natalie stare at me.

Slowly, a wicked smile spreads across Sky's face. "I like the way you think." She backs away, a fierce determination in her eyes. "There's a place for you here, Katie. Even if Fiona and the others don't see it yet."

I nod, my throat tightening. I want to say thanks, to tell her how much that means to me, but I can't find my voice. Her acceptance, her belief in me, is everything I need right now.

The sirens grow louder, their long wails rising in all directions and competing with each other. Down the street, flashing lights approach, painting the ruins in red and blue.

"Katie?" Hazel warns.

"Coming," I say, resigned.

Sky takes her cue and disappears into the steam clock, giving us a final salute before the earth swallows her in a haze of particles.

Natalie squeezes my hand, her touch reassuring.

I squeeze back, my heart already aching at the thought of leaving her. "Come with me."

"I can't," she says, barely audible.

"But why should I run away and leave you to face them down there?" I ask, frustration bleeding into my tone. "Won't they punish you?"

She tilts her head, a sad half-smile on her lips. "They'll hear me out, and any punishment will be nothing I can't handle. You, on the other hand, I'm not as confident about. You're too new to the coven, and not as… immune. It's better if you get out of here, at least for now."

The truth is bitter, but I appreciate her honesty. "But how long until we see each other again?"

She leans in, whispering into my lips. "As soon as possible. Promise."

I close the distance, kissing her gently, trying to pour everything into this one moment before we part. There's so much I want to say, but not now—not when this devastating, harsh reality is blazing around us, and not when I'm so terrified of what's going to happen next. The Madsens aside, most of the coven is furious about our decision, and we'll have to answer for it in some way. 'As soon as possible' might be months or years—or never.

My throat tightens. *No, I can't think like that.*

When we break apart, Natalie hesitates, holding my gaze like she's seeing right into my core. She cups my cheek, and her lips part as if she's about to say something more.

But too soon, she drops her hand and steps back, and there's nothing left to do but get in the car. Without another word, I climb into the back seat and let her shut the door.

My heart is ready to burst as I watch her through the window. She jogs to the steam clock and disappears with the rest of the witches.

As more emergency vehicles arrive, Hazel speeds off in the opposite direction—taking me away from Natalie, away from the steam clock, away from the coven.

A thick, suffocating silence closes around us, making my ears ring. Pain zaps through my body like lightning, hitting every limb and every inch of exposed skin.

My phone lies on the back seat where I abandoned it earlier.

I pick it up. A text from an unknown number arrived five minutes ago.

We'll find another way to get what we came for, sweetheart. And when we catch up with you, you're going to wish it was you instead of Freddie today.

I scoff, but even as I try to brush off Oaklyn's threat, a chill rolls through me like snow sliding down the back of my shirt. I don't doubt that I'd be in trouble if the Madsens got their hands on bio magic.

But I'm not going to let that happen.

As Hazel takes us onto the highway, I reach forward and squeeze her shoulder, a silent thank-you. She pats my hand. No words necessary.

Through the windshield, high above, the wings of an enormous creature spread as wide as a jet, carrying it up and away from the city... free from the laws that kept it imprisoned.

I feel the same, somehow. I've broken free from the cage of my old life and am ready to embrace a new version of myself.

I brush my fingers over the enchanted gauntlet still on my hand, feeling as if it were meant for me all along—like it's become a part of me I don't want to let go of. Its magic trickles through my veins like an IV drip, rooting me in a bone-deep sense of purpose.

What comes next is clear, appearing before me like an illuminated path. As soon as I can see Natalie again, we'll need to rescue her dad and make Sophia and Oaklyn pay for what they've done.

I clench my fists, ready for it. I might not be a witch, but I have the ability to see magic where nobody else can, and I'm going to use that for all it's worth.

The thing is, I'm done being pushed around by people who think they're stronger than me. The coven wants to punish me for protecting the world from dangerous magic, the Madsens want me dead for killing Freddie in self-defense, and I've just been forced to leave behind the woman I'm head-over-heels in love with. None of this is fair. I've been used, lied to, hurt, and hunted down, all for trying to help.

I glare at Oaklyn's threat on my phone, fury pulsing through my veins until I'm trembling. If she thinks she can get to me, I hope she's ready for what she finds. She has no idea what I'm capable of.

Author's Note & Acknowledgments

Thank you, dear reader, for supporting an indie author! If you enjoyed this book, please leave a review online, as it really helps me out.

The idea for this story came about when a spider nest hatched in my bathroom, leaving me screaming as a thousand creepy-crawlies scuttled up my wall. After I calmed down, I joked that I must have been cursed by a witch... and then immediately became inspired to write. I wrote a short story about bringing cursed items to an attractive witch as an excuse to see her again, and my husband had funny ideas about some not-so-cursed kitchen appliances the protagonist could bring her. What started as a fun idea about curses turned into an entire novel about a secret coven!

So, Toshi, thank you for helping to inspire the story and for being an excellent sounding board. Thank you also for your help with writing about Katie's experiences as an Asian Canadian teenager. Thank you Ashley Reiter for your help with this as well. I couldn't have created Katie and Hazel without your voices to guide me.

Finally, thank you to my family for your love and support!

Keep Reading

Continue Katie and Natalie's story in the sequel, *How to Charm a Coven*.

Read *How to Flirt with a Witch: The Webcomic* on Tapas, WEBTOON, and Patreon!

You might also enjoy:
Ice Massacre (Mermaids of Eriana Kwai #1)
The Valkyrie's Daughter (Sigrid and the Valkyries #1)
From Fan to Forever
The Road Trip Agreement
Snowed In With Summer
Striking Gold

Don't miss a new release. Sign up for Tiana Warner's newsletter:

tianawarner.com/newsletter

About the Author

Tiana Warner is a multi-award-winning sapphic romance author and outdoor enthusiast from British Columbia, Canada. She is passionate about animal welfare and is an active volunteer with local dog rescue organizations. You can often find her cuddling a foster dog, riding her horse Flynn, or exploring nature.

Instagram @tianawarner
TikTok @tiana_warner

tianawarner.com